ALL His WRAth

BOOK TWO:
THE GARGOYLE CHRONICLES

BRANDON KING

ALL HIS WRATH

Book Two: The Gargoyle Chronicles

For inquiries, please contact:
Prepare For Rain Press, Boise ID
prepareforrainpress.com

Editors: Stacy Ennis, stacyennis.com;
Kim Foster, kimfostereditor.com
Cover by the graphic design team at Prepare For Rain Press; background image by Alan Frijns
Interior Design by Fusion Creative Works, fusioncw.com
Fireball illustration by Jessica Lund

ISBN: 978-0-9889537-6-5

First Printing, 2015
Revised cover, 2023

Published in the United States of America

ALSO BY BRANDON KING

The Quest for the Temple Key;
Book One of *The Gargoyle Chronicles*

Coming Soon!
The Ten Pinnacles;
Book Three of *The Gargoyle Chronicles*

DEDICATION

This story is dedicated to Conrad Lund.

A superb example of grace under fire.

A supremely creative man.

A wonderful father.

We miss you.

ACKNOWLEDGEMENTS

Writers are a curious people. Few things are more mentally painful than creating characters, dialogue and worlds out of nothing. Yet, few things are more exciting and deeply fulfilling. This story was all of that for me. The fact that it is "Book Two"—representing the second volume in what must then be a series—is, well, amazing. And scary. Plus delightful.

As was true in *The Quest for the Temple Key: Book One in the Gargoyle Chronicles*, this story's greatest influence has been my daughter. But unlike the first volume, *All His Wrath* has been long-expected by more readers than just her. What is most special is that because of Book One's impact on her, she developed her own skill as a fantasy novelist, publishing her first novel, *NeverSeen; Book One of the Faeland Legends* in 2014. It immediately won an award and received a strong recommendation from our local newspaper's book critics.

As always, the enduring support of my wife has helped me pursue my passion for writing. She graciously permits me absurd amounts of time in my writing cave. Then she gleefully reads whatever I've woven together over too many hours. Without her constancy, giving up would be too easy.

Several truly wonderful professionals helped bring you something better than I am capable of. My heartfelt thanks to each of them:

Stacy Ennis and Kim Foster are superb copy-editors. And they are wonderful friends.

We're grateful to Stuart Bache for his amazing cover design training, which provided the tools for our publishing team at Prepare For Rain Press to create the cover you have in your hands now.

Shiloh Schroeder and Rachel Langaker took lots of ink and white space and morphed it into a lovely interior.

I've been blessed by many fans of the gargoyle realm. I thank you all for your enthusiastic, rock-solid support. To all of you, my enduring gratitude.

Brandon King
Boise, ID
2015
Revised 2023

CONTENTS

CHAPTER ONE

DISTURBED

"Bother," she exhaled quietly into the darkness of her bedroom. "Fourth night in a row."

Danielle didn't like the new dream any more than the old one. With the destruction of the Key of Kahrnahrgx, she thought she'd no longer have those awful nightmares. As she bitterly wiped the sleep from her eyes, she realized how wrong that assumption was.

She sat up sluggishly, rotated her legs so they swung over the side of the bed, and hopped to the floor. Although she knew better than to look at her alarm clock, she glanced anyway.

"Double bother!" she grumbled. It was 3:52 a.m. She stared at her clock, motionless except for the movement of her lips as she muttered under her breath.

A thump from the darkest corner of her room brought Danielle out of her spin-cycle of gloom. Quickly, she dropped to her knees. "Quiet, girl!" she whispered, patting her legs softly.

In the dim light of the waning moon falling through the window blinds, an enormous dog appeared out of the shadow, canine nails clicking on the hardwood floor. Her tail wagged gently, almost dreamily. The great beast nestled her nose into Danielle's neck and rubbed against the teenager for a moment.

Then, she sat down before her mistress, her eyes level with Danielle's.

"Hi, girl! I'm sorry to have woken you up again, so early in the morning..." Danielle's words came unevenly as she struggled through the weariness that builds over several nights of interrupted sleep. "Oh, but that's a good Anja." The dog's tail swished back and forth across the floor, while her mistress gave Anja a long hug and many loving pats on her head.

Anja had been added to the Wheelens' household within one day of their return home from their terrible adventure. It was crazy to think about: the strange key her parents had unearthed during an expedition just before Danielle was born was actually from another race of creatures. Gargoyles had burst into their lives, some seeking the key to complete its evil purpose, while others protected Danielle and her parents in her quest to destroy it. Still, their house was destroyed early on in the struggle. When Danielle's parents met with the police to file a report on what happened to their old house, they came up with a convincing story that didn't include gargoyles. Then, they had to meet with their insurance agent, too, about what would be covered—and what wouldn't—and when they could get into a new house. To the great relief of the Wheelen family, the fire department had already concluded that something went terribly wrong in the kitchen that had led to the fire that destroyed most of their house. But even with those important meetings during that first day back, they made sure to get to the pound to find a dog. As big and fiercely protective a dog as they could find.

The staff at the shelter introduced them to Anja, an unusually large Akita. This breed was known to make excellent guard dogs, being suspicious of strangers but very affectionate towards their own family. Anja and Danielle hit it off instantly. Danielle loved Anja's dark, wide and thoughtful eyes, bordered by a heavy coat of brown and black, all the way back to her corkscrew tail. When Peter, Danielle's father, found out that Anja weighed nearly as much as he did, he took a deep breath, smiled wide at his wife and daughter, and declared, "Perfect!" Amy, Danielle's mom, had smiled back, her eyes filled with tears. Anja barked enthusiastically.

For several months, they had stayed with friends. Good friends, indeed, to let Anja stay there, too. Danielle remembered her mother's tears when the insurance agent had come over and informed them that their old house was condemned. It would have taken too long to wait for their house to be rebuilt. And because they all knew the real reason the house was destroyed, they really didn't want to remain at that location, anyway. So, on the weekends, when her parents weren't grading their university students' papers, the Wheelens ran all over town with Ms. Sally, their real estate agent, in her compact car.

It had nearly driven Danielle mad looking at house after house after house for more weekends than she could remember. But she was so happy with the house her parents chose. It was a two-story building, with a beautiful, granite flagstone floor on the ground level and hardwood floors at the top of the stairs, where all the bedrooms were. Some of her friends thought it was strange that her new house didn't have any carpet at all. They also thought it was weird that you could hear a pin drop, even between floors. Danielle had even proven it to them. But then Danielle's friends didn't know why that acoustic characteristic was so vitally important to the Wheelens.

The backyard was large, because their new house was at the edge of town, where the lots were large. This made the commute to the university longer for Peter and Amy. But the trade-off was that Anja had room to play with Danielle, which both of them loved to do as soon as Danielle got home from school. Peter liked the chain-link fence, not for its beauty, of course, but because he could see long distances through it. Even though there was little risk of anyone—or anything— sneaking up on their home through the open fields beyond the fence, Peter liked the idea of both Anja and himself being able to see that far.

So it was that the Wheelens spent several months getting "all moved in" to their new house. Naturally, their moving was different than most people's moves, since it meant replacing just about everything they'd had in their old house. In the weeks that followed, the family established comfortable routines and habits. Enough so, in fact, that they'd just about lost all of their anxieties about the disastrous adventure that destroyed their home and nearly cost Danielle her life.

That was, until Danielle's nightmares came back.

"Well, girl," she whispered to Anja. "Should I tell them? Mom and Dad, I mean. I suppose they'd want to know that I'm having creepy dreams again. But I hate to do that. It'll ruin Mom's day. Maybe her whole week. She'll get pretty upset, you know?"

Anja kept quiet and wagged her tail back and forth through the moonlit stripes on the floor.

"OK. You're right," Danielle continued. "That will be up to her, whether she freaks out or not. Dad always helps with that. Although he probably won't like the news much, either."

Anja licked her mistress's hand encouragingly.

"Good girl!" Danielle patted her dog gently. "It really is too early to get up. I'm crawling back into bed. Come on, Anja!"

Moments later, Danielle was breathing quietly, straight as a post along the edge of her bed. Anja was happily sprawled across most of the bed, her breath warming Danielle's neck.

The enormous dog gazed out the window as best she could through the partially closed wooden blinds. Maybe her sleepy eyes were playing tricks with her. But Anja was certain she'd seen something perched on the roof peak of the Rumples' house. *It is big enough to be Mr. Rumple! That could not be right, could it?* Anja wondered. As sleep stole over her, Anja determined she must nose around the neighbors' house the next morning. *I will investigate. I will sniff things out. I...* Anja began snoring softly.

She didn't see the grotesque shape on the roof turn and stare through her mistress's window. She didn't see two eyes blaze red.

CHAPTER TWO

HAUNTED

In spite of her disrupted sleep, Danielle woke up feeling refreshed. Yet she was a bit cramped from being wedged up against the edge of her bed for the past few hours, due to Anja's bed hogging. When she hopped onto her bedroom floor, Anja quickly followed by leaping off the bed full of spunk and mischief. Danielle grinned wide at her wagging friend. Both girls—human and canine—tore down the hallway at a sprint, turned hard at the wide stairwell and vaulted down the steps as fast as their legs (two and four) could carry them. Halfway down the steps, Danielle grabbed the wrought iron handrail and hopped over it, landing on the entry's polished floor just before Anja slid wildly into the kitchen next to it.

Peter, his cup of coffee hovering just a few inches from his mouth, had first listened to the ruckus overhead, and then witnessed the unbridled glee of his daughter being chased by their enormous dog. Grinning from ear to ear, he said, "Well, looks like your summer gymnastics class taught you how to dismount properly!" Then, he took a big gulp of coffee.

"What on earth was that?" Amy's voice bellowed down the stairs from the master bedroom. A moment later, she came shuffling around the corner. Her tousled hair lay heaped wildly over her pink and exceedingly fluffy bathrobe. Giant bunny slippers, in matching pink, slid loudly back and forth beneath the robe. Peter loved that his academically brilliant and fiercely competitive wife wore such outrageous sleepwear.

"One guess," he grunted, quickly standing up to give Amy a peck on the cheek as she shuffled by.

"Of course. I needn't ask, really," Amy intoned with mock solemnity. She bowed towards her grinning daughter, who had just gotten the toaster going. "I suppose you had something to do with it, too, didn't you, Anja?"

Anja said nothing, but her jowls formed what appeared to be a smile. Then, the dog leaned into Danielle so hard that Danielle slid a few inches across the somewhat slippery floor.

"Well," Amy continued, now in a truly solemn tone, "just make sure you always land with your knees bent, Dani, OK?"

"Yes, Mom." Danielle had heard enough times about the damage she could cause to her legs by a bad landing that she could probably present it back to her mother, verbatim.

Danielle's toast popped up and she set to slathering them up with butter and jelly.

By now, it was nearly 7:00 a.m. The sun was out and it looked to be a wonderful day. Everyone would be out of the house within the next forty minutes. Or at least they should be if they were to be on time. But the look on Amy's face stopped Peter's cup of coffee midway to his lips the second time this morning.

"What's up, Ames? You feeling off today? You look kind of pale."

Amy shuffled her slippers on the floor as if she couldn't get comfortable. Then, she leaned heavily onto the granite-top island, her hands propped against the cool stone. Peter and Danielle, sitting on stools on the other side of the island, glanced at each other and waited. Something was coming.

Finally, she looked up at her family. "No…well, yes. Oh, bother. I don't know how I feel! All I know…is…darn it! I haven't wanted to say anything about it. You know, because of last time. Right? But it's just that—I hate to bring this up at *all*—it's just that I've been having nightmares the past four nights!" Her eyes were wide; her forehead furrowed with worry.

"What?" Peter replied. "Why haven't you said anything until now, Ames?"

"For the same reason I haven't," Danielle interjected, sheepishly. "I didn't want to cause any alarm…"

"You, too, Dani?" Her father looked troubled. But there was something else in his look that—

"What is it, Dad?"

"Uh, well, the thing is…so have I."

"Oh, dear," Danielle and Amy said, simultaneously.

Danielle quickly unlocked the front door and breezed through the quiet house. Anja was already wiggling with excitement, staring from the other side of the sliding glass doors that opened onto the backyard. Her mistress flipped the latch, slid the door open and burst through the back door. The two of them leapt, laughed, chased, growled, sprinted and rolled for the next fifteen minutes, until both laid on the cool autumn grass, panting hard with their tongues hanging. After a brief rest, Danielle attached a leash to Anja's strong leather collar. Her dog still needed a good, long walk, even after such a rumpus.

"OK, girl. Let's go!" Anja was well behaved on a leash. She didn't pull, mainly because she wasn't in a hurry to get anywhere. She loved going for walks with her family. The other reason she didn't pull was because she knew better. She weighed about the same as her master and, of course, was much stronger than any of her humans. It wouldn't be difficult for her to hurt them by pulling. So, she didn't. Instead she matched her pace to her mistress's—which, today, was oddly uneven. She glanced up at Danielle and could tell her person was distracted.

Indeed, Danielle had found it difficult to concentrate on her studies at Parkside Junior High. Normally, she was a top student. This came quite naturally to her, but there was always pressure to do well because her parents were university professors. Some of her classmates gave her a hard time about being "soooo suh-mart!" But, most days, Danielle ignored their razzing. Today, she'd pretty much ignored everything. She'd been upset since learning her parents had been having nightmares, too. That was bad enough. But that they'd all started four nights ago—*What's that about?* she wondered. That one question had nagged at her all day. Even horsing around with Anja hadn't dislodged it.

Danielle stumbled, but quickly caught her balance. She'd tripped on a rock jutting out of the dirt path that ran along Heather Ridge Drive, the rural road that passed by their home. Anja looked up again at her mistress. Danielle was muttering, annoyed at the rock.

Split rail fences ran for miles along either side of the road. Many of the folks who lived out on the edge of town, beyond the crowded subdivisions, had a horse or two, even some cows. Quite a few folks in their neighborhood called themselves "gentlemen farmers." Danielle's dad sniffed at this title and said they were "mentalmen farmers." He considered all of them—including himself—to be crazy for trying to farm anything as a hobby. Still, they liked the slower pace of life out here and the general neighborliness of the area. For one thing, there weren't as many cars on the road. So, it was the large number of cars blocking Danielle's path that should have gotten her attention.

"Hey there! Watch where you're going, lassie!" a strong voice hollered.

Danielle's head snapped up abruptly. She'd nearly walked into the back of a police car! "Huh?"

"Lost in thought, eh?" the voice continued, but not as loud since it was now right next to her.

Danielle turned and looked at the man who had warned her. He was a policeman. His eyes were covered with large, dark sunglasses and overshadowed by a dark blue cap. His matching uniform was crisp and clean, but only to his knees. From there down, his pants were covered in mud, as were his shoes. But he was smiling, so Danielle smiled back.

"Hi! And thank you for the warning! Uh, yes, I am distracted, I guess. More than I realized," Danielle laughed nervously, feeling self-conscious. Over the patrolman's shoulder, she could see other men clustered closely together in the field behind the fence. "So, what's going on over there?" she asked.

"Never you mind, young lady," the policeman replied. "It's a police matter. Nothing for you to be concerned about. Probably best to head back the way you came. That sure is a big dog you have," he continued, as if seeing Anja for the first time.

Danielle could feel the sudden tenseness in Anja. The dog's stance was defensive. She growled, glaring at the man. There was a queer, very unpleasant smell wafting over from where the group of men was standing. It made Danielle want to plug her nose. She'd never smelled anything so terrible.

"Yes, OK, officer. We'll be on our way," she choked out. Danielle spun on her heels, grinding them into the dirt, and walked briskly back towards home. She hadn't gone far when she cast a furtive glance over the fence. She was trying to see between the legs of all those men. "What are they looking at?" she said out loud. She couldn't be sure, between all the limbs and the shadows the men's bodies cast on whatever they were looking at. But it looked like there might be a body of a cow, or perhaps a horse. Whatever it was, its legs splayed up into the air. "Oh, that doesn't look good," she whispered to Anja.

She didn't know that the policeman had watched her steal a look. She didn't see him make notes on his metal clipboard before hopping back over the fence and talking to one of the other men.

Their return trip was at a much faster pace, so Danielle was winded by the time they got home. After letting Anja into the backyard to do her business, Danielle ran upstairs. It took several minutes of frantic searching before she finally found her father's binoculars. First, she tried looking out her bedroom window, but the oak tree blocked the view to the far-off field. Next, she tried the west-facing window in her parent's bedroom. The view was clear! Quickly, she adjusted the binoculars. Then, she aimed them towards the field and scanned madly back and forth. The men were gone. Whatever they'd been standing in front of was gone. Everything was gone!

"Dang it!" she yelled. "Now we'll never know what happened over there." Whatever had been there must have been trucked off, because there were deep, dual tire tracks and numerous footprints in the soft soil. A soft clicking sound filtered up the stairs. It was Anja tapping her paw on the glass door. She wanted back in.

Danielle tromped down the stairs, frustrated with not knowing what had happened so near their home. She was certain that it must have something to do with her nightmares—well, all of their nightmares. Without thinking, she threw open the sliding door so hard, it crashed into the huge, rubber safety bumper and slid violently back, just as Anja stepped through the opening.

Anja yelped in fright and leapt into the kitchen.

"Oh, Anja! I'm so sorry, girl!" Danielle cried, dropping to her knees and hugging her dog. "I'm just upset about what we saw—or didn't see—this afternoon. Goodness, girl!" What with a few minutes of vigorous patting and snuggles from her mistress, Anja soon forgot about the incident entirely.

Absently, Danielle glanced at the clock by the refrigerator. "Oh, no…it's already 5:15. I need to get cracking on supper." Ten minutes later, Anja had been fed, and a whirlwind of action—with Danielle at the center of the storm—swirled around the kitchen island. By the time her folks got home from the university, she was humming loudly. The Beatles were her favorite!

Anja was lying next to the window, just beyond the path of activity, looking happily at her mistress, her dark sienna eyes shining brightly. She jumped up when Peter and Amy came in from the garage.

Danielle greeted her parents with a big, "Hi!"

"Hi, back," her father replied. He sprawled out onto the couch, dropping his briefcase on the floor, unceremoniously. "Wow, what a day!" he declared through closed eyes. Amy stood quietly, her nose almost against the front room window facing northwest.

"Well, how about you tell me all about it…after I tell you something you won't believe?" Danielle asked.

"Honey," her mother said, without turning away from the window, "you better hear what we have to tell you first."

CHAPTER THREE

SOME ENCHANTED EVENING

Even before the sun set the horizon ablaze in orange flame, the conversation in the Wheelen home fell to ash and smoke. Danielle felt like she'd just witnessed a horrifying car wreck, and then discovered that none of the occupants survived. It was hard to believe what her parents were telling her.

"Really? I mean, that's crazy, Dad!"

"Honey, we've been over this more than once. It's…"

"Awful. That's what it is!" Amy interrupted her husband. "We can't know for sure. Right? Can we?"

"Not that I can think of, Hon," Peter replied. "In fact, I don't think we need to. Aren't we all pretty certain what's happening?"

"But Dad! You're saying that today, just down the hall from your classrooms, the police conducted an autopsy on a…cow? And they did that because the science lab at the university is large enough—and has the best equipment—to handle this kind of investigation?"

"Yes."

"But what exactly do they think they're investigating? I don't get that part."

"Well, at first, they thought it was a simple cow mutilation. You know, crazy people. Drugs. Nut jobs."

"But then they found the farmer," Amy whispered.

"And he…was…also mutilated?" Danielle asked, her voice a bit higher than normal.

"That's not what Professor Antrim said," Peter replied. "We found Doc Ant in the hallway, pale and sweating, just outside the lab room. He said that it appeared the farmer died of a heart attack, perhaps caused by fright."

"I don't understand why then…why they think swords were involved," Danielle said, tension swelling her throat. "You lost me," she murmured, twisting her hands.

"Look, Honey, I don't know. Your mother and I didn't actually see"—Peter shifted around on the couch nervously—"see the bodies. But they said they've never seen anything like this cow before. Even with a sword, they can't imagine how these…how…how…"

"It was in sections, Danielle," her mother continued quietly. "Like it had been dissected. Except with a huge blade, not a scalpel. 'Intersecting, downward sloping lines, razor sharp,' Professor Antrim said. Horrible…like it happened all at once."

Danielle felt nauseous. Anja whimpered quietly at her feet. The dog didn't like the tension in her home.

"Except," Peter said, and then paused, eyes closed, for such a long time Danielle wondered if he'd fallen asleep, "except for the door to the farmhouse." Indeed, her father's eyes had a sort of dreamy, faraway look. "It was the door—or *lack* of it—that drew the attention of the police in the first place. Because where the door had been—you know, just a normal front door, vertical rectangle with a knob, lock, dead-bolt, hinges and casing around it—it simply wasn't there. The door was gone. Poof! Just a perfectly round empty hole where it had been, with light from the front room streaming out of it. Like those hobbits have in that story you've been reading, Dani, except what it would probably look like with that kind of door swung wide open. And if it wasn't strange enough that there was this perfect, circular hole where a rectangular door should be, it was the leftover wooden rings, three of them, each just a few inches wider than the original hole, that's got the police in a twist. Really puzzled! They're so perplexed as to what could cut through a door, studs—walls, for crying out loud!—not just once, but four times simultaneously...and in a nice perfect circle." His eyes looked glassy.

"And when they went in to check things out, that's when they found him? The poor farmer." Danielle suddenly found her throat to be very dry.

"Yes. That's what we overheard," her mother answered, just above a whisper.

"Later...the cow," her father added. "Except not all of it could be found."

Danielle was suddenly cold. She shuddered.

No one said anything for a long time, each lost in their own thoughts. Anja fidgeted nervously. She didn't want her people to be fraught with fear. But her own thoughts were troubled by the man earlier in the day, the one that spoke with her mistress. Anja didn't like the smell that was on him, any more than the stink coming from where the other men stood in the field. She knew that smell. It was a sad smell. Many an evening she'd laid on the back deck since they'd moved in and watched the cow wander aimlessly in her field, content-edly chewing grass. Anja knew she would miss that cow, even though they'd never been properly introduced. But she didn't like something else about the man in the uniform. *What is it about him?* she wondered to herself. She realized it would take some time to sort out. Anja wasn't hasty about making judgments regarding people. There were some dogs that did make snap judgments, she knew, but those dogs also generally snapped at people, too, as a habit. And she'd been raised better than that.

Finally, Danielle stirred. She shifted her weight between her feet, swaying back and forth like an aspen tree in a slight breeze, and looked at her parents intently. After a moment, her voice tightened so it sounded strangled and higher than normal, she blurted out, "They're here, then. Right? Somehow they followed us?"

Peter murmured and then slowly inhaled, breathing deeply. "It sure looks that way. We've been discovered. Our secret is gone."

"But is it Kahrnahrgx out there?" Amy asked, hysteria shimmering at the edges of her eyes. "Or one of his minions?"

Peter shrugged and shook his head, but said nothing.

"At least we have Anja." Danielle patted her dog for a moment, her hand trembling. Then, she dropped to her knees to give Anja a fierce hug.

"That's right, Dani." Peter smiled wanly. "That's got to count for something."

"I hope so," Amy muttered under her breath, so quietly the others didn't hear her. "I hope so."

CHAPTER FOUR

In the Wee Hours

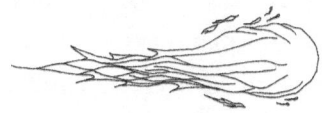

About an hour after their discussion, Danielle watched her parents quietly pull her bedroom door nearly shut. Although her friends would have made fun of her if they'd known, she liked that her parents still tucked her in, especially on a day like today. But she'd had to convince them she'd be safe on her own with Anja. They had wanted her to stay with them in the master bedroom. She'd made her case to stay in her room on the fact that they had adopted Anja for just such a time as this. By the time her parents relented, her mind was so full of the news they had shared with her that she forgot to tell them about her own, strange day. Even though she didn't feel like she could sleep because of all the unsettling things that happened during the day, she still yawned.

"Whew, Anja. Maybe I'm more tired than I thought." She patted her dog's head. Anja sat on the floor next to the bed, her head resting on her mistress's pillow.

"At least you can sneak out of my room if you need to, girl, for a late-night snack. I just hope all this news doesn't ruin another night of sleep for me."

"What do you think, Hon?" Peter asked Amy from their huge closet next to the bedroom. "Do you think she'll be OK?"

"How do I know?" Amy snapped back, brushing her hair even as she walked in from the bathroom. "None of us has slept well for the past four days, apparently. Now we have strong—and frightening—evidence as to why. None of this should be happening." There was a shrillness to Amy's voice that reminded Peter of when they'd first found the cursed Key years ago. He was troubled by her tenseness. Now, he realized it was probably foolish of him to believe that, with the Key destroyed, his wife would be rid of the clawing fear that had haunted her during Danielle's early years. Apparently, the deep-flowing, silent fear had gnawed at Amy until it left a permanent mark upon her. He reached out and gently stroked her anxiety-lined face.

"Well, then, let's turn in and do our best to remedy that problem," he replied, quietly. "Let's get some sleep. As much as we can, in fact."

Amy twitched at the touch of her husband. "Oh, I'm sorry," she murmured. "I don't know what's come over me, Peter. I had just thought…hoped…prayed…this business was over! *Why* shouldn't it be over? Didn't we destroy him? You know, when Dani destroyed his evil Key?"

"Uh, no, Hon. Not destroyed. At least, the others didn't think so. I mean, yes, it diminished his power. And yes, the Key was destroyed. But he, himself, wasn't. That's why the others were concerned about us."

"But then why," her voice pitched higher than before, "haven't they done anything to protect us?"

Peter shrugged dejectedly. He didn't have an answer that would be satisfactory to his wife. In fact, he didn't have any that satisfied him either. "I…I don't know, Ames. Somehow,

I didn't think we'd be left to our own devices. I mean, you know, they became friends. I just don't think…ah, I'm just too tired to think, frankly. Let's turn in, or I'll fall asleep here in the closet."

He took her hand, walked to the bed, lay down and draped his arm around his wife, and then fell immediately asleep, dead to the world.

"Dagnabit!" Danielle fumed. "Why doesn't someone turn the dratted alarm off?" She was in the school library, which was her favorite place on the campus of Parkside. The solitude helped her think. It had lots of books about foreign countries, which had become both important and interesting to Danielle since last year. She'd intently studied those books, highlighting the lands of Scandinavia, especially those with a broad sweep of the history of Norway. In fact, she'd just been reviewing a book focused on Norwegian communities of the nineteenth century when the alarm had sounded. And awakened her. She'd been asleep, her face nestled by the book.

"Turn it off!" she yelled. Then she realized she'd just broken a cardinal rule in Parkside Junior High's library. Horrified, she looked around quickly to see if the librarian, Mrs. Uffante, had heard. "Hm, that's odd. Where is she? Come to think of it, where is…anyone?"

Immediately, Danielle felt a wave of fear roll over her. She couldn't remember when she'd last seen someone in the library, or even if she had ever seen anyone. And that blasted alarm kept ringing.

"Wait a minute! Maybe everyone else got out of here already!" She jumped up out of her chair so quickly she caught her foot on the table leg.

She fell out of bed in a heap, blankets strewn around and under her.

"Huh?" she cried. "Oh, blast. I've been dreaming!" Except the incessant, high-pitched beeping followed her from the dream into wakefulness. Anja whimpered at her bedroom door.

Danielle quickly extricated herself from twisted sheets and blankets and ran to her door. As she yanked it open, her father went racing by and sprinted down the stairs, jumping them three at a time. Only then did Danielle realize the annoying beeps were actually coming from the doorbell. Whoever had been relentlessly pushing the doorbell had just started pounding on their door. Anja lunged past Danielle, almost knocking her over, and chased after Peter.

Without thinking, Danielle bounded down the stairs after her father and dog. By the time she reached the first floor, Peter had already opened the door. A policeman filled the opening, his nose just inches from where the door had been. Silver streetlight glowed behind him, casting him in silhouette. But enough light from their entryway shone on his face that Danielle recognized him at once. It was the same officer from the crime scene earlier that day. Anja must have also recognized him, too, because she dropped her head down, spread out her stance, bared her glimmering teeth and growled so low it rumbled.

Peter was startled by Anja's growling almost as much as by the policeman stepping into their house. His mouth still open to speak to the officer, Peter twisted his head to shush the dog. But before Peter could say anything, Anja launched herself at the man. At the same moment, the officer abruptly flung his bare hands out at Peter, with palms out and fingers aimed at the ceiling. Even though his hands never touched him, Peter was hurled up and backward. As if in slow motion, Danielle watched in horror as her father sailed violently past her, flying through the length of the house until he crashed into the rear wall, narrowly missing the picture window looking onto the patio. The look on his face told her everything she feared. But what drew her attention was Anja impacting the policeman, chest high, with enough energy to knock him off the front step and into the grass beyond. Furious barking was quickly drowned out by an unearthly howling. Danielle's blood ran cold.

"Oh, no! It can't be!" Danielle screamed. "Daddy! Anja!"

Moments later, she heard a great yelp from Anja and then her faithful and brave dog hurtled through the house, knocking Peter back down, just after he'd stood up. Both slid, piled into a heap, and crashed into the back wall. Danielle heard a sickening crunch. Her father grunted, struggling for a moment to get out from under the unconscious dog, and then passed out.

Danielle's feet were leaden. It took great concentration to move them. Worse, paralyzing fear clouded her mind. She couldn't decide which she wanted more: to see to the welfare of her dad and beloved dog or flee from the policeman. She took too long to decide. A scraping noise at the door drew her eyes back to the front of her home.

Danielle blinked and shook her head. Her eyes must be deceiving her. Had the man grown taller? He was nearly as tall as the doorway! How could that be? His clothes were ragged and torn. His shoes! The man's feet had burst through them. Leather flopped at either side of the soles. And his skin began to change color, first from a tanned, blond man to the mixed colors of granite, then deepening to dark slate, until he finally shimmered obsidian. His features changed as his body expanded. No longer did he resemble a normal human man, but a horribly disfigured one. Finally, his black leather jacket, emblazoned with insignias and officer's stripes, burst into shreds as wings erupted behind him. The silvery light from the streetlamps fell into darkness, choked off by his out-stretched bat-like wings. At the last, the man's pale blue eyes closed, then reopened bright red and luminous, like the glow-ing center of a house on fire.

"We meet at last," a voice cracked, as stone upon stone. A wicked sneer spread across the creature's face.

"Wh—" Danielle's voice caught from dry fear. "Who are you?"

"I am your benefactor."

"How's that?" she squeezed out.

"I am Sedig-Tahr. I am come to rescue you, child, from... all this." His voice oozed malevolence and sarcasm.

Danielle was light-headed. It was difficult to breathe prop-erly. She forced herself to relax and inhale deeply. She couldn't hope to run if her body was so tense.

Sedig-Tahr noticed the subtle change. "My dear, you are not planning on such a silly and hopeless effort as attempt-ing an escape? By now, you should know better. Yes? Did you learn nothing from my less competent brethren?"

Despite her heart telling her to be quiet, she blurted out, "What's it to you, beast?" She immediately turned on her heels and sprinted towards the back of the house, hoping against hope either her father or her dog was recovered enough to help...to fight. Better yet, both.

"Oh, you can't escape, child. I will have you!" She could hear Sedig-Tahr behind her, a crunching sound on the stone floor...and then a sharp twang.

"Not without paying a high price!" Amy bellowed, her face pressed up to the wooden banister. She'd stolen down the stairs, armed with her bow, while Sedig-Tahr threatened her daughter.

Danielle slid sideways in her stocking feet, at the same time twisting her head around. Sedig-Tahr arced his body back and forth, one heavily muscled arm flailing wildly. With the other, he clutched an arrow stuck through the side of his neck.

"There, you hideous creature!" Amy jumped down the final steps in one leap, racing first to her daughter and then to her husband, with Danielle right behind her.

Peter eyes squinted through pain, but he was lucid enough. "Nice shot, Ames," he moaned.

Danielle gently stroked Anja's large head, trying to assess what damage the dog had suffered.

Only moments had passed since Amy's bow shot. But no one's attention was on Sedig-Tahr. A rough gargling noise re-directed their focus back to the entry area. The creature leaned heavily against the honey-oak paneling in the hallway. His left hand wrapped tightly around his neck, while his right hand slowly—horribly—pulled the embedded arrow out of his throat.

"Oh, no," whispered Peter. "He's not going down, Amy." Needing her complete attention, he grabbed his daughter's wrist and twisted it hard. Danielle whimpered. "Honey, you need to run. I'm in no shape to...you just need to run. Now!" He tried to shove her towards the back door and into the garage.

In spite of her father's urgency, Danielle turned slowly to face the front hall. Sedig-Tahr still held the arrow in his right hand. His left hand was now pressed hard against his throat. From their experience with gargoyles, the Wheelens recognized that he was healing his own wound.

Amy shrieked, "He's almost healed himself, Dani. Go! Now! You know what he can do. You've seen it! You must leave before—"

But it was too late. Sedig-Tahr unexpectedly straightened himself, his head nearly brushing the tall ceiling. Sweeping his arm left to right, he flung the arrow so hard it pierced the opposite wall. It quivered, humming slightly, next to a large family picture. His eyes grew large and bloomed in fiery rage.

"Now, where were we, girl, before your mother so rudely interrupted us?" he asked quietly, in mock reverence. He pressed his muscular arms toward the ceiling and pushed his hands into the beam overhead. They could see dust erupt from the force. Ragged sharp talons emerged from the tops of his hands. "By the way, woman," he said, seething at Amy, "that arrow of yours did *hurt*. You will regret—*terminally*—your actions here tonight."

All at once, Amy screamed, "Run!" and shoved Danielle violently towards the back door. Peter bellowed, "No!" and leapt to his feet, hauling Amy up with him. Roused by Danielle's gentle strokes, Anja howled defiantly at the gargoyle—for Sedig-Tahr's transformation was now complete and unmistakable. The huge Akita coiled into a trembling mass of teeth and rippling muscle, prepared to hurl herself at the vile creature threatening her family…her mistress!

The gargoyle lunged forward, his talons thrust towards Peter's face. Instinctively, Peter dodged to his right while pushing Amy to the left, in the direction of Danielle, who was moving agonizingly slow. Even as he assessed where the gargoyle's strike would land, he computed the miserable chances that his daughter had of getting through the door before he and Amy were overwhelmed by their foe. They'd be no match for—

"What the...?"

The flagstone floor midway between them and the advancing gargoyle surged upwards with a shattering eruption of jagged rock, dust and broken grout. Immediately, the cloud of debris began to take shape, then halved into two shapes and solidified. Through the gloom of shifting forms between him and Sedig-Tahr, Peter could see the eyes of their enemy widen in horror and despair. But his momentum was too great to redirect away from the shapes now before him. With a cry of wrath and fury loud enough to break the windows in front of him, Sedig-Tahr slammed into the two shapes, now also formed into gargoyles, with full force. But these gargoyles had burst forth on bended knee, thus avoiding his outstretched talons. Their talons, in turn, were aimed straight at his chest. His own thirst to bring violence and death to the humans instead brought it unexpectedly unto himself. Skewered, unable to move, mortally wounded, Sedig-Tahr's last vision was of the enormous dog hurtling towards his neck.

Anja slammed into the dying gargoyle, knocking him loose from the impaling talons. But, before Sedig-Tahr crashed to the stone floor behind him, he vanished. A swirl of dust enveloped Anja, as she slid to a stop, looking back for the gargoyle, fury and confusion in her eyes.

"The beast!" Amy cried. "He's parted!"

CHAPTER FIVE

Friends Well Met

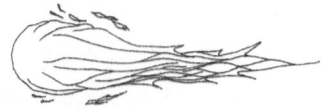

"You've what?" Amy asked again.

"We've been waiting," Conomorg repeated flatly.

Peter stared, slack jawed. While very pleased that Danielle was unharmed because of his unexpected houseguests, it was still an unnerving discovery.

"We're sorry, Conomorg," he blurted out. "And to you, Ita-Mudak," he continued, bowing to his friend. "It's just... just so..."

"Fantastic!" cried Danielle. "Wow! To think you guys were laying in our floor the whole time we've been living here. That's just *fantastic!* Really!" Danielle began spinning around the flagstone floor, her arms outspread, a huge smile dancing across her face. Anja ran happily around her in mad circles.

"You see, Peter," Ita-Mudak, the larger of the gargoyles replied, smiling at Danielle, "after the battle for the Temple of Kahrnahrgx, and after we saw you off, several of us returned there with squads of our soldiers. We needed to look for any surviving friends—as well as enemies—and dismantle the temple structure, buildings and prisons. We also had to collapse Kahrnahrgx's tunnels and caverns. Great foolishness it would have been to allow him or his minions to return there.

Yet, it was during the destruction of his temple facility that we found it."

"And what was that, again?" Amy interrupted, her voice edged with frustration and tension.

"Evidence, Amy," Conomorg interjected. "Unmistakable. We found, without any doubt, disturbing…compelling… gruesome evidence that Kahrnahrgx had successfully combined *fundamentals* of gargoylekind with humankind."

Danielle abruptly stopped dancing. Anja, immediately sensing something had gone wrong, nestled against her leg.

"Remind me what that means, exactly?" Peter said, his face the color of chalk.

Ita-Mudak shifted on his enormous taloned feet and pointed to the area where Sedig-Tahr had vanished into dust. "It means that our enemy, through unspeakably vile and wicked devices, has created a gargoyle adaptation—an abomination—that can *appear* human *because* it is. At least, the creature shares in sufficient fundamentals of humankind that it is nearly untraceable by us. From that terrible discovery until this moment, we have guarded you and your family," he said, looking at Danielle.

"In your world," Conomorg added.

"This creature only became known to us when he stepped into your house," Ita-Mudak continued. "But there was no question that one of these hybrids would come for you."

"So, then," Danielle choked, "you believe there's more than one of these creatures?"

"Yes," both gargoyles replied in unison.

Danielle leaned into Anja for support. Her legs felt like rubber.

"Well, how many?" Amy's eyes widened, anxiety washing across her face. Her voice had a shrillness to it that reminded Danielle of fingernails on a chalkboard.

Peter was also filled with fear, of course. Still, he was amazed—and oddly comforted—when both gargoyles struggled to soften their slab-like faces out of fondness for their human friends.

Ita-Mudak answered quietly, "We don't know for certain, but we believe there are only two hybrids."

"Only one, now," Conomorg added, with what Peter took for a valiant attempt at a smile. "Your foe tonight, this Sedig-Tahr, was mortally wounded, without doubt. Yet, in parting at the last moment, he foiled our ability to discover more about his kind. Also without doubt, his goal was to take news of your whereabouts with him to Kahrnahrgx. Or his minions. It matters not. You are no longer safe here."

"Are you not able to trace him, then?" Peter asked. "I thought you were able to do that."

Again, Peter observed an effort at smiling. This time it was from Ita-Mudak.

"We are sorry, Peter. No. It is difficult for all but the strongest of gargoyles to trace another's parting. Lately it has grown very difficult indeed. The enemy has grown skilled, as have we, at disguising the destinations of their partings. With these mutant creatures, it appears impossible to trace them. What we are more successful at, as you experienced before, is sensing our foes prior to their arrival, especially when they part in large numbers. However, with this creature, we didn't know of his presence here—in your world, in your time—until he physically stepped onto the stone floor of this house. Even so, we were not sure we would be able to sense him at all." The gargoyle paused for a moment and stroked his strong jaw thoughtfully.

"Do you have any idea when he may have appeared? Have you observed anything unusual or out of the ordinary?" Conomorg continued.

All at once, each of the Wheelens tried to tell the pair of gargoyles about the strange events of the prior day. After several minutes of interruptions, side explanations, revisions and lots of pent-up energy, they had provided a sufficient-enough recounting that Conomorg nodded his massive head.

"So, the beast must have come only recently, then. It is not difficult to conclude that the farmer was stricken unto death from fear. How could he not? Advanced in years, frail in body, only to see his doorway cut away in ribbons, like one of your machines might do? Of course, the cow was simply food to Sedig-Tahr. Crude, yes, but functional. However, his main intent was to strike terror into this part of your world—this *community*, as you say—in the hope that he'd flush you out somehow. Yet, I think he already had located you, or near enough, to be so close to your home as the nearby farm…"

"But when you spoke to him, Danielle," Ita-Mudak interrupted, "it was then he knew his prey was found. It is a wonder that he didn't simply seize you and part with you at that moment! For that we can be most grateful."

"I'm confused, Ita-Mudak," Danielle said softly. "Why… why…I thought…you know…" Her heart drummed in her ears so fast that she found it hard to concentrate. What with several nights of shattered sleep, challenging days at school, frightfully disturbing news from earlier in the day—*Actually*, yesterday, she thought—not to mention the terrors of this long night, her mind was rummy with fatigue. She wasn't even sure what her question was. Or did she have more than one? Why hadn't the creature snatched her when she stood in front of him, unwittingly, when she'd been walking Anja near the farm? Why not?

Sensing her thought, Conomorg bent over at his waist until he was eye level with Danielle. "I am not certain, you see. But I believe when these hybrids are in their human form, they are powerful and dangerous, as we have seen, but they are unable to part. For that, it appears they must be fully transformed back into their gargoyle nature. They are greatly disguised by taking on human characteristics, as we have witnessed. Yet at a high price. They set aside much of their innate powers."

"From what I saw, it didn't take him long to transform back into his full, nasty self," Peter scoffed, limping over to where Amy's arrow stuck out from the wall paneling. He pulled at it several times unsuccessfully, straining hard, until his face turned red.

"True," replied Ita-Mudak, who walked over and pulled the arrow out of the wood panel, like a warm knife from soft butter. He handed it to Peter, then walked to the front door and closed it. His talons clicked loudly with each step. Turning back to face Danielle, he said, "It is possible, as Conomorg has said, that these mutant gargoyles cannot part when in human form. Of that, I have my doubts. However, have you surmised another reason he may have left you untouched at the side of the road?"

Danielle noticed Ita-Mudak glance at Anja, who was now resting on her feet. "Are you saying that Anja had something to do with it?"

"Did she not indicate that something was 'not right'—as you said earlier—with the man in the uniform?"

"Well, yes, that's true! At first, the policeman—Sedig-Tahr, I mean—seemed fine. Kind of intense maybe. But, with the situation, it seemed normal, I guess, that he'd be intense. But Anja wasn't really indicating anything about him...wait! She was tense, herself. But I figured it was from the nauseating smell coming from the field. So, it wasn't the smell that bothered her, after all, now that I think about it! It was *Sedig-Tahr!* Now, it makes way more sense." She patted Anja's head affectionately. "Good girl!"

Anja swished her tail thoughtfully. *Of course I didn't like him. He smelled, too.*

"OK, then," Peter said, looking at Ita-Mudak, while scratching his head. "What's next?"

"Well, I know one thing for sure," Amy replied. "We're not leaving until you've been looked at! You and Anja."

It only took a few minutes for Conomorg and Ita-Mudak to assess the wounds and damage that Sedig-Tahr had inflicted on Peter and Anja. In just a few more, Danielle's father and dog were healed by the still-strange powers of their gargoyle friends.

Amy was amazed at how subtle and gentle the gargoyles' hands were as they held them pressed against the wounds. She flinched as she watched them push their slate-grey palms directly against the scrapes on her husband's face and arms. *He doesn't even flinch. They must not only have the ability to heal—quickly!—but also desensitize the area,* she marveled to herself. And then, not even a scar to speak of! *Wow!*

Anja simply flopped over for Conomorg, as if waiting for a good tummy rub. Danielle thought her dog would purr, if she were able to.

"Boy, fellas!" Peter exclaimed to Ita-Mudak and Conomorg. "If people weren't frightened to death of you two, we could open a gym or maybe a physical therapy clinic with you two as masseuses." Peter twisted his right arm back and forth, studying it intensely. "It feels great! I can't even find where the damage was."

Amy stepped over to her husband, slid an arm around his waist and kissed him on the cheek, smiling. "Honey, even if they were dressed up nicely, I think most folks would blanch at their long nails, don't you think?"

Before Peter could reply, she quickly went to the gargoyles and—almost as if she didn't want to think about it too long—stood on her toes to reach Conomorg, then Ita-Mudak, kissing them each on the cheek, too. "Thank you," she said quietly, her eyes glistening. "Thank you!"

"Quite right," Peter added. "All kidding aside, we are in your debt yet again."

Danielle, who had been watching all this while patting Anja's wide head, jumped up from the floor, ran over to Ita-Mudak and jumped as high as she could to hug the monolithic creature. Securely attached to his neck, Danielle's legs merrily bobbed up and down.

The sudden movement of Danielle got Anja very excited. She jumped and ran crazy circles around Conomorg. This was such an odd scene to behold, just minutes after being faced with the seething malice of Sedig-Tahr that all the Wheelens burst out laughing. Even Conomorg smiled slightly, apparently amused by the surprised look on his comrade's angular face.

Danielle released her grip on Ita-Mudak, fell to the floor and then repeated the maneuver on Conomorg. Then it was Ita-Mudak's turn to grin at the sight of a fearsome, mighty lord of gargoyles reduced to a puzzled, awkward recipient of earnest gratitude by a human girl. When Conomorg, at a loss of what to do, began gently patting Danielle's back, carefully splaying his talons up and away from her, Ita-Mudak actually began laughing. The sound vaguely reminded Peter of the clattering of large stones being emptied from a dump truck, during a landscaping project on the university's campus a few years earlier.

Amy, seeing that the gargoyle's laughter was from genuine mirth, also began laughing again. Which, of course, got Peter laughing. Finally, Danielle began laughing, too, her nose just inches from Conomorg's wide, flat nose. After a moment, she hugged him tightly around the neck and dropped back to the floor.

Peter noticed Ita-Mudak actually wink at Conomorg. He found this to be immensely comforting, even though he was surprised to see this moment of lightheartedness between these gargoyle guards.

"So?" Peter asked. "Since Anja and I are healed up now, what's next? Staying here seems like a really bad idea."

"Indeed," replied Ita-Mudak. "We've tarried here long enough." Noticing Amy's glaring eyes, he added, "However, it was well advised to look after you and your four-legged companion properly before parting."

"Come! Join hands," Conomorg said, as he reached out his enormous hands, his left to Amy, then his right to Danielle. Quickly, the others finished forming a circle. Danielle called for Anja to come stand next to her. Instead of joining hands with her father, Danielle grabbed the thick, heavy scruff on Anja's neck, while Peter did the same. In this way, they added Anja into the circle.

"Where are we going?" Danielle asked Conomorg.

"To see Lohxnahr."

"You know," Peter chuckled, "I'm a scientist and still find this parting so, well, so—"

"Awesome!" Danielle finished.

"Yes, Dani! It is awesome indeed. And somewhat frightening, while also being absolutely—"

"Intriguing!" Amy interrupted, grinning wide.

Peter cocked his head to one side and grinned back. "Was I saying something, Ita-Mudak? Conomorg? No, I guess not," he declared with mock anger. "Still, sometime I'd like it explained more thoroughly, because intriguing as it is, it would be a truly awesome—and terrible—power in the wrong hands. Folding, or parting, space and time, like going through a doorway…"

And with that, the inhabitants of the Wheelens' home—human, canine and their long-hidden gargoyle guests—vanished into thin air, just as dawn broke through the rear porch windows.

CHAPTER SIX
THE GLIMMER

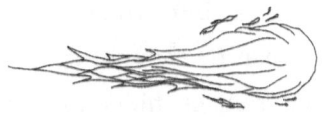

There wasn't any sound. Nor was there any smell. If there also hadn't been any light, Paign would have thought he was entombed in a coffin, dead. But he could see, although not much. *Wherever I am, it's dim, like twilight, or maybe predawn. How long have I been here?* He ordered his hands to reach out in front of him and sweep away the gloom. His brain registered movement, but that was only because he felt his shoulders contract as his arms swung up from his sides. *Why can't I see anything?* So, he held his right hand up in front of his eyes. As before, he was certain that his hand did, in fact, swing up directly before his face. Still, he saw nothing but the pale orange shimmering that had been twinkling all around him for what seemed like ages. *It's like being covered in dry, orange water!* Growing more anxious—and in an effort to confirm his mind's command—this time he ordered his right hand to strike his nose.

"Ow!" Paign cried. "Svarte! Why can't I see my hand when I just hit myself with it?" The sound of his voice was odd, like it had been bellowed into his pillow.

Still, all that registered in Paign's view was the pale orange glittering. By now, Paign was fully worked up and agitated. He struggled to move his feet, but they seemed to be bound, or stuck. Of course, he could no more see them than he could the hand he'd just given himself a bloody nose with. At least he assumed the warm, moist sensation dribbling down his upper lip was blood. Furious now, Paign pushed down with his left foot as hard as he could, while pulling up with his right leg. Not seeing what bound him in this bizarre, glistening place angered him all the more. But, straining as he did, even mustering more energy than he thought possible, Paign still was unable to break free from his hidden bondage. However, he could tell that if he tried much more, he would do serious harm to himself. Something had already popped in his left ankle, which was now throbbing.

"Aaaygh!" he screamed. "What is this place?"

A cracking sound startled Paign. It instantly reminded him of when deep winter's expanding ice sometimes caused the granite to crack near his home, nestled near the base of Ruar's Ridge. It was a rare event but always one that commanded attention because splitting stone often came just before an avalanche. Instinctively, Paign clenched his fists together. He wasn't home, so the cracking wasn't due to ice. In fact, he had a bad feeling about the noise.

The second round of cracking sounded less like rock on rock and more like the longshoremen back home when a ship came into port. Many of them would shout at the same time to each other along the pier or up at the sailors leaning over the gunnels of incoming ships. Paign had observed this many times, always amazed the dockmen could understand anything over the enormous racket of so many voices shouting. But, of course, by now Paign knew that the cracking sounds were coming from a voice, not from stone.

"You are collected within the Glimmer." The words crashed into Paign's ears like thunder.

Finally, the orange shroud changed in appearance. Like someone ripping fabric from top to bottom, a tear formed directly before Paign, just enough for him to peer through the gap into a stone room beyond. As Paign had feared, standing in the foreground was a gnarled, hulking gargoyle, the color of basalt; his eyes glowed with an intense, fiery red. Without the muffling of the orange glittering substance in his way, Paign could plainly tell the beast was laughing at him. So low and guttural was the gargoyle's voice that it again sounded something like a rock slide.

"What do you want with me?" Paign bellowed at the beast, his anger winning over his fear.

"With you?" the gargoyle rumbled. "What makes you think we want you?"

Confused, Paign fired back, "How did I get here?"

"So, you don't remember? Ha! Even better."

Without thinking, Paign impulsively twisted his legs, as if avoiding an obstacle while telemark skiing, in a renewed effort to break free. Immediately, there was another, louder pop from his ankle, and he twitched in agony, screaming.

The gargoyle stepped forward until it was just beyond Paign's reach, at the outer edge of the Glimmer. Paign, in spite of his anguish, registered that the gargoyle's feet–talons had come up before him.

Against the bitter ache pulsing up his leg, Paign raised his head and glared at his foe. "No! I don't remember, you beast! Who are you and why should I care?" Paign yelled through the gap in the orange shroud that still enveloped him.

"I am Rance-Dahl, keeper of the Glimmer," the gargoyle replied, suddenly reaching into the gap with his enormous hands and long talons, and then pulling the folds of the gap further apart. His head thrust through until it was a bare inch from Paign's.

"I am your captor and keeper, human! It matters not to me that you remember how you got here. It matters even less to me if you understand your purpose. All that matters to me is all that *should* matter to you: the Master wishes to use you as a lure for another. Beyond this singular function, he cares not what happens to you. The Master has given me free rein in my dealings with you, so long as you do not expire prematurely. While I don't expect you to long linger here, it is certain that your stay in the Glimmer will feel like an eternity. That I promise you."

Before he could respond or react, Rance-Dahl reached into the glimmering orange that held Paign, seized him by his shoulders and yanked him out, throwing him across the room. Paign flew more than half the length of the room before crashing to the rough floor, then slid hard into a stone wall.

"Shall we begin, then?" sneered Rance-Dahl. With one snap of his leathery wings, he quickly sailed over and reached down to pick up Paign.

CHAPTER SEVEN

SOLACE

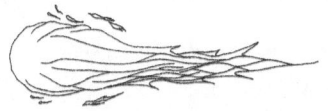

"What do you mean, Anders? When was the last time you saw Paign?" Freida was worried. Very worried. She could plainly see that Anders was agonizing about the welfare of his best friend, Paign, who also happened to be his cousin.

"I...I, uh," Anders muttered, shaken. Fear clawed at his mind, making it difficult for him to think straight.

The two sat on the porch swing in front of Anders's home. Everything, it seemed, was in full bloom across the Honellaken Valley. Just across the road, the forest of mostly maple trees swayed gently, reminding Freida of wind blowing through a ripe wheat field, with the canopy of leaves gently waving to and fro. The breeze itself was very pleasant, because it brought cooled air down from Ruar's Ridge. Normally, Freida loved to listen to the gentle rustling of the maple leaves. She'd sniff their slightly waxy, honeyed scent and think of sipping tea, along with a winter breakfast of pancakes.

But recent events made enjoying such moments impossible. Anders's right knee bobbed up and down like a manic sewing machine needle. His right hand was balled up in a fist and bounced rhythmically off the top of his knee. Freida thought the combination looked like a bobbing, upside-down exclamation point. To Anders, the rustling in the trees was like fingernails on a chalkboard.

Freida, despite her own gnawing worry for Paign, was overcome with pity for Anders. She reached out and wrapped her slender, long fingers around Anders's right hand. His leg immediately stopped moving, and his fist rested on his knee.

"It was three days ago…no, four. That's right," Anders said with difficulty, his voice strained. "Yes, it was four days ago. We'd been arguing. You know, like the other times."

"I was afraid of that," Freida murmured. "About—"

"Yes!" Anders interrupted her, his eyes fiery. Then he shrugged, glanced briefly at Freida and muttered, "Sorry."

Freida smiled reassuringly and waited.

"You're right, of course, Freida," Anders continued. "You always are about us." Taking a deep breath before continuing, Anders shrugged again. "It was about Danielle."

"Paign hopes to see her again, correct?" Freida asked quietly. "He still believes she'll come back here?" In her own way, Freida missed Danielle probably as much as Paign. But she knew neither she nor Paign missed Danielle as much as Anders. Suddenly, Freida didn't know what to say.

The only sounds for a few minutes were Anders's bobbing leg creaking the floorboards of the front porch and the maples rustling with the breeze.

Freida struggled with what to tell her friend that might be helpful. She wanted to comfort Anders. But she, too, was frightened for Paign. Uncomfortably, she found herself admitting that she missed Paign the same way Anders missed Danielle. She didn't know whether she liked the feelings she had for Paign. They'd been friends for so long now—her whole life, really. What would happen if he discovered how she felt?

"Why does he have to keep bringing her up, Freida?" Anders cried. "She can't come back here. Not on her own, certainly. She'd have to have help—like last time—to cross several hundred years!"

Abruptly, Anders jumped up from the swing and began pacing back and forth across the porch. His fists were balled up, mindlessly pounding against his hips. Freida watched him, her grey eyes blinking quickly.

"It just makes me so...*crazy*, Freida!" Anders slapped the stout, knurled oak post nearest the porch swing. She wasn't surprised to see him wince. After all, these posts had held up the porch's roof for decades before Anders was even born. The Knutsons' farm had been home to Anders's father and his father's father. "What chance is there of ever seeing her again? What chance, Freida?"

Freida had no idea what to say. Staring at her feet, she slowly shook her head and muttered, "I don't know, Anders. I just don't—" When she looked up at Anders and saw his eyes welled up, she impulsively jumped up and hugged him fiercely.

Then, she pushed him suddenly away. "There's something you don't understand, Anders! That's why I'm here. Paign's gone! I mean, I know you haven't seen him for four days, but he's not been home, either, since three days ago. His mother came over today looking for him. She's still with my parents, I suppose. My mother, at least. My father went off to look for him at the same time I came running over here to see you."

Freida glanced away and stared down the road that led to her farm. When she looked back at Anders, her eyes revealed a growing anxiety. "His mother said he'd gone camping but was supposed to come back last night. He'd been upset about his argument with you, I guess, and wanted time alone. He's gone."

"But I didn't mean anything, you know," Anders sputtered. "I had just told him to stop talking about Danielle," his voice trailed off, so that he barely whispered Danielle's name.

Anders seemed even more distressed than a moment earlier. Freida stared at him, with no idea of what to do.

"I didn't tell him to leave! I just...I just didn't want to hear him talking about her like she'll be back soon. Or ever. Well, he didn't like that, as you might guess. He shoved me down. I yelled something at him—I don't remember what. He yelled something back. Then he stomped off."

Thoughtlessly, Anders slapped the knurled post again. Yelling out in pain, he tucked his stinging hand under his other arm.

Freida winced. The distress of seeing Anders's self-inflicted suffering resonated with her own conflict.

"With Paign gone," she choked out, "maybe we will see her again, Anders. Maybe soon." Her eyes shimmered as she stared into his. "You know?" she pleaded. "To help find him," she said, the words tumbling out in little gasps. "With Paign...gone."

And then the fear that had been hammering hard against her heart finally swept over her. She collapsed to the porch floor, curled up on herself and sobbed against Anders's legs.

"With...Paign...gone..."

CHAPTER EIGHT

REUNION

This landscape is almost lunar, Peter thought. It was difficult to make out much in the near-total darkness. In the silvery glow of a waxing crescent moon, he could see nothing that resembled vegetation. The air was warm enough to be comfortable, and the arid terrain reflected moonlight off of stone and glittery soil. Peter felt a tingle steal down his back. *Otherworldly...man, this place kind of gives me the creeps.* He was cross with himself for feeling uneasy, even with Conomorg and Ita-Mudak standing like sentries nearby. And he knew he was being absurd. *How do I know what "lunar" looks like? Watching the moon landing on TV hardly makes me an authority on the subject.* Still, he couldn't shake the feeling that they'd come to a place...to a place—he couldn't put his finger on it.

Danielle, looking somewhat ghostly, showed no concern on her face, for which Peter was grateful. But then she had Anja next to her, an imposing sentry in her own right. He again felt a rush of gratitude to Amy for picking out such an enormous beast of a dog. Anja was panting but seemed happy.

Amy stared unblinking at Danielle stroking Anja, but her mind wasn't on Danielle. In fact, Amy was fully engaged in the memories of her previous experiences with their gargoyle protectors. While the outcome of those encounters was positive—they were alive, after all—she found her reminiscing was not pleasant or encouraging. They'd all been so close to a horrifying end. *What's going on? Where's Lohxnahr?* Amy shuddered. *Are they after Danielle, again? And what about the others?*

As if he'd heard her thoughts, Conomorg said, "Lohxnahr will be here soon."

"Hey, wait a minute!" Peter yelled out, startling Danielle and Amy. Anja barked at him. "I figured out where we are! At least, I think so. Isn't this ridge near the village of Taksar Bhojpur? Ames! Look around, Hon. Don't you see? Smell! Take a deep whiff! Can't you smell the sissoo and sapwood trees? It's just like when we were here years ago!"

Amy stood quickly and took a deep breath through her nose. "You're right, Peter! I'm sure of it," Amy replied, excited. "That explains this headache I've got. How high do you think we are?"

"Hm." Peter thought for a moment. "Best as I can recall, if we're where I think we are, we'd be at least 2,800—maybe 3,000—meters."

"Dad, that doesn't help me," Danielle said, irritably. "You should know by now that I haven't learned metric yet. How high are we?"

"Dani, if I'm close to being right about our location, we might be just a tad below 10,000 feet up. We're certainly high enough to experience altitude sickness." In the thin moonlight, Peter couldn't tell if his daughter's face was truly pale. "How are you feeling, Honey?"

Danielle yawned and stretched her arms over her head. "Oh, OK, I guess, Daddy. I'm just tired. Sleepy, you know. And I have a whopper of a headache. What time is it, anyway?"

"I don't know, Dani," Peter yawned back. "Sunup should come soon, I think. Looks like the horizon is starting to lighten a bit," he said, trying to sound unconcerned. But he got up and carefully picked his way across the uneven ground, finally sitting down next to Conomorg.

"So, how long will we be here, Conomorg? And is here where I think it is?" Peter asked, talking over the building breeze. "This air is pretty thin for us. It seems to be affecting Danielle, Amy and even Anja. So far, I'm doing alright with it."

"Hm," Conomorg replied. "I was not aware that you humans had restrictions with elevation. As far as our location, it is where we were commanded to be. We know not the human name of it." The massive gargoyle stretched his wings out and twisted at his hips. Even though the movement was slow and gentle, it disrupted a plume of dust on both sides of him.

Peter bent over in a fit of coughing. "Well," he choked out, "at least, I was doing fine in this thin air until you covered me in dust." His coughing resumed immediately.

Conomorg smiled plainly enough, understanding Peter's humor by now. "I don't know how long we will be here, Peter. I expected Lohxnahr at the darkest hour of the night. But, as you can see, it is now growing light."

The ridgeline on the other side of the deep valley was sharply defined against a cold, dark azure sky.

Peter kicked at the ground, then shook his head at the dust he kicked up. "Do you find that troubling? Lohxnahr, I mean. Being late and all." He resumed coughing from the new dust cloud, a victim of his own making.

Even though the night was vanishing very slowly, Peter could see that Conomorg stared at the ridge top as if expecting a pair of wings to come sailing over it. While all gargoyles seemed capable of flight—as he'd witnessed firsthand—he thought it unlikely that Lohxnahr would fly to meet them. He was about to ask Conomorg a second time, when he saw the gargoyle turn his head back and forth. *No? He's stumped!* Peter couldn't remember a time that he'd seen such a simple human gesture come from one of these creatures. He found it very unsettling. *Somehow it seemed better when everything about them was foreign*, he thought.

So quiet was Conomorg's reply that Peter nearly missed it. Then he wished he had.

"Yes. Very troubling."

Freida had lost track of time. All she knew was that her face hurt from where it had lain against Anders's boot and that her heart hurt worse.

Slowly, she rose to her feet and smiled weakly at Anders, rather embarrassed that she'd revealed so much of her feelings about Paign to him. But, then, this was Anders. She'd been friends with him since birth, just like Paign. In those thirteen years, though, she'd never shared something this personal with either boy.

"Oh, my!" he laughed. "You've got my bootlace imprinted on your cheek! Sorry about that, Freida."

"Why would you be sorry?" she snapped, feeling even more awkward about her openness. "You didn't do anything. Your boot did!" Freida straightened out her rumpled clothing. Noticing the lengthening shadows of the trees, she blurted out, "I need to be going home now. It's time to feed the stock."

"Uh, sure. Of course." Anders replied, feeling like he'd done something wrong, while having no idea what it was. He shrugged.

"So? What's next?" Freida asked.

"What?"

"What's *next?*"

"Uh…"

"Anders! What's next? What are we going to do about Paign? We need to find him…wherever he is!" Now Freida's hands were balled up, planted on her hips.

"How would I know where to find him, Freida? He could be anywhere, you know!"

"We need help." Freida's face was clouded with fear, even as she looked to the sky, hoping against hope.

CHAPTER NINE

BLACKNESS

Slowly, ever so slowly, Paign regained consciousness. The throbbing in his head was matched by the perfectly timed eruptions of light in his closed eyes. When he twisted to roll over onto his chest, Paign nearly threw up from the nauseating pain that shot through his left leg. A groan escaped his throat in spite of his overwhelming desire not to make a sound.

His nose touching the dirty stone floor of his prison, Paign whispered to himself, "Well, I would have changed my name if I'd known it would be prophetic."

Taking a deep breath and little consolation from his dark humor, Paign steeled himself for the onslaught of suffering he'd absorb. Then, resolutely he stood up. And nearly passed out again. Yet, he stood.

Rance-Dahl stared motionless for a moment, then smirked. "Hm. Not bad, boy. It only took you two attempts this time. Your first effort resulted in passing out again, I believe. Although, you took so long to rise this second time I thought, perhaps, you were—how do you say?—*napping.*"

Paign's captor squatted on the gritty limestone floor, roughly thirty feet from the boy. The Glimmer twinkled behind the gargoyle, providing the only light in the chamber.

"Your leg seems to be seeping again, eh?" Rance-Dahl asked with mock concern.

Paign could feel a fresh trickle of blood crawling down his left ankle. When Rance-Dahl had thrown him across the room earlier, Paign's upper left leg had been the first part of his body to impact the rough surface of the cave floor. He guessed that he'd slid for more than ten feet on that leg. His pants shredded immediately, leaving his skin exposed to the abrasive stone and grit. Most of his upper leg, from the hip to the knee, was skinned and raw. His left knee was gashed and the source of the trickle.

"So it would seem." Paign's eyes smoldered, but his voice was firm and calm. *Was that the fourth time he threw me? Or the fifth?* Paign was having trouble concentrating.

Rance-Dahl smiled. "Perfect."

"Jah, OK, then. Let's go over this again, Anders," Johann asked, tension clearly on his face.

"Father! We don't have time!" Freida cried.

"Honey," Heidi said gently, "until we have a complete picture of this situation, there's nothing you, Anders or we can do." She reached out and laid her hand softly on Freida's shoulder, but her daughter twisted away from her, walked to the window, yanked away the blinds and stared outside, her cheeks flushed red.

Anders sighed and looked at Freida's profile, hoping she'd turn to look his way. Competing feelings stormed within his chest. It was hard to breathe. Growing fear for Paign pummeled him like the tidal surges he'd seen at the sea's edge. But he didn't know what to do for his cousin. Anders was smart, a thinker. He could solve problems. He was very handy with a bow and forceful with his sword. In this situation, though, he was powerless.

"What can I say, Mr. Skulstad, that I haven't already told you?" he replied, more heatedly than he wished. "The long and the short of it is that we need to find Paign. He's been gone too long to simply have been camping. Like I said before, I believe the smartest thing for us to do is head up to western rim of Ruar's Ridge, you know, where Paign loved—*loves*—to camp."

Anders immediately felt terrible for his stupid word choice. He already was choking down the lump in his throat when Freida whipped her head around with a stricken look when she'd heard "loved" in the past tense.

Idiot! I am an idiot! Paign will be all right…he will!

"We need to go now, Mr. Skulstad!" Anders begged Freida's parents. "If you must, join us." Again, he regretted his word choice. Freida scowled at him.

"Johann," Heidi said, touching her husband's elbow, "I believe that Anders—"

Everyone's heads snapped towards the front of the house at the high-pitched scream coming from outside, "Heiiiiiideeeee!" They all jumped at the sudden thudding on the wooden steps below the Skulstad's large porch. Again, an alarming, unearthly howling, "Heiiiideee!" came just as the front door flew open.

Wild-eyed, disheveled and filthy, Paign's mother, Gudrun Macy, burst into the room.

Heidi Skulstad, whose name was being screamed, ran to her friend.

Johann and Anders jumped up.

Freida stared at what Gudrun held in her right fist, so tightly her knuckles were ghostly white.

"I've been to the ridge!" Gudrun gasped. "I've been to his favorite—he wasn't there. All his things...all of it un-touched...no sign of...only...THIS!"

The woman's eyes finally were overcome with panic. Her wraith-like fist thrust out from her, clutching an enormous black, leathery feather.

Still gasping for breath, a choking noise suddenly burst from Gudrun, and both hands reached towards the farmhouse ceiling. "Paaaaaignnnn!" she wailed, then fainted, collapsing into Anders's arms.

Freida went cold all the way to her heart.

CHAPTER TEN
WICKED THIS WAY COMES

Danielle saw that she was smiling. She smiled, as one does when holding a picture of a happy time. *I'm dreaming, she realized. Isn't it odd that I'd be dreaming of me dreaming?*

She heard a rustling behind her, of someone stepping on gritty rock. But she didn't turn. She recognized the steps. Her smiles widened, both the smile on her own face and the one on the dreaming self that she observed.

"Why is it odd?"

Danielle spun around on her heels, delight painted across her face like the sunrise finally breaking over the Nepalese mountains.

"Lohxnahr!" she cried. "You are here at last! We've been waiting so long for you!"

The small gargoyle now hovered a few feet in front of Danielle. His gossamer wings whirred like a hummingbird's, so fast that they appeared nearly colorless. His glistening, pale lavender eyes were framed by his chubby face.

"Hullo," Lohxnahr said happily, his voice raspy, "and good morning to you, and to us all, as you can see," his right hand pointing over Danielle's shoulder, toward the sun rising over the dark, ragged ridge. "It is a morning of wonder and a wonderful morning."

Danielle so wanted to hug her friend but knew she couldn't. If nothing else, it would get in the way of his wings. *And he's not a pet!* Embarrassed at this thought, she recognized that there had been times she felt like hugging Lohxnahr like she did her friend's big cat. *How foolish of me...*

"Why is it odd?" Lohxnahr repeated, flying closer to Danielle, so that he was just two inches from her face.

"Uh...what?"

Smiling from ear to ear, Lohxnahr replied, "You said, 'Isn't it odd that I'd be dreaming of me dreaming?' Why is it odd?"

"Well, you know, it's just"—Danielle abruptly stopped—"Wait a minute! I didn't *say* anything about that. I was *thinking* it, Lohxnahr."

Lohxnahr's beaming face still hovered just two inches in front of Danielle's nose.

"Are you listening to my thoughts?" Danielle giggled.

Lohxnahr's head tipped a little to one side. "That *would* be interesting!"

Danielle could have sworn that her hovering friend winked at her. Instinctively, she reached out and gently laid her hands on the little gargoyle's shoulders, pulled him toward her and hugged him. She felt his hands reach around her neck, grateful he took care to avoid her with his long talons. The thrumming of his wings caused a buzzing in her ears and vibrated all the way down her back.

Releasing him, Danielle giggled again. "It is so good to see you! Where have you been, Lohxnahr? We've been waiting for you," she swept her arm around in the direction of her parents, Conomorg and Ita-Mudak. "We've been worried."

The gargoyle's lavender eyes narrowed slightly. "Worried? Worried, please be not! For worry solves nothing. It only distracts our minds and saps our strength." Although it didn't seem possible, Danielle thought Lohxnahr's smile grew even wider.

"Yes, I suppose that is true."

"Of course, it is not odd."

"I'm sorry?" Danielle replied, perplexed.

"Of course, it is not odd to dream that you are dreaming."

"Oh," Danielle said, grinning as she caught up to Lohxnahr's meaning. "And why is that?"

"Because you didn't answer my question, I chose to provide it myself," Lohxnahr intoned solemnly. His body leaned slightly to the left, and he began circling around where Danielle stood.

"No, no, Lohxnahr." Danielle replied, giggling again. "I didn't mean, why did you answer the question you asked me? I meant that I am curious why you don't think it is odd that I was dreaming about me dreaming."

"Because you still are." Lohxnahr continued to slowly fly around where Danielle stood.

"I…what?"

"You are still dreaming that you are dreaming."

Danielle blinked, confused.

"But…but…we're talking," she cried, immediately feeling stupid for saying something so obvious.

"Of course!" Lohxnahr replied merrily. "I most enjoy our conversations, whether you be awake or asleep."

Danielle opened her mouth to speak but snapped it shut. A moment later, she blurted, "So, this is all a dream!"

"Of course," Lohxnahr beamed. The new dawn breaking over the ridge glittered off of the gargoyle's wings, reflecting tiny, random bursts of light.

Danielle squinted. "But I—"

"Have you not noticed everyone sleeps, still?"

"Ah, well, I do now," Danielle muttered, feeling thick. Now that she looked around, it was obvious that all the others had not moved during her "conversation" with Lohxnahr. "Oh, bother!" Danielle hated feeling stupid.

"Shall we go now?" Lohxnahr's pace had increased, Danielle realized. He circled around her faster.

Danielle trusted Lohxnahr completely, so she wasn't alarmed about going anywhere with him. But she was greatly annoyed with herself and frustrated by this conversation.

"Why?" she sighed, squeezing her head in her hands. She'd almost shouted at her friend.

"Because you are dreaming that you are dreaming, of course!" Lohxnahr chirped. "This is a very strong path to awareness. This, we need."

By now, Lohxnahr spun around Danielle so fast that dust and grit funneled high over her head. An uncomfortable throbbing pulsed in her ears. She could no longer see anyone outside of the swirling dust-cloud.

"Where are we going, Lohxnahr?" Danielle shouted. She could no longer focus on him; he was spinning too fast. But she caught brief glimpses of him within the churning plume of dirt and thought he'd brought his hands directly over his head, just a few inches between them.

Then she heard a clap and they were gone.

Gudrun's weariness hadn't grown any less, even with whatever sleep she'd gotten. Running her hands through her hair, she realized several things. First, her hair was filthy, but she didn't care. Second, it was now night, and she was in the home of Heidi and Johann Skulstad, her dear friends. She guessed that Johann had carried her to their modest sitting room, where she'd slept, although she had no memory of passing out. Third, the ache in her heart for her missing Paign was just as excruciating as before. When her husband, Roald, had been killed just three years earlier, Gudrun had felt such despair she expected it to kill her. In fact, there were days she'd hoped it would. Oh, she'd missed him so. But she found purpose in caring for her young son, Paign, and Bettina, his older sister. She had something to live for. Someones to love for. That love had carried her through the ending of the War of Dominance. Of course, there was great rejoicing when the war ended. But she, like many widows, continued to mourn their lost husbands while raising their young children the best they could. Now, her only son was missing.

Gudrun sat up, leaning on her left elbow, but wasn't quite ready to get off the comfortable sitting couch next to the fireplace in the Skulstads' modest parlor. Too many months it had been since she had visited her friends, she realized. She ran her calloused hands down her face again, wondering what time it was.

The dying glow of burning coals sent faint shadows chasing around the room. *It must be quite late. Or very early.*

Still exhausted, she eased her legs off the couch, but quickly pulled them back up. She'd felt something other than a hardwood floor! A moment later, a huge dog's head rose up before Gudrun. It was Tiny, the Skulstads' family dog, an enormous mastiff. Gudrun could hear the dog's tail swishing on the hardwood floor of the parlor.

"Ah, Tiny!" she whispered. "Forgive me for nearly stepping upon your tail."

But Tiny could tell the woman didn't have much feeling in her apology. It was plain that she was weary and careworn. He licked her nearest hand. *Maybe this will help her a bit,* Tiny hoped.

Gudrun absentmindedly patted Tiny's head with her free hand. She was vaguely aware that the dog continued to lick her other hand. Yet, she didn't mind. There was comfort in receiving attention from a dog. "Dogs could just as well bite you, after all," she sighed. *But not this dog. No, not this dog! Tiny helped save my Paign from those beastly, gargoyle-creatures last year.*

"Tiny," she whispered, "you kept Paign safe, didn't you?" Tears quickly welled up in her eyes and streamed down her troubled face. "Didn't you, Tiny?" she murmured, barely audible.

The great mastiff lifted his left paw to Paign's mother as a token of his comfort and offer of friendship. The woman urgently took his paw in her right hand, sobbing. Then, his head was enveloped in her tousled hair, as she laid her head on top of his. She wept for a long time, clutching Tiny's scruff for support.

"Where's my boy, Tiny? Where's my boy?" she breathed into Tiny's ear, over and over again.

Amy awakened to the sound of a clap. The sun was breaking over the far ridge of the Himalayas. Everyone else slept or, at least, she didn't know what else Conomorg and Ita-Mudak were doing. They sat motionless, looking very much like large stone statues, completely out of place in the wild, high steppes of west-central Nepal. All except Anja, who was tearing around their campsite in a crazy rush, her nose to the ground. She had a wild look in her eyes.

"Anja!" Amy whispered, with as much authority as she could muster with a whisper. "Anja! Come!"

But Anja didn't stop. She didn't slow. Madly, she tore back and forth, with only the sound of her feet kicking loose grit and stone. Her ears were flat back against her head, which was angled upwards. Her eyes were wide.

What has gotten into her? The last time she had that look in her eyes was—Amy caught her breath the instant the thought crossed her mind—*when the hybrid stepped into our house!*

"Where's Danielle?" Amy screamed. "Where's Danielle?"

Within minutes, the entire area had been thoroughly searched. No sign of Danielle was found.

Peter was seething, furious with himself for not protecting his daughter. He held Anja's neck with his hands and kept her immensely strong body pinned between his legs. For the moment, the dog appeared mostly content to remain in front of her master. Still, her body quivered uncontrollably. Peter figured she could feel him quivering, too.

Conomorg paced back and forth. Given his immense size and weight, he'd quickly worked a minor trench into his path.

"Do you not agree, then?" Ita-Mudak quietly asked his fellow guard, as his comrade strode by.

Conomorg said nothing, continued pacing away from their camp, came to the end of his path, turned and stopped. Amy could not determine the look on his slab-like face.

"But, why, Ita-Mudak?" Conomorg replied, tension constricting the tone of his voice. "Why would he not alert us to his arrival?"

Before Ita-Mudak could answer, Conomorg continued.

"Not only that! *How* could Lohxnahr have come without our knowing it? How?" Conomorg began pacing again, his chin almost touching his chest, looking at no one.

Ita-Mudak strode across the camp until he stood in Conomorg's path. When Conomorg was forced to stop, he finally looked up.

Ita-Mudak laid his long-taloned hands on Conomorg's broad shoulders. "I do not have an answer for any of your questions, my friend. Like you, I am very puzzled that Lohxnahr returned to our camp without a word and that he was able to take Danielle with him…without our awareness."

Ita-Mudak turned so that he could include Amy and Peter in what he wished to say next.

"However, I am not 'worried,' as you humans say. For Lohxnahr is a High Priest of the Order of Ancients. He is, above all else, worthy of our enduring trust and complete obedience. That he came as he did—and left in the same manner, with Danielle—is something I accept, although I do not understand it."

Peter looked at Amy, wanting to believe that Ita-Mudak was right. Or, at least, he desperately wanted to believe in Ita-Mudak's faith in Lohxnahr. Amy stared hard at Conomorg, as if waiting for a more compelling opinion before coming to her own decision.

Slowly, Conomorg's head rose up. He looked at Ita-Mudak intently, for what felt like an eternity to Amy. Finally, Conomorg nodded.

Immediately, Danielle knew where she was. The smell of candles in Zarentil's chamber, in the tallest peak of the Ten Pinnacles, had a pungent but sweet and comforting aroma. Again, the beauty of the spherical room, with dazzling stalactites and stalagmites all reaching towards the center, literally took her breath away. She couldn't think of anywhere else she might see such an explosion of colors—pale blue soapstones, travertine oranges, quartzite purples, jade greens, onyx silver-whites, granite pinks—except maybe a coral reef. She'd read about them in her science class.

Lohxnahr had parted them directly into the chamber of Zarentil.

For some reason, I didn't think we could do that, she thought. *Last time we walked in from the entrance because we had to, right?* Before she could consider the question further, she realized they were not alone.

"Kimar!" Danielle cried. "Ercen! You're here!" Without thinking, she ran over and hugged both of her friends, first Kimar, then Ercen.

Ercen smiled and held Danielle close for a moment, long enough to whisper into the girl's ear, "Hush, Danielle. We seek guidance from the mystic, Zarentil. This is a place for reverence…and discretion, my dear." Then Ercen gently pushed her away and looked closely into the girl's face. "But it is good to see you again."

Kimar, the bravest gargoyle that Danielle had encountered in her adventures the year before, placed a hand on Danielle's head. Although she knew he hadn't allowed any weight from his arm to push on her head, Danielle still felt as if a small boulder had rested on the top of it. But she nevertheless found it comforting that he did so. Lifting her eyes, she smiled up at him.

He turned Danielle's head to face the stone chair. She hadn't seen Zarentil come in and was very surprised to see him there.

The Mystic of the Ten Pinnacles for generations upon generations, Zarentil's importance could not be overstated. This much Danielle knew from her previous experiences with gargoyles. So, his visions and insights were critical now. She guessed that Kimar's leadership was central to those gargoyles who were committed to defeating Kahrnahrgx and his minions. Still, she was puzzled about why she'd been brought here.

"Peace, Zarentil," Kimar said, bowing slightly at the waist.

"Peace, Kimar. And to you all." Zarentil replied, in a voice that Danielle had never heard the likes of before meeting him. The tiny gargoyle's voice, even though he was no bigger than a human infant, was very deep, as if it came from the base of the peak named after him. And yet, his voice had the quality of an infant, too. It reminded Danielle of the preschool children's cries in the playground. *Zarentil seems like an extremely old and wise child…with a deep voice*, she thought, grinning.

He was beautiful to look at. His eyes—*the exact color of a brand-new penny!*—were what revealed Zarentil's vast age. Nearly all of the gargoyles that Danielle had met already, good and bad, were the color of darker stone, like granite, slate, basalt. Obsidian seemed to be the primary color for almost all of Kahrnahrgx's followers. So, a lighter colored gargoyle stood out from the others, at least in her experience. But Zarentil! His body had a leathery look to it, like the stone itself had gotten wrinkled to a glimmering, pearlescent white. Strangely, Zarentil was cloaked in a robe of pale lavender. Danielle wondered if the ancient creature had wings any more. *Maybe he never did*, she thought.

"I bring greetings from Quarastohr and the other members of the War Council," Kimar continued.

Zarentil said nothing but tipped his head slightly.

Danielle noticed Ercen fidgeting on the other side of Kimar. Out of the corner of her eye, Danielle could see Ercen's toe-talons pushing very small piles of grit around. But Danielle didn't dare sneak a direct look. She was, after all, supposed to be on her best behavior.

"What do you seek, Kimar?" Zarentil asked, serenely, his voice both deep and innocent.

Without any idea why, Danielle felt the hair on the back of her neck stand up.

Ercen's fidgeting was becoming very distracting. Danielle fought the urge to stare at her. Maddeningly, Kimar didn't seem to notice.

"We seek your guidance, O Mystic."

"Guidance regarding the other?" Zarentil asked, now in a voice pitched high but with a queer undertone. Danielle thought he sounded like he was mocking Kimar. The skin on both of her arms immediately popped goose bumps.

What is going on here? Danielle felt her breath coming in short gulps. She turned to stare at Kimar, hoping for an answer either from his words or on his face.

Danielle screamed as Kimar's face turned towards her and morphed into the face of a gargoyle she never wanted to see again, Gahrspat. *But he's dead! Isn't he?*

Kimar's eyes changed from amber to glaring red.

Danielle screamed with everything she had in her. Yet no sound came. *Why can't I make any sound?* Danielle's heart was pounding in her chest so loudly it was hard for her to hear anything else.

But she heard Zarentil speak—and wished she hadn't.

Guidance? The Mystic asked directly into her mind.

Numbing fear surged through Danielle, like tidal waves crashing into a primeval shore. Oh, she did not want to look at Zarentil, for fear of what she would see. But she was powerless not to look. *Am I choosing this? What is happening?*

Stricken, Danielle watched the petite, pearl-like, ancient gargoyle grotesquely change shapes and colors, until he was Sedig-Tahr, the terrifying gargoyle that posed as a policeman, leering at her. She had no doubt of his intention to kill her, mercilessly. The malice on his hard, cold face was all too clear.

Every cell in Danielle's body recoiled at the sight of Sedig-Tahr. She knew he could not have survived the grievous wounds delivered by Conomorg and Ita-Mudak in her home. Yet, here he was.

With primal force, Danielle spun around on her heels to run. Little confidence she had in her chance of escape, but it didn't matter. This was all mindless impulse.

But she couldn't turn. Gargoyle hands pressed down on her shoulders, holding her fast to the chamber floor. Ercen's hands! Danielle twisted around, hurting her back, so she could see with her own eyes that her friend was holding her captive. Danielle gawked at her friend, trying to speak. Ercen stared blankly at the ceiling.

When she turned her head back, Zarentil-Sedig-Tahr stood directly in front of her, his hot, acid breath pouring, heavy with malevolence, onto her long hair. His eyes blazed the red of lava, the red of death. Danielle gasped and, in doing so, inhaled the acrid fume of the hybrid gargoyle. In panic and fury, she screamed one last time, for she knew it would be her last.

"Nooooo!" she screeched.

Ercen twisted Danielle's shoulders back and forth.

"Nooooo!" she screeched again.

Ercen shook her more urgently.

Danielle heard Ercen calling her name.

In the middle of her third scream, Danielle stared at Ercen's hands, expecting to see her talons splayed out...but... but...

These aren't Ercen's talons!

"Danielle!" cried a raspy voice. "Danielle! It is time. Come home!"

What?

"Now, Danielle!" The raspy voice sounded so comforting, so calm. "You have done splendidly, child. Return now!"

Lohxnahr? "Lohxnahr?" Danielle cried.

She twisted her head around to see Lohxnahr's cherubic face and soft, kind lavender eyes smiling into hers. His hands were holding Danielle in midair, while his wings thrummed rhythmically.

"Oh, Lohxnahr!" Danielle burst into tears. "Please, please, get me away from—"

Peter could see that Amy was seething, and he couldn't blame her. He was incensed with what Lohxnahr—High Priest or not—had put his little girl through.

"And this was necessary, *why*?" Amy asked.

Lohxnahr beamed, undisturbed, apparently very pleased.

Ita-Mudak watched impassively. Danielle sat directly in front of him, as if finding protection from his bulk. *Just what I want to know!* Peter thought, *I'm angry, too, Ames.* Anja sat like a sentry in front of Danielle.

Conomorg replied, "If I understand your meaning, Lohxnahr, you needed to take Danielle, while in her sleeping state, to investigate the health of Zarentil?"

"Of course," Lohxnahr replied merrily.

"And this," Conomorg stole a glance at Amy, "was because the human child has the power of discernment, pertaining to certain...matters?"

"Indeed!"

"Well," Peter snapped, "it would have been appropriate to tell us about it before whisking her off without a word, you know!"

"This we could not. The risk was too great," Lohxnahr replied with a lilt in his voice, almost like he was singing.

"And that was—" Conomorg began.

"Because we were no longer clear on who was untouched," Lohxnahr interrupted.

"Meaning us, right?" Amy asked, her voice betraying the growing fear she was beginning to understand.

"Yes, of course." Lohxnahr launched off the boulder he'd been perched on during this conversation and hovered a few paces in front of Danielle and Ita-Mudak.

"So, does that mean someone was *touched* by whatever?" Amy blurted.

"Indeed!"

"Uh, OK, I'm getting lost here," Peter grumbled. "Can you just tell us plainly, Lohxnahr, what this is all about? What's going on? Who has been 'touched,' and what difference does it make?"

"We needed Danielle's vision to confirm what we feared to be true. Zarentil suspected that a hybrid gargoyle, like that which attacked you not long ago, had infiltrated our clan. But elusive this creature is. It is as if he can know our thoughts and melt away before we are able to identify him. Diligent we have been. Dedicated. Deliberate. But craftier is our foe."

"Oh, Great One," Conomorg intoned. "What did your taking Danielle to visit Zarentil provide in the way of insight? What knowledge did her dream-state give you?"

"That Zarentil is dead. The hybrid has killed the ancient Mystic and taken his form."

CHAPTER ELEVEN
THE BEST DEFENSE

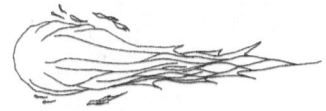

Gudrun woke up with a start. Her head still resting on Tiny's and her mind still cloudy from a strange dream she'd just left, Gudrun couldn't tell if she'd really heard something or if it was Tiny's swishing tail that awakened her.

Yawning, Gudrun sat up. Then, she reared back into the sitting couch.

"Please, do not be alarmed," said the gargoyle, standing at the end of the room.

At first, Gudrun wondered why she hadn't screamed. Then she realized that it was, at least in part, because Tiny hadn't barked. In fact, Tiny trotted over to the gargoyle and sat next to it, wagging his tail vigorously. The gargoyle's voice was surprisingly comforting to Gudrun, almost lyrical in tone.

"Are you…are you one of Paign's friends?"

"Yes. I am Ercen."

Gudrun breathed deeply, not realizing she'd been holding her breath. The voice of the gargoyle was pleasant, though gravelly.

Before she could say anything, Gudrun and Ercen both turned their heads upwards, towards the second floor of the Skulstads' farmhouse. Sounds of chaos thumped on the ceiling overhead, followed by shouting. Finally, many feet thundered down the narrow stairs and Freida, then Anders, bounded into the living room.

"Ercen! Ercen! We heard you through the floor!" Freida cried.

It was clear to Gudrun that they were delighted to see Ercen. Finally, Heidi and Johann came into the room, welcoming their gargoyle friend enthusiastically.

Several hours later, the humans had finished a speedy breakfast, completed the farm chores, cleaned up and quickly packed. They had finalized a plan to find Paign with Ercen's help.

Gudrun's nerves were shot. Her hands had a constant, mild shake to them, which embarrassed her. Still, she felt so much more focused than the day before. She was utterly relieved—almost hopeful, she realized. It was so much to take in, these gargoyles. She'd always been a simple woman, with simple needs and goals. Gudrun had loved being a farmer's girl, even more a farmer's wife.

Her years with Roald had been full of joy. They felt so blessed when they became parents to two children. "One of each!" Roald liked to say. Bettina had come first, then Paign. Losing Roald in the war, especially so near the end of it, was bitter and had been hard on all of the family. Gudrun was proud of how Paign had stepped into the role of the "man of the house," even as a young boy. Of course, he couldn't do much of a man's work, but he tried so hard. It was Bettina who withdrew. She'd become quieter as the weeks after learning of Roald's death grew to months, and finally years. When she'd asked Gudrun for permission to move away, to live with her cousins in the large city of Trondheim, it nearly broke Gudrun's heart. But she sent Bettina to Trondheim, nevertheless. Her lovely daughter needed to live somewhere else; being on their farmstead held far too many painful reminders that her father was never returning home.

It's simpler this way, I suppose, Gudrun had thought at the time. *At least Bettina will be safe where she is, away from all of this. Perhaps she will smile again.* Now, with Paign missing, Gudrun ached for her daughter's comfort.

Heidi had packed extras of everything for Gudrun. Ercen made it clear the humans needed to make haste. She could hear the others busily making preparations.

Ercen waited outside the farmhouse next to the barn, motionless. Freida and Anders sat at the foot of the kitchen's porch doorsteps. Tiny lay next to Freida, his chin flat against the dirt, nothing moving but his eyes.

Most of the farmsteads in the Honellaken Valley utilized a mudroom between the kitchen door and the door outside. In it the family kept their work coats, boots, gloves and a walking staff or two. Often, the farmer kept a rifle in the corner and bullets on a small shelf next to the window. When the house didn't yet have a water pump inside, the water was kept in a large lidded can, with a ladle, next to the outside door. In the Skulstads' mudroom, Johann also kept his sword and a pair of bows with full quivers, hanging on wooden pegs.

Anders absentmindedly fingered the fletches on the arrows in the quiver lying in his lap. "I'm grateful your father is letting me borrow his extra bow," he said, looking at Freida. The bow was slung over Anders's right shoulder.

Freida barely heard Anders or the odd, rhythmic sound his fingers made running down the fletches. Her mind was full of memories of the battle she'd seen last time—when she had been the one needing rescue from the minions of Kahrnahrgx. Although she'd been rescued, these memories were not comforting; she knew how close she'd come to death. Her rescuers, too.

"What?" Freida asked, turning to focus on Anders.

"Oh," Anders replied softly, "I was just saying that I'm grateful to be able to use this bow. It might prove useful. You know…if…when…"

"We'll find him, Anders," Freida said, sounding more confident than she felt. "We'll find him and he'll be all right. Now we have Ercen here to help us."

"You know, Freida," Anders replied, "we had a lot of help the other times. Ercen didn't seem all that certain that Kimar and any of the others were able to go with us this time."

Before Freida could say anything, her mother and Gudrun came out from the kitchen and onto the stone landing, packs slung over their shoulders, with her father right behind them. He was awkwardly holding his pack, bow, a quiver bristling with long arrows and two, long walking staffs.

Anders jumped up. "Jah, Mr. Skulstad! Let me help you with all that."

"*Tusen takk*, Anders!" Johann bellowed, grateful for the help.

A moment later, each human stood, forming a rough circle facing Ercen. They all held whatever gear wasn't slung over an arm or on their backs.

I'm glad to see Mrs. Skulstad's brought her staff! Anders remembered well the woman's skill with a simple walking stick; this one had been made by Ercen especially for Heidi from the branch of an old tree, high up on the sides of the Ten Pinnacles. It was infused with the strength of a gargoyle and virtually impossible to shatter. *That stick, with her skill, we can definitely use.*

While Anders and Freida held Tiny's scruff, the rest joined hands with Ercen. A sudden, momentary fence-high uptwirl of dirt marked their departure.

Paign was awash in misery. Where his pant leg had been torn away above his knee, a large contusion was already the color of black, blue and blood. He couldn't hold back one slight chuckle, grimacing as he did so. *Where don't I have bruises, welts…or worse?* But it was the breathing that was proving to be a real problem. He was pretty sure he had at least three broken ribs, which made it exquisitely painful to breathe. In a perverse twist, Rance-Dahl himself had fixed the very shoulder dislocation that he caused; when he had thrown Paign back across the room, Paign felt the shoulder snap back into position upon slamming into the rear wall.

Oh, new problem! Paign felt Rance-Dahl pick him up, yet again. By the look on his captor's face, it appeared the gargoyle had said something witty, but all that got through to Paign was acidic breath and a muffled rumbling. Other than that, Paign heard nothing but a loud ringing in both ears. *I suppose it's just as well I can't hear him,* he thought. *Probably just more of the same drivel.* But, deep inside sprang a devastating doubt that he'd survive his capture.

It was stupid to go camping on my own. I wonder if anyone knows I'm gone?

At precisely the moment that Rance-Dahl again sent him flying through the length of his cell, it hit Paign.

Even if they realize I'm gone, how would they ever find me?

Paign couldn't hear the crunching sound of his impact against the stone wall. But he felt it. Sharp, spiking, searing pain.

The boy slid to the floor in a heap and moved no more.

CHAPTER TWELVE

COLTON

Kimar was invisible on the gymnasium roof. The night sky shone brightly with stars, but the new moon cast no light. The small town of Colton, Washington, had few street lamps and none near the all-grade public school. Kimar could only be seen by looking directly where he sat and only if someone noticed the lack of stars behind his hulking frame.

Perched for several hours atop the tall, brown-brick structure, all that Kimar had seen was a prairie coyote hunting deer mice across the track infield. Once in a while, the coyote leaped high into the air, like it was going to dive into the nearby community swimming pool. Then it fell back down, front paws first, intending to pounce on its prey. So far, Kimar saw it jump and pounce five times with no success.

With nothing else to distract him, the gargoyle deliberated all that had been recently discovered.

Although he could not explain how, Lohxnahr had convinced Kimar that Danielle would be able to discern whether Zarentil was still Zarentil. Several of Kimar's closest and most faithful companions, including Ercen, had received during their nightly dreams a very disturbing vision revealing the demise of their ancient Mystic. Yet, Lohxnahr would not risk Danielle's safety to an actual visit to Zarentil's chamber. For if it was true that their great spiritual leader had fallen, as the shared vision seemed to indicate, then great indeed would be the foe who had killed him. Worse, these visions hinted at the enemy's ability to masquerade as Zarentil completely. Only in an enhanced dream-state could Danielle—and only Danielle—discern the truth of Zarentil. At least, so said Lohxnahr. Kimar was obligated to obey Lohxnahr since he was the High Priest. There were times Kimar wished the cherubic gargoyle would simply utter a clear command. Kimar preferred action over discussion. He'd rather have a direct task to accomplish, or perish in the attempt, than to be given hints and riddles.

Of course, the problem was that there were other dreams that involved other gargoyles being absorbed by hybrid creatures. At least one gargoyle had convincingly posed as a human policeman, nearly killing Danielle and her family. What wasn't certain was whether there were more of these hybrids. *And what if these creatures could pose as other gargoyles, not just as humans?* Kimar wondered. *How would they be discovered? How many might there be? Is this just a trick of Kahrnahrgx? Is his hope to cause such fear or distraction that we drop our guard?*

"Perhaps they have been infiltrating our ranks for some time, yes?" Kimar remembered clearly the dread he'd felt when Lohxnahr posed that question to him, in spite of the resolute lilt in the voice of his High Priest. "We must be watchful. Open. Most aware. In this, we will be tested, Kimar. And in this, we can rejoice since closer we must become. Closer than we have ever been before. In this, the enemy's cunning bears a gift, if we maintain our hope and our faith in one another. Until the ending of this duplicity, we must accept that anyone who has left our sight may return to us as another. Trust will be most precious and still more difficult. Even your finest lieutenants you must suspect. You would do well not to speak of this matter to anyone, Kimar. Not even to Ercen."

Kimar had glowered at Lohxnahr. The little gargoyle had hovered before his hulking friend, his lavender eyes beaming. Kimar was deeply skeptical about withholding information from his mate, Ercen.

Lohxnahr had shown no outward discernment of Kimar's feelings.

"You will do as you wish, Kimar. This is as it should be. You are a great commander. I could dictate to you but I would not do so. And yet, my guidance to you is stealth. Secrecy, Kimar! Our enemy has employed the most devious of methods to work against us. To not respond with the greatest concealment would be, I contend, rash. Quite possibly to our ultimate downfall."

"What action do you recommend, Lohxnahr?"

"That the leaders—you, Ercen, a few others of my choosing—stay hidden, even from each other, until I summon you."

"There is a way for you to find us? To summon us?"

"No. And yes."

Kimar had understood his meaning. There was no way to find a very strong gargoyle's location—that he was aware of—once they parted. Thus it was that Osberg the Great vanished into the deeps of time with their enemy's key of power. What surprised Kimar was that Lohxnahr was still able to somehow summon these concealed gargoyles.

"And you, Lohxnahr? Where are you going next?"

"Where, I will not say, even to you, my commander. But this I will tell you: it is imperative that I find Danielle quickly. We must know of Zarentil."

The solitude of the small town brought him little solace. So deep in thought was Kimar that, at first, he didn't notice a bright-colored tanager landed on the school's roof next to him. Enough light now crept over the rolling hills, ripe with pungent alfalfa, that Kimar could easily make out the bird's head was a ruddy orange, with a brilliant yellow and black body. Immediately, the bird began singing in the coming day.

Kimar shrugged his massive shoulders to loosen the tension in them. He'd tarried long enough.

The coyote saw the movement and crouched abruptly when it realized that what was perched on the high, flat roof was more than large enough to hunt her. She scampered away, leaving the quivering deer mice for another night.

The bird continued to chirp and sing happily next to Kimar, unconcerned by his presence.

Time to part. I wonder how they fared?

Kimar's parting momentarily dislodged the tanager from his perch. Quickly resettled, the bird went back to its urgent welcome song for the rising sun.

Ercen and her group were the first to arrive at the rendezvous point chosen by Lohxnahr. Ercen explained that Lohxnahr had told Kimar, unless he summoned them, they were all to meet at the Cave of Osberg on the morning of the third day of the mission.

It had troubled Ercen deeply that Kimar, her mate of many human generations, had given her and the other gargoyles so little information. She felt untrusted. From the looks of the others at the time, especially Conomorg and Ita-Mudak, she was not alone in that feeling. Something was very wrong, apparently, that Lohxnahr sought secrecy above trust. Besides this decision causing a rupture between her long-time comrades, Ercen was also troubled by what the need for this level of secrecy meant to their order.

But there was no more time to indulge her concerns or recollections of that difficult conversation. The third day had arrived with no word or summons.

"Johann! Heidi! Please make your camp behind that tall cluster of stalagmites." Ercen aimed both arms straight out in the direction she alone could see, due to the abject darkness within the cavern beyond where she stood. Her hands tilted down toward the cave's floor, so that her talons pointed back slightly at her own feet.

From the fast-growing light diffusing into the floor around Ercen, Johann's eyes followed where Ercen pointed to; an orange glow was building just beyond the stalagmites, near the far end of the long cavern.

"Jah, very well! *Tusen takk* for the lighting!" He jogged across the gritty, uneven floor, his pack hoisted over one shoulder, his long bow and quiver slung over the other. The sword at his side, which he'd just retrieved from his pack, occasionally thumped and clanked into stalagmites in his path. Heidi trailed slowly behind him as she helped Gudrun follow.

"You three," Ercen said to Anders, Freida and Tiny, "come this way. Leave your packs here. You'll return for them later."

Freida and Anders glanced at each other; both felt the disquiet in Ercen but had no idea of its source. Their own tormenting anxiety over Paign's welfare didn't help. Tiny darted along close to Ercen, his head up and eyes alert, quickly scanning their surroundings.

Ercen turned and stopped once she reached the middle of the chamber. Anders and Freida waited. Tiny nosed around, sniffing the ground in a wide circle.

"Here, we wait," Ercen said, distracted. "Although not for long, if our plans hold true." Her hands were interwoven; her talons clicked rhythmically.

"What plans are those?" Freida asked, troubled by Ercen's behavior.

Anders glanced around their immediate surroundings and realized that the others would not be able to see them because of the tall, wide stalagmite directly behind them.

"To wait."

"But, we are waiting, Ercen," Freida replied, more heatedly that she expected. Hearing her own anxiety out loud, Freida suddenly felt angry. "In fact, that's about all we've been doing! Waiting for Paign. Then waiting for help. Waiting for you!"

"Freida," Anders murmured, gently touching her elbow.

She twisted away from his touch.

"I'm sick of waiting!" Freida looked back and forth across the cave, now fully defused in the orange glow Ercen had set upon it. In a different mood, Freida would have thought it beautiful. Now, she hated it. She looked back and forth, her head twisting, searching furiously for a way out.

Anders found himself also looking for an opening in the cavern. While he had no idea what Freida's plans were, he was going along with her. That decision required no thinking.

"Now that you *are* here, we're still waiting!" Freida seethed. "I'm leaving!"

"Wait." Ercen reached over and laid her slate-colored hand on Freida's head, gently turning the girl around, while dropping her own head low, so she'd be on the same level with the girl. Freida found herself staring directly into the gargoyle's wide, amber eyes.

Ercen spoke tenderly. "Freida, we must wait, although it is hard to do so. You are a girl of action, thus this demand is difficult."

"You don't understand, Ercen. Paign is in grave danger…I can feel it." Freida's resolve began crumbling.

"Yes, child. I do understand. For I also believe this to be true. Something is happening that I—we—are trying to discover. Our enemy is devious, deceptive. Kahrnahrgx is on the move. It is likely that, soon, we will all be in grave danger."

"But, Ercen," Freida whispered, leaning her head against Ercen's cheek, "what of Paign?" Freida's wave of anger dissipated as quickly as it had come. Now, she struggled to stem the flow of tears stinging her eyes.

"Child," murmured the gargoyle, "I don't know where he is. We wait for Kimar. Perhaps he will know or have word from another."

"Shouldn't we be able to see the children?" Gudrun asked, her voice shrill. Already, she regretted coming along.

"Eh? What's that?" Johann had nearly finished laying out their camp with Heidi's help. He wished he knew how long they might be here.

"These gargoyles have never been what you might call *talkative*. But this time, wouldn't you say that Ercen is very closed about her business, Johann?" Heidi interjected.

"Jah! You said just what I am thinking," Johann replied, as he stood up to help Gudrun. He quickly scanned the vast cavern.

"Now, where have they gotten to?" he growled.

Quickly, Johann and Heidi fanned out, jumping on top of small stalagmites to get a more expansive view. Heidi shimmied up a tall one. Neither could spot Ercen or the kids.

"Hei! There's Tiny sniffing around that far corner. Did you see him, Heidi?"

"I think so. But where are the others? Why can't we see—"

Gudrun's shriek spun their attention back to where they'd just been.

"Nei!" Johann roared, as he sprinted between the maze of stone he'd just woven through. "Nei! Nei!"

"Gudrun! Flee! Flee!" Heidi wailed at the top of her lungs, still clinging to the mineral spire she'd climbed.

To his horror, Johann saw, fleetingly, Gudrun flailing her arms at two obsidian gargoyles soaring down from a high, dark recess in the cavern's ceiling. He was still blocked from her by columns of rocks. He swore many oaths at himself for laying down his bow and quiver as he set their camp. Now, he had nothing to defend the woman with from this distance!

"This way, Gudrun! Run!" Johann bellowed, still sprinting toward her. "Run! This way! Now!"

Three strides later, a gap between columns of rock allowed him another glance at where Gudrun had been. She was no longer there! A black wing swung down where she'd been flailing. Another gap. Wing. In just a few more seconds, Johann would blast into the clearing where he'd left Gudrun. His plan was no more complicated than to hurtle in fast and low. Beyond that, he'd hope to providence. And his sword. Already, his strong fingers were wrapped tightly around the hilt, his right arm holding it straight up in front of him as he ran.

A strange whistling roared over Johann's head, followed immediately by a withering heat and brilliance that forced him to drop down, sprawling on the floor. An explosion of fire and broken stone erupted from the direction he'd been racing towards. A cloud of fume and grit enveloped him. Coughing on the dust, Johann jumped up and raced for their camp, which was now roiling in a plume of dirty smoke. Steeling himself for sword-to-talon combat with the obsidians, Johann burst into the open area of their camp at a dead run.

CHAPTER THIRTEEN
THE TESTING OF PAIGN

It hurt to breathe. Oh, it hurt. Paign tried to take a deep breath, but searing pain almost made him pass out. *Wonderful! I think Rance-Dahl has broken several of my ribs. How much more of this can I take?* Paign wondered.

Rance-Dahl stared at the boy across the room, his clothes tattered and stained. The gargoyle was surprised that the object of his "attention" was still moving. This level of tolerance to suffering was…unexpected. While the senior minion of Kahrnahrgx didn't have extensive experience at torturing humans, he had enough to concede this boy was stronger than any other human he'd encountered. Rance-Dahl even felt a grudging respect for the boy.

But he had his orders: cause suffering. And Rance-Dahl was exceptionally skilled and practiced in his craft. Indeed, he enjoyed his work. In no hurry, since Paign remained on his hands and knees staring at the floor, the beast stared at the boy, puzzled. The gargoyle's arms were folded across his chest, the wicked talons of his left hand drumming on his much-scarred right side.

Paign sighed deeply, despite the anguish it brought him. He knew it couldn't be long now. Although his captor had said something about it being important that Paign not die from his torment, it seemed that Rance-Dahl had forgotten that detail of his mission. So many places on Paign's body were damaged—he was painted in bruises, contusions, scrapes and blood, both crusted and fresh—it required intense concentration just to move. Paign refused to lie down on the floor, even though he desperately wanted to, because he would not give his captor the satisfaction. However, standing up again was proving beyond Paign's capacity. So, he continued staring mindlessly at the floor, still on his hands and knees.

As much hurt as Paign had already absorbed on the outside of his body, it didn't match the tumultuous suffering inside of him. Even the mind-numbing misery from his broken ribs was no match for the despair engulfing him like the monstrous winter storms that buffeted the Norwegian coast near his home.

Paign was still shocked that his closest friend, his very own cousin, Anders, had railed at him about Danielle. The confusion he'd felt when Anders exploded at him for even speaking of Danielle hadn't diminished when Paign had stomped away from their argument; it had only intensified.

The turmoil that surged through Paign, as he hiked for hours after leaving Anders, was not a new feeling. Indeed, it was all too familiar. But that didn't make it any easier.

Memories, bitter and frenzied, washed over him like salt in a fresh cut. When Paign had first learned of his father's death in the War of Dominance, it was as if someone had, at that very moment, poured smoldering ash into his soul, melting it into slag. He'd felt all burnt inside, purged of all that was good. He'd felt only raw, cloaked in shrieking loneliness. Unlike a severe sunburn, there was no salve that Paign could have applied to his broken heart. But like the way a sunburn throbs until the skin is twisted—at which point the pain magnifies itself, almost as a most bitter punishment for having skin—Paign's heartache and grief at the loss of his father had throbbed without respite. When by himself, the ache of it became so habitual that he had become mostly numbed to it. But when with others—who always seemed compelled to make some kind, sympathetic remark—Paign's heart was again twisted into fresh agony. Their comments never helped. Never.

Arguing with Anders had been a reflex action and surprised Paign. It left him unsettled, confused and very agitated. After his bitter departure from Anders, Paign hiked for many hours, mindless of weather and totally unaware of his location. When he stopped, it was only to seize a fallen branch to shatter across the nearest tree or to hurl a rock at a nearby innocent, unsuspecting—and then very frightened—animal. Haunted, Paign muttered terrible things, hateful and vile things, at his cousin, at his friends, at his mother, even at his dead father. By the time he had utterly vented his rage, Paign's hands were bruised and bloodied from the bark of a particularly rough, sessile oak branch twisting in his hands as he slammed it into a boulder. Dirt from the hurled rocks had wedged into the wounds caused by the coarse bark. His voice had become raw and hoarse by the time he finally sat on an outcrop not far from the high cave on Ruar's Ridge that Freida had discovered the year before.

Finally, Paign saw that the sun would be down within the hour. He didn't care. He was exhausted physically, more from the violence he'd perpetrated on the forest than from the rage-filled hike. The great weariness in his soul felt as cold as the snow-chilled draft falling down from the ridge top. Abruptly, he sat down.

Though he'd rehearsed the conversation countless times already, in his mind, Paign again listened to Anders yelling.

Paign, you must stop talking about her! She's not coming back. Even if she wanted to, it won't happen! Don't you get it, Paign? Danielle is not coming back here. She lives in a time way beyond ours, right? We're as good as dead to her, from her time frame, anyway. So, she's as good as dead to you…and to me! She's gone, Paign. Gone!

At that point, Paign's body was spent and unwilling to smash anything more, and he found himself reflecting more on Anders's words and actions. He turned their conversation over and over in his mind.

Why was Anders so worked up over this? We've never really been angry at each other before now. Sure, he's annoyed me sometimes, but so have I to him. What of it?

As the sun neared the mountains to the west, it set the evergreen forest below into a fire of brilliant oranges and reds. Paign shifted on the flat outcrop he sat on and ran his fingers through his thick, scruffy hair. Behind, his long shadow mimicked the motion.

"You…and to me," he said, as his shoulders slumped.

"And to me." Paign ran his fingers through his hair again, but this time he pulled hard on it. He didn't notice the clump of hair entombed under his knuckles, whitened by the ferocity of his grip.

"And to me," repeating the words again, but now in the tone Anders had used.

Paign jumped to his feet. "What a thick, dense twit I've been!" he roared, his voice breaking, already damaged and hoarse.

Picking up a large shard of stone, he hurled it far over the edge of the outcrop. It clattered into the tree line below.

"How could I have not seen it? Anders! My own cousin! My best friend, no less—he's after my girl. He's after Danielle!"

Three more shards flew down the steep slope below Paign, like wickedly fast arrows from an expert bowman. Paign's face was bathed in the sinking sun's flaming colors.

"Danielle! Nei! Nei! You can't have her, Anders! Not her!" he shouted.

With a furious rush of jealous rage, Paign arched his back, thrust his fists skyward and bellowed, "Danielle!"

It was at that moment, perched high above the Honellaken Valley, very near the cave below Ruar's Peak, that Paign was seized by Rance-Dahl.

The sound of his captor's talons scraping on the floor of Paign's cell brought his attention back to his dire situation. Utterly dejected, Paign slowly shook his head.

Brooding about the hours leading up to his capture was poisonous to Paign. After days of torment, remembering the final words he'd had with Anders brought a terrible darkness over Paign's heart. His cousin had betrayed him! Even now, Paign was certain that Anders was busy planning a way to reach Danielle. After all, Paign was now out of his way! And he also had been betrayed by his friends and his own mother! For more time than Paign could remember now, he'd expected a rescue mission. He'd found strength in visualizing Kimar, Ita-Mudak, even Lohxnahr, parting into his cell with his friends and Mr. Skulstad's sword already swinging. But there'd been no rescue. No one came. No one cared. Perhaps they were all busy rescuing Danielle...for Anders?

Paign was still alone, just as alone as when his dad died. Alone. But now, he'd been betrayed and abandoned. By those closest to him.

Staring down at the top of his wounded hands, still on his hands and knees, Paign again shook his head slowly.

I have been a fool…a pathetic, idiotic fool.

The scraping sound of Rance-Dahl's talons drew nearer. Paign could see the gargoyle's feet approaching out of the corner of his left eye.

Volcanic, blinding fury surged through Paign, as hot tears burned his eyes. His breathing quickened.

I have been a fool, but I will no longer be!

Rance-Dahl paused next to the object of days of his hatred and scorn, momentarily bewildered by the boy's shaking body. The beast witnessed, with wicked pleasure, the human's tears staining the gritty floor. Smirking, the gargoyle reached down, intending to hurl the boy across the torture chamber another time—mistaking the boy's quivering for manifested terror.

But Paign's shaking wasn't from terror.

CHAPTER FOURTEEN
GATHERING STORM

Gudrun was gone!

Johann's head was already turning back and forth, scanning their campground, even as he slid to a crunching stop, grit and dirt flying up from his boots. The canvas bag holding the remains of their cooking kit smoldered on the shelf of rock where Heidi had left it minutes earlier.

Spinning around, his sword at the ready, Johann quickly scanned the area, hoping to spot some telltale of Gudrun. His mind swam with questions, dismayed at the prospect that his wife's childhood friend, the mother of Paign, might now be captured. Or worse.

Muttering under his breath, he frantically hastened around their camp, peering behind outcrops and stalactites.

"Did the obsidians get her, then? Why would they want her? Why would Ercen risk a fireball when Gudrun could be killed?"

Johann stewed on these questions, his head down low, while grinding grit under his right foot.

With barely a whistle of wind, Ercen flew into the ring and alighted on a squat, charred stalagmite. She quickly lowered Freida and Anders to the ground. Anders's hair was mussed up from the flight.

"Why did you fire on her?" Johann asked Ercen, his face tight with anxiety.

"Fire on who?" Heidi asked, trotting into the camp ring, with Tiny just in front of her; they'd run not far below Ercen's flight path with the children. Quickly looking around, she faced Johann. "Where's Gudrun?"

Johann first stared at Ercen, then turned to his wife. "Gone. Gudrun was gone before I could reach this place. She...I couldn't see whether..." He paused, struggling to actually say out loud what he feared in his heart. "The obsidians were flying very fast and low. My view was obstructed most of the time."

Heidi's face wrinkled with care. Her shoulders slumped as she anticipated the meaning in her husband's troubled eyes.

Anders walked silently around their camp, quickly leaning to the right or left of roughly a dozen stalagmites, as if hunting for something. Freida was motionless, except for her eyes, as they moved from her mother to her father.

Johann breathed deep. "Look, I couldn't see...she may have been taken by the obsidians. But I believe she was destroyed by Ercen's fireball!"

Heidi dropped to her knees as if her legs had been knocked out from beneath her.

Ercen immediately stepped off the stone stump and in three steps reached Heidi, enveloping her in her wings. "My dear," she murmured to Heidi, "my dear."

Freida ran to her father and took his hands in her own. Her eyes filled with tears. His were squinted, staring far beyond the confines of the cavern.

Anders scratched his head, dismayed and overwhelmed by this turn. Could it be that Paign's mother had been killed?

Worse, was she killed by an ally? He sat on the stump Ercen had stood on, his eyes focused on nothing. He wished there was something—anything—he could do for his friends. Absentmindedly, he ran his fingers through his hair.

Was she really killed by the fireball? Anders wondered again to himself; then before he knew it, his mind turned to a hateful notion. *But wouldn't there be evidence? Wouldn't there be something? Some...remains?*

Unconsciously, Anders stood up and scanned the area immediately around him. It was the only area he'd not inspected before because Ercen had been in the way. Tiny stayed close to him, sniffing.

The others heard him gasp, and they turned to look at him. Tiny was next to Anders, his front paws spread wide and his nose to the ground.

Anders stood stiff, pointing at the charred stump of stone. "This was a stalagmite," he whispered. He twisted around. "I mean, this was a full-height stalagmite—until Ercen's fireball blasted into it."

"So?" Freida replied, her voice strangled. "What of it, Anders?"

With an edge of excitement in his voice that sent a thrill down Freida's back, he continued, "Well, none of us noticed it. Why should we?" His voice grew stronger, quicker. "We're surrounded by hundreds of these things. They're everywhere!"

Anders's arms swept around, indicating the entire cavern.

"Notice what?" Johann barked. "Notice what, Anders?"

Anders bent down suddenly into a squat, quickly picked up something and stood back up. "This!"

His light blue eyes twinkled triumphantly as he smiled, thrusting his hand out in front of them. Wedged tightly between his forefinger and thumb was a frayed and singed, shimmering black feather fragment.

"Don't you see?" he continued. "Ercen's fireball left quite a mark on at least one of the obsidians, just as they parted out of here with Gudrun! Look!"

Following his gaze, they all saw many such fragments all around the shattered stalagmite, which moments earlier they'd all taken to be a stump. The feather bits were so numerous and evenly distributed that, in their haste, no one had recognized them for what they were. Without thinking, they'd all assumed the cavern's color simply included dark speckles.

"You mean—" Heidi began.

"Jah!" Johann exclaimed. "Gudrun wasn't killed by the blast! It destroyed at least one obsidian, though."

"Which is great news, but—" Freida started, her voice shrill.

"Gudrun is still in greater danger," Ercen finished, sounding only a little relieved. "And where are the others? Kimar should be here by now."

Paign surged off the floor, ramming his left shoulder into an unsuspecting and very startled Rance-Dahl, throwing his captor off balance. Before the gargoyle could regain his footing, Paign shoved his straightened left arm into the rough floor, quickly pivoted around on his wounded left hand, and delivered a powerful, double side kick into Rance-Dahl's abdomen. The furious gargoyle sailed backward, unable to fight the boy until the laws of physics returned him to the chamber's floor.

Too late did Rance-Dahl realize the angle that Paign had kicked him. Glancing behind, the gargoyle twisted violently in the air, vainly trying to swing away from the Glimmer.

As his captor hurtled into the bizarre device that had earlier kept the boy locked within, Paign was already on his feet, racing at the flailing gargoyle.

Rance-Dahl's head, torso and legs were nearly engulfed in the Glimmer, as if he were sinking into a thick porridge. Only the front of him was uncovered by the glowing orange mass. His right arm was trapped, halfway up his massive, twitching forearm. His left arm was encompassed to the elbow, leaving his forearm unbound and free to slice wildly at the Glimmer.

Paign slammed into the beast's left forearm, seizing the gargoyle's wrist with all of his strength.

Rance-Dahl wailed in fury and pain, his left arm compressed suddenly into its immovable elbow. Frantically, he tried to slice at Paign's head with his right-hand talons; only the right wrist was free of the Glimmer. His flaming eyes grew wide, enraged that he couldn't reach the impudent boy.

But Paign's rage was the greater. Already, he was viciously twisting Rance-Dahl's left wrist so that the beast's talons were aimed at his own throat, bearing down with all the strength his will could muster.

"Aaargh, I see your game, boy! I commend your creativity and spirit," the gargoyle grunted. "Nevertheless, in a moment, you will die for this insolence!"

Sweat ran down Paign's forehead, his arms barely maintaining against his captor's mighty resistance. Out of the corner of his left eye, Paign could see talons furiously sweeping at his neck. The effort of holding the gargoyle's arm in place made Paign's chest ache. He winced from the spasms coming from his broken ribs.

Rance-Dahl hissed at Paign, just inches away. "Losing already, human?" Slowly, a wicked smile widened across his face.

"You are such weak creatures. Pathetic. Your frail bodies are matched only by your dim wits. Soon, I will also *instruct* those of your little fellowship. Particularly, I look forward to teaching my lessons to that troublesome girl..."

Paign grimaced and stared at Rance-Dahl. "You will not harm the girl, you vile monster," he wailed, then wrenched at the gargoyle's wrist with all of his waning might.

"Ah! I see it now. Before I did not, so focused I was on your learning," Rance-Dahl purred. "She is of importance to you! Of great importance, in fact!" He burst into harsh laughter.

"No!" Paign cried, wincing as he pushed on Rance-Dahl's arm.

Seizing on Paign's obvious misery, the gargoyle suddenly yanked his left arm up, hoping to dislodge the boy's grip. Somehow, Paign hung on to the fierce pull off the ground. His captor, furious at his lack of success, thrust his arm back down.

By the time Paign hit the floor, his own rage exploded upon his captor, renewed by his overwhelming fear for Danielle. In a twinkling, even as he felt his right ankle break upon the floor, his physical pain merged with his personal anguish and sense of betrayal.

A primal scream erupted from Paign's throat.

Appalled, Rance-Dahl watched in horror as his wrist, bent by the unexpected power of the boy, inched closer to his own neck. Impulsively, the gargoyle pushed back. But the Glimmer's force held his body in place, so that he could not leverage his superior strength and weight against the human.

As the talons moved ever closer, it dawned on the gargoyle that he would have less and less power to resist his opponent. His greatest strength was in a straightened arm. Desperately, he tried to slice Paign with the talons of his free hand. Here, too, the Glimmer worked against Rance-Dahl.

Sweat dripped off of Paign, but he now showed no sign of weakening. Strength surged through him as he struggled to make this chance—his one chance—to survive.

As fear flooded Rance-Dahl's mind, the gargoyle spontaneously twisted within the Glimmer, to the left. His massive strength, inhibited by the unyielding nature of the Glimmer, did what Paign's could not. A deep rip formed in the orange matter, about a meter to the left of the gargoyle.

Simultaneously, Rance-Dahl's eyes and Paign's head jerked towards the sound of the tear that ripped the Glimmer. Paign's face filled with dismay. Rance-Dahl's filled with hate. Both knew the fight was nearly over. In a moment, the gargoyle would be free of the Glimmer, and Paign would be dead. All Rance-Dahl needed was one more twist, and the rent would open wide enough for him to fall free of the Glimmer.

Although his body was nearly spent, his energy so depleted, Paign's mind felt sharper than it had ever been. In the span of a heartbeat, he realized what his tormentor's next move would be. He also knew his chances were still terribly grim. But one possibility yet remained. With his last ounce of strength, even his last ounce of life, Paign willed himself to spend it protecting Danielle.

Leaning his face towards Rance-Dahl's, leaving little space between them, he spat, "You will *not* have her!"

The idle boast of the idiot human flooded Rance-Dahl with overwhelming confidence. His face curled up into a fiendish snarl, completely baring his long sharp fangs for the first time. "You pathetic excuse for something worthy of my attention, I *will* have her, right after I dispatch you! You fool!"

As if time slowed to a crawl, Paign felt the pressure of Rance-Dahl's body swing violently to the right, just as he had expected. The gargoyle's intention, of course, was to complete the tear in the Glimmer and be set free of it.

What his tormentor failed to recognize was that his own violent movement finished what Paign started. The momentum of the gargoyle's massive rightward twist built on Paign's increased pressure on the creature's own wrist.

"No, you will not!" Paign exulted into the face of a wide-eyed Rance-Dahl.

Paign's ankle finally gave way and he fell backwards, landing hard on the floor.

Rance-Dahl remained motionless, except for his darting, flame-red eyes. The gnarled, glistening knuckles of his left hand pressed hard against his neck. Far behind, the talons protruded through the base of his head. His right hand, still embedded in the Glimmer, vainly tried to reach over to remove his impaling wrist, the talons twitching for a moment. Abruptly, they drooped, still.

As Paign, utterly spent, slipped out of consciousness, he heard a voice whisper, "No, you will not…no, you will not… no, you will—"

Then, all grew quiet and he knew no more.

CHAPTER FIFTEEN
FLAME AND WRATH

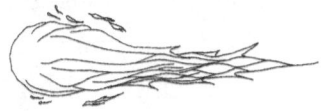

Gudrun's nerves were no match for what she faced. Still greatly overwrought by Paign's disappearance, her own lack of sleep and the madness of the previous days, all she could do was shiver uncontrollably. She could not form any words in her mind, let alone send any from her lips. Her being was reduced to her most basic elements: she breathed—shallowly—when she wasn't able to scream anymore.

Her face the hue of pale ash, Paign's mother looked at the countless gargoyles surrounding her. One lay in a smoldering heap, struck dead by Ercen's fireball, just as it had parted away with her. Had Gudrun been capable of greater attention when she was in the company of her friends, she would have recognized these gargoyles as different from those seeking to help her rescue her son. With her mind seized by numbing fear, Gudrun hadn't noticed that these gargoyles were glistening black, like flint knives. All she noticed now was their cruelty.

"Aaaygh!" Gudrun wailed, her head facing the cavern ceiling high overhead. "Why? Why?"

The obsidian gargoyle fiendishly clutching both of her wrists twisted them towards the floor, while leaning down and into her, his face pressed against hers.

"Have I your attention, human?" Sepanyahd hissed into Gudrun's cheek. "Where did your group take your son?"

The woman twitched in a frenzy of torment, her body recoiling at her captor's touch. Her mind was stunned by the severe anguish pulsing through her arms. It was if all she had ever known in life was suffering. Almost. Like tatters of a shredding dream, vague images bolted through her, carried on the stabbing pains clouding her mind. Yet, the images anchored her. Deep inside, Gudrun realized her sanity would soon be crushed if she didn't focus on these fleeting images.

Dimly, she was aware of her captor's hot and languid breath on her face as he shouted and shouted at her.

The images...the images. I must remember! Gudrun fought to gather her wits to her defense. *I must—Roald?* Her husband's face floated before her. He smiled at her gently but with profound sadness, his dark blue eyes holding an unexplained urgency. *My beloved Roald! Oh, how I have missed you. My darling...no, please wait!* The apparition frayed, dissipated and reformed. *Heidi! Please, Heidi! Why do you not intervene?* Her friend's face was lined with care, anxiety filling it with an agedness unfitting of her. *Heidi?* Gudrun's body convulsed as Sepanyahd twisted her wrists again, bellowing into his mindless captive's face. *Heidi, I am so weary. Roald is coming, you will see! He will return from the front, I know it in my heart—oh, no. No, Heidi!* Again, the flitting image swirled in Gudrun's tortured mind, fragmented and then vanished. Darkness now encroached on her, where she'd before been sustained by images of those she loved. It was oppressive, weighing on her heart like a cloak of stone. As the final, vaporous shred of Heidi disappeared, another quickly formed. *Paign! Oh, my lands! Paign, my darling! What has happened to you?* Horror swept through Gudrun's soul, struck the deeper by the wounds her only son plainly carried on his body. Gudrun convulsed and wept bitterly.

"Human!" Sepanyahd thrust Gudrun away from him violently, to the extent that her arms could move while he still clutched her wrists brutally. Immediately yanking her back, he screamed again into her bloodied ear, "*Where* did your group take your son, you human refuse?"

Vaguely, Gudrun's mind cataloged something had just shattered in her right wrist; the anguish had changed somewhat. But, much more clearly, as if for the first time, she attended her gargoyle persecutor's words.

Son? Take? What is this beast saying? It was so difficult to force her mind through the waves of pain sweeping over her. *Son? Can he be speaking of Paign?*

Suddenly, her mind focused, snapping everything into sharp contrast. *Yes!* Gudrun exulted. *He—they—don't know where Paign is! Yes! Perhaps he is safe, then.* Gudrun felt as if she were at that final, breathless moment before breaking the surface of the water after a deep dive. The internal pressure was nearly beyond her constraints. An overwhelming desire to spit on her cruel harasser swept over Gudrun. Fear, rage and anguish smashed together within her aching chest. She desired to taunt Sepanyahd, to fling back at him impudence, to mock him and his cohorts for their inability to locate and contain one, solitary human boy. A fury unlike anything she had ever known rose within her. Just as she gasped into her lungs the air sufficient for her triumphant, defiant rejection of Sepanyahd, a new image quickly formed in her awakened mind, even as she glared at her subjugator.

Like thick mists rolling up from an ice-chilled marsh, a ghostly specter took shape, nearly obliterating Gudrun's awareness of the hellishness surrounding her. The vaporous shape was unknown to her and peculiar, yet she felt no fear of it. Only a deep sense of serenity and curiosity. Similar to the other images she'd seen, this one also floated before her in a greyish, fog-like cloud. Yet, it differed in its clarity and sharpness. The others Gudrun knew to be grounded in memories, while this one struck her as being somehow real, as if she were really seeing a winged creature flying at little more than arm's length, directly before her face. She could plainly see that the creature was a gargoyle, and yet she knew instinctively that it was unlike those acting as her jailers.

How can this be? she wondered. *By what magic could I be seeing this gargoyle while these other creatures seem not to?*

"Fear not! I have been sent to you, mother of Paign," said the small gargoyle, his voice making a curious, buzzing sound.

His eyes shown in brilliant copper. Like a new teapot from the shops in Røros, she marveled.

Then it hit her. Shocked, Gudrun realized the being had spoken to her, but without actual speech. At least, not speech her captors could hear.

Gudrun knew not what to do, so she simply stared at the pearlescent wings of her visitor as they gently undulated back and forth. Feeling a tightness in her chest, Gudrun finally softly exhaled the deep breath she'd inhaled several seconds earlier.

"Ah, good! It is well that you are calm, mother of Paign," the tiny gargoyle hummed to her. "I am Zarentil and I bring you tidings of your son."

For reasons that Gudrun could not explain, the misery and ache in her wrists immediately diminished.

"Your son has been in the clutches of the gargoyle known as Rance-Dahl. From the area you know as Ruar's Ridge, below the very peak of the same name, your son was taken captive by Rance-Dahl to the Glimmer. This gargoyle is known to me over the span of many, long generations. He is a vile beast, ruthless and forgiving, not."

Gudrun's heart leapt within her, both from the pure joy of news of her son and sheer anguish over his suffering. She had the distinct impression that Zarentil paused his speech to allow her time to fully experience these feelings. Then, he continued.

"I have come to you, mother of Paign, for help in recovering your son. For while he is near the Glimmer, he is hidden from us. Rance-Dahl, the Keeper of the Glimmer, is capable of transporting it to locations pleasing to him, thus he could be in places innumerable."

Before she could stop herself, Gudrun blurted out, "How am I to find my boy? I have no special powers! Paign, my beloved son! How am I to find him, Zarentil? How am I—" Suddenly, Gudrun stopped, overcome by fear that her captors had heard.

"Fear not! They cannot hear. Sepanyahd and the others are, as yet, unaware of my presence, for I have slowed time that we might commune one with the other."

Gudrun simply nodded to Zarentil, as she would do with her parish parson, when presented with something beyond her understanding. Again, she realized she'd been holding her breath, so she exhaled slowly.

"Although the powers of the Priestly Order are great, mother of Paign, and mine are greater than any other in this matter, it is not possible for us to sense your son's location."

Gudrun's heart grew heavy, overpowered by despair, and plunged into darkness. Faintly, she heard the queer, fuzzy rasping of Zarentil, so faintly.

"Mother of Paign! While it is not within our power to detect your son's place in the world, it is within yours! Fear not, human, for you hold within you a power unmatched by our race—that of a mother's love for her child. It is through you—and only you—that your son will be reclaimed."

Gudrun's knees nearly buckled under her. "What? Zarentil, what are you saying to me? I don't have any...I can't..."

"I am not able to locate the boy but I am able to assist you," he replied sympathetically. "Have a care as you take my hands."

Gingerly, Gudrun reached around the gargoyle's out-stretched hands, avoiding the glistening talons. His skin was leathery yet surprisingly soft and warm to the touch.

"Please now, mother of Paign, listen deeply with your heart. Listen for the who of your son. Fix your heart on the sounds of his heart. He is in great pain, this much is known to me. Physical anguish, yes, there is. Yet, there is something more...something deeper...great suffering of a different kind."

Gudrun experienced sensations unlike anything she'd felt before, as if she inhabited not only her own body but also that of another's. She assumed that her connection to Zarentil provided her increased sense of time and place. Even as simple as she was, she knew she could not be in two places at the same time. And yet, she was. Her eyes still took in the fiendish gargoyles around her, unmoving, with Sepanyahd's snarling visage just inches away from her.

Strangely, her new vantage point was not seen through Zarentil's eyes. It was, somehow, the sum of the two. While she could, if she wished, see things as the little gargoyle did—looking at her as she looked at him—her vision now took flight, encompassing beauties and horrors that defied description or understanding. Gudrun choked momentarily at the realization that she was empowered to see everything. Whatever she wished. Whoever she wished. That this power had come upon her unbidden, to a poor, uncultured, military widow, distraught and weary of torment, was intoxicating. Gudrun's senses grew dull and sluggish. In a stupor, her mind wandered impulsively to times, places and people she sought something from. Forgiveness she sought from some. With others, it was forgiveness she sought to bring. But as she scanned the horizons of her life, Gudrun began to search out those she wished for retribution. Quickly, she searched for those officers who had commanded her beloved Roald into the battle where he was slain. Before she could pursue this thought, an enormous desire to see Roald swept over her. Perhaps, she could save him from the battle! Could it be that with this newfound power, she could intercede and direct her husband to a different end? Wild hope bloomed inside of Gudrun as she bent her will to see into that specific time and place where she could save her husband.

If only this terrible ringing would stop! I can't hear myself think! The sound hammering against her wasn't the ringing of the church bell she sometimes heard, especially in the quite of a still evening. This ringing must be more like standing within the huge, iron bell of their stave church, she thought. *Oh, my head will shatter soon!* Nausea assaulted her. Her eyes still open, seeing through time and place, Gudrun instinctively made her mind go blank. The severe ringing immediately stopped. Zarentil's voice broke through.

You must listen! Seek not these other cares of your heart. There will be time later. You must listen for your son, mother of Paign! His need is urgent! Please, listen your way to him. I will take us to the there *he is.*

Revulsion and loathing crashed through Gudrun; her intuition told her the terrible ringing had been Zarentil trying to break through all along. She'd wasted precious time, indulging her sense of importance and power. Guilt surged up within her like bile.

Stop! There is no time for this, either! Nei! Gudrun bent in on herself, pulling Zarentil's hands close to her, and collected every shred of energy remaining, intent on one thing: finding the heart of her son in the vastness of the universe.

Paign! My son! Let my heart reach out to your heart, dear one. Son of Roald, your mother seeks you. Paign, you are…broken! Gudrun felt pangs throughout her body. Encouraged by the knowledge that she was, in truth, sensing echoes of her son's physical being, she pushed herself harder.

My son, we are coming. We are desperately searching for you, Paign! We are—

As if struck by a falling brick, Gudrun suddenly reeled back, kept in place only by Zarentil. *Oh, Paign! My dearest, no! No! Oh, no!* Wave after wave of self-loathing and despair pulsed into Gudrun's heart from the very heart of her only son. Withering rage, too, and crushing heartbreak. Convictions of abandonment. Betrayal! Oh, betrayal. *Paign! We are coming! We are, my dearest. Child, I am coming!*

Gudrun pulled Zarentil close. "Paign is dying! We must go to him, now! Now! Now!"

The shiny copper eyes blinked. *I have him! I can see him through your heart's eye!*

They parted away in that instant, leaving Sepanyahd and his compatriots startled and stupefied.

Ahkzita, just moments into his promotion to take Sepanyahd's place as Hunter-Seeker unit commander, hoped that Kahrnahrgx didn't observe his shuddering. Or that any of those most highly skilled soldiers in his freshly minted command bore witness to his "weakness."

"You there!" Ahkzita bellowed at his squad, shocking them from their preoccupation. "Clean this up!" With a wave of his talons, he indicated the remains of Sepanyahd, which were strewn about the cavern like so much fleshy carnage after exploding from cannon shot.

Turning slowly and veiled in shadow from the cavern's brightly lit center, Kahrnahrgx leaned down slightly and stared at Ahkzita. Only the impenetrable fiery-red eyes were clearly visible.

"May I trust *you* to not repeat his mistake?" Kahrnahrgx intoned, his voice so deep it reverberated in the stone floor of the cave.

Straining against the terrible impulse to shudder again, Ahkzita's throat tightened so that he squawked out, "Yes, my Mas—" Roughly clearing his throat, he stated flatly, "Yes, Master! Of course, my Liege."

"It will be better for you," Kahrnahrgx replied. "I'll not be as inclined to show you the mercy I gave to Sepanyahd. He was my trusted friend."

Heidi paced back and forth, nervously wringing her hands. Gudrun lay fast asleep next to her. Except for the gentle smile on her face, she looked terrible. Her clothes were tattered and stained from the terrors meted out upon her by Sepanyahd and his followers.

Of course, Gudrun had originally wanted to immediately go with the rescue team to retrieve Paign. But, when she'd parted into their cavern alone a few hours earlier, it had been an enormous struggle to piece together what had happened during her absence.

Unfortunately, Gudrun had appeared mostly incoherent to the others. For their part, Johann, Anders and especially Freida were not as patient as they needed to be to actually learn anything useful. Heidi had been hard put to it to mediate their conversations. Ercen quietly worked on Gudrun's most serious injuries, saying very little.

The intensity and frustration of trying to make clear to the others what Zarentil had said and done finally exhausted Gudrun. The weariness that swept over her was, of course, empowered by Ercen's healing touch. As Gudrun's pain diminished, the more her body cried out for rest.

Johann stepped in front of his wife and whispered, "So, what do we know? Tsk! I've run over this in my mind for the better part of this hour and still don't know what to make of it."

Before he could finish, Heidi seized him by the arm and walked him to the far side of their camp.

"Shush…Gudrun needs to rest," she hissed softly to her husband. Still, Freida and Anders could hear her. Heidi's eyes were framed in worry and care. But, as she looked into

Johann's ruddy face, she squeezed his arm and her own face quickly softened.

"I'm sorry, my husband," she whispered. "It's just that I was so worried for my friend"—she paused to take a deep breath before continuing—"and now that she's back here with us, I...I...how do we rescue Paign?" Burying her face in Johann's shoulder, Heidi wept.

Freida listened to their conversation, agonizing over the same question. She assumed Anders had been working on a solution as well. He hadn't moved so much as a hair since he'd sat down soon after Gudrun fell fast asleep.

Freida started when Anders whispered distinctly into her ear, "That's exactly what I want to know!"

"Well, how should I know?" Freida hissed into his face, distressed.

"Hey, look. I'm on your side, you know!" Anders replied. "It's just that I'm confused about why this character, Zarentil, is able to find Gudrun and then is able to locate Paign—through his mother, no less. Yet, he drops her off here with us...to do what? He needs her help to find Paign, but he doesn't need ours to rescue him? That just doesn't make any sense!"

"No, it doesn't, Anders," Freida whispered. "No, it doesn't."

CHAPTER SIXTEEN
CRACKS AND FISSURES

Paign drifted up to the edge of awareness. Ephemeral shapes moved in and out of his vision, like strange shadows set fluttering within a cavern when struck by lantern light. Voices. He heard voices…with the movement? It was a struggle to focus his attention. *Remember. So hard. To wake up?*

There was awareness of pressure. *Someone is touching me. Someone is pushing on my*—Paign gasped—*my ribs! Oh! This is intolerable*—

He passed out.

More light, shapes and shadows swam at the rim of Paign's perception. Again, he struggled to break through to wakefulness. A roundish shadow off to the right moved towards the center of his understanding and quickly grew, until it nearly filled Paign's still-unfocused vision. He could almost make out a face. *Whose? Don't recognize him, do I? Like Lohxnahr, in a way. Lohxnahr? Is that you?* But no sound came.

The face briefly came nearly into focus, although still vague. Paign could see for a moment a lovely smile on a gargoyle, but it was looking away, towards something or someone on Paign's left. For some reason, this annoyed Paign greatly. He must have twitched or made some movement, because the gargoyle's smile turned toward Paign and then vanished into a veil of concern.

*No, not yet...*Paign heard the gargoyle speak directly into his mind. But the boy couldn't be sure of what he heard.

As Paign again felt consciousness slipping away, his last thought was, *I really must have done it this time. I feel terrible.*

"She's making me crazy, Anders! Really, she is!" Freida hissed, not terribly concerned about whether Ercen could hear her.

Anders was concerned. "Please, Freida! Keep your voice down. I mean, I understand that she's not helping right now." He turned to watch the hulking gargoyle pace back and forth on the far side of their camp. "She's been doing that since Mrs. Macy returned. Or was returned, I should say."

Freida's eyes burned hot. "But she doesn't believe it! Isn't that what you hear her saying, without saying it that plainly, of course?"

"Well, uh, yes," Anders replied. "That is what I hear her saying, Freida. And who's to argue? It's pretty cussed strange that Mrs. Macy was returned and Paign was not, don't you think?"

Freida glared at Anders, her lips pursed tight.

"Well, don't you?"

"Of course I do, Anders!" Freida relented. "But I am vexed...so highly vexed by this that I can hardly think! Here, we should be feeling splendid about Mrs. Macy's safe return—from a really horrifying and abominable testing—rather than doubting and questioning whether her redeemer is, in fact, the hybrid demon of Kahrnahrgx's making!" Tipping her head toward where Ercen paced, she added, "At least, that is what *she's* questioning."

"Sure, Freida. Sure. It is, as you say, completely vexing!" Anders ground his right boot toe into the loose stone at his foot. He looked at Freida pointedly, adding, "And you must admit that it is a question worth asking,"

"Except that it's made Mrs. Macy into a miserable mess, or a liar, or both," Freida replied, staring affectionately at a woman she'd known her entire life. A woman of deep suffering, to be sure, but also a woman of decency and strength.

"We should go listen in," Anders suggested.

"You're probably right," Freida conceded.

The two walked over to a wide, broken stalagmite roughly in the shape of a bench. This put them just to the left and behind where Heidi and Johann sat on either side of Gudrun, while Ercen paced before them.

"Then why isn't he *here*?" Ercen said heatedly.

"If we knew that, Ercen, we wouldn't be having this conversation!" Heidi replied in kind. "And which he do you mean? Lohxnahr? Or Kimar?"

Ercen continued to pace without answering. Anders thought he heard a growl come from her direction.

"Jah, well," Johann began, gently patting Gudrun's knee before standing up and walking over to Ercen. "Let's see if I have this straight. Ercen, you were made to understand that Lohxnahr spoke with Kimar some time ago about concerns of a *high-breed*, as you call it. This creature is believed to be made somehow by Kahrnahrgx out of a gargoyle beast and a human."

Johann stood staring up at Ercen for a moment. After a moment, he thrust his large, gnarled hands out, until his arms flung out his annoyance: "Jah?"

"Yes, that is so," Ercen replied, her voice even.

"All right, then," Johann resumed. "According to Kimar, Lohxnahr also put across the notion that this high-breed beast may have—how do you say it, Heidi…*skifte?*—*become* the gargoyle priest called Zarentil." Johann was pacing now. Ercen stepped out of his way, since he unwittingly was using her recently made trench.

"Good, then!" Johann muttered, his head aimed down, as if watching his pacing feet provided greater clarity. "Where was I? Ah, yes. Lohxnahr asks Kimar for great stealth and secrecy, naming his fear that this Zarentil imposter could destroy everything that much of the gargoyle and human worlds hold dear. Correct?"

"It is as you say, Johann!" Ercen said, dejectedly. "I should not, absolutely not, have told you all this."

Anders quickly leaned over to Freida and whispered, "Wow! We missed a lot when we were—"

"Shush, Anders!" Freida hissed back. "They're not done, yet!"

"Finally, Lohxnahr sends all of you off to different places, so he can search for this Zarentil-not-Zarentil with the help of Danielle…"

Anders stared at Freida, his eyes wide. Before he could blurt out anything, she quickly put her hand over his mouth.

"While you all waited for a summons from—"

"Johann! Please cease speaking!" Ercen commanded. "*I should not have told you any of this!* Do you not understand? Kimar was told by Lohxnahr to keep this information to him-

self. He chose to disclose these matters to me in the strict-
est confidence. It was my weakness, in my growing unease,
I transgressed and broke Kimar's confidence." The great gargoyle shook her head back and forth, utterly disconsolate.

Johann stepped forward sharply and took her enormous
hands into his, gingerly avoiding the razor-like talons. Lifting
his head, he looked straight into her wide face.

"Forgive me, Ercen. In my eagerness to find resolution, I
have spoken out of turn. Let me say this, however. It is not for
ill that you have shared this information with us. You see it as
a break of confidence, a breaking of faith with Kimar. I say it is
not so. It was *meant* to be shared, perhaps?" He smiled reassuringly, hoping to convey some peace to his hulking friend. "We
know you meant no harm from sharing this with us. Rather,
the opposite."

"I agree with Johann, dear Ercen." Heidi added. "It is not
for naught that you disclosed this to us. Consider that you
have simply extended the confidence to us that Kimar placed
in you. As you know, we have a stake in this, too."

Ercen, her face a display of wonder and hope, replied, "Yes.
Yes, you do have a stake, my friend Heidi, as well as you, Johann."

Quickly, the gargoyle dropped to her knees directly in front
of Gudrun. "Please know, Gudrun, that I do not doubt your
truthfulness, nor do I question your experience or what your
eyes and heart have told you." Her large, limpid amber eyes
blinked just inches from Gudrun, whose own eyes ran freely.

Freida leaned forward to hear better, grabbing Anders's
hand and squeezing it tight.

"It is *my* experience that I doubt," Ercen continued quietly. "It is *my* truth that I call into question. It is *my*—" The
gargoyle's head dropped down and she became silent.

Gudrun wiped away her tears and stared at the top of Ercen's head, noting for the first time the infinitesimally delicate feathers interlacing between the gargoyle's short horns. Without thinking, she reached up and stroked them gently, as more tears flowed afresh.

Abruptly she stopped, her fingers lingering in midair, unsure.

Ercen raised her head and looked softly towards Gudrun. Freida could see the woman's back facing the children. "It is *my* doubt that I should, rather, question. My doubt of your story. My doubt of Lohxnahr's story. My doubt of"—her voice breaking—"Kimar's story. In these have I proven faithless."

Ercen stood up. More firmly now, she continued, "While I have no explanation for how Zarentil came to you, nor how he affected your rescue and return to us, I believe he did so. It is profoundly unclear why he would not also return Paign to you…and us. Finally, it remains a great mystery how it is that the same Zarentil who redeemed you should also be the one we so greatly fear now. Nevertheless, it is beyond question that only one of the Great Ones could affect a rescue of such magnitude. Though you may not believe it, I am convinced that Zarentil snatched you back from nothing less than the inner sanctum of Kahrnahrgx himself!"

Freida could stand it no longer. Without letting go of Anders's hand, she ran over and stood next to Ercen, dragging Anders along.

"But where was Paign? Where is Paign?" she cried, clutching Ercen's hand.

"I know not, child. Caverns beyond counting could have held him. Based on what Gudrun has shared with us, Zarentil returned her to us prior to seeking out the boy.

Through Gudrun's heart's eye, Zarentil knew where to retrieve Paign. But, with no description of his place of captivity, I have no way of guessing it." Seeing the obvious fear in her eyes, Ercen added softly, "I am most sorry, Freida."

Tiny, who had been sitting at the edge of their camp, walked over to Freida and curled up at her feet, actually covering them, while his long, bushy tail swept back and forth over his mistress's feet.

Freida dropped to her knees, releasing Anders's and Ercen's hands as she did so. She folded herself over Tiny and wept.

Gudrun leaned over to stroke the girl's disheveled mane of red hair, tears streaming down her own weary, careworn face.

Heidi squatted down to hug both her daughter and her friend.

Anders looked at Johann, feeling quite hopeless, saying, "So, even after all this, we know nothing more than before, do we?"

At first his mouth opened, as if he were about to say something back to Anders. Then, his mouth closed and Johann shrugged.

Ercen turned away from watching the women. Quietly, but with surprising intensity, she replied, "Yes! Yes, we do. We know that Lohxnahr may have erred in his conclusion that Zarentil was brought unto death by the hybrid gargoyle. We have much evidence that the Great One, Zarentil, is in fact very much alive. And that is certainly more than we knew before."

For a moment, Anders stared at Ercen, appearing unconvinced as far as Johann could tell. Suddenly, Anders's eyes grew wide and he stepped back awkwardly, like a sailor on the wave-washed deck of a heaving ship.

He gasped. "Oh, no. No. Oh, no. What if…"

Freida's head lifted up, her tear-stained face stricken by the sound in Anders's voice. "What if what, Anders?"

"What if it isn't Zarentil who's the counterfeit?" Anders cried. "What if it's Lohxnahr?"

CHAPTER SEVENTEEN

ALLUVIUM

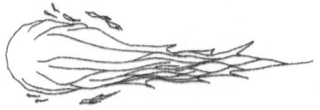

Tiny was pleased that everyone had finally stopped talking. Well, yelling was more of what they'd been doing and for much of the afternoon. Even though he'd been in a cavern, shut off from the light of day, Tiny could still tell what time it was. And he could tell when humans needed to calm down. Apparently, gargoyles sometimes needed to calm down, too. That had been an unpleasant surprise.

In the first few moments after Kimar had suddenly parted into the Cavern of Osberg, for the same reason that Ercen had brought the others, there had been much rejoicing in the reunion. But that all turned quickly sour as Kimar learned the details about Gudrun's abduction and, particularly, her return.

"Ercen! You should not have told these humans about Lohxnahr's suspicions!" he roared.

Tiny dropped his head onto his paws, looking exceedingly forlorn. That one comment by Kimar had set off a storm of angry words and protests—by his master, in particular. *He is not easily heeled, once his mind is set! And he did not like the bark of the big gargoyle pack leader! Master did not even care about my other person's concern for his safety. Ho! His bark was loud!*

Johann had exploded at Kimar, actually forcing the gargoyle captain to step back a few paces from the raging farmer, whose arms flailed around to punctuate his speech. Insulted, he bellowed into Kimar's face, "What mean you by *these humans*? Are we not friends anymore? Are we no longer to be trusted with this crucial information? After all that we have been through together? Do you really mean that, Kimar? I am not believing you have said this thing!"

Johann dropped his head and furiously spat into the dirt. "Ah, *spytte, Kimar! Spytte!*" He abruptly turned on his boot heels and stormed off into the maze of mineral spires surrounding their camp, his face the color of a plump strawberry.

"That was not well spoken, Kimar!" Heidi had hissed. She then trotted off after her husband, leaving Gudrun and the kids with Tiny.

Kimar said nothing more for what seemed an eternity to Tiny. *At least he knows when to stop barking*, the dog thought.

There were periods of time when Tiny closed his eyes, bored with the hushed, but intense, conversations taking place at the same time. Ercen and Kimar spoke in forceful but low tones at the far side of their campsite; their wide noses were often just inches apart. Anders and Freida spoke hurriedly in high-pitched tones nearby as they tried to console Gudrun, who seemed to feel to be the cause of all this unhappiness. Of course, with Tiny's sharp ears, he also heard from a distance that his master still railed about Kimar's poor word choice. He also heard Heidi saying little more than, "Hm, I see," and the like, but whenever she tried to say more, Johann cut her off and launched into another long speech, punctuated by sporadic spitting. Occasionally, there was also the sound of clattering rock, which Tiny assumed was caused by his master.

If you just snarled, barked and snapped at each other a few times, you could then be done with this, make friends again and go back to playing! Tiny marveled that no one took his suggestion to heart. A moment later, he was snoring softly.

"But how do you support that, Kimar?" Anders asked, with more heat in the question than he really intended. He sat facing Kimar, with everyone else sitting in a rough circle. The gargoyles squatted, as was their habit during discussions.

Before anyone had a chance to say anything, Anders added, "Please, forgive me. We've already had enough to get upset over. I'm just trying to understand all of this. Based on the evidence we have at this moment, we have as much reason to suspect Lohxnahr has been undone by Kahrnahrgx and replaced by an altogether evil impersonator! Because Mrs. Macy was rescued and returned to us by Zarentil, it seems we have more reason to question whether it was really Lohxnahr who was speaking to you."

"As I have said already, Anders," Kimar replied, his voice tightly measured, "I have known Lohxnahr for many generations of men and I trust my senses. Beyond this, I do not need to justify my decision."

Anger flashed across Johann's face, and he cleared his throat loudly. Heidi quickly laid her hand on his knee and pressed down hard.

Tiny lazily opened his eyes, curious if everyone was ready to play again.

"Look," Freida interjected, "it seems to me we also have good reason to believe that Lohxnahr is Lohxnahr and that Zarentil is Zarentil." Quickly she raised her right hand, palm out toward Kimar to cut him off. "And we have good reasons to disbelieve both of them are who we so desperately want them to be!"

Anders jumped up. "Agreed! Nice stroke, Freida! All right, then. Can we all agree that both Lohxnahr and Zarentil are suspect, until proven otherwise?"

"While I also agree with you, Honey, how do we go about proving otherwise?" Heidi said, smiling ruefully to Freida.

"Jah! That I wish to know, also," Johann retorted.

"Please, all of you," Ercen spoke softly, "let us consider these things we do know of a certainty. We know that Kimar—and I—have known Lohxnahr, lo, these many ages. We know that Gudrun was spirited away by the minions of Kahrnahrgx and most certainly rescued and returned to us by Zarentil, so she says, and we have no sound reason for doubting her." Here, Ercen bowed slightly to Gudrun.

Ercen continued, "Further, we know that, at any moment, we should be prepared for the arrival of none other than Lohxnahr, as well as Ita-Mudak and Conomorg. At that time, we should learn much and answer many riddles that currently vex us." Here, Ercen bowed slightly to Kimar.

"Finally, would it not be prudent to accept the arrival of our friends as friends, while also being at the ready for come what may? For it is also possible that Ita-Mudak or Conomorg have been overthrown."

Tiny had his answer. *Too bad. They are still not ready to make friends and play.* With that, he went back to sleeping.

Hunger woke Paign. Ravenous hunger. He was lying face down in a darkened room and his stomach growled. *What time is it?*

He sat up, suddenly. Taking in his surroundings, his jaw dropped open. Paign glanced quickly at his bed, lifted his hands as if they were on a hot burner, and jumped off, twisting around to stare at the bed. It was made of fine, clean cloth and blankets woven from a material he'd never seen before. Rather than straw piled on a wooden slat bed like he was used to, this bed appeared to be made of a huge rectangular pillow, stacked upon a second rectangle. Sliding out of bed, he dropped to his knees, laid his hands on the floor and looked under the bed. He gasped to see interlacing bands of metal and wire supporting the rectangles. *What is this place? Where am I?*

Paign glanced quickly down at his hands and stared at the floor he kneeled on. Running both palms back and forth, he marveled at the texture. This little room didn't have a dirt floor, but something shiny and patterned. He'd seen pictures of the interior walls of the Royal Palace, and this reminded him of the pattern.

Rolling off his knees and onto his bottom, he spun around on the slippery floor and surveyed the room. A rough-hewn wooden table stood in the opposite corner. That looks right, at least! he mused. A single, high-backed wooden stool stood beside the table, with a brightly colored woven blanket draped over it. While the blanket looked to be made from spun wool, the brilliant colors were in a pattern he'd never seen before. A large candle rested in the middle of the table, flickering gently, with what looked like a tin platter underneath. Grotesque shapes, made up of spent candle wax, littered the platter. The room wasn't hot, but neither was it cold, so Paign wondered where the heat source was. *Nearby, I guess. Probably just on the other side of the door,* he thought, imagining a cast-iron wood stove or fireplace.

"Well, either I'm dead and ended up in a rich man's home, or this is heaven. At least I'm not with that ghastly Rance-Dahl anymore!" Muttering only to himself, he was still comforted to hear his voice and smiled at his joke.

Paign swung his head back and forth, puzzled by the strange pictures on the walls and peculiar items on shelves that seemed to float in space.

"How'd I get here, I wonder? And where is it I am, exactly?"

"You are where you needed to be!" a raspy voice came from the area of the stool hidden behind the woven blanket.

"Hey! Is that you, Lohxnahr?" Paign cried, a smile bursting across his bruised face.

"No."

Paign saw the woven blanket shift on the stool. Talons, followed by their fingers, wrapped over the stool's high back, and then a pair of bright, copper-colored eyes suddenly peered over the top of it.

"And who would you be, then?"

"Zarentil, I am."

Paign felt better as he lay on his strange bed. At least physically. Zarentil had spent what felt like hours pressing against the numerous wounds on Paign's body. While the pressure was uncomfortable for every single wound, the sensations that came with the healing touch were very strange and wonderful. At first, the area being pressed on tingled, with a slight burning sensation. The tingling grew to an increasingly ticklish feeling. That, in turn, soon changed to a prickly twitching, like when his foot fell asleep.

The most difficult time for Paign was when Zarentil pressed on his ribs. All the prior sensations swept over Paign, but with a breathlessness he found hard to tolerate. Paign quickly discovered, to his regret, that squirming only made the healing process hurt almost as bad as the original injury.

When Zarentil was finally finished, so was Paign. Although the outcome was tremendous—for which Paign was exceedingly grateful—his healing didn't come without a cost. Paign was exhausted, falling asleep even as Zarentil was saying something about leaving on an important trip.

Of course, when Paign woke up, he had no way of telling what time it was and, thus, how long Zarentil had been away. Taking a long and luxuriously deep, pain-free breath, Paign rolled onto his back. Staring unfocused at the ceiling, his thoughts went again to his situation. The more he thought about all that had happened since his argument with Anders, the more deeply his mood sank. It was as if, with a newly healed body, all of his attention could finally focus on the emotional pain he felt.

With surprising and sudden vengeance, the feelings surging through Paign in the moments before he killed Rance-Dahl erupted from deep within him. Like the agony that comes with a freshly shredded scab, Paign convulsed from the throbbing waves of loss and betrayal. His friends, his family, even his best friend—he was abandoned by them all.

Rolling back onto his side, his body faced the wall. But he saw nothing, for his eyes were squeezed tightly shut as he wept, his face contorted, mirroring the writhing of his soul, and his body convulsed as anguish swept through his heart. Paign had grown to hate time when he was in the clutches of Rance-Dahl. It proved to be his enemy, as his wicked captor meted out physical misery again and again. Although this internal suffering was far beyond Paign's comprehension or experience, an awareness was growing in his mind that it somehow sharpened him. In the white-hot rage spewing up within him, Paign sensed the massive scope of its power. At the same moment, he also realized there was something wrong—even perverse—that he so desired this raw, pulsing energy. Quickly, he rejected these misgivings as weak. Even the warning of his heart made him angry.

No! His mind screamed. *Not again! I will not be—ever again—at the mercy of someone else! It is caring for others that has brought me to this place…THIS place! I utterly reject this impulse. I…I…*

Paign's body abruptly curled tightly on the bed and he sobbed uncontrollably.

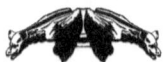

"Yes, my master, Lord Kahrnahrgx." The tall, muscular gargoyle who knelt before Kahrnahrgx shimmered as he unhurriedly nodded. The orange glow that infused the enormous cavern subtly danced on his glistening, obsidian skin. The subservient gargoyle knelt in the center of a large clearing devoid of stalagmites. Instead, multitudes of much smaller obsidians encircled him. They also knelt, facing their liege lord.

Kahrnahrgx stared at the gargoyle, as if considering the viability of his affirmation. He said nothing, remaining motionless, except for his arms. Hanging straight down at his sides, his thick forearms flexed slowly as his talons flared out, stiffened and returned to a relaxed position.

Finally, Kahrnahrgx folded his massive arms across his chest, apparently having come to a decision.

"Very well, Lement-Nor," Kahrnahrgx said, articulating slowly. "There can be no mistake."

"Yes, my master. This is known to me. There is no mistake. He has no reason to doubt me, nor does he harbor any awareness that he has succumbed to my will." Lement-Nor spoke as one with supreme confidence.

"Indeed."

"Yes, Lord. Even now his rage deepens and expands, like blood stains water."

"And the others?"

"This, too, is known to me, my liege. The female's mind was easily thrown down. She fully believes me to be the other."

"She doesn't concern me, Lement-Nor," Kahrnahrgx hissed. "What of her *companions?* Not all of them are as simple and weak as she."

"My master," murmured the obsidian, bowing his head slightly. "It is for this very reason she is such an effective weapon. None of her companions have cause to suspect she is nothing more than a tool now. It is their love for her that provides such fertile soil in which our ruse grows. It is from their love that their undoing comes swiftly."

"Make it so, Lement-Nor."

"As you wish, my liege."

In a twinkling, the obsidian transformed into a gargoyle less than a third in size, pearlescent in color, with bright, copper-colored eyes. A low murmur erupted from those encircling Lement-Nor and Kahrnahrgx. Most knew of a special plot their supreme commander had implemented, but only a handful knew of the hybrids, and none had seen their transformation. So thorough and convincing was the result that those less intelligent in the assembly felt compelled to attack the now fully exchanged obsidian. With a flick of his head, Kahrnahrgx commanded them to stop.

With a nearly imperceptible nod, the Zarentil hybrid parted and was gone.

The expansive cave grew immediately still, while Kahrnahrgx remained motionless. A few seconds later, he pivoted on his heels, his rear-facing talons scraping the stone floor, and waved over one of his most-trusted lieutenants.

"You are tasked, Ahkzita, with dispatching the obsidian hybrid, Lement-Nor, upon the completion of his mission. Not a moment before," Kahrnahrgx commanded, "and not a moment after."

"I understand, Eminence. It will be done."

"If not, the consequences will be dire—not only for you."

"Well, I just can't believe it!" Danielle bellowed, her face flushed red. "How could you? How *could* you?" Her hands formed into fists and thrust down, as if to emphasize her dismay.

Anders blanched at the intensity of her rebuke. Several hours earlier, his nerves had been a disaster, when suddenly, Danielle, her parents, Ita-Mudak and Conomorg, along with Danielle's new dog, Anja, parted into their midst, with none other than Lohxnahr leading them. On the one hand, Anders was thrilled beyond his greatest hope to see Danielle again, for he'd never expected to. Indeed, he'd vehemently argued with his cousin Paign about this very thing. Anders also felt nearly crushing guilt and remorse now that Danielle stood before him, while Paign was suffering unknown but unspeakable torment somehow because of their argument. And now Danielle stared at him defiantly, questioning his allegiances to her companions—and herself.

As Anders shook his head, searching for what to say, Freida rose from where she'd been sitting. Her great mastiff lay next to her with his head across her feet.

"Oh, bother! Tiny's made my foot go numb!"

Gingerly, she hobbled over to her friend, taking her hands into her own. She gently unclenched Danielle's fists and wrapped her hands around them.

"Please, Danielle," Freida said softly. "Please understand that we don't want to believe this. But we feel we *must*. Do you understand?" Freida squeezed Danielle's fingers in her own.

For a moment, Danielle's hazel eyes continued to glare into Freida's grey ones. Then, Danielle's chin dropped, as she looked at Freida's fingers wrapped around hers. Without thinking, Danielle stroked Freida's rough farm hands with her thumbs.

Not looking up, Danielle replied, "Yes, I suppose so." She shook her head as she looked up into the eyes of her friend. "It just seems so wrong to question Lohxnahr." At the mention of the little gargoyle's name, both girls turned toward where Lohxnahr was being held.

Still speechless, Anders also turned. It was an utterly mournful sight to him. Lohxnahr squatted on a stump of stalagmite, about the same height as he was. Conomorg and Ita-Mudak flanked him, each with a large, powerful hand resting on one of Lohxnahr's shoulders. Ercen stood behind

Lohxnahr, with her right hand upon his head. Kimar paced back and forth in front of them all, with his head hung low and his brow furrowed. The other gargoyles wore similar expressions. Except for Lohxnahr, who beamed at Danielle.

"Yes, my child!" he rasped, approvingly. "It is to be supposed!"

Still stroking Freida's hands, Danielle stamped her left foot on the ground. "But, Lohxnahr, how can you be so... so...aren't you upset about being held prisoner? You, of all people? It's, well...I just can't get over it."

"Me, too!" interrupted Peter, who was sitting to one side, along with Amy, Johann and Heidi. "Doesn't it make more sense to *not* doubt Lohxnahr is, well, Lohxnahr? But instead to cast doubt on any of the other gargoyles here?"

"Based on what, sir?" Anders replied, finally finding a topic he felt comfortable discussing. "As you have heard over the past several hours, there's another hybrid gargoyle running loose, presumably just like the one you told us attacked you in the past day or two. Except this one is not impersonating a human but another gargoyle, almost certainly a—"

"High Priest, yes!" Lohxnahr interjected, enthusiastically.

"Uh, yes," Anders agreed, without any enthusiasm. Blinking at Lohxnahr a few times, he continued, "If Kahrnahrgx could hide one of his hybrid minions right in front of us in plain sight, well, there's no telling what he could do. But we all agree; the end result would be very bad."

"Yes, of course, Anders," Amy said, with no little amount of impatience in her voice. "Yes, it would be bad. But it is sheer madness to consider Lohxnahr as the greatest threat here! And, really, what do you hope to accomplish by holding him in such a way? Can't Lohxnahr simply part away from you, by only wishing it so? Are you seriously expecting to keep him here by laying hands on his shoulders? This is ridiculous!" She then slapped her leg. "Ridiculous!"

"Jah, it is so," Johann concurred. "Why is it that the others do not fall under suspicion?" he asked, staring at Ita-Mudak and Conomorg.

Danielle immediately let go of Freida's hands, spun on her heels and replied, "I could ask the same!" She threw a glance at Ercen and Kimar. Just as quickly, she exclaimed, "Oh, no! What have I said? I'm sorry, I didn't mean that!"

"And that, right there, is our dilemma," Anders said firmly, stepping over to Danielle and laying his hand on her shoulder.

Peter's left eyebrow rose at the sight of Anders's hand on his daughter.

"It is difficult—perhaps impossible—to provide compelling evidence to discount anyone, I mean, any of the gargoyles, but especially so with Lohxnahr," Anders continued.

Gudrun, who sat alone across from the others and accompanied only by Anja, coughed violently. Anja looked up at the woman, concerned.

"I am sorry," Gudrun said, just above a whisper, "that all this difficulty should come from me...it is something so terribly regrettable. I am so very sor—" Another fit of coughing overtook her.

Quickly, Heidi jumped up and hastened to her friend, murmuring, "Gudrun, no, no, this isn't anyone's fault." She patted Gudrun gently on the back until the spell passed.

"And yet it is!" Lohxnahr said with so much cheerfulness, it sounded almost like singing. "Fault to assign, this you seek."

Kimar abruptly stopped pacing. "Lohxnahr is right!" he barked. "Consider the extent of your distrust of us! Those who protected you at great peril and rescued you"—Kimar looked first at Danielle and then at Freida—"at even greater peril. What else would serve to convince you of our trustworthiness?"

"Ah, come now," Johann cried. "This must be resolved!"

"Just what I wanted to say!" Freida agreed, disgust coating her words. "We keep wasting more precious time arguing this, while Paign suffers what I'm afraid to think about!"

"Well, two things occur to me," Peter interjected. "First, if one of you is a hybrid spy, what hope really do we have of disarming you, assuming we could figure out which one of you is the bad guy?" He winked at Danielle, hoping to bring some relief to the heaviness of the moment.

"Second, it seems the only reasonable way forward is to use simple logic and the process of elimination to determine whether one of our gargoyle friends is a demon in disguise."

"Agreed!" Anders replied earnestly.

A chorus of "agreed" followed.

"With a certainty!" Lohxnahr proclaimed. "It is to be supposed, as I said some time ago."

Anders grinned at the little gargoyle, first at his comment and then at the incongruous image of the High Priest being literally held by two huge gargoyles, Conomorg and Ita-Mudak, who plainly didn't believe it was necessary.

"So, let us suppose, then!" Anders began, as if making a speech. "Perhaps we should start at the start. Based on what you have shared with us, the gargoyle called Sedig-Tahr became known as a hybrid only when he transformed from your inquisitous—and apparently very human—policeman into a horrifying threat, yes?"

"Correct," replied Peter. Amy and Danielle nodded but remained quiet.

"And a policeman must be like our konstabel," Anders added.

Peter nodded.

"Very well," Anders continued. He looked at the members of the Skulstad family. "So, would we agree, while it might be possible that Conomorg or Ita-Mudak could also be a hybrid, that it is very unlikely? They both lay hidden in the Wheelen's home, as part of the stone floor no less, for a great long while. Would a hybrid really hide that way, given that at any point it could dispatch the whole family?"

Anders scanned the faces of his countrymen to gauge their judgment.

"Good! We're making progress!" he cried, winking at Ita-Mudak and Conomorg. The two gargoyles remained completely passive, as if the verdict meant nothing to them.

Ignoring them, Anders forged ahead. Energized by this turn of events, he started pacing.

"Yes, good! Next up for our consideration would be Ercen, I think."

"Wait a minute!" Danielle interrupted. "Shouldn't Lohxnahr come next? I met him before the others were aware of his arrival."

Before Anders could reply, Amy jumped up, "Not so fast. This is just what still bothers me about his arrival," she snapped, pointing at Lohxnahr. "He sneaked in and took Danielle before making himself…without…it nearly gave me a heart attack to discover Danielle missing, right under the noses of our sentries."

"I suppose that's true," quipped Lohxnahr.

Amy was plainly very unamused and glared at the little gargoyle for a moment before sitting back down. Peter could almost see smoke coming from his wife's ears.

"If you'd permit it, Mrs. Wheelen, I'd like to come back to Lohxnahr last, since he is the primary focus of our concern," Anders replied.

"I thought Zarentil is," Gudrun whispered. Anja lifted her head at the sound of Gudrun's voice, licked her hand and laid her head back down. Tiny lifted his head, in turn, to watch Anja.

"Yes, ma'am," Anders quietly acknowledged. "I have not forgotten him. I believe we should discuss him after we've settled the matter of Lohxnahr, since they seem intertwined with each other."

"Continue, lad," Johann muttered. "My head is hurting and I, for one, would like to be done with this."

"Right. Of course, sir." Anders began pacing again, his hands folded behind his back. "So, if we use the same course of reasoning for Ercen that we used to dismiss Conomorg and Ita-Mudak, then wouldn't it be fair to say that by now Ercen would be found out, as the little saying goes, by one of you other gargoyles?"

"Ah! A master stroke, Anders!" Johann exclaimed. "Well done! 'Tis so! Makes perfect sense. We're done then, eh? Let's eat!"

"Sorry, my friend," Peter said, puzzlement crossing his face. "How'd you get from the one to the other?"

"Well, if it is true that Ercen would be discovered as a hybrid by now, so close to the other gargoyles, as yours was *felt* in your homestead by Ita-Mudak and Conomorg, then wouldn't all other combinations of possible high-breeds also be made safe?" Johann replied.

"I suppose!" Lohxnahr beamed. "With one exception."

"And what might that be?" Danielle asked hopefully.

"Not what. Who. Gargoyles who have not been in the presence of others," Lohxnahr hummed.

"What do you mean, Lohxnahr?" Freida asked.

"Not all gargoyles who have been named here today have yet been in the presence of the others," he replied gleefully.

"Uh," Peter began.

"You mean Zarentil, don't you?" Amy asked.

"I suppose," Lohxnahr beamed.

Amy shook her head. *There are times when his happy nature is just so out of place!*

Anders shifted his feet on the ground, which drew everyone's attention. "Okay, Lohxnahr," he said, "let's explore that option now. You're saying that, while we know Zarentil, or something posing as him, has been apparently helpful to Mrs. Macy, he is still suspect because he hasn't made himself known to us, right? He *behaved* like Zarentil would, but until you all can confirm he's not a hybrid, he's a suspect."

"Hmm," Lohxnahr hummed.

"Come on! Really?" Danielle snapped. "How about the fact that Lohxnahr and I saw the hybrid posing as Zarentil in my dream? That's obviously more important than whether he's 'made himself known' to us, isn't it? If not, *it should be.*"

Again, Anders was stung by Danielle's retort.

"Honey," Peter broke in, much to Danielle's annoyance. "As you know, your mother and I weren't—aren't—too happy about how Lohxnahr snuck you away from us in the middle of the night, only to find out that he took you on a very risky clandestine mission—"

"A *what?*" Johann asked. "What on earth is *clan-dust-nine?*"

Grinning, Peter slapped his friend on the shoulder. "Forgive me, my friend. It's a fancy, unnecessary word. I mean, secret mission."

Johann nodded and grinned back at his friend. "Ah. 'Tis so."

"Yes, dad, I know that," Danielle cut in. "What I mean is, unless you plan on questioning my word, too, then it *should* be settled, you know, about how to feel about Lohxnahr. Because I have no doubt about him."

"Hmm," Lohxnahr hummed yet again.

Anders dared to smile at Danielle, despite his misgivings. "Yes, Danielle, I believe you. We believe you. It's just that we needed to walk through this maze to sort out where our suspicions should be aimed, given there is a hybrid still loose."

"Indeed!" Peter exclaimed. "To pick up where I got...so, here's the thing. We got our undies in a twist when Lohxnahr removed you for that mission of his—which, apparently, had both a physical and metaphysical component to it."

Peter saw the puzzled look coming from Johann. He realized there were at least two things he'd said that likely confused his friend.

"It is supposed to," murmured the little gargoyle.

Peter heard Amy's sigh of frustration, but didn't know if it was from Lohxnahr's cryptic comment or from something he'd said. He quickly kept going. "Yeah, okay, then. My point, Dani, is that while we didn't like his taking you, it isn't enough of a compelling reason to doubt his authenticity...that he really is Lohxnahr. Good? Like you said, if we doubt him, then there is a corollary doubt that falls on you. It's just logical."

"What of me, then?" Kimar asked.

"And me?" Ercen added.

"Well, the same logic applies to both of you," Anders replied. "Again, if we assume the recognition factor, if either of you were a hybrid, then Conomorg or Ita-Mudak, or most likely both of them, would recognize you for being false, just as they did with Sedig-Tahr."

"And that is exactly why you should release Lohxnahr!" Danielle cried, as her hands balled into fists.

"Makes sense to me," Anders agreed. "How do the rest of you feel about it?"

"Jah," Heidi and Johann said together.

"Yes," Amy and Peter nodded, smiling.

Turning to face Paign's mother, Anders was shocked to see tears streaming down her face. "Mrs. Macy?" Heidi still had her arm around Gudrun's shoulder.

"Based on your deductions, then, you have no reason to not suspect me," she muttered.

"Sorry?" Anders said.

"I follow her meaning," Heidi offered quietly, "because only she's seen Zarentil. So, then"—her hand rose to her mouth, almost as if to hinder the words about to come out—"not only is Zarentil still suspect, so is she."

"Whoa!" Peter exclaimed. "Because if the Zarentil-hybrid brought her back from the clutches of Kahrnahrgx—which in itself doesn't make any sense to me—the hybrid could have just as easily stayed here...as Paign's mother!"

"One might suppose so," Lohxnahr chirped, "if you believe that a hybrid could so successfully imitate human emotions."

"Please, Lohxnahr, what do you mean?" Danielle whispered, nearly too afraid to hear his answer. "Would you explain?"

"Certainly, my dear! This I have been doing from the beginning. Only now does it appear you are ready to hear it." Having been released moments earlier by the other gargoyles, Lohxnahr flew almost silently into the middle of the group. He stopped before Danielle, who still stood next to Freida, with Anders just a few paces away.

"Your logic has already determined that Paign's dear mother could not be a hybrid, for the same reasons that I could not be, nor Ercen or Kimar, Ita-Mudak or Conomorg. We would know of the other. If we are not all of us hybrids of Kahrnahrgx's abominable making, then none of us are. This be true as well for the humans here."

Danielle became very flustered, waving her hands as if trying to clear away smoke. "But Lohxnahr, when Sedig-Tahr was in human form, neither Conomorg nor Ita-Mudak could identify him as anything other than human."

Ita-Mudak's deep voice rumbled from behind her. "Child, perhaps you misunderstood my meaning when I told you that we only identified him as a hybrid when he stepped into your house. You were not aware of our presence, even as we were disguised as part of your stone floor."

"A very large part of it," Conomorg quipped.

"Yes, my comrade," Ita-Mudak acknowledged. "We certainly could feel that the hybrid was nearby. Yet we waited until we could engage him directly in battle. For once we rose from the floor, both you—"

"And him!" Conomorg interrupted.

"Would know of *our* presence," Ita-Mudak finished.

"Clever! Well done, lads!" Peter cried, a wide smile across his face. "Well done, indeed!"

"So, we're finished, then! Right?" Anders looked around, smiling hopefully.

"I suppose not," Lohxnahr buzzed.

"Oh, dear. And why not?" Heidi asked, tension in her voice. Gudrun hadn't looked up during this latest round of debate.

"It was with Danielle's clarity that the hybrid posing as Zarentil was exposed. We have no reason to doubt that it is the same creature that brought the mother of Paign away from her tormentors. That he was able to locate her is not in question, since as the special one of Kahrnahrgx, he would know all that his master wishes him to."

"Okay," Peter responded, leaning forward.

"Jah?" Johann added.

"It is reasonable to suppose that something went wrong with the plans of Kahrnahrgx," Lohxnahr replied, fluttering gently up and down.

"How's that?" Amy asked.

"The hybrid was needed to locate the mother of Paign because only she could locate Paign. Clear this makes the hiddenness of Paign to Kahrnahrgx. Why she is returned, this remains hidden to us."

Her voice quavering, Freida asked, "What do you think this means for Paign?"

"Something has happened that even Kahrnahrgx didn't suppose," Lohxnahr replied, turning to face Freida. His smile was wide and reassuring to her.

"So, you're saying that the hybrid used Mrs. Macy to find Paign—" Anders began.

"Like you used our Dani to locate the hybrid in the first place," Amy interrupted.

"One could suppose so."

Gudrun's shoulders started to heave up and down under Heidi's comforting arm.

Nearly choking on her words, Freida dropped to her knees and cried out from the anguish in her heart, "But Lohxnahr, how…how…do we…find Paign?"

Heidi's heart was already breaking for her friend, but now she felt for her daughter. *How could I have not seen this before now? Oh, my dearest, my Freida! She's in love with him.* Before she could reach out to her daughter, Heidi felt Gudrun's back stiffen and looked to see her head rise.

"Do you mean this, Lohxnahr?" Gudrun asked, her entire face glistening from tears. "My Paign was damaged—so deeply wounded—when the Zarentil creature found him through me. He was so alone…so terribly broken…"

With a merriment that uplifted even Amy, Lohxnahr nearly glowed when he replied, "Find Paign we will, mother of Paign. As the hybrid was able to locate Paign through the eye of your heart, so shall we, *together.*"

Something about the tone in Lohxnahr's voice when he said "together" gave Danielle gooseflesh down her back. Shuddering, she whispered, "What else is there, Lohxnahr? What is it you aren't saying?"

"Hmm, yes." The gargoyle's small wings undulated faster than before, although his position didn't change. Danielle's hair wafted up from the wings' airflow, distracting Anders.

"It is reasonable to suppose that Paign has been touched by the hybrid in harmful ways…with results terrible and deep. Remember, we must, that the hybrid not only poses as Zarentil, our Mystic. In truth, the false creature is Zarentil, having absorbed much of who Zarentil was. What he knew. That essential good has now turned to wicked ends towards Paign."

Freida gasped. Heidi reached out and drew her into the same firm embrace that still encircled Gudrun. Amy hastened over and wrapped her arms around all three of the women. Danielle stood leaden, struck numb. Anders, a dark and grim look on his face, stepped next to her.

No one said anything for several minutes. The only sounds were those of the women crying and the humming of Lohxnahr's wings.

The humans all jumped at the sound of Kimar's strong, deep voice. "Then it is time for us to go, Lohxnahr. We have tarried long enough."

Seeing the forbidding faces of the four gargoyles, especially those of Ita-Mudak and Conomorg, Peter wondered how the hybrid would fare when they all showed up with Lohxnahr to rescue Paign. He'd seen what each one was capable of the year before, during the storming of the Temple of Kahrnahrgx.

"It is not to be other than the mother of Paign, she with me. And Danielle."

A chorus of protest exploded. The gargoyles argued that they should accompany Lohxnahr as guards to protect not only the human women, but also their High Priest. Of course, the most vocal of the humans were the parents of Danielle, although Freida's parents came in a very loud and supportive second.

Lohxnahr, with his pale lavender eyes gleaming at Danielle, finally angled higher into the air. When he'd reached a point slightly higher than the tallest of the gargoyles, he held out his hands so that the palms faced the group. "Peace now and still, be. It must be thus."

Amy would not be stilled. "Why?" she demanded. "Why does Danielle need to go with you?"

Lohxnahr dropped down suddenly to Amy's height, stopping right in front of her. It was Amy's turn to have her hair fanned by his fluttering wings. Amy was struck again by how deep his eyes were, yet childlike and innocent. The lavender was the loveliest she had ever seen. She felt her roaring fear quickly dissipate—for that's what she was truly feeling, a great fear, not anger. Her heart opened to what Lohxnahr had to share with her.

"It must be so because Danielle knows me, as well as the deceits of the imposter. She will not become lost, as I fear Paign has. See, mother of Danielle, that when Danielle joins me in the not here—as you describe her leaving this *physical* realm with me—she is yet not there. I would not have risked Danielle's presence in the actual chamber of Zarentil. It was in the in-between place we went. There, great insights may be found by the wise. The hybrid took the mother of Paign to the in-between and, while there, was able to find that which Kahrnahrgx could not: Paign. Yet, it was not the hybrid who knew to seek him in the in-between, but Zarentil. However clever has the hybrid been bred, only Zarentil—a Mystic— would know of the power of the in-between."

As Amy stared into the calm, limpid eyes, she marveled to see them grow even softer, as if mercy itself came from them.

"As Danielle has plunged deep into the mysteries known to the Ancient Mystics to her benefit, so has Paign been plunged into the *other* depths, where brokenness, loneliness and despair are found. This is the place of perversions and great suffering."

Amy's heart skipped a beat; she closed her eyes, overcome with pity for the boy. *How is it that Danielle can help?* In the very asking of the question, she realized that Lohxnahr had been speaking directly into her mind. *This must be like what Danielle has described to me.*

Yes, mother of Danielle. This is the Oneness. It is possible that even the mother of Paign will not be able to reach her son through the place he's been taken by the Zarentil-not-Zarentil. It is for this need that Danielle is required.

I understand, Amy replied.

Yet, that is not all.

Amy waited, fear clawing again at her heart. The lavender eyes were beautiful and soothing.

It is quite possible that the mother of Paign may seek to plunge into the darkest place in her last great effort to ransom her son.

Amy swallowed hard, her heart pounding wildly. *Is there no other but Danielle who can do this? Please, Lohxnahr, please...*

Only she. For in her is the deepest experience of compassion. In her, the spirit of the Widow Vellhelmina was released, even in the very depths of Kahrnahrgx's Temple. Only she. If not her, we risk losing both the mother and the son.

Amy struggled to take in a deep breath. It came haltingly. She was aware of reaching out blindly for Peter's hand. Finding it, she was comforted.

I am here, Ames. I...I heard everything. He squeezed her hand again, reassuringly. *She has to go.*

Yes, I know it. I know. Lohxnahr, please keep her safe.

Hearing a familiar clap, Amy opened her eyes, only to find Peter staring back at her. Knowing in their hearts even before they looked, a quick scan of their camp confirmed it: Danielle, Gudrun and Lohxnahr were gone.

CHAPTER EIGHTEEN
BESET

Freida was inconsolable. And Anders wasn't in much of a mood to try comforting her, even though he felt he should. His initial shock at seeing Danielle was, literally, breathtaking. Now that she'd gone with Lohxnahr and Mrs. Macy, he felt as if he'd been left terribly sunburned on the inside. Burnt and raw. He figured that was pretty much how Freida felt, too, but didn't have it in him to do anything about it.

As bad as they felt, Anja was in a much worse state. In the minutes following the rescue parting, Danielle's parents had explained to everyone their experience with Lohxnahr, since no one else "heard" their conversation with the gargoyle. Not that Danielle's parents seemed content with what happened, but at least they'd known what was coming: Danielle's parting. Of course, Anja knew nothing of the sort.

For several minutes, Tiny had chased around after Anja, hoping to bring her some comfort. Only with strong intervention by Mr. Skulstad did Tiny finally seem to understand that chasing was only making Anja even more distressed. With that problem resolved, at least for the moment, Peter was eventually able to coax their family dog into sitting down. He was not successful, however, in keeping her still. Anders thought it a pitiful sight—Anja's quaking body and darting sienna eyes.

Anders shifted his gaze to watch Mrs. Skulstad stroking Freida's hair, as her father stood stolidly next to his womenfolk like a palace guard. *But why should I even bother with trying to comfort Freida? She's well taken care of at the moment.* Anders felt an acute sense of isolation. He was bereft of his cousin's companionship. His good friend, Freida, was very upset and paying him no heed. Her parents focused on her alone, while Danielle's parents were huddled in hushed conversation with Ercen and Kimar, with Anja now lying at Mr. Wheelen's feet.

"So, everyone is provided for, except me," Anders muttered into his lap, his head bent low.

"Only if you don't count us," Conomorg said quietly.

Anders recoiled at the gargoyle's voice.

"We walked over here a few minutes ago," Ita-Mudak added.

"You were, to our eyes, very distracted," Conomorg continued, "as you still appear to be, even now."

"It is not well to be friendless at times such as these," Ita-Mudak said flatly. "The others have family with them. We would not wish you to feel on your own."

"Uh, thank you," Anders mumbled. "Tusen takk. I would have been…I mean, I'm fine."

"Perhaps," Ita-Mudak stated.

"Anders," Conomorg began, "it not for naught that we have spent much time with you and your countrymen. In solitude and community, in the midst of great joy as well as much grief, through mountain chills and valley's heat, welcome serenity and unwished-for battle, all of these we have shared with you and your kind, one among the other."

Ita-Mudak nodded solemnly.

Anders blinked, uncertain what to make of this unexpected visit.

"We mean you no discourtesy, Anders, by accompanying you now," Conomorg continued. "We, too, understand the warmth and encouragement of a friend near to hand in times of great challenge. Thus, we know the vacancy felt within at times of forced separation."

"Uh," Anders said softly, "I...uh—"

"Let us speak of Paign," Ita-Mudak said, his voice low and purposeful. "Chronicle for us what has come to pass between you and he."

Quietly at first, Anders recounted for his massive, slate-hued companions what transpired between Paign and himself only a few days earlier, although it felt more like a lifetime ago to Anders. Even though these gargoyles were not of the priestly order, Anders knew he needed to be as candid and forthcoming with them as he could. Even if they didn't share Lohxnahr's uncanny ability to see into the "in-between," as Danielle's parents had just reported, he recognized these gargoyles would know if he fudged his report in any way. So, he held nothing back, disclosing his own feelings throughout his argument with Paign, as well as what he sensed of Paign's feelings. It was embarrassing at times, very humbling and utterly awkward. Now and then, he paused, trying to tease the right word out of his muddied mind. And yet, Anders realized the more he talked about it, the less guilt he felt, given that neither Conomorg nor Ita-Mudak showed any ill will toward him.

But then they've never been all that obvious about what they're feeling, have they? Ah, bother. Maybe I am in for it after all.

"No, you have done well in this, lad," Conomorg said, as if reading his mind. "Is it not as we suspected?" he added, glancing to his tall colleague.

"In truth," replied Ita-Mudak, bowing slightly at the waist.

"What do you mean?" Anders cried, twisting suddenly so he could try to see what the faces of the gargoyles might reveal.

"Yeah, what do you mean?" Freida asked abruptly.

Whipping around at the sound of her voice, Anders, already startled, was horrified to see not only Freida but both sets of parents standing right behind him. All wore a look of apprehension.

"Oh, great. Just great!" Anders exclaimed, shaking his head in dismay. "And I suppose you heard everything?" Frantically, his head snapped back and forth, searching everyone's face. *What are they thinking? How much did they hear?* But did he really want to know? He felt wholly wretched. Exposed. Something so much worse than embarrassment exploded inside of Anders. He just wanted to bolt, to run away as far and as fast as he could. He looked down at his hands, which he clenched and unclenched nervously, his face deepening to the red of an overripe apple.

Before his body could follow through with what his mind had decided, Anders felt a squeeze on his left shoulder. Unwillingly, he turned his head to look at the hand that now slowly patted his shoulder reassuringly. A man's hand, with an elaborate ring on the third finger on the right hand. Slowly, Anders's gaze followed the hand to the arm and then up to the man's face.

"It's all right, Anders," Peter said softly, the corners of his mouth curled up into a small smile. He shrugged sheepishly. "We didn't know. At least, I didn't," he added, tossing a momentary look at Amy.

Amy's maternal instincts, already stretched taut by everything having to do with Danielle, couldn't help but notice Anders's hands, still clenching and unclenching like a kneading cat. She leaned over impulsively and kissed Anders on the top of his head.

"Yes, Honey," she said, her lips still gently pressed on his thick, charcoal hair, answering her husband's implied question. "I guess I've actually known a long time." Then, she kissed Anders's head a second time, embracing his shoulders in the process.

A maelstrom of emotion swept up from within Anders, overwhelming him. Not knowing what else to do, he curled over and wept, overcome. For several minutes, he was powerless to stop the hot tears. Even more embarrassed than before, he ached inside still. Yet, he felt less pressure than before, like a great log had been lifted from his knotted chest. Keeping his head down, he pulled his sleeves over his hands and vigorously wiped his face, hoping he wouldn't look like he'd been crying. Staring at the ground, he saw feet approach and stop in front of his own. Small feet. Girl's feet. Freida's feet. He took a deep breath, trying to center himself. Freida's knees dropped to the ground directly between his boots. He felt her arms wrap around his neck, just after Mrs. Wheelen's arms released him.

"Anders," she whispered into his ear, "it *is* all right...and it *will* be all right."

He lifted his head and faced her nearly nose to nose. He had a splitting headache from the stress he'd been feeling, as well as the intensity of his crying. He gave her a wan smile.

"I guess I always knew, too," she continued, tears in her eyes.

"Hey, I know this place," Danielle said in tight, hushed tones. "It's the Hudsons' cabin at Strahl Lake. Why are we here, Lohxnahr?" she asked, anxiety darkening her face. Her words turned to vapor in the chill air of a new spring morning. Twigs crackled under her knees as she shifted around for a better view through the bush.

Gudrun's eyes darted between the girl and the gargoyle.

"It is where Paign is," Lohxnahr replied.

"Dear child," Gudrun gasped, seizing Danielle's hands, "doesn't that mean we are in a different time? *Your* time?" She shuddered.

Danielle looked into Gudrun's eyes, who was plainly in great distress and suffering, and realized—astonished—that they reminded her of the Widow Vellhelmina's. *Well, not exactly. It's more...more...*

The increased squeezing on her hands brought Danielle's attention back to the present moment.

"Uh, yes ma'am. I believe it must mean that." Danielle looked beseechingly to Lohxnahr. "Right?"

"Indeed!" Lohxnahr replied. A plump, black bumblebee flying by hummed along perfectly with the natural buzzing of the gargoyle's voice.

"But why?" Danielle sighed. "Why now? You know, now, in my time? And why here of all places?" She freed up one of her hands and patted Mrs. Macy's hands as gently and comfortingly as she could.

"It is where Paign is," Lohxnahr repeated, looking off towards the cabin.

Gudrun was still having difficulty facing Lohxnahr. Danielle was convinced that the poor woman might never trust her dear gargoyle friend and protector. The girl patted the woman's cool, rough hands again. While Danielle was accustomed to Lohxnahr's cryptic style of communicating, Gudrun was not. It showed in the tension in the woman's shoulders.

"Child," she began falteringly, "are these people friends of yours? These Hudsons?" Clutching Danielle's hands so tightly that the girl winced, Gudrun gave a choking cry, "Are they safe? Why do they have Paign?"

"I...I..." Danielle stuttered.

"Because this is a terminus of the hybrid Zarentil-not-Zarentil," Lohxnahr murmured.

"A terminus?" Danielle interrupted.

"Ah, yes," Lohxnahr quipped. "Think of it as a destination point, like the end of a train track. An end point. Quite specific and determined."

"How peculiar this would be that kind of place...for him," Danielle replied, keeping her voice low.

Lohxnahr smiled and continued. "It was difficult to locate, but we have done so, thank the Gaudium. It is known to me that there are several stations like this of which the hybrid makes use. It is a fearful thing, in truth. For"—he paused, looking most intently at Danielle—"it requires the welcoming of the human host, willingly or not."

Danielle's forehead tightened as she tipped her head. "What does that mean, Lohxnahr? How can someone welcome a guest, or whatever, *unwillingly?*"

"Forgive me!" Lohxnahr chirped. "My meaning is that humans may be persuaded into accepting something otherwise quite unacceptable."

"You mean *forced?*" Danielle replied. "The Hudsons have been forced to keep Paign?"

Gudrun's head swung back and forth to follow the flow between Danielle and Lohxnahr. Danielle felt the woman's hands grow cold and tremble spasmodically. The sun was climbing high enough to break through the new leaves blooming overhead in the aspen grove that kept them hidden from the cabin.

"What do your senses tell you, child?" Lohxnahr asked.

"Well, the Hudsons are really nice people, Lohxnahr," her voice animated and intense. "There's no way they'd just *welcome* some creep—or worse," Danielle swallowed hard, as the vision of what may have happened to the Hudsons settled in on her. She shuddered like an aspen in a stiff wind. "I, well, I just *know* they wouldn't willingly be a part of anything bad."

The frost encasing the elderberry and buttonbushes surrounding them fought a losing battle against the sun's advancing warmth.

"Excellent!" Lohxnahr replied. "And what else?"

"Do you mean about my senses?"

"Of course!"

"Hm, well, I don't sense anything else."

"Truly?"

"Lohxnahr, I'm becoming confused by you," Danielle huffed. "What is it you want from me?"

"Trust!"

This time, Danielle's eyebrows furrowed so deeply that her bangs moved. She stared at the diminutive gargoyle's eyes until her head hurt. He smiled back blissfully. While a part of Danielle wanted to lash out at her marble friend because of her anxiety about Paign, another part struggled to understand him. He was, after all, the most senior gargoyle Mystic—if, in fact, Zarentil was dead. And she, of course, was the person who had declared Zarentil overwhelmed by the hybrid. In many respects, Lohxnahr was also *her* mystic. He was certainly her mentor and guide. She'd been through enough with him to know that, while he seemed small physically in comparison to the other gargoyles—especially the towering Ita-Mudak and Conomorg—he was every bit as powerful. *Maybe more so?* she wondered. *What if, somehow, things worked in reverse in the world of gargoyles—the smaller they are, the more powerful they become?*

The left side of her mouth turned down as she considered him, as if for the first time. "Trust?"

"Indeed! How wonderful it is to trust!"

Gudrun's body curled closer upon itself, as if she was retreating into her skin. She muttered something unintelligible to Danielle.

"Sure. Trust is good, Lohxnahr," Danielle said somewhat sharply, "important, even. But shouldn't we be going in? Mrs. Macy really needs to see Paign." Danielle wasn't sure the woman even heard what she'd said. She felt bad for her friend's mother, for she seemed to be mentally somewhere far distant. Giving her cool hands a squeeze, she whispered into her ear, "It's time, Mrs. Macy."

For a moment, there was no reaction. Then, Gudrun quivered and moaned, "Oh, dear Paign. My boy." She stared into Danielle's face, her own face deeply lined with sadness. "My boy," she exhaled loudly. "What shall we find, dear? I am fearful for him."

Danielle took a deep breath and held it, trying to calm her mind. Quietly, she replied, "Oh, I'm sure everything will be fine, Mrs. Macy. Would you rather stay here while Lohxnahr and I go to the cabin?"

"Certainly not."

Standing in front of the cabin door, melting snow dripping onto her ear, Danielle felt as if a jackhammer were pounding in her chest. Blood surged through her so fast she could hear it rushing past her eardrums. *Do I knock? Or do we just go in? Will Mrs. Macy hold up? Will I?* She struggled to maintain her composure and rubbed her hands up and down on her pants. She hoped the others would think she was warming them, not drying the sweat off—and trying to get them to stop quivering.

Glancing over her right shoulder, she was surprised to see Mrs. Macy staring at the door's wrought iron door handle, her lips moving soundlessly. Lohxnahr stood as tall as he could, his long toes providing a secure base with his talons splayed out, so that he could rest a comforting palm on Gudrun's back. Danielle wondered if he did so only for moral support, or if he somehow transferred calm or strength to her, as well.

"Danielle," Lohxnahr rasped. "Paign may not be as you expect him."

Turning back, it was Danielle's turn to stare at the wrought iron handle. She inhaled slowly, realizing it was a simple-enough decision to make. Knock? Or not?

Lohxnahr noticed Danielle's shoulders rise slightly. Gudrun swallowed loudly.

Danielle turned the handle down, hoping to open the door like a robber might. She'd decided on stealth.

Just as the handle reached the point that she felt the door come free, it squeaked like fingernails on a chalkboard. Before she could even think about gasping, the door surged away from her, wrenching her hand still clinging tightly to the handle.

Danielle cried out, not for the pain stabbing in her wounded wrist, but for Paign standing before her. For only the span of a heartbeat, she *saw* him—taller and bulkier, more man than the boy she knew. His hair, now longer, framed a face scarred and hard. Behind his imposing presence, she could see the cabin's kitchen as she remembered it: the cedar logs with their warm satin finish, the cabinets in a welcoming light-oak color, the stout-built island and countertop in glistening black marble.

The coldness in his eyes stopped her arms midreach—instinctively stretched out to hug. She hadn't noticed them until they were pushed out of the way by Gudrun.

Paign's eyes remained focused on Danielle, his brow furrowed, even as his mother enveloped him in her embrace, wailing loudly in words Danielle didn't understand.

Even as Danielle saw that Paign was about to speak, out of the corner of her eye, she observed the sunlight falling through the kitchen's large window begin glinting randomly off the counter top.

Gudrun's sudden collapse was arrested by Paign, while he held her close. He gently lowered her to the hardwood floor.

Danielle's mind worked at a feverish pace, trying to sort out how to feel about—and what to say to—Paign, while also taking in her surroundings. She wanted to look at Paign; she wanted to speak to Paign. But the sunlight continued to fracture off the counter, distracting her. Then, all at once, the black marble became elastic and poured onto the floor behind the island.

Just as a scream erupted from her throat, she saw light glinting off of Lohxnahr's talons as he swiftly reached around her waist and pulled her back from the entryway.

"*No!* Not again!" Danielle screamed, frightened and furious. Slowly, a short-horned, obsidian head rose from behind the kitchen island, until it stood as high as the cabinet tops.

There is a second hybrid, after all! Feared clawed at her mind as the beast grinned at her.

"Ah, here you are!" Lement-Nor gloated. "And how thoughtful of you to bring friends!"

Only at the sound of the gargoyle behind him did Paign turn, his hands still firmly placed on his mother's shoulders.

"What the—" he cried. "Who are you? You're not Zarentil!"

"How quick of you, boy," the hybrid sneered. Tilting its head to one side to peer around Danielle, it added enthusiastically, "How nice of you to join us, Lohxnahr! Another plan happily coming together."

Danielle violently exhaled—all the wind squeezed out of her—as Lohxnahr hurled her back towards the thicket they'd come from just moments earlier. She landed on her side in a thick pile of leaves. Twisting her head to stay focused on him, she was stunned to see Lohxnahr soundlessly blown back from the cabin's porch. But even as he sailed backwards, his wings wrapped around him from the force of the blow, Danielle saw the framework around the cabin door explode out from where she'd just been standing, splintered wood reflecting sunlight almost like snow. A moment later, the door swung out on its still-attached lower hinge, twisted and fell hard. Lohxnahr smashed into a large, thick aspen, completely sheering off the upper third of the tree. Slack jawed, Danielle gasped as the treetop crashed into the ground below.

Rolling onto her knees, Danielle could only gape. If Lohxnahr was defeated by the hybrid, what would become of the three humans?

Surrounded by a cloud of the shattered tree's detritus, Danielle clearly saw Lohxnahr's speed slow as his body's trajectory began arcing downward. It was then she saw his wings shimmering back and forth.

Without warning, his voice exploded in her mind. *Run, Danielle! Run! To the thicket, child!*

Just as she jumped to her feet, Paign and his mother tumbled out through the destroyed entry, tripped and fell onto the damp meadow. The hybrid stepped out, chuckling at the destruction he had wrought.

Keeping her head low, Danielle called on everything she had and ran as if she was escaping a burning building. She'd always been an able runner but had improved greatly the previous year during her school's track season. Track had helped to get her life feeling "ordinary" again after her first adventures with gargoyles. And it had helped her run faster. She needed that now.

Even before she saw it, she felt the sudden pressure as a wall of air pushed past her right shoulder. A moment later, a tightly packed trio of aspens exploded as if they'd been hit by a rocket. Danielle instinctively angled hard to her left. *The flying fists! What hope do I have of avoiding those?*

Anticipating that her adversary would fire another one of the most powerful gargoyle weapons she'd encountered, she veered back to the right. The year before, Danielle had seen the flying fist used on both sides of a gargoyle battle to terrible effect. In the hands of the most powerful, it could rupture even the hardened minerals of stalagmites and stalactites. No sooner had she leaned her body into a right angle, she spun around and fell hard. The hybrid's second flying fist had come so close to her that its violent wind had twisted her around in its dust devil. Now only fifteen feet from the thicket, she rolled back up on her knees, not expecting that she'd make it in time. *And even if I do, what difference will it make against his weapon…against him?* she agonized.

Stealing a look back at her enemy, she felt all hope fade. "He's smiling! He's enjoying this! He's—oh, oh!" The hybrid abruptly pulled his right elbow back, his palm facing out at her, his talons aimed at the pretty blue sky overhead.

Launching off the uneven ground like she was sprinting from the blocks during a track meet, Danielle ran zigzagging towards the gently blowing aspen thicket. Her mind raced as she counted to three; she hoped to leap hard to the left just before the flying fist hit her in the back.

Instead, a roar of heat and flame blew her high off her feet. Tumbling in dismay, she fell headlong into a dense cluster of elderberries. As she fought through the tightly woven branches, Danielle stole a glance at three fireballs exploding between her and where the hybrid stood. Following the smoke trail back to its source high above her, she shouted, "Lohxnahr! Yeah, Lohxnahr!" The tiny gargoyle glittered in the sunlight as he hovered nearly at the treetops, firing again and again between her and the hybrid.

"Why don't you shoot the beast, Lohxnahr?" she bellowed.

The others, child!

Horrified, Danielle realized her friends still lay near the hybrid. "Oh, no! No, no, no!" she cried, flailing the elderberry branches that acted like a cage. In a moment, she was covered in the black juice of its berries. Twisting high into the air, she thrust her legs hard to one side, catapulting feet first over the top of the bush. Her boots squished into the soft, shadowed ground. Immediately, she turned and ran behind the nearest tree and stole a glance around it.

The hybrid's left hand was already pulled back, ready to fire another wicked flying fist. But when she looked at the hybrid's right hand, Danielle gasped and staggered out from behind the tree and fell to her knees. Like a collar of knife blades, the long talons of the hybrid's right hand encircled the necks of Paign and Gudrun, even as they clutched each other tightly at the waists.

In the very back of the Cavern of Zarentil—lit softly by the colors of its multitude of stalactites and stalagmites—a small patch of ancient dust gently swirled upward from the ground. With only the myriad colors of the chapel's variegated stones, awash in travertine oranges, onyx silver-whites, pale blue soapstones, brilliant jade greens, quartzite purples and granite pinks, no living thing witnessed the first pangs of rebirth.

Unthinking, Danielle threw her hands in the air, hoping beyond hope that the hybrid would recognize her meaning: surrender. Immediate and total surrender. Heedless even of Lohxnahr flying somewhere above her, she sprinted awkwardly towards the cabin. Only blind terror filled her mind. Every cell in her being recoiled at the sight of her friends encompassed by the talons of their opponent. She stumbled headlong over an unyielding clump of field grass, landing splayed out. She rolled over onto her knees, still crouched over, her forehead nearly touching the grass, unable even to gasp. Rocking back on her heels, she stared helplessly at her friends, certain their fate was sealed. Her body spasmed, curling her back down into a kneeling fetal position, struggling to force air back into her throbbing chest.

What is this? Danielle wondered, nearly faint. She felt the ground thumping under her knees. Desperate for more air, she looked up and immediately fretted if her mind was playing tricks on her. Mom? Dad? Were her parents really running towards her?

Huh? Freida and Anders? What are they doing here?

She could feel consciousness slipping quietly away, but she kept moving her head from side to side, astonished at what her eyes were communicating to her faltering mind.

Even Freida's parents...

Whoa! Kimar, Ercen and—what are their names again?—Cono...Mudak.

As her mind shredded into black and her head tipped forward, she had the final odd sensation of being lifted by the shoulders and her face being licked from both sides.

Anja! Did I see Tiny with you?

CHAPTER NINETEEN
THUNDER HERALDS

Her eyes still closed, Danielle smiled. It felt so pleasant to have her hair stroked like this. The cool air flowed gently across her face, carrying the pleasant aroma of elderberries and the honey scent of buttonbush—*Wait a minute!*

Danielle sat up abruptly, nearly smacking her mother's face with her own.

"Hi, Dani!" she heard her father say enthusiastically, his voice tinged with relief.

"What are you—I mean, when did you—"

Her mother placed a finger gently across Danielle's lips, indicating clearly that she was being shushed. But the huge smile on her mother's face told her everything else she really needed to know.

"Honey," Amy said gently, "we arrived just moments before you passed out."

Anja's wet nose smooshed into Danielle's left hand, insistent that her mistress respond. Danielle smiled wide, reached over and hugged her imposing dog. Anja's tail, already swishing merrily, picked up its tempo.

"Jah!" Johann barked. "And 'twas a good thing, too, it was! That nasty creature had you pinned down by the looks—"

"Hey, wait a minute!" Danielle cried out, interrupting the brawny farmer. Jumping to her feet so she could see better, she hurriedly scanned the area around the Hudsons' cabin and surrounding meadow. Anxiety clouded her smudgy face.

"Where are Paign and Mrs. Macy?" she shrieked. "I mean…he didn't…they're not…where are they?"

"Honey," Amy said again, this time gently patting her daughter's hand, "they're not here. They're—"

"Gone," Peter interrupted. "Gone, Dani. That hybrid thing parted out of here in a hurry when it set eyes on who just dropped in to join your fight."

"Something about Kimar, Ercen, Conomorg and Ita-Mudak all flying straight at him seemed to put the fear of the Lord into him, as the saying goes," Anders finished, his face strangely flushed. Danielle wondered for a moment if he'd been running.

"Hey, I didn't know you were here, too!" Danielle grinned at Anders, then at Freida standing next to him. She gave each of her friends a big bear hug but didn't notice the winks that went around the grown-ups. Tiny trotted around the three in a jaunty circle.

"So, they're gone, then," Danielle said quietly, processing what she'd just been told. She didn't know what to say, especially now that her human friends from another time were joined again. She didn't want them to know how desperate Paign looked in the brief moment she'd seen him. Of course, they already knew how dire the situation was for Mrs. Macy's emotional stability. Or, at least, they thought they knew. Now, it could only be worse. Much worse.

"We know you're worried, Dani," Peter said. "How could you not be? That thing is a piece of work!"

"Ah, now," Johann muttered, eyebrows raised high. "What is this work of his that is in pieces?"

Peter stared at his friend for a moment before a grin cracked his face wide open. Chuckling, he slapped Johann on the shoulder. "Ha, my friend! Forgive me once again. It's just a phrase that means the hybrid is like, well, like a…" Peter looked at Amy for reinforcements.

"Like something else!" she blurted.

Now it was Johann's turn to smile, but he still looked puzzled. "The beast looks like something else? Like what else, then?"

"This is no good," Peter grumbled, rubbing his head with both hands but still grinning at Johann.

"Oh, dear," Amy said, trying again. "You know, 'something else' is out of this world!"

"Oi!" Johann shouted. "Jah, that's good! Very good! Let us have that vile beast out of this world as soon as possible. Good idea!"

Danielle stomped her right foot down, startling Tiny and Anja. "OK, fine, then. Where is Lohxnahr?" she asked, her hands clenched at her sides.

"I believe that is what the others are discussing now," Peter replied calmly. He glanced at Amy to confirm she, too, was noticing Dani's agitation. "Over yonder," he added, tipping his head in the direction of a massive tree fall.

Twisting around to follow her father's direction, she observed Kimar and the others step from behind the aspen's shattered top, now broken to bits near its base. For a moment, she considered telling the others what caused the "tree fall," but the impulse to learn more was greater.

"I'll be back in a minute," she said loudly to her father, as she sprinted over to the gathering of gargoyles. Danielle didn't notice that Freida and Anders followed her. It was impossible to not notice the dogs, though, because they were so often in her way. Both dogs grinned, their tongues lollygagging in the warming air of the morning.

Ercen, whose back was nearest to where Danielle ran, turned. "Greetings, child!"

"Hi, Ercen," Danielle responded. "Hey, everyone." She looked intently at Kimar, Ita-Mudak and Conomorg. "So, what are you doing?"

"I believe the correct term to use in answering is *speculating*," Conomorg replied lightly.

"That's right," Anders said, "if your meaning is that you've been investigating and you're now trying to draw conclusions."

"Indeed," Ita-Mudak said, his low voice felt as much as heard.

Danielle often wondered if the huge gargoyle was teasing her when he solemnly bowed to her. *Nearly every time he says anything to me, he bows!* she thought.

"Indeed, we have drawn conclusions," he continued, "but because we have little to speculate on, perhaps a better word to use is *guess?*"

Anja plopped down next to Ita-Mudak, her head tipped up to watch him. The dog's ears were also tipped up expectantly. Immediately, Ita-Mudak's slab-like right hand was patting Anja's head, its long talons glinting in the dappled sunbeams.

"Yes?" Freida asked. "What have you guessed?"

"Where is Lohxnahr, Kimar?" Danielle interrupted. "Was he hurt?"

"He is not hurt, Danielle," Kimar replied. "Not in a material way."

"What does that mean?" Danielle asked, her hands splayed across her hips and her eyes flashed. "You didn't see him hit this tree so hard that it sheared off as he went through it."

"He what?" Anders and Freida cried out together.

"Yes, dear," Ercen said softly, as she laid her hand on Danielle's shoulder. "It would have been upsetting to witness. Remember, though, that we are not like you. It is this poor aspen that fared the worse from its encounter with little Lohxnahr."

"You mean, Lohxnahr's not—" Danielle, Freida and Anders asked, simultaneously.

"Here," Conomorg cut in. "He is not here, young ones. That is all."

"And he took no physical hurt," Kimar said, with natural authority.

Looking first at her Norwegian friends, Danielle turned towards Kimar. "Then where is he? Where is Lohxnahr?"

"That's what we're speculating on," Conomorg said.

"Very well," Anders sighed, annoyance framing his face. "What is it then that you speculate happened to him?"

Both Freida and Danielle nodded in agreement. But Anders saw out of the corner of his eye that Danielle also smiled broadly at him. Feeling blood rushing to his face and suddenly desperately uncomfortable that Danielle would notice, he quickly added, "Come now, don't you have any suspicions? At the very least, a thoughtful guess?"

Kimar tipped his head slightly to one side as he considered the boy. His amber eyes revealed nothing.

Anders felt intensely awkward. Glancing away from Kimar, he noticed Danielle's head turn back towards the hulking gargoyle captain.

"Yes," Kimar agreed. "We believe that Lohxnahr is pursuing the hybrid."

"'Giving chase,' as you might say," Conomorg quipped, plainly smiling as he spoke.

"By himself?" Danielle asked, dismayed.

"That's what I was wondering, too," Freida cried.

"He is not without his powers, child," Ita-Mudak replied to Danielle.

"Indeed not," Ercen added.

"And they are substantial!" Conomorg quipped again.

"Okay," Danielle interjected. "Okay! So Lohxnahr's powerful, I know. I've seen him in action, you know. Remember, in the chamber beneath the Temple of Kahrnahrgx? I saw Lohxnahr do amazing things, like taking out a whole squadron, or flock, or whatever you call a group of those nasty Vanntorden creatures—all at once!" As she spoke, Danielle's voice grew more shrill. Her arms flailed, animated by the anxiety pumping through her.

She felt a hand on her right shoulder. Glancing at it, she realized it was her father's. She turned around and saw that all the grown-ups had joined them.

"Tell us what your concern is, Dani," he said softly. "What's on your mind? Are you worried about Lohxnahr? What has you so revved up?"

Johann's head snapped over to stare at his friend, puzzlement clearly stamped on his face.

Danielle's head turned back and forth as she looked first at her parents and then at each of her friends, human, canine and gargoyle. She felt the pressure building inside, her clawing anxiety coming into full bloom. Her skin prickled up from her feet all the way under her disheveled hair. Anja sensed something was very wrong with her mistress, walked over with her head lowered and began nuzzling up against Danielle, first pressing into her thigh and then the hand hanging just above it.

Struggling to find words to express her gnawing fear, Danielle felt her face warming quickly. Embarrassingly. *Will they think I'm silly? Will they even believe me?* Her eyes darted back and forth, even as her breath got shallower. How can I tell them? For a moment, her eyes settled on Freida's, whose face showed anxiety—for Danielle, her dear friend. *How can I tell them?*

"What is it, Danielle? What is it we must know?"

Danielle followed the voice and turned to stare at Anders. *How can I tell...him?* Her forehead crinkled as her eyebrows lifted in misgiving.

"Honey," her mother murmured. "It's all right. It's all right. You can tell us."

Danielle heard, almost from outside of herself, the sounds of shifting weight, the sounds of bodies moving uncomfortably. The sounds of growing unease. The pressure inside was making it hard for her to breathe. As quickly as she'd felt her face grow flush, she felt it now growing cold.

"I, uh," Danielle began. Her hands trembled. Anja nuzzled the one closest to her, trying to comfort her mistress. "It's... it's..." she tried again.

In a way she could never describe later, Danielle felt pressure, such enormous pressure, to balance two incompatible forces. *How can I tell them?* She couldn't bear the thought of what it would mean to them—how terrible a revelation—and yet, she could feel her mind collapsing as she, herself, finally allowed the truth of what she witnessed to sink in. To sink lower and lower. Beneath her unwillingness to face it. The vision of what she'd seen through the doorway of the cabin filled her mind. All else faded from view. *Could it really be?* Tears, hot and throbbing with blind fear, clouded her vision so that she couldn't actually see Kimar move in front of her. Still, she could feel his mass, his warmth…*his acceptance? No, no, it's his courage. His courage…he's giving me his—*

"It's Paign!" Danielle heard her voice shrieking. "It's Paign! It can't be—it just can't! But I saw it. Don't you understand? I saw him! I saw him! It's Paign!" Not realizing her eyes had been closed, she popped them open, looking wildly at each of her companions, and shouted again and again: "It's Paign!" Until she came at last to Anders, when her voice became suddenly quiet.

"It's Paign," she whispered. "He's turning into a hybrid."

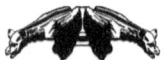

The sounds of loose grit and crunching stone echoed down the narrow entry into the multihued chamber. Sometimes using the outermost pinions of his mottled grey wings, the small gargoyle navigated the uneven path like a mountaineer would utilize a walking stick. It was utterly silent but for his movement further into the cave. A large gyrfalcon descended onto the lip of the cave's small entrance, perched high above the remote valley floor. Unseen by human eyes, the opening blended into the dark vein of minerals cutting diagonally across the huge peak, named Mount Thor after the Scandinavian god of thunder.

The gyrfalcon's head tipped back and forth as it watched the gargoyle slowly vanish into the far reaches. *It's been quite some time since he's been here. What brings him back?* the gyrfalcon wondered. *Why his return? Perhaps he is seeking the last visitor? Unwhole was that one. Like a wingless youngling. Something missing.*

Lohxnahr hummed softly, in a sing-song but rather tuneless voice, as he made his way back into the chamber of Zarentil. A soft lavender glow emanated from his face. The meter of his song matched his awkwardly meandering pace perfectly.

"Wonder...we...do...wonder...yes...what...comes... next?" The cherubic creature skipped on the penultimate word of his hummed song, briefly losing his balance as he did so. A moment later, the gyrfalcon launched off its dizzying perch, as the sound of crashing rock and a cloud of dust spewed out of the cavern's entry.

"Dear me!" Lohxnahr cried. "Wonder...we...do...yes," he hummed again, "why...that...fell...down?" What had been a thin stalactite lay shattered behind the small creature. "Pity. There isn't time now to renew the aged spire."

Lohxnahr walked more quickly towards the deep recess of the chamber, still using his wings to right himself on the uneven floor, in spite of the unfortunate incident with the spire. The gentle colors of the nearly luminous stones bathed him in a kaleidoscope of pastel hues.

CHAPTER TWENTY

TEMPEST

A horrible cry—her own cry—frightened her out of a troubled dream. Slapping her right hand over her chest, Bettina's eyes brimmed over. Her breathing was rapid and shallow. In the glum predawn light, her body quivered like a mouse pup separated from its mother's warmth. The horrible vision played in her mind even while she knew her eyes to be open.

"Oh, Momma!" she wept. "Oh, Momma. What is happening?"

It had been years since Bettina felt this sense of utter and crushing hopelessness. It was a feeling she'd never wanted to feel again. The death of her father in the waning days of the war had delivered such a cruel blow to the family.

Knowing that only a handful of weeks remained before their father's return, Bettina and Paign had eagerly helped their mother begin preparations for his arrival. Although Paign was big for his age and exceptionally strong like their father, Bettina's view of the world was practical: Paign needed help from his older sister, or some things just wouldn't get done. So, she'd done them. This wasn't uncommon in recent years, since so many families in the Honellaken Valley also had missing fathers and brothers. For too many, their menfolk would never return.

Still, Paign had great difficulty in accepting help from anyone, especially his sister. There'd been hard feelings. Sometimes, even harder words. In spite of their good intentions, even in their efforts to help their mother prepare for their father's return, a lot of strain had grown between the children.

Then came the dreadful news: their father had been killed. Besides dealing with her own grief and heartbreak, Bettina watched helplessly as her mother grew quiet and remote, aging before her very eyes.

Her closeness to her brother had already suffered during their time of preparations. Now the siblings, too, were distant and cold. Paign began spending all of his free time with his cousin Anders at the Knutsons' farm. In some ways, Bettina was pleased for him, grateful that the boy had a close companion his own age who understood the loss of a father, since Mr. Knutson was also never coming home again.

But with the emotional withdrawal of her mother and the physical retreat of her only sibling, Bettina had been on her own to resolve her grief. And the grief shattered her.

She knew, of course, the importance of sons to her farming neighbors, for their strong backs working alongside their fathers and uncles could make the difference between a highly productive farming enterprise—even eventual wealth—and total failure.

There was the constant pressure from all sides. The vagaries of crop prices. Unpredictable weather. Uncontrollable pests. Theft.

Perhaps it was this ever-present worry that nurtured the importance of daughters. Certainly, daughters were vital to successful farms in their own way. They helped their mothers with the cooking and cleaning. But they also helped with farmhouse operations: feeding the livestock, mucking the henhouse and stable, tending the garden. There was always more than enough work that needed doing.

Yet, there was a special bond of love between many fathers and their daughters. Bettina had seen it often, especially on Sundays after church, when families lingered to chat with each other. The fathers of her girlfriends had a certain gleam in their eyes when talking to their daughters. She'd always thought it was a look of hope for the future. There was a lightness and joy in the conversations that revolved around the girls. A special twinkle in the ruddy faces of the farmers as they observed their girls.

Bettina also noted a common look for the boys, although it was different. Not bad—just different. With the boys, it was a look of strength for the present. She could see confidence in the farmers' eyes—most of them, anyway—confidence that they'd make it through whatever challenges came their way, because they had their boys to help.

Bettina had known that sparkle in her own father's face, every time he looked at her. Her earliest memory was of her father smiling at her. She must have been only an infant, lying in her crib. It was Bettina's favorite memory of her father. Indeed, it was her favorite memory.

With the closeness in her family ruptured, Bettina was overwhelmed with grief when her father died. She would never see that sparkle again. She wouldn't feel the wonderful sense of sanctuary that had been to her like water to a parched flower. The gentle touch of his gnarled hands patting her on the head, just before kissing her forehead at night, would never come again. Her father's smell—a mix of sweat, earth, livestock and strong coffee—was gone. It had been a bitter draught for her to swallow, like a pleasant holiday cider gone sour. Even so, not having her mother or brother to share this loss with her to blunt its cutting edge—was bitterer still.

Eventually, she'd withdrawn, too. Just as Paign adequately, if mechanically, performed the farm duties required of him, Bettina scrubbed, cooked and mucked as before. And, like her mother and brother, she wandered through the day like their cows—aimless. Quiet. Days of routine grew to weeks. Then months.

Finally, there was an argument. Bettina couldn't remember who had suggested it, her or her mother. It didn't matter really. As best she could recall, less than a week later, she was on her way to Trondheim to stay with relatives.

After that, there wasn't much communication, to her or from her. A few scattered letters written in her mother's spidery script about Paign's far-fetched adventures with Anders and others. What her mother reported in these letters was so strange and otherworldly that Bettina worried about her mother's health. Her mind seemed to be going.

Now, Bettina strove to catch her breath. "What is happening, Momma?" she cried again.

Clutching at her temples, Bettina squeezed her eyes shut and pressed against her head, impulsively trying to force the vision to stop.

It didn't help.

Like an annoying theatrical play where the actors repeat the same scene over and over, Bettina again saw the cabin at a distance. She was looking down on it from near the aspen grove's tallest tree. She could see below through the branches an oddly dressed girl, her mother and a queer creature. It reminded her of the demon-shapes on the huge and famous Nidaros Cathedral in central Trondheim. She couldn't hear what they were saying, but she looked back at the cabin when the girl pointed in its direction.

Then, suddenly, she was staring at the cabin's door, standing right in front of it. The same feeling of dread washed over Bettina, causing her to clutch at her chest again, for she knew what came next.

As before, the vision revealed the door opening abruptly. Her brother Paign stood before her—except it wasn't her, but her mother—the odd girl and the creature.

Bettina moaned loudly as the vision revealed the second creature—far worse than the first—glistening black and seething malice towards her mother and those with her, even as it rose from behind her brother. Bettina's mind recoiled at how the horrifying creature came into existence; she simply couldn't understand it.

"What does it mean, Momma?" Bettina wailed into the darkness of her simple bedchamber. Even though the room was cool from the crisp night air coming through the open window, her skin was damp with sweat.

Again, her viewpoint changed. She was flying backwards, as if she was a life-size marionette, yanked hard by a puppet master. A great ache exploded in her chest. Just before she smashed through the tall tree, her mother and brother fell—far below her—in a heap near the cabin's door.

"Momma! Paign!" she cried out, her voice echoing off the walls of her bedroom. Her hands clawed the air in front of her as she sought to fly back to them, to rescue them. From it. Even at this distance, with a cloud of the broken tree's dust and debris obscuring her view, Bettina could feel his malevolence.

Out of the corner of her eye, Bettina saw the strange girl tumble out of the aspen grove and run towards the cabin, only to hastily turn back. But she couldn't understand what was happening to the girl, as explosions of fire erupted near her.

Another moan came from deep within Bettina. Fear, confusion and horror washed over her. She was staring at Paign again. At first, he appeared as she had last seen him: his tousled, charcoal hair framing his sunburned cheeks as he had leaned against the pasture's fence. The morning's fog had been breaking behind him as he turned to look back at her. "It's time for breakfast," she'd called. He had stared at her for a moment, saying nothing, his pale blue eyes perfectly matching the color of the quickly shredding mist. Bettina remembered how vacant her brother's eyes had been. It was as if he, too, was dead. Dead inside. He turned away from her and walked into the barn. In his silence, he'd yelled: "I'm not coming in for breakfast." But it felt like more than that. Like he was never coming back, period. Like his emotional distance would be permanent.

For just a moment, that was the face of Paign she'd seen framed in the cabin's doorway. But even as the horrendous demon-creature had risen behind him, Paign's face had slowly changed, as if the beast's rising brought forth from him the full bloom of Paign's suffering and hatred.

Bettina's breathing came in gasps now.

"What—

"Is—

"Happening?"

Her vision, she knew, was surging again to the place where she'd wakened in a sweat.

"Oh, Momma…please, no. Please…"

She looked across the sun-drenched glade. Her mother and brother tightly hugged one another. The hellish creature stood beside them, chuckling without mirth. He was saying something, something mocking from the defiant stare on his face, but she couldn't hear it. She saw his muscular body stiffen and flex. Imperious, his talons—for Bettina could see them clearly, knife-like and horrible—were stretched around their necks, a shimmering necklace of doom. Despair strained at her heart.

"Please, no. *Please!*"

And then, as before, the vision ended. Screams still rising in her throat, her mother, brother and the captor were gone. Bettina knew not whether to believe they were abducted by the creature or outright killed by him.

A second horrible cry—again, her own cry—frightened her completely awake. Bettina slid onto the lovely hardwood floor, rolled onto her knees to face the bed, and buried her head into the cool, sweaty bedcovers. Her shoulders bobbed up and down, and she wept as she'd never wept before.

Lohxnahr turned at the sound of the gyrfalcon launching off the ledge, even as the final bits of stalactite continued to come to rest nearby. *Until next time, my friend.*

"So, what's next?" Danielle asked. She was embarrassed about her outburst, but still shaken. Her shoulders hunched involuntarily as a chill ran down her spine. She didn't want to believe what she'd seen on Paign's face. As she and her parents walked back into the meadow to rejoin the others, Danielle pushed down her anxiety about what the others thought of her outburst. It helped to have Anja trotting at her side.

Kimar, whose back faced Danielle and her parents, turned to face them.

Before he could say anything, Anders replied, "I believe we just arrived at the answer to that question!"

Kimar stretched his wings wide, not unlike a human stretches their arms when getting up from a nap.

"It is time for us to convene at the Valley of the Ten Pinnacles."

"Why there, Kimar?" Peter asked.

"Are you planning a war council, then?" Amy added.

"Of that, we are uncertain," Ercen replied. "For where would we take the battle? Unlike last time, when it was clear that we need assault the very Temple of Kahrnahrgx, we do not know where the hybrid has taken Paign and his mother."

Danielle stepped forward, stopping two paces in front of Kimar. Glancing quickly at Ercen first, she asked, "What do you hope to accomplish, then? What will going there bring us?"

"Clarity," he answered.

"How so?" Peter followed.

"Well, we're all agreed that there's very little time for us to do something," Anders interjected. "Mrs. Macy was already unwell before she came here. And who can blame her? If we believe what she told us, she's been to an inner chamber of Kahrnahrgx himself. None of the rest of us can claim as much!" Quickly, Anders glanced around at the gargoyles. "Well, I mean, at least among the humans…none of us have seen such a place."

Kimar bowed slightly to Anders.

"And I don't want to," Freida quivered. "Ever!"

"Nor me!" Johann roared.

"But…" Peter began quietly.

"You somehow think being there will bring us clarity?" Amy added, completing the sentence for her husband. She'd heard the increasing wariness in his voice.

"More than we have here, my friend," Heidi replied, pulling Amy's hand into her own.

"So, kind of like going for reinforcements?" Danielle said.

"That's a good description for it, I should say," Anders replied.

"Okay, then. What's keeping us?" Danielle asked.

Without a reply, Kimar nodded his head, and everyone shifted where they stood until all were in a loose circle. Anja squeezed in between Danielle and Peter, while Tiny did the same between Freida and Anders.

A moment later, a swirl of leaves and needles spun up into a funnel about half the height of the surrounding trees, hovered a split second and then fell to the ground. They were gone.

Not only had the rescue of Paign Macy failed miserably, now his mother was also captured again.

CHAPTER TWENTY-ONE
EPHEMERA

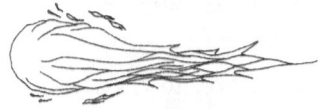

"When do you expect them?"

Uud-Rement observed that Prohximus wasn't looking his way, but rather staring into the high western reaches of the encircling ridgeline they called the Ten Pinnacles. With the sun just peering over the eastern edge, the orange limestone hue of Prohximus's back made it look like he'd been set on fire. Indeed, the curved horns on his head gleamed nearly white from the shower of sunlight falling on his head.

I suppose I'm glowing like a hot red coal, then, the fierce general grinned, before answering the question.

"Soon."

"Come now, Uud," growled the voice of Quarastohr, his hulking soapstone body casting a vivid light blue onto the deep green grass surrounding all of them. "You have more than that, yes?"

"Soon," came the reply.

Prohximus chuckled and turned to face the companions he'd known since his youth. "We have seen too many battles together to begin one of our own."

Uud-Rement grinned, still squatting on the dewy grass, his hands and talons splayed out in front of him. "You speak great truth, my friend. With you I would not quibble and joust."

Leaping like a frog, Uud-Rement sprang to his left just as Quarastohr's fist swung through the space his friend's head had just occupied.

Prohximus's chuckling doubled. "As always, old friend, your reflexes are still faster than Quarastohr's quickest swing."

Uud-Rement rolled over in the soft earth, leaving a small impact trench, and jumped fluidly to his feet. "My reflex speed is ever dependent upon my surly friend's legendary lack of humor." He winked at Prohximus, adding, "And dull mind."

It was Quarastohr's turn to chuckle. "Ha! Is that so? Please explain to us, if you would, how it is that *your* body—not mine—looks like a terrible accident from a young one's stoneware exercise?" Shifting on the grass, Quarastohr placed his meaty hands on his hips. "But rush not your explanation, out of thoughtfulness for my slow wits."

Uud-Rement, scarred from head to toe, did indeed look as if his body was assembled from leftover parts. He folded his arms mockingly and tipped his head to one side. "If only there was enough time in the universe to go *that* slowly!"

Prohximus burst out laughing and leaned back to face the deep blue sky above. A moment later, he was laying face-first in the meadow, pushed there by a smirking Quarastohr.

"That will teach you to side with the likes of a troublemaker like Uud-Rement, an aging commander who has seen his best days pass befo—"

Quarastohr didn't see the leg sweep of Uud-Rement coming and landed on his back with a moist thud. By then, Prohximus had already rolled onto his back. Both gargoyle commanders propped themselves up, their long hands behind them, and glared at their comrade.

Uud-Rement stared down at them, smiling. "Well, I am still the youngest of us, you know. Shouldn't you have learned that several centuries ago?"

"What difference does that make now, after all the centuries that came before?" Quarastohr growled in mock anger. "We're all old now!"

Prohximus reached up to Uud-Rement for a hand in getting up. "He has a point, Uud."

Uud-Rement laughed and reached down to assist each of his friends.

Prohximus stole a quick glance at Quarastohr, who winked.

A moment later, Uud-Rement was sailing over their heads, wailing as he went, "Treachery!"

The sound like a wet towel slapping a brick wall echoed gently back from the nearby trees.

"You've made quite an impression in the world!" Prohximus said with great solemnity, as he towered over Uud-Rement. "And with no effort on your part. Well done!"

"Indeed, he has!" Quarastohr quipped. "Not unlike a human young one in the snow. What do they call that shape, again?"

"A snow angel," groaned Uud-Rement. Now, it was his turn to reach out to his friends for help in getting up. A moment later he was trying to wipe the mud and grass off of his back, not very successfully.

"So, when *do* you expect them?" asked Prohximus.

"Let me guess," Quarastohr intoned.

"Soon!" all three voices bellowed together.

"Ah!" Lohxnahr murmured. "Not done yet, I see."

In the back recess of the Cavern of Zarentil, only a dim yellow light came from the nearest stalagmite, about a meter away. The cavern's anemone-like stone formations, usually pulsing with the subtle colors of their mineral source, were dimmed and shared a uniform dull grey. Countless candles surrounded the raised dais. Many were stacked on the dais itself; many more were nestled into the numerous recesses within the chamber's walls. None of the candles were lit but, at one point, all had been used. They had all melted to about the same height. It was if all had been blown out at the same time.

Lohxnahr squatted down onto his knees. Before him was a swirling sphere of dust and grit, about half a meter in size. While the dust whirled around in an intricate pattern of intersecting lines, the sphere itself undulated gently up and down, about a meter off the rough floor, slowly rolling top to bottom. From time to time, dazzling lavender light would break through between an intersection of lines, like volcanic faults cracking the earth. A deep hum punctuated the cavern's silence precisely when light emitted from the orb of earth and minerals.

Carefully—almost reverently—Lohxnahr reached out as if to hold the orb. But he stopped short of touching it, like a child might seek to gently capture a dandelion's floating seed in an open hand. Humming softly at first, Lohxnahr smiled and his eyes gleamed from the reflecting lavender. Then, in a lilting chant, he sang.

In order to be, see.
Attend your ear, hear.
Withhold not, free.

Defeat fear, run near.
Ambiguity, embrace.
Throw open, heart.
Radiance upon your face.
The evil, part.

"My friend, these words you spoke to Danielle. I now borrow them from you—with a few changes, if you will pardon me. You were always better with words. I believe the time is come."

In order to free, again be.
Attend your ear, draw near.
Withhold not, free.
Defeat fear, return here.
Ambiguity, eliminate.
Throw open, start.
Radiance, stimulate.
Then evil, part.

Lohxnahr's wings fluttered outward slightly as he chuckled. "Truth, you see! You rhyme better than me."

Leaning forward, so that his flat nose was nearly touching the orb, Lohxnahr breathed on it. Immediately, the orb's motion ceased. The intermittent crackling increased in speed and width. Bright lavender beamed out from the cracks nearest to Lohxnahr's face, while intense yellow-white shards of light stabbed out from the back of the orb.

The rhythm of Lohxnahr's continued humming matched the pulsing light emitted from the orb. As the meter of his humming increased, so the speed at which the light bursts also increased, as if the tune and the light together created a shared dance of wonder.

Lohxnahr's hands shifted ever so slowly until they cupped below the pulsing orb. More and more, light throbbed outward as the cracks flared wider.

Shadows burst across the stillness of the chamber, brought into being from the lavender and white-gold explosions of orb light. Most of the shadows formed, for the briefest of moments, from the orb's flashing against the many stalactites and stalagmites within. As a result, all shadows were long and slender like the mineral column casting it. But three shadows came not from the material of the chamber, for their shapes were like that of Lohxnahr.

"Greetings, my old friends!" Lohxnahr hummed, stealing a glance toward the left of the dais. "It is good of you to join me at this time of renewal."

Though the bursting light did not alight on any visible creature, the three shadows bowed slightly in unison as their wings overlay each other to form a thinner-shadowed, vaporous canopy.

Lohxnahr leaned in one last time and breathed on the now fully glittering orb. Then, he spoke again the words of his prophecy:

In order to free, again be.
Attend your ear, draw near.
Withhold not, free.
Defeat fear, return here.

The intensity of light within the chamber bloomed, sparkling but for a moment. Then, it faded back to the level it had been but continued dimming, with an occasional small burst.

About a half-minute passed, until there was a final flare of lavenders and yellow-whites.

Even as the chamber dimmed, the three shadows darkened. But now they stood upright with their wings folded and tucked. In unison, they bowed and were gone.

Lohxnahr's eyes and face were immediately washed over by a rich, warm copper hue.

Paign held his mother tightly at his side. She alternated between being momentarily awake and passing out. The strain of being abducted by this creature, Lement-Nor, had brought such a terror into her that she was simply incapable of much more than a quick gasp before falling again into semi-unconsciousness.

For his part, Paign could not conceive of anything but revenge. Although he was painfully aware of his mother's need for protection, his mind was consumed by rage at the hybrid. *Again! Again! Again, I have played the part of the fool! Perfectly!* Thus, his focus was more on how he might replicate the conditions under which he'd killed Rance-Dahl. Then he could take care of his mother.

But like a nagging burr in his work boots, Danielle's face kept playing in his mind. The shock in her widening eyes. The revulsion spreading across her face. Revulsion…of him.

"Paign," his mother's voice whispered into his ear, tickling him so that his back quivered.

Gently, he pulled her head into his shoulder. "Yes, mother. I am here." He felt her shudder next to him. The stone bench upon which they sat was warm, so he knew it was not the cold that shook her.

"What will become of us?" she replied, barely audible. "What do they want?"

Part of him wanted to snap at her, *To kill us, mother! Isn't this much obvious?* Instead, he caressed her face, saying, "I don't know, mother," because it was the truth.

For the past several hours, they'd been alone. At least in terms of having Lement-Nor or one of his minions standing nearby. Or tormenting them. This had surprised Paign. His experience with Rance-Dahl was nearly constant harassment. The beast seemed to *enjoy* his work, to revel in it. But with this hybrid creature, Paign sensed that all of its actions were driven by some hidden purpose. Not that the hybrid didn't bring physical hurt to Paign. It simply didn't seem to be driven by it like his captor did. While very grateful, Paign was also exceedingly puzzled by the hybrid's ignoring of his mother, for he knew that Rance-Dahl would have enjoyed nothing better than to torture the mother while the son could do nothing.

So it was that even as Paign repeated, "I don't know," to her, he puzzled greatly over this new enemy's behavior.

In the first few hours of their capture, Paign was able to painstakingly piece together much of what his mother had been through since he'd left their farmhouse only days earlier. He'd gained some knowledge of the actions of the others, as well as what she claimed was an abduction to the headquarters of Kahrnahrgx himself. Consequently, he learned that she believed it was Zarentil who had come to save her. But he also knew that the hybrid had successfully convinced him that he was Zarentil. Which left many questions unanswered for Paign: Was it truly the hybrid who had saved his mother? Or was it the real Zarentil? If it were the hybrid, why would it "save" his mother? To what purpose? If it were Zarentil, why did he not do a better job of rescue?

Amongst all of these doubts festered those that had been there before: *What of the others? Where are my so-called friends? Even my neighbors, the Skulstads?* Most pointedly, *Where is Anders?* Paign didn't want to even think about Danielle or her parents.

Still, the unbidden thought came anyway. *Why did she look at me that way?*

In spite of the desperate seriousness of their situation, Danielle's heart felt lighter. She had fallen in love with the Valley of the Ten Pinnacles during her first visit here the year before. It helped, of course, that Anja slept in front of her, so close that she lay on top of her mistress's feet. Besides the protecting comfort of her dog, Danielle reminisced about flying around the valley on Kimar's back, even diving into the lake for a swim. It had been magical.

Danielle took a break from munching on her supper of simple farm food and smiled at Freida, who was sitting next to her on a long flat stone near the edge of their eyrie.

"Isn't this place great?"

Unfortunately, Freida had just taken a big bite of her bread loaf and gotten a much bigger chunk than she'd expected. Bits of bread fell from her lips as she struggled to get it all in. She waved her hands in mock distress. "Hmphf," was all she could manage to say.

"Absolutely!" Anders interjected. "This place is just fantastic! Just fantastic."

Their eyrie was perched along the lower half of the nearly vertical face of grey rock that soared more than five hundred meters up behind the war council's dais. It was wide enough that they couldn't hear the conversation of the adults, who were sitting some thirty meters away to their left, next to the squatting gargoyles. Tiny sat next to Ita-Mudak, apparently listening to the conversation, his head turning back and forth as Ita-Mudak patted it.

Freida finally choked down her bread and added, "I love this place. It's so…so…"

"Fantastic!" Anders quipped, his wide smile revealing a bright bit of carrot lodged between his teeth.

The girls laughed. It was a shrill, merry laugh, loud enough that it turned the heads of the adults. A laugh of lightness and joy that disguised the very real anxiety all of the kids held for their friend, Paign, and his mother.

"What? What?" Anders asked, uncomfortably aware that the girls were not just laughing at his witty remark.

Both girls pointed at his mouth. "Carrot!" came the reply, in perfect unison.

A moment later, the offending bit of carrot flicked away, Anders said, "Wouldn't it be interesting to know where they get this food from?"

"You know, I've been thinking the same thing," Freida replied. "In so many ways, the food is very much like our own!" Glancing at Danielle, she added, "You know, quite like the food that Anders and I are used to."

"Farm food," Anders added helpfully, his eyes twinkling. Quickly, his face became more serious. "The question is—or questions are, rather—Who owns the farm? Where is the farm? And *when* is the farm?"

"But should we assume that our friends go to only one place—one farm—when they are providing for us?" Danielle asked.

"No, I suppose not," Anders replied as he bit off some cheese.

"Although it does seem to come from the same *when*, don't you think?" Freida added. "It's been quite dependable that way, it seems to me."

"That's true, I think," Anders agreed. "Particularly the bread loaves. They've been very consistent."

"Well, I don't know about you, but I feel sorry for the farmer who is called upon to provide enough food for a bunch of teenagers! Especially boys!" Danielle joked.

Immediately, the smirk on her face vanished.

"I mean, boy," she added softly.

"Everything will be right as rain," Freida replied, patting Danielle's knee. "Anders can testify that I've been nearly feverish with worry about Paign before now. And now we must also worry about his mother."

Anja leaned her head upwards to lick Freida's hand in thanks. *That's nice of her! That's just how my mistress comforts me.*

Freida's cheeks rose as she smiled, deepening the little crow's feet at the edge of her eyes. She leaned over and hugged Anja around the dog's rough. "That tickles my skin, girl!"

"It's like Freida says, Danielle. She has been a wreck and, in truth, so have I," Anders faltered. Without warning, he brought his right fist up to his mouth, clearing his throat. Then coughed into it several times.

"I think it has something to do with this place," he continued, waving his arms around to encompass the valley surrounding them. "There's something magical about this place. It's so...so..."

"Encouraging!" Freida interrupted.

"Yes! Yes, that's it, Freida!" Anders replied, conviction and strength returning to his voice.

Danielle said nothing, but she smiled at her friends. In spite of the fear gnawing at her heart, she couldn't argue that the Valley of the Ten Pinnacles did bring her a deep comfort and a sense of rightness in the world.

For a few minutes, they sat silently munching their simple supper, comforted by the presence of their companions and the strange normalness of this world they found themselves in.

From the height of their perch, they could see hundreds of gargoyle families doing what humans families do at such times: preparing for the close of the day. From their adventures the year before, the kids remembered that their winged friends didn't usually eat in the manner humans did. Instead, they could take nourishment directly from the earth, from which they were also formed. Danielle thought of it as similar to a plant drawing its life from the ground. What was different about the gargoyles was that they didn't need good soil like a plant does. In fact, they didn't need soil at all. She hadn't noticed much of a rhythm to gargoyle feedings, either. It was a much more sporadic and unpredictable happening, as if the desire to be renewed had more to do with communing with nature than with a demanding, unavoidable need for nourishment.

From this height, the children could see many, many gargoyles motionless, some standing while others squatted. Most often, their heads would be tipped down slightly and always with their eyes closed. Their hands were pressed flat together and held parallel to the ground. In the glow of the setting sun falling upon some of the adjacent eyries, the talons of these gargoyles glittered bright yellow, as if fire was leaping sideways out of their blunt fingertips.

For reasons she didn't understand, Danielle reached out for Anders's and Freida's hands. Anders stared at Danielle's hand holding his and then hoped neither girl noticed. The three stood together, quietly watching the gargoyles, as the sun slipped behind the high western rim of the valley.

After a few minutes, Anders said softly, "You know, it's almost as if they're not just renewing themselves—I mean, I know it's their way of eating, but it's hard to see it that way. They look, well—"

"Like they're showing reverence," Danielle interrupted.

"Like they're worshipping," Freida whispered.

"It is good to have you returned to us, my friend," Lohxnahr said, bowing slightly. "I have missed you."

The once darkened chamber now glowed an intense copper.

"And you appear to be none the worse from your adventure," he continued. "Indeed, you appear to be more you than you once were."

"Do I?"

"In a way. You are less matter than before, I can see, but you are more meaning than even you were."

"How so, my friend?"

"Ah! Well, yes," Lohxnahr chirped. "As even you can see, there is less of you to block the view of what's beyond you."

Zarentil lifted his small hands up between his and Lohxnahr's faces. While not completely translucent, they had become nearly transparent, as had the rest of him.

"And your eyes carry the ages of time in them!" Lohxnahr continued, almost singing.

Zarentil tipped his head. "I must accept your word, Lohxnahr."

"Of course, you have no need for talons anymore."

"Not at such a time as this, it appears. Perhaps at another time. Yet, in this way, I am less matter than before, am I not?"

"In truth."

"As I am regathered, there is yet some—unsettledness. Thus, it is clear not how I come to that which you describe as being of more meaning."

Though Zarentil was much smaller than Lohxnahr—not much bigger than a human infant—Lohxnahr bowed. Smaller did not mean less significant.

"My lord, it is of a certainty that you are of less matter. Yet, it is also of a certainty that your meaning is greater. For you passed from this world willingly. And this not only for yourself, nor for greater glory, nor for the benefit of all peoples. Nay, this you did not for even the ransoming of a friend. In truth, you permitted yourself to be slain for the redemption of an enemy!"

"It returns now, memories full," Zarentil's deep voice rumbled as he closed his eyes. "Remember, I do."

When he reopened them, Lohxnahr beamed, bathed in coppery iridescence.

"What do you want with us?" Paign snapped at Lement-Nor. The boy's mother nestled behind his shoulder, partially squeezed between him and the rough stone wall.

The gargoyle gave a dismissive wave, his long, muscled arm swinging past Paign's face. "I don't want you, boy. You and your whimpering mother mean nothing to me."

"Then why are we here?"

Lement-Nor leaned down so his face was only inches from Paign's.

"Have a care, human! Do you forget so quickly how I surprised you at the cabin? Do you already disregard how it was I deceived you as to my actual shape? I am Lement-Nor, a special hybrid, able to absorb the being of another—gargoyle or human! I am the ultimate spy and assassin."

Gudrun cowered behind Paign and shuddered violently.

"But what would *I* want with you? Nothing! Your kind cowers and snivels. You are soft, weak and pathetic."

Lement-Nor stepped back from Paign and began pacing the length of the humans' cell.

"You are *fragile*. Your bodies are fragile. Your minds are fragile. And your spirits are fragile. In a word, you are repulsive—a pox upon the earth," he spat, glowering at Paign.

"It is an abomination that he wants any of you for any reason. And it is a vile command that I should have *any* part of this. That is why—"

"You mean Kahrnahrgx, don't you?" Paign interrupted.

Although the hybrid was more than three meters away from them, in only two strides he was again face to face with his captive. Paign's blood ran cold at the sight of the hybrid's nimble movement, a combination of a light step and winged glide.

"Are you simply incapable of learning, boy? Have you not an ounce of wit in your head?" he spat, his hot breath blowing Paign's hair back.

"I am Lement-Nor!" he bellowed.

As the echo bounced down the long halls far beyond Paign's sight, he felt his mother quiver spasmodically and then grow still. *She's passed out, you idiot! Why are you egging him on?* Paign scolded himself. *This isn't Rance-Dahl. He's different. He's worse, much worse. More calculating...more dangerous. And it's not just me this time!*

"Yes, sir," Paign replied quietly. While he didn't wish to honor the beast in any way, Paign was unwilling to allow the creature's temper to rise further on his account. The risk to his mother was too great. "You are Lement-Nor."

His captor's forehead furrowed and he slowly stood. Rubbing his chin, his talons glittering light in all directions, Lement-Nor studied Paign for a full minute.

"Conformity? No, I think not. Placating? Perhaps, but that isn't it, either. Grudging respect? From this one? Never!" The tone of the gargoyle grew more mocking with each question.

"Appeasement! You wish to soothe me, boy? Out of fear for your female progenitor, perchance?" At this, Lement-Nor exploded in raucous laughter. "Ha! That's it, isn't it? You wish to *quiet me down!* Me, Lement-Nor, the all-powerful hybrid, more powerful than even his unsuspecting 'Master'! Ha!"

Suddenly, Lement-Nor reached his right hand out and placed it on Paign's head. "I'll give you this, human. Whatever your intent, you *have* amused me."

Pulling his thick hand back, he patted Paign's head with his talons, only once. Four tufts of black hair slid down onto his shoulders, and blood slowly oozed from the wounds. Paign cringed but made no sound. He had his mother to consider.

Bettina stared out the window. Her breakfast had grown cold, but she hadn't noticed. The intensity of her night terrors made her feel slightly nauseous. She took another sip of strong, black coffee, fortunate to not spill any as her hand trembled.

It was quiet in the house. She'd risen much later than normal, so much so that her uncle was already at his work as a dock foreman. Her aunt would be shopping at the market near the wharf. Her cousins, all older, had taken jobs away from Trondheim and recently moved away. It didn't bother Bettina that she was alone, since it provided her time to think. It also meant she didn't need to explain anything about her outbursts in the small hours. Apparently, she'd been quiet enough in the night that she hadn't awakened them. Otherwise, there would be a note on the square kitchen table, written in the flowing script of her aunt.

Bettina loved them, her aunt and uncle. They were some-what less stoic than the people in her village. The townspeople were quicker to laugh, she'd noticed, probably because there was more interaction between people, just because they lived closer to each other. The town was more neighborly. Nevertheless, her relatives weren't exactly talkative, preferring to let their actions do the speaking for them. So the dinners they shared together were rather quiet and predictable. Common topics included weather predictions, especially about the conditions of the sea, and lots of town gossip. Bettina wondered how much of the gossip was accurate, but she avoided getting into the discussions.

She appreciated the freedom they gave her, as well as their support of her studies. She wasn't charged anything for her room and board, which made staying with them an excellent choice because her mother had little in the way of money. All that was required of Bettina was weekly housecleaning and occasional yard work.

Today, Bettina was unaware of the beautiful morning, with the sun shimmering brightly on the harbor. The mountains on the far side of Trondheimsfjord were bathed in yellow-orange. She took another sip of coffee and abruptly held the delicate, flowered cup away from her.

"Bother," she said. "Now my coffee has grown cold." She quickly tested her breakfast of lefse and smoked salmon and determined it had suffered the same fate as the coffee. Unwilling to waste it, she ate it halfheartedly. The coffee she poured out into the cast iron sink and replaced it with a fresh cup from the enameled tin pot on the stove.

In the light of a new day, it was difficult to believe in the dreams she'd suffered through. Bettina recognized that they certainly *felt* real at the time. But could they be true? Did they actually portend the future? Worse still, did they describe the present? She'd always trusted her intuition, but this was just so hard to absorb.

"Could the letters Momma sent be true?" she whispered. "What if Paign really did encounter gargoyle creatures?" Too frightening to speak, the thought came nonetheless. *I've never dreamt of them before last night, so why do they come now?*

Filled with nervous energy, Bettina got up and walked quickly into the parlor. The curtains were still drawn, so she pulled them open. She was careful not to disturb the potted plants on the window sill. Light filled the quaint, wallpapered room tastefully arranged with intricately embroidered chair covers and lacy tablecloths and set floating flecks of dust shimmering.

"What do I do? What do I do?" she murmured, pacing the length of the rectangular room. "Should I go home? But what can I do?"

Unaware that she'd stopped moving, Bettina nearly jumped out of her skin when the housecat, a black-and-white longhair forest-cat named Petra, rubbed against her leg.

"Oi!" she cried, leaping to one side, startling the cat. "Oh, it's you, Petra. I'm sorry, girl. I didn't see you in here." Kneeling down low, she coaxed Petra over. Bettina plopped down into the small couch behind her, then patted her lap until the cat leapt up.

"That's my girl," Bettina hummed. Petra immediately set to purring loudly, enjoying the consistent petting she received from her distracted companion.

Again, Bettina stared blankly out the window to her left, with its commanding view. Petra's warmth was calming to the girl and gave her something to do with the energy pulsing through her.

"What should I do, Petra? What should I do?"

Because Bettina's attention was turned away from the feline, she didn't notice the cat's head swing to the right toward the kitchen.

"May I suggest that with us you come?"

Bettina's heart leapt in her chest at the sound of the buzzing voice. She protectively clutched Petra and turned to face the sound.

Immediately, she felt as if she'd been plunged back into her night terrors. There stood two creatures. She couldn't be sure, but the larger one looked very much like the one from her nightmare, the one she'd seen from overhead in the tree. Except now she could see his face. He was smiling at her. The smaller creature—not much larger than a child—glowed with a fresh copper hue and, Bettina realized with great astonishment, was nearly translucent.

She stared for a moment, speechless. As her forearms bumped into gooseflesh, Petra slid off her lap and walked over to the creatures, stopping in front of the larger one.

"You're gargoyles," Bettina uttered, breathless.

"Indeed yes, young lady! Please permit me the honor of making our introduction. This is Zarentil. I am Lohxnahr. You are Bettina, the beloved daughter of Gudrun Macy and the loving sister of Paign Macy."

"Yes," Bettina replied quietly. Despite her misgivings, she was feeling herself relaxed. Perhaps it was the way Petra reacted—or didn't—to these otherworldly visitors. Or perhaps it was the serenity that exuded from both creatures, especially the one named Zarentil. She sensed no threat from them.

"What's happened? Has something happened to my family?"

"What does your heart tell?" Lohxnahr replied.

"Something terrible, something...I don't have words for."

"Now, wait a minute, Kimar!" Peter replied, his face flushed. "Does it really have to go this way?"

Again, Tiny wished the grown persons—biped or winged—would just settle down. A nap would do them all good. Although he liked the idea of trotting to the other end of the eyrie to join the kids, he liked the sound of a nap so much that he went back to sleeping.

"Peter," Kimar replied. "There is no answer for a question such as that. At all times, there are options. At all times, we must weigh those options and determine which appears best."

"We don't know where they are being held," Conomorg added.

"But when we do—and I am certain that soon we will know—we must make all haste to launch a rescue," Ita-Mudak said.

"And you recognize, Peter," Ercen offered, "that it will be more difficult than the efforts needed last year to rescue either of Danielle or Freida, because they weren't held together at the same time or place."

"Not to mention," Amy added, as she held Heidi's hand, "aren't they likely to be held at a more secure location?"

Johann cleared his throat, waiting a moment to see if his wife would speak. She simply stared at the ground. "And Gudrun has not the strength of our little Freida...or your Danielle."

"Hmphf," Peter snorted. "I suppose you're all right." While conceding the logic of the argument, Peter was still filled with disquiet. It had only been about a year since they were first thrust into the world of gargoyles. Before that, their lives had been nice and predictable. They had lived in a nice house in a nice neighborhood, had nice friends, and lived a nice, respectable life together. He'd liked it that way: predictable. No big surprises. No drama. He'd sensed people looked at the Wheelen family and wished to be like them. Who wouldn't? Two acclaimed college professors with a bright and gifted daughter, living a life of purpose and comfort. It's what everyone dreamed about. He rather liked being the epitome of that widely held dream. And yet—

"How *do* we find them?" Amy asked, breaking Peter's train of thought.

"That is our dilemma," Ita-Mudak answered.

"We have not discerned a way to locate them," Kimar continued. "We know that Lohxnahr was working through a plan he had devised, but we do not currently know where he is or whether he has made any progress. We also know that the Zarentil-not-Zarentil hybrid successfully utilized Gudrun to find her son. Beyond these known factors, we can only suspect certain things."

"Like what?" Peter wondered, hoping for a better reply than his heart expected to hear.

"We have much confusing information," Ercen replied.

"Agreed," Peter conceded. "Nevertheless, you have suspicions. Let's hear them."

Kimar stared down the length of their eyrie, watching the kids as they laughed while having their supper. He turned back towards Peter. "It is unclear how, but we believe that the hybrid can—even without absorbing its host—access the memories and feelings of his victims. Thus he was able to see through Gudrun where Paign was being held…"

"But?" Peter asked.

"It begs the question as to why such a senior minion of Kahrnahrgx doesn't already know where an important captive is being held. Further, he utilized a human to find another human, rather than pursue his inquiry through normal channels."

"You mean like military channels?" Amy said.

"It is as if the beast was avoiding normal protocols!" Johann cried. "What does *that* mean?"

Tiny raised his head to see what all the upset and tension was about.

"That is our puzzle," Kimar replied firmly. "The hybrid's behavior seems to reveal he is working out an agenda based on secrecy and stealth."

"But if that's the case—and it sure appears to be so," Amy said quickly, "is the creature conducting a special mission for Kahrnahrgx that somehow involves Paign and Gudrun?"

"Or is he working *against* Kahrnahrgx?" Peter gasped.

"The latter," Kimar replied. "We believe he's running a rogue mission."

"To what end, Kimar?" Heidi said, choking on the words.

There was no answer. Again, Kimar looked away at the kids, just as the girls pointed at Anders and burst out laughing.

"I believe he intends to overthrow Kahrnahrgx."

"Does Kahrnahrgx know of this?" Johann asked.

"We have no way of knowing," Ita-Mudak replied. Tiny was again fast asleep next to him. "But given the intelligence of Kahrnahrgx, it is certain to me that he does know or must soon suspect so."

"But why would the hybrid want the Macys?" Heidi cried.

"The same reason that Kahrnahrgx does, we think," Ercen replied.

"And that is?" Johann followed.

Kimar turned again in the direction of the kids. "Bait."

"To capture Danielle," Peter whispered. He was sure that Amy's skin also went cold as he reached out for her hand.

Ercen dropped down on her knees in front of Amy and Peter.

"Yes," she said, "but we fear for different purposes."

Johann and Heidi gathered next to their friends.

"Kahrnahrgx, we believe, seeks Danielle for revenge over the destruction of his temple. His method for approaching her was by means of the hybrid's stealth, as you have seen. His ability to shape himself into the form of another makes him elusive and frightening. His creation by Kahrnahrgx is a master stroke of deception."

"Except—" Conomorg began.

"Except that the tool of deception that my brother created," Kimar interrupted, "has become the deceiver to his master."

"To what end?" Peter asked, as if from outside his body.

"I believe that the hybrid seeks to usurp his master. To do so, he believes he needs the power of one who has already thwarted him. This hybrid uses the Macys as bait, as he seeks to capture Danielle for his own ends."

"What ends?" Amy whispered.

Sounds of laughter drifted over from the far end of the eyrie.

"To absorb her. He will then have all of her knowledge, memories…and, we believe, her power."

"You *believe*?" Peter coughed out. "You don't know?"

"No," Kimar replied. "We have your report of the first hybrid and his failed attempt within your home. He appeared to have absorbed all of the knowledge of the peacekeeper he dispatched.

"Ah, yes," Johann cried out. "The constable!"

"But you can't prove that the hybrid somehow took the man's power," Peter declared.

"No. But based on what we know, it is very reasonable to conclude that it could—and did—in effect, become the man, while yet retaining itself."

"What matters most," Ercen cut in, "is that the hybrid believes it can obtain Danielle's power…by absorbing her."

CHAPTER TWENTY-TWO

RADIAL

Paign could feel his body wanting to contort, badly. But he didn't allow even a flinch. Lement-Nor's face was just inches away. His breath was foul, with a smell like burnt tar and sulfur. Still, Paign didn't want to give his captor any satisfaction and willed his body to remain motionless.

"Do you understand me, boy?" he hissed. "Not a word. Not a glance. Not a hint. Not even an unfettered thought."

Twisting his head ominously, the gargoyle continued, "Because you may know that your mother's life is instantly forfeit if you betray me in any way!"

"Yes, sir," Paign said quietly.

"Yes, *what*?"

"Yes, I understand, Lement-Nor. There is no reason for concern since, first, I don't know anything to disclose, and second, I'd be crazy to make an alliance with the likes of Kahrnahrgx."

Lement-Nor leaned in even closer, so that Paign felt the heat coming off of the creature.

"I'll be the one to determine that, human."

Paign wondered which of his two reasons was "to be determined" by his captor. Then he wondered if Lement-Nor heard his unfettered thought. There was no sign that he did.

Seeing that Gudrun was unconscious, the gargoyle spat at her feet. Again, Paign controlled his body from reacting.

"See to it that she doesn't hinder our departure. We leave at the next rising of the sun."

Lement-Nor abruptly pivoted on his heels, chewing up the stone floor as his rear talons dragged the shape of half-moons into it. Paign was grateful that his own feet were tucked beneath him, or he would have likely lost a few toes as the talons swept over where his feet had been.

"So, how long does that leave us?" Paign muttered. "Sitting here in a cave, who knows where, how am I supposed to know when sunrise comes?"

Both of the obsidian guards left to monitor Paign and his mother turned and stared at him, but said nothing.

"Never mind. Not talking to you," Paign gave a dismissive wave of his hand. "This is just great. We get to meet Kahrnahrgx."

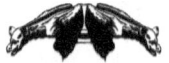

Paign couldn't discern the look on her face. Danielle looked startled, even alarmed. "What's gotten into her, anyway? I haven't done anything!"

He stooped down and picked up another chunk of stone and hurled it into the dark corner of the chamber. A series of loud crashes followed.

Glancing again at Danielle, Paign saw she was now glaring at him. Her legs dangled from the long, stone altar. Rubble was strewn across the surface and littered the dais encircling it.

Mindlessly, he picked up another chunk and flung it the same way as before. More crashing.

"Oh, oh. Here she comes."

Indeed, Danielle had hopped off the altar and was coming straight at Paign. She was heedless of the rubble obstructing her way. She should have been careful but, instead, looked crazed. Twice, her legs went askew in an unnatural way, yet she didn't slow. *Her legs should have broken right there!*

Paign felt a shudder ripple down his back. He started backing away from the approaching girl and immediately tripped on a large, flat stone broken away from the altar itself. Landing hard on his tailbone, he cried out.

Then she was on him, grabbing him by the collar. Aghast at her strength, Paign was hauled up to his feet. She flared her eyes at him.

Wait a minute! She's not as tall as I am. He looked down at her feet to confirm she wasn't standing on a rock. His skin crawled at the sight of talons jutting through her shoes.

She was shaking his shoulders violently and yelling at him. "Stop it…stop it!"

"But I haven't done anything!" he cried.

An otherworldly wail shocked Paign awake. His mother's wail.

Shaking off the sleep, he quickly surveyed their cell. An obsidian held his mother off of the floor, her feet dangling. She was screaming hysterically. The other obsidian guard held Paign by his shoulders, mercilessly pinching him.

"Awake now, human!" he sneered. "We wouldn't want to delay Lement-Nor from keeping his appointment with Kahrnahrgx." A wicked smile split its head. "Or *would* we?"

Danielle couldn't believe how much Bettina looked like Paign. She had the same high cheekbones and strong nose. Even in all of the chaos of her visit to the Hudsons' cabin, Danielle remembered enough of Mrs. Macy's face to realize that her daughter's nose was different, softer and rounded. Now, she had a sense of what Mr. Macy would have looked like. He must have been quite handsome. But Bettina was all girl, and a very pretty one. Her hair was wavy and dark like Paign's, but had a red-brown shimmer when sunlight hit it. She sounded a lot like Paign, too, just in a higher register.

Why am I thinking so much about how she looks? How she sounds? Danielle shifted her feet, making a scuffling sound. *I need to pay attention!*

Anja glanced up at her mistress, licking the girl's hand out of habit. *Hm. She tastes tense,* the dog noticed.

The conversation had been going on for much of the morning. When Lohxnahr had parted, unheralded, into the Valley of the Ten Pinnacles at dawn, there had been quite a ruckus, in no small part because he'd caused so many questions in the preceding days.

And then there was Zarentil! The center of so much doubt and distress, he'd remained passive and content during the entire debate over his authenticity. Even Danielle had needed assurance from Lohxnahr that Zarentil was legitimately Zarentil. It was hard to accept, since she had—in her own vision—witnessed his being overcome by the hybrid. It helped that he looked different than before, almost angelic in his transparentness.

Finally, there was Bettina. During a break in the conversation, primarily so the adults could have coffee, Danielle learned that Freida and Anders knew of Bettina, of course, but didn't actually know her personally. Since she was older, they hadn't moved in the same circle of friends. Most of their experience of her had been bumping into her at Paign's house: brief and unrevealing.

So, she's really kind of an unknown factor here. Danielle shook her head and refocused her attention on the dialogue.

"So, it is your intent that the four of you—and only the four of you—will plunge into the realm of the enemy to effect the rescue of the captive boy and his mother?" Quarastohr asked.

"Indeed," Lohxnahr replied with a lilt.

"Why not take more? Why not a strike force?" Uud-Rement growled. "It will be in a formidable fortress that they are held. Is it not rash to go with such a small force?" The morning light cast harsh shadows on the gargoyle's many deep scars.

"Indeed," Lohxnahr replied with an even greater lilt. This seemed to completely nonplus his audience. Immediately, many feet began shifting around.

"What?" Peter cried. "Pray tell which part are you 'indeed-ing'? That they're held in a formidable fortress or that it is rash to go with such a small force?"

Danielle knew her father's blunt question was mostly from his concern for her, but it was also borne out of his need for clear logic. Often, the manner in which gargoyles reached decisions—or at least argued a position—seemed to have no logical basis. She knew that was hard for both of her parents. They'd often talked, or more accurately, complained about such behavior from their university students. But Danielle had come to understand in her adventures the prior year that life doesn't always follow a logical process. Sometimes, it is more important to follow one's instinct, even when it flies into the face of what makes "logical" sense. Danielle knew somehow, not from her mind sorting out all the elements of the argument but from the confidence of her own intuition, that Lohxnahr's plan was best. Even so, she knew it would be difficult for her scientist parents to accept. Hearing their teenager argue, "Well, I *just know* it's the right way to handle this!" wouldn't be very compelling to them.

"Yes!" Lohxnahr replied, his wings fluttering as he remained squatted on the dais.

"Bother!" Johann grumbled. "I gather you mean that you agree, Lohxnahr, that yes there will be a nasty fortress to deal with and that yes it is rash—rash, mind you!—to go after our loved ones with but four rescuers?"

"Perfect!"

Heidi, whose face was already lined with care for her dear friends, Gudrun and her son, Paign, sat next to Amy. Their friendship provided needed support for each other, as both had loved ones in great peril. Heidi rocked gently forward and then back, as Amy rolled her eyes at Lohxnahr's quip.

"Lohxnahr," Amy spoke first, gently patting Heidi's hands. "You know that I have had my doubts about you on more than one occasion and that I haven't hidden them. This plan is madness. All the evidence and experience I have of Kahrnahrgx and his soldiers is that conducting a rescue mission with anything other than a massive force is, well, reckless and foolish!"

Lohxnahr said nothing, but smiled and bowed to the mothers.

"And yet it resonates in my heart," Heidi added, her voice breaking, "despite the skepticism in my mind. I have had a terrible foreboding that Gudrun's mind is slipping, even now.

It's like she faces a torment of fear so great…that Paign…."
Abruptly she swung her head down into Amy's lap and wept.

"That is why it must be so," Zarentil said. "In a fortress of great dread opens a door for great courage."

The other humans flinched at the sound of the deep resonance of the voice. Only Danielle and Bettina had heard the gargoyle before. Peter and Amy gawked at the cherubic, translucent Mystic, their eyes wide in dismay.

"Oi!" cried Johann like he'd been stung.

Anders and Freida grinned, politely amused that the deep, rich sound that came from the undersized gargoyle was even better than the low-toned pipes of the organ at their country church.

Tiny's head popped up at the sound. He gazed for a moment at Zarentil and then lay back down next to Freida. Anja slept through the surprise, nestled up against Danielle's legs.

Prohximus sighed. "Be that as it may, Lord Zarentil, while dispatching a small party may prove wisest for scouting and reconnaissance, perhaps even stealth and ambush, would you be kind enough to reveal the wisdom of comprising your rescue party with two elderly gargoyles and two female children?"

"That which is least expected carries the greatest quandary," Lohxnahr chirped.

"But for whom?" Peter shot back.

"For our opponent, Dad," Danielle replied, softly.

Lohxnahr beamed at her.

"Now, I'd be lying if I said that this idea doesn't chill me to the bone," she continued, rubbing her hands briskly on her jeans. Before continuing, she took a long, even breath. "But here's the thing…we know both Paign and his mother are in growing danger, even as we talk. Right?"

Peter nodded reluctantly.

"So, we're basically wasting precious time. We need to go as soon as possible…just the four of us, so the party is small. We already know that Zarentil's hybrid—uh, you know, the hybrid that was posing as Zarentil—was able to find Paign through Mrs. Macy. He told her it was through her 'heart's eye' or something. Now, of course, he has Mrs. Macy, too. That's why we need Bettina, right? To locate where her loved ones are through *her* heart's eye?"

This time, Lohxnahr nodded at her.

"And if I'm understanding things, Zarentil needs to come because, just as the hybrid gained the knowledge within Zarentil when he absorbed him—that seems to strange to say when you're right here," she said, shrugging at the Mystic, "so Zarentil absorbed the knowledge *and plans* of the hybrid!"

"Excellent!" Lohxnahr cried, levitating off the ground for a moment.

Danielle glanced around at her friends and companions. "Lohxnahr and I need to go," her head dropping down so that she was barely audible, "to bring him back. Not just physically, I mean. But bring Paign back as Paign."

Freida's eyes welled, but she said nothing.

Anders nodded fiercely and said, "I volunteer to go, Lohxnahr! He's my cousin…and best friend." Though his voice cracked, there was fire in his eyes.

"I would counsel that you accept his offer, Lord Zarent—" Quarastohr started.

"If he's coming, then so am I!" Freida interrupted.

"Great hearts would bring great action," Uud-Rement stated.

Bowing, Prohximus said, "We stand in support of these two additions to your squad. The stature of each member remains small and, thus, you retain the key element of stealth."

"What's their size got to do with anything?" Peter asked.

"Jah, that was my question, also," Johann agreed. "Isn't it the size of the group that matters? Not the size of each comrade?"

Kimar shifted his weight on the dais, and his talons screeched across the stone. All eyes turned toward him.

"Peter," he said, "it has to do with a theory—as yet unproven to my satisfaction—that the size of a gargoyle scout is central to its success at stealth. If there is less mass, there is less to sense. If this be true, the presumption is that this will apply also to humans. The smaller the stature, the greater the stealth."

"Meaning that because the kids are smaller than Johann and me, for instance, they're less likely to be spotted. Or sensed, as you say. Is that it?"

"That is the belief."

"So, that's why this rescue team includes the two smallest gargoyles I've ever met?" Amy asked. "Is that in line with this belief?"

"Yes and no," Lohxnahr quipped.

"What's that mean?" Amy replied, annoyance in her voice.

Again, the low voice caused most to be startled. "Yes and no," Zarentil repeated. "Our small stature benefits the secrecy of our mission, for we are more difficult to see with the eyes of the sentries."

"As well as with their minds," Lohxnahr added.

"How's that?" Anders said.

Danielle stepped forward.

"I think I might understand," she began. "Because the sentries guarding Paign and Mrs. Macy serve the hybrid, they would expect visits from their master periodically, right? In other words, they'd expect to *sense* him."

"Of course!" Anders exclaimed. "Brilliant! I see the game now. It's brilliant!"

"Fine, then," Johann grumbled. "Help out an old farmer. How does this all work?"

"Oh! Yes, sir," Anders replied. "It's clever, simple and devious, all at the same time. The sentries would expect to sense in advance a visit from their master, the hybrid."

"Granted, Anders. This even the farmer knows."

"Well," Danielle said, gently, "Zarentil *is* the hybrid."

"Ah! That *is* clever!" Johann cried. "Our Zarentil's arrival will feel like the imposter's. How I would like to join you just to see their surprise."

"It *is* agreed, then," Prohximus said. "The rescue company will comprise of these six: Lohxnahr, Zarentil, Anders, Freida, Bettina and Danielle. Its purpose will be the liberation of Paign Macy and his mother. Its method will be stealth. Its strength will be in surprise. Its success will be in its determination."

"Well, I wish I was determined it was a good idea," Peter groused, "but I don't see a better way." Looking at Amy, he shrugged.

She chewed her bottom lip while gently nodding her head.

Yep. She feels it, too, Peter thought.

Kahrnahrgx stood at an angle to the humans, his arms crossed in an x-pattern, so that his long talons flared past his ears. Lement-Nor stood to the left of his master, his nearly closed eyes revealing nothing…and everything.

"Suffice this, boy," he said, "long have we grown weary of protecting such an unworthy race as yours. You are, all of you, self-possessed, caring only for your own petty concerns and abandoning others to fend for themselves, even those ill equipped to do so."

Turmoil bubbled inside Paign like a pot of overheated porridge. Taken aback, he found that he agreed with many of the arguments Kahrnahrgx posed. How often had he felt abandoned by those purporting to love and care for him? Yet he didn't like being on the same side of any argument with a creature like Kahrnahrgx. *What would that say about me?*

There was also his mother to consider. Paign knew that the life of his mother hung by a gossamer thread. It was imperative that he keep his temper, no matter what. But here, in this temple of dread and darkness, his chest was tight with terror and quickly growing rage.

Kahrnahrgx continued, "Even your own scriptures declare this:

Your love is like the morning mist,
Like the early dew that disappears.

"I know nothing of that, sir," Paign said softly.

"I know otherwise," the gargoyle leader snapped.

Paign swallowed hard and glanced at Lement-Nor. His eyes were wide and glowed red.

"Yes," Paign nodded.

"My trusted lieutenant informs me that you, more than most humans, know deeply what it is like when the love of another disappears like the morning mist."

"Yes, sir."

"So, would you argue with the human poet who declared of your kind:

You have planted wickedness,
You have reaped evil,
You have eaten the fruit of deception.
Because you have depended on your
own strength
and your many warriors,
the roar of battle will rise against your
people,
so that all your fortresses will be devastated?

"I don't know, sir. It seems like this is how it's always been." Paign felt his mother stirring next to him. He hoped she would remain unconscious. Her sanity was fragile enough without waking to the very leader of their enemies.

"Precisely. That is how it has *always* been. And that is why the time for our serving humans must reach its end. Your worthiness for our protection was ever false. You have sown the wind. Now it is time to reap the whirlwind!"

"What are they talking about now?" Freida asked. Bettina sat next to her, patting Tiny on his wide head.

They sat in the same meadow about a hundred meters from the dais where they'd gathered the year earlier, just before launching their assault on the temple of Kahrnahrgx. Freida knew nothing of that event since she was the captive at that time.

A gentle breeze whispered in the trees, and a pleasant aroma filled the warm air.

Bettina had never seen the place before and didn't know what to do with herself. It was deeply comforting to run her slender fingers through the dog's thick coat. Tiny certainly didn't mind.

"Plans for a massive diversionary attack, based on what I overheard," Anders replied.

Danielle squinted as she looked at the assembled gargoyle captains and the four humans gathered with them. Sunlight glinted randomly off the talons of the captain—*Quarastohr, I think*—who was apparently supporting his argument with rapid hand motions.

"Don't they trust us?" she asked.

"Oh, I think they trust us just fine," Anders replied, glancing at Bettina. "They just don't want to be left out of this fight."

"And wouldn't it help our cause by distracting the enemy?" Freida wondered.

"Well, I believe that is exactly their thinking, Freida. How could it not help us, right? Better to have as many of those nasty fellows occupied with defense, with loads of chaos thrown in for good measure, to gum up the works of guarding our friends!"

Bettina opened her mouth, but then closed it again.

Anders leapt up from the rock he was sitting on and deftly pulled his sword out its scabbard in one motion. He proceeded to thrust, jab and parry, working through offensive and defensive moves as he practiced against imaginary foes.

A quiver ran down Danielle's back. Anders's fierceness was quite thrilling to her. His movements were fluid and confident. *And he is fast! Really fast*, she marveled.

"Have you been practicing, Anders?" Danielle asked. "I mean, you were always good with that, as I recall. But look at you! You've improved!"

A sheen of sweat had formed on Anders's face as he went through various offensive and defensive forms.

"Sure have!" he grunted, breathing heavy. "Paign and I mostly, but sometimes with Mr. Skulstad, too…we'd practice a few times a week."

Anders's sword arm flew back and forth, blocking, sweeping, stabbing. The meadow was filled with the sound of the blade cutting through the air.

"He taught us—Freida's dad, I mean—Paign and me, he taught us everything he knew from his military training…"

Sweep. Spin. Sweep. Block. Reverse. Stab.

"…and he knows a lot!"

Slice. Rising block. Sweep. Reverse. Reverse. Ground swing.

"He was—*is*—very good," Anders huffed.

Bettina marveled at the neighbor boy she'd hardly known. *Well, he's certainly grown up!*

Two-fisted block. Spin. Duck. Sweep. Stab.

Freida smiled at Anders. She was proud of what her father's training had accomplished. She'd known about the training, of course, but hadn't watched since the first few lessons, many months ago. *Anders is fast!*

Tiny had sat up minutes earlier to fully enjoy the show. Anja was mesmerized by the sword's motion and sound.

"And Paign is *also* very good…"

Rising block. Downward slash. Swing. Spin. Stab.

"…so, I've gotten very good, too!"

Suddenly, the intensity of his movements increased. Danielle sucked air through her teeth, imagining the number of opponents Anders could be fighting.

Sweep. Slash. Reverse. Block. Block. Stab. Slice. Sweep. Reverse. Upward stab. Hold.

"Turns out I have a knack for this," he spat out, breathing heavily as sweat ran down his face.

"Bravo, Anders!" Freida cried.

"Marvelous!" Bettina said.

"Unbelievable, Anders!" Danielle said breathlessly.

"Well done, lad!" Johann bellowed. "That was some pretty work, I declare. You took my lessons to heart…and then some! You've become a better swordsman than I am, boy."

"Perhaps he was a boy, Johann," Peter quipped, "but what I just witnessed was no boy playing at a game. Before us is a man and a desperately dangerous one, at that!"

"I didn't see you come up, Dad," Danielle said.

"How could you," Peter replied, "when Anders's display was so hypnotic?"

Anders wiped his face off on his sleeve and dipped his head down. He was unaccustomed to this much attention. But a moment later, he stood straight and squared his shoulders.

"Thank you, sir," he said to Peter, his grin quickly widening.

Turning to Johann, he bowed. "You taught us well, sir."

"Ha!" Johann cried, overjoyed. "The student has become the master, Peter. Don't you agree?"

"Well, how could I know that, Johann? I haven't seen you with a sword since last year, and I've never seen you fight Anders."

"Trust me, then, my friend," Johann laughed. "Trust me."

"What about showing us, Daddy?" Freida asked.

"Now, Honey, the boy has just worn himself out, as you can see. It wouldn't be fair," Johann gently mocked.

Anders grinned at his mentor and then reached out with his free hand. *Come on*, it invited.

As Johann slowly removed his sword from its scabbard, Peter backed out of the circle and stepped onto the toes of his wife.

"Oh! Sorry, Hon! Didn't see you had come to join us," he said, his voice rising as he saw a large host had gathered quietly. Not only was Amy there, but so was Heidi, the gargoyle leaders and a great many residents of the Valley of the Ten Pinnacles.

"And you brought all of our friends, I see!" he added.

"Wouldn't want to miss this, would we?" Amy winked at her husband.

"I would not," Uud-Rement growled.

Prohximus nodded.

A murmur of agreement rose from the assembly, as a large circle of observers formed around Anders and Johann.

Protocol dictated that the younger swordsman bow and hold the tip of his sword out and level with the ground. The senior fighter would then tap the outstretched sword with his own and also bow.

Even though his head was bowed towards his elder, Anders watched Johann closely and held his sword firmly by the hilt but loose with his arms. Ready.

Johann stepped forward, stopped, and lifted his sword until its tip was level with Anders's. But, instead of tapping it gently and then bowing, he flicked his sword tip up at an angle, jerking Anders's sword high to his right. At the same time, Johann lunged at Anders with a howl.

Anders leapt to his right and spun, clockwise, so that his sword blow came down hard onto Johann's stabbing thrust. The clang of metal rang out across the meadow, and a collective gasp rose from the audience.

With huge smiles on the faces of the opponents, they went hard at each other, blocking, sweeping, stabbing, circling and slicing. Soon, Johann was also drenched in sweat.

"Nice rhythm they have!" Uud-Rement declared.

"Do you mean their swordsmanship, their footwork or the clashing of their swords?" Quarastohr replied over the din of clanking steel.

"Yes!" Uud-Rement bellowed.

"Good thing they like each other!" Peter shouted at Amy over the growing roar of the crowd.

Sweating freely now, Johann jumped back and pulled off his shirt. He clearly had more power than Anders. Already a tall man and heavily muscled and brawny from his daily farm labor, he was awesome to behold.

"For pity's sake, Ames," Peter said into Amy's ear, "his biceps are nearly as big as my thighs!"

But it didn't matter. Anders was lightning fast, and the joy of battle lit his face. Most of Johann's mighty swings he simply dodged. Those he didn't, he deflected with easy confidence.

A final flurry of clattering swords ended when Johann found himself staring at the tip of Anders's sword, just an inch from his throat.

"Ah, I've been bested, Peter!" Johann roared. "It is as I said earlier, yes? The student has become the master!"

Peter nodded vigorously.

Gently, Johann pushed Anders's sword away from below his chin.

Before he knew it, Anders was crushed in the farmer's bear hug. A few slaps on the back from Johann and Anders found himself short of breath.

"That's a fighter before you, good citizens and guests of the Valley of the Ten Pinnacles!" Johann said as he beamed at Anders. "Indeed, yes!"

"Impressive!" Uud-Rement declared.

"Agreed!" Quarastohr and Prohximus cried out together.

"That was something, don't you think?" Freida said. She and the other girls were freshening up at the lake's edge, not far from where Anders had sparred with Johann. The sun was skidding behind the western edge of the Ten Pinnacles. The most prominent spire, Mount Osberg, split the sun in half.

Danielle finished splashing water on her face before answering, "I'll say! Boy, he's so much faster than he was last year."

"You've seen him fight, then?" Bettina asked softly. She gazed around the valley's high walls, many more than a thousand meters high. As an afterthought, she added, "I just can't get over this place."

"It *is* beautiful, isn't it?" Danielle answered. "And, yes, I have seen Anders fight before. Actually, several times. He was good with a bow then, as well as the sword. Except his sword work is many times better than before, and it's not like he was bad a year ago."

"So, Freida," she continued, chuckling, "have you seen Anders with a bow recently?"

"No," she replied, "but if he's anywhere near as good with the bow as he just proved himself to be with the sword, then I pity his opponents."

"Forgive me," Bettina said, rubbing her forearms, "but do you think Paign is as good as Anders? Do you think he—" She stopped midsentence, her voice cracking.

Danielle quickly put her hands on Bettina's shoulders and felt her quivering.

"No, no…please forgive me, Bettina," she said. "I'm so sorry. Freida and I aren't meaning to make light of the danger that Paign and your mother are in. We're just kind of shocked at how…how skilled Anders is now. He's provided a nice bit of distraction, I guess—and, for me at least, encouragement, especially since he's going with us."

Freida walked over and also put her hand on Bettina's shoulder. "Danielle's right. In the back of my mind, there's always a gnawing, maddening itch—one that I…I…I'm that concerned about your family. I can't begin to put into words just how much…how much…"

Freida folded over with her hands pressed against her face.

Danielle patted Freida on the back, trying to smile. "I think you've expressed perfectly how we all feel, Freida."

At least she assumed so. Danielle figured that her own sense of conflict was similar to the other girls: a largely unpleasant mix of excitement and nervousness about their quest, combined with an overwhelming urgency to do something. *I suppose this is what my dad means when he talks about being stuck between a rock and a hard place.*

As she patted Freida's back and also observed Bettina's faraway look, Danielle felt isolated from the others, alone with the horror of her vision. It was as if what Lohxnahr said about the hybrid—his ability to absorb his prey, changing its very nature into himself—was being done to Paign, but very slowly, methodically. Involuntarily, she shuddered, the fear of it clawing at her heart like a frightened dog scratches at the door, wanting in on a cold, stormy night.

It's one thing to rescue them from the cavern, but how do we rescue Paign from himself?

She took what comfort she could from the company of the other girls.

CHAPTER TWENTY-THREE
COUNSELS

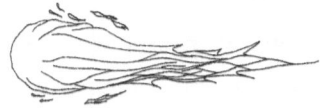

Kahrnahrgx's face betrayed nothing of his thoughts. His senior commanders stood in a half circle around his massive throne. With his thick palms pressed together in front of his face and his elbows planted on his knees, he peered past his talons, standing like sentinels directly before his eyes.

Finally, he turned toward Lement-Nor, stationed below and to his right, nearest the dais.

"Are they prepared, then?"

"Yes, my lord," the hybrid asserted.

"Your assessment?"

"The female's mind hangs by but a thread—"

"And the boy?"

"His transformation requires only the final step."

"He suspects nothing?"

Lement-Nor snorted. "He is nothing but an assemblage of anger, confusion and unruly hormones."

"You answer a question I did not ask," Kahrnahrgx murmured slowly, his eyes flaring like melting flint.

Lement-Nor bowed slightly and tipped his head low.

"No, my lord. He suspects nothing."

"It would be well for you he doesn't."

"Yes, my lord."

Turning to his left, Kahrnahrgx signaled to his palace marshal. The marshal's place was three paces to the left of the throne and one pace back, a deferential position but still near at hand when his master required him.

He stepped forward to the edge of the dais and called out in a clear voice like a trumpet, "The Lord Kahrnahrgx summons General Uu-Descah."

From the rear of the great hall, a mammoth gargoyle stepped forward and moved towards the throne. The general's width nearly matched his height. While not tall in comparison to other accomplished warriors, his massive shoulders spanned almost half again the next strongest fighter. There was an awkwardness to his gait. His shoulders undulated up and down, as his torso swung resolutely back and forth. Where his right foot should have been was lashed a worn leather boot.

Uu-Descah was of the basalt class. His back, chest and left leg revealed columnar lines, while the back of his head and right thigh were marked with the holes and pockmarks common in scoria rock.

Sunlight shone down on the chamber floor, directly in front of the dais, from a tunnel punched through hundreds of feet of solid rock. Uu-Descah stopped in the center of the unfiltered shaft of light. Sunbeams glinted off of his long, twisted horns as he tipped his head in obeisance.

"Your servant, my lord Kahrnahrgx."

"Your assessment, commander."

The general's weight shifted slightly as his left knee bent, allowing him to stand for long periods of time with his remaining foot. "The holding cell is secured. As the humans slept, nine of my finest soldiers stole into their chamber and melted into the walls, completely hidden from the captives. In addition, there is a squad stationed outside the cell, flanking the entry. Thus, the dungeon's interior is well fortified. Further, the dungeon's periphery is guarded by a full host. Should our enemy send a large force against the citadel, they will soon be hard pressed." Though the general spoke normally, his voice was easily heard throughout the acoustically perfect stone hall.

"And of the other matter which we spoke?"

First tipping his head, the ancient soldier stared hard at his commander. "Yes, my lord. It has been arranged."

"Very well. The trap is laid. All contingencies are covered. Let them come. You may go, General Uu-Descah."

As the warrior hobbled back to where he'd been stationed, Kahrnahrgx leaned on his right elbow and scratched his forehead with his shortest talon. A moment later, he propped his chin on his fist. Whether he waited or was thinking was unclear. None of the officers arrayed around the room had reached their command level by being stupid. If any felt the need for haste, they did not show it.

Long after the general's motion stopped, Kahrnahrgx surveyed the group, as if conducting his own assessment of each soldier's readiness and commitment. For several minutes, only his head and eyes moved as he scanned his commanders.

Abruptly, he stood up and leapt to the floor, his wings flaring out, landing within five paces of the first row. Dust and grit blew into those nearest him.

"This must be done!" he growled. "We *will* be vindicated!"

"Vindicate!" the commanders shouted back.

"We *will* conquer our foes."

"Conquer!"

"We *will* prove right our claim!"

"Prove!"

"We *will* vanquish our foes!"

"Vanquish!"

"It must be done! These humans are but bait for the girl they call the Chosen One. Through her, we will mete out our revenge!"

"Revenge!" They roared back.

"We *will* defeat them!"

"Defeat!"

"We *will* rule!"

"Rule! Rule!"

"We will conquer those who stand in our way, whoever they be!"

"Conquer! Conquer!"

"We WILL conquer!"

"CONQUER! CONQUER! CONQUER!"

The tumult was deafening within the confines of the stone chamber. Several thin stalactites cracked and fell, exploding across the floor of the hall. In the exultant din of his commanders' response, Kahrnahrgx did not notice his hybrid's smirk.

Kahrnahrgx lifted his right hand, palm out, with his talons pointed at the roof.

The captains, commanders and generals immediately became still. It took a moment for the echoes of their chant to recede.

As Kahrnahrgx lowered his hand, the full complement of fighters saw a wicked grin spread across their lord's face.

In a low growl, he said, "Yes, we *will* conquer. We *will* vanquish our foes. We *will* have our revenge. And we *will* rule." With each declaration, the assenting roar increased in volume.

Kahrnahrgx held up his hand again for silence. Again, the hall echoed angrily.

Turning on his heels, Kahrnahrgx walked slowly to his left, then spun around and walked right. With his head lowered as he paced, he bellowed, "But it is not enough for us to pass the time—like servants waiting for the return of their master—plotting our revenge."

An angry murmuring rippled across the assembly of soldiers.

"It is not enough for us to develop our stratagems, arguing the merits of troop placements, while lingering like an old woman whose tea grows chill while she daydreams."

The murmuring grew louder.

"It is not enough for us to dawdle within this fortress—as a feeble old man, tottering around his cottage as his life slowly ebbs away."

Many now grumbled loudly, while some shouted defiantly.

"It is *not enough* for us to slumber and sleep—contented like an infant suckling at her mother's breast—while our enemy makes plans for our demise!"

"Not enough!" the company roared.

"It is *not enough* for us to wait...to linger...to slumber. It is time for us to attack!"

"Attack!"

"Yes, attack!"

"ATTACK!"

When Kahrnahrgx's pacing brought him to the center of the hall again, he abruptly wheeled to a stop. His wings unfurled high and wide and he leaned forward, his eyes blazing red.

"We *will* surprise and dismay our enemy!" he bellowed.

"Dismay!"

"We *will* launch sorties against multiple targets!"

"Launch!"

"The time has come for us to take the fight to the humans…"

"LAUNCH!"

"…especially those humans who have collaborated with our enemies!"

"LAUNCH!"

Even before the echoes had died, Kahrnahrgx snarled, "Each of you was given orders before you entered the chamber. You know your missions. Go now! Make your final preparations. We are about to make history—a new history—a *better* history! In bringing our battle to the very doorsteps of human collaborators, we will draw out our enemy's forces—spreading them thin, while delivering an important lesson to the humans they will not soon forget!"

"LAUNCH!"

"Go now! Our attack will commence tomorrow at the zenith of the sun."

"LAUNCH!" still reverberated throughout the hall as the commanders with troops stationed nearby walked swiftly out of the throne room. Many other commanders immediately parted away. Several plumes of dust and grit slowly twisted back down to the floor.

As he strode out of his hall, Kahrnahrgx motioned for his marshal to join him. In a fluid motion, the marshal flew off the dais and alighted on the narrow surface of the stone bridge next to his master, matching his pace.

"Yes, my lord?"

"I will see him in a quarter hour. Make the arrangements."

"The hybrid, lord?" *What is he so agitated about? The council was a great success, was it not?* the marshal puzzled.

"No, fool! The other."

"Yes, my lord. It will be done," the marshal replied, before stepping off the bridge and plunging into the vast abyss below.

Had Kahrnahrgx turned back from whence he came, he would have observed his hybrid step out from the massive stone column he'd melted into during the final moments of his master's speech. Kahrnahrgx would have seen a cloaked figure, shrouded in a shimmering robe with a long hood, step out of the shadows.

"A rousing speech," a deep voice rumbled from under the hood.

"It is necessary for the simpletons he commands," Lement-Nor scoffed.

"It is unwise to minimize the power of Kahrnahrgx."

"Yes, Preceptor," Lement-Nor replied, bowing low.

"So, he suspects nothing?"

Having just been reproached for his arrogance, Lement-Nor paused to reconsider his planned retort.

"No," he said, demurely. "He suspects nothing, my master."

Danielle sat bolt upright, her head pounding to the same rhythm as her heart. Moaning softly, she rolled onto her knees. In the cool predawn air, she wrapped her blanket around her shoulders as a cloak against the chill. Most of the silver light falling on the meadow came from thousands of stars hanging low over the valley, with some scarce help from a fingernail moon.

"You, too?" came a girl's whisper.

Danielle turned and saw Bettina also wrapped in her blanket, leaning against an oak tree trunk with Anja lying at her feet.

"Yes. Bad dream?" she whispered back.

Bettina nodded twice as her right knee bobbed. She was petting Anja with an almost manic fidget.

"Would you like to talk about it?" Danielle asked softly.

Again, Bettina's head nodded twice.

"Should we walk? We don't need to wake the others."

Anders, Freida and Tiny slept soundly in the stillness of the night.

Several sentries perched high up the walls observed the girls walking, hand in hand, with a huge dog by their side. The girls wandered slowly across the wide meadow, stopped before the war council's dais, turned and sat on its edge.

For several minutes, neither girl spoke. The starlight shimmered on the surface of the lake where the mists didn't cover the water. A gentle breeze stole through the treetops, fluttering the dappled maple leaves into a dance of nocturnal light and shadow. Both girls pulled their blankets snug and huddled closer together. With a hand signal that Anja understood well, the dog followed her mistress's wish and lay down on the girls' feet. The pungence of the damp grass blended with the faint scent of columbine, mountain laurel and larkspur.

"This place is harsh and hard at night," Bettina said.

"Do you think so?" Danielle replied. "I think it's pretty tonight, in spite of my dream."

Bettina said nothing for a moment, but Danielle noticed her knee begin bobbing again. "Yes, I suppose that is true," she whispered.

"Do you want to talk about it?" Danielle asked.

"It is…difficult."

"I understand. There's no rush. And we're safe here."

"Is there no rush?" Bettina replied, a shrillness edging into her speech.

"Tell me, Bettina. Get it out." Danielle felt strange speaking to an older girl this way. "What is your dream about?"

"Death," came the nearly inaudible reply. "It's about death."

Danielle smiled wanly, hoping to look encouraging. She patted Bettina's hand.

After waiting a moment to see if Bettina was going to share, Danielle said, "Well, how about I start then? Here's the thing…my dream was about death, too."

She paused, then continued, "I mean, it seems like *all* of my dreams have been about that for ages. But this one tonight was different. Really different. Because the other dreams—*the regular ones*, so to speak—are about us…about Mom, or Dad, or me, even Anja, being chased by some awful creature. Being attacked. Fighting for our lives."

As Danielle's voice drifted off, Bettina turned and gawked, plainly dismayed by what she'd heard.

"I had no idea, Danielle," Bettina said in a hushed voice. "How terrible. How simply terrible for you."

Hearing her name, Danielle glanced again at Bettina.

"Hm," she replied. "Yeah…yes, in fact, it is terrible. Quite terrible, really. But that's not what I wanted to share with you, as long as we're discussing such an awful topic."

Bettina nodded.

"The thing about my dream tonight, Bettina, was that it wasn't about us. We weren't the ones being chased. We weren't the ones being attacked. It was—"

"Your friends!" Bettina cried. "Friends of your family!"

Danielle gasped, her heart pounding. "Oh no! This is the dream you had, too?"

Bettina's eyes welled up immediately.

"Troubling this is," Lohxnahr murmured, as he stepped out from the darkness of the forest that abutted the dais.

Both girls recoiled at the sound of the rasping voice.

Anja looked up at her mistress, puzzled. *You did not see the little ones?*

"More treachery this may foreshadow," Lohxnahr added.

"My goodness, Lohxnahr!" Danielle cried, laying her hand across the nape of her neck. "You've nearly given us a heart attack! How long have you been there?"

"Harm we mean not," he replied. "Alone you two should not be, even here in this valley."

A rustling in the brush soon revealed Zarentil.

"But aren't we protected here, Lohxnahr?" Danielle said.

"Of a certainty, yes," he replied.

"And no," Zarentil added.

"We don't understand," Danielle said.

"The valley provides physical protection and safety, such as we have for its inhabitants, as well as its guests," Zarentil murmured. "Yet in the dark hours, one can be at risk and threat not from outside."

"From inside, you mean?" Danielle asked.

"Indeed," Lohxnahr replied.

"So, you mean our dreams can put us at risk?" she continued.

"Yes," Zarentil responded.

"But aren't they just dreams? Even if they are bad ones?"

"Child, do they feel like just dreams?"

"Well, no, they feel real," Danielle whispered. "Too real."

"Indeed," Lohxnahr repeated, his smile lit silver by the night sky.

Bettina's knee began bouncing again. "Are they real then, our dreams? Are they...visions?"

"This we know not," Lohxnahr replied lightly. "This is a matter of utmost concern, for which a solution we must in haste create. Yet, that is not why we are here with you."

Danielle reached out and clutched Lohxnahr's hands from the sides, avoiding his talons. "Why then?"

"The answer you have provided, dear one. Your dreams feel real. In so doing, your perspective in the day may be influenced from the night. Agitated feelings born of the fevered darkness may direct the actions during the light of day. The feelings become more forceful than the dream that birthed them."

"Okay, that makes sense," Danielle replied softly. "Sort of. Sometimes, I've had a bad dream leave me in a bad mood pretty much all day."

"Even when the dream is forgotten," Zarentil said.

"Even when the dream is false or broken," Lohxnahr added.

"Broken?" the girls asked in unison.

"Humans often dream in broken shapes," Lohxnahr replied. "Concerns of the day grow into fears in the night. Simple problems transform into frightening evils. Fragments of fading dreams mutate into inhibiting insecurities."

"Which can then become concerns of the day—" Danielle began.

"The next day?" Bettina interrupted.

"Quite so!" Lohxnahr chirped.

"And you're here to keep that from happening?" Danielle asked.

"We already have!" Lohxnahr cried.

"Okay, but you said something about treachery," Danielle said, stroking Anja's head.

Anja's tail added a gentle swishing to the sound of fluttering leaves.

Immediately, Lohxnahr grew serious. "It is our fear the enemy has great mischief afoot, or soon will. We have felt it in our dreams."

"Your dreams?" Bettina asked, incredulous. "Gargoyles *dream*?"

"Absolutely!" Lohxnahr said.

"So, you're here to make sure we're safe from our dreams becoming more powerful than they should be—" Danielle began.

"And to keep ours from the same fate," Zarentil interjected.

"We need each other," Lohxnahr finished. "Broken dreams are made whole with insight from another. Conclusions chosen in twilight are most often void of depth and, thus, shapeless. Phantoms swirl around them. And when is a phantom not frightful?"

Danielle smiled broadly in spite of herself. "Well, with you all being here, I think I could face any phantoms. In fact, a whole mess of them!"

"Let us then speak of our dreams and bring them into submission," Lohxnahr beamed.

Johann was not surprised to see that Peter and Amy were already rising. He and Heidi had learned the year before enough about the lives of "university professors" to know that they were early risers. Something about "gaining an hour or two" for grading papers or preparing for class.

"Hi, hi, my friend," he said, walking over to sit with Peter, who was perched on the edge of their eyrie.

"Good morning, Johann!" Peter replied cheerfully. He tipped his head quickly to one side, indicating he meant over the edge of the eyrie. "Take a look."

Johann stood at the edge of the massive natural stone shelf they'd sheltered on during the night. Peering down, he scanned the floor of the valley.

"Well!" he exclaimed. "How about that! Did you ever expect to see such a thing as that?"

"As what?" Amy asked, sitting up next to Peter.

"See for yourself, Hon," Peter said softly to his wife, his eyes twinkling.

Amy wormed out from under her blanket and crawled to the edge of the shelf.

"Well, isn't that sweet?" she murmured.

Almost directly below their high perch was the War Council's dais. It was there the girls had walked in the smallest hours of the night. Where the dais bumped up against the edge of the forest, Danielle and Bettina were sleeping. Anja lay between the girls for warmth, her paws beneath her head like a sphinx. Danielle's head rested in Lohxnahr's lap, while Bettina's was nestled in Zarentil's.

Paign hadn't slept at all, near as he could tell. Dead tired, he was too preoccupied even to yawn. There were few clues to go on as to when night came to the cavern, but he'd determined that, of the three shifts, one group of guards was routinely sleepier than the others. That was the shift on duty now, and they'd been on duty for many hours.

Twice during the night, a great rumbling had reverberated through their cell. Although not particularly loud where they were, Paign judged that whatever made the thick walls of stone shake from sound must have been very loud, indeed. It was a confused and muddy sound, like hearing a rockslide tumbling down Ruar's Ridge back home, except with his pillow on top of his head. But Paign's intuition told him that the protest hadn't come from a rockslide.

"It sounded more like the bellowing of an angry mob," he whispered.

"What, dear?" his mother asked.

"Oh, nothing, mother," he smiled reassuringly.

Stroking her hair as her head rested in his lap, Paign wondered how much time she had left. With little water and even less food, her strength was waning. But then, so was his. It pierced him, her presence here. It was so wrong that she would be held captive and suffer so.

Soon, his mother was breathing evenly again. Paign gently held her head steady under his palm and shimmied out from under her. He lay his shirt beneath her head as a pillow. It was warm enough in their cell that all he'd needed was his undershirt. The temperature had not varied since they'd arrived. *Which was...when? Days ago? Or is it weeks now?*

He got up and began pacing. One of their guards peered around the open doorway. Paign took no notice of him.

He was tired. It was physically exhausting, of course, to be trapped in a cell with next to nothing to eat and drink. But it was also boring with only one's thoughts to pass the time. And Paign was tired of his thoughts. He was tired of thinking about Danielle's dismay at seeing him. He was tired of wondering what that look on her face meant. In some ways, he was even tired of being angry. *What's wrong with me?*

"Nothing!" he hissed.

Gudrun stirred and moaned.

Paign swore under his breath and abruptly stopped pacing. When he saw her body relax, he went back to pacing the length of their cell.

"Nothing," he repeated, this time in a whisper accompanied with a shrug.

Sighing, Paign muttered softly, "You've been a fool, Paign Macy. A fool. Anders was never against you! He was trying to tell you the truth, you idiot. What chance—really—was there of seeing Danielle again? Next to none...next to none. There could be no way to guess that she'd come back."

Paign reached the end of the room and stopped inches from the wall.

"Why *did* she come back? She was there at the cabin. She was with Lohxnahr, after all..."

Paign's forehead touched the wall as he sucked air through his teeth. Placing his palms against the harsh granite, he buckled his knees and slid his hands down until he was in a squatted ball, his forehead again touching the rock.

His body was compressed so tightly he could hardly breathe. But Paign didn't care. As the recognition of why Danielle was at the cabin finally crashed through his mind, Paign knew that, had his mother not been held captive with him, he would have made a run at the guards, wishing to end his misery.

Tipping onto his left side, Paign thudded onto the hard floor while holding his knees tightly against his chest.

"She came for me!" he whimpered. "She came for me. She risked her life *for* me. I brought this on."

With only the slight sound of scraping grit as Paign's body convulsed with racking sobs, the stone beneath his head darkened from the dripping flow of tears.

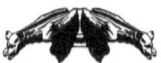

The sun was nearing its zenith when Prohximus dismissed the group for lunch. Due to the meager sleep that Danielle and Bettina had managed during the night, they yawned through much of the proceedings that they, inadvertently, were responsible for.

Lohxnahr had alerted the High Council even before the sun had risen over the horizon. Soon, he and Zarentil were explaining to the commanders—along with a bleary-eyed cast of humans and canines—their growing apprehension that Kahrnahrgx and his followers were soon to launch, or already had, a campaign against the friends and countrymen of the humans who had defied him the year before.

"A campaign of retribution?" Kimar had asked in disbelief. "He's a better field commander than that!"

"Nevertheless, Kimar," Lohxnahr said, bowing, "there is but one conclusion to draw from the night terrors of the young women here. We believe them to be premonitions."

"Is there actual evidence upon which to base your conclusions?" Amy asked quietly, stepping back.

"Mom? What do you mean? This isn't something we'd make up."

Amy's face grew pale as she stared at Lohxnahr, apparently not hearing Danielle.

"Mom?"

"Hm?" Amy murmured, turning to look at her daughter. There was a dreamy look in her eyes.

"What is it, Mom?"

"We…we never stopped to wonder why the beast took Paign and Gudrun to the Hudsons' cabin…we never stopped…the Hudsons…"

"Oh, God preserve us!" Peter cried. "She's right! How did the hybrid know about the Hudsons' cabin without first knowing about the Hudsons?"

Striding quickly over to his daughter, Peter laid his hands on her shoulders. "Is this what you saw in your dreams, Dani? The Hudsons? In danger?"

She nodded.

"Oi! Well, then, Bettina," Johann blurted, "I fear your dream…vision…premonition—whatever we call it—is about your uncle and aunt. Are they in danger, as well?"

Bettina slowly shook her head.

Puzzled, Johann looked at Heidi.

"All right, dear," Heidi said softly. "If not your relatives, then who is it that your dream warns about? Is it a neighbor back home?"

Bettina nodded as tears welled up and flowed over the dark circles under her eyes.

"Yes…my dream is of…you."

Johann blinked and rubbed his hand against his hair vigorously.

"But we're not in any danger. We're here!" he said.

"Your farm is not," Bettina replied.

"I say again to the Council, this is not something my brother would do! Tactically, it is madness. He would have his forces assembled for greatest advantage, not spread them across space and time."

Kimar's argument didn't get far. The Council needed to gain a deeper understanding of whether the girls' dreams were nothing more complicated than unpleasant bedtime imaginings or were, in fact, premonitions of terror.

And the Council's need was not nearly as strong as the humans'. Johann and Peter were both wrought with the impulse for action. Standing around and discussing the merits of going or not going, or whether or not Kahrnahrgx would do such and such, exasperated both men.

"Can we not implore a simple soldier to help us part home?" Johann cried. "Can we pay them something to help us?"

"What would they need with our money?" Heidi countered, edgy, her face flushed.

"I've seen nothing that would even hint that gargoyles have any type of what we would call commerce between themselves, so throwing money around won't help," Peter stated flatly.

Fueled by the extreme worry the adults struggled with, their conversation continued, with many words and little listening.

Anders waved Danielle and Bettina over to a small stand of trees thrusting out from the main forest like an archipelago. The girls' departure, along with Anja and Tiny, went unnoticed by the agitated parents.

"First off, I just want to say how sorry I am that both of you've had these really horrible dreams," Anders began, speaking quickly. "They sound awful, and it's plain to see that they've robbed you of a decent night's sleep for too long."

"Second, Freida and I just can't help believing this isn't about retribution. In other words, I agree with Kimar's position. But what's really strange is that, if it isn't about vengeance, what is it about? The next logical choice would be that it's a trap, right? Get us back home to our respective times and places, under duress, so we're not careful enough and we get caught. But that doesn't make sense to me, either."

"Why not?" Danielle asked as her stomach lurched.

"He already has an elaborate trap set. We've already spent a lot of time problem solving how to rescue Paign and his mother—a lot of time because it's a really complicated mission. Why set these other traps? It's like setting out mousetraps after you've dug out a huge hole in the ground and disguised it with sticks and leaves. It just doesn't make sense."

"So, what do you think might be going on?" Danielle replied.

"Well," Freida said, glancing at Anders and then across the meadow at the group of parents, where Kimar and Ercen had joined the group, "it's as if someone else is involved."

"Someone is working against Kahrnahrgx," Anders added.

"But that's crazy!" Danielle exclaimed. "Who would do—"

She was cut off by the call of her father. They were being summoned to join the others.

"There is no question we go!" Johann demanded, the knuckles on his fists a pale white. "I must see to my farm. There is no question."

Quarastohr tipped his head slightly. "We understand your wish to visit your homeland, but deem it unwise."

"Unwise or not, we must go," Heidi replied. "Will not any of you help us?"

Conomorg and Ita-Mudak stepped forward. "We would go with you."

"You are free to determine your own fates," Prohximus said to the two gargoyles. "But your strength is needed for our diversionary assault. Your departure now is ill considered."

"And ill advised," Quarastohr added.

Uud-Rement shifted his weight, which caused a screech when his heel-talons skidded on the marble surface. "Nevertheless, they will go to the farm," he stated. "It is the foremost duty we have to protect those entrusted to us." With a wink, he added, "Therefore, I will accompany them. Given their youth and inexperience, they might need looking after."

His forehead wrinkled and after a moment, Quarastohr said, "As you wish, old friend."

"Then it is decided," Prohximus declared. "With misgivings expressed, I release you to investigate the truth of the nocturnal vision."

"Hey, what about us?" Peter cried. "We *must* check on our friends! Who will get us there?"

"We will," Kimar and Ercen said together, stepping forward.

"I want to go, too," Danielle said.

"That cannot be, child," Lohxnahr rasped. "You and Bettina must remain behind, for you have your own hazard to engage in very soon."

"Well, *that's* not a comforting statement, Lohxnahr!" Amy snapped.

"Agreed, Ames, but it appears we have only crummy options to pick from," Peter replied, shaking his head.

"But it's *our* dreams that have caused all this upset," Danielle protested.

"Even more reason you must not go," Zarentil rumbled.

Danielle's mouth opened and then closed a moment later.

Bettina said nothing, her brow furrowed deep, as she glanced back and forth at who was speaking.

"Look, Dani, we need to go. You need to stay," Peter continued.

She nodded, none too happy.

"Go then with all haste. The nighttime riddles vex and distract," Lohxnahr said cheerfully. "Perhaps they need to remain in the slumber from whence born they were. But this we cannot know until with your eyes confirmed they are."

Danielle winced as Bettina grabbed her hand tightly. With the other, she reached out to Freida, who already patted Tiny's head with her free hand. Anders stood next to Tiny. Anja sat on her haunches directly before Peter and Amy, whimpering.

Amy squatted down on her knees so she could be at eye level with the dog.

"It will be okay, girl," she said comfortingly.

I need to go with you!

"That's a good Anja!"

Anja growled and barked, *I need to go with you!*

Amy glanced at Peter.

Anja barked again.

"Uh, this is weird," Peter mumbled.

Anja barked a third time and dropped her head down as she splayed out her front paws.

"Dani?"

"I think she needs to go with you, Dad," she answered.

"Very well," Conomorg said.

All it took was a slight bending of the waist from Ercen, and Anja's rear legs started pumping furiously, slipping wildly on the slick marble of the dais. When she finally got traction, she bounded over to her and lurched into the gargoyle's arms. The force of the dog's weight rocked Ercen back on her heels.

"All right, then!" Peter exclaimed. "I guess she does need to go along."

"Good thing she jumped into Ercen's arms," Amy quipped, "because it would have ended badly had she done that to you."

Peter chuckled, "True enough."

"Indeed, enough," Johann snapped. "Let us go at once."

In a moment, Freida's parents parted away with Conomorg and Ita-Mudak.

Danielle mouthed "I love you" to her parents, as they parted away with Kimar and her beloved dog held by Ercen.

CHAPTER TWENTY-FOUR

ASSAULT

Johann's first thought was that his gargoyle companions had mis-parted them into hell. Smoke and ash choked him. He heard Heidi hacking next to him against the blackened, putrid air. Through the shredding gloom, he could see that four of his eight recently harvested hay mounds were fully engulfed with flames sprouting twenty meters into what otherwise would have been a brilliant blue sky.

The hair on the back of his neck prickled from heat, even though he was facing the burning hay. Instinctively, he threw himself into Heidi, forcing both into the field's leftover stubble, just as a fireball roared over their heads and crashed into the fifth hay mound.

Rolling onto their knees to assess what they were up against, the Skulstads' eyes glittered from the licking flames nearly surrounding them.

"Oh, Johann!" Heidi cried.

Johann had already counted seven gargoyles in his field, not including Conomorg and Ita-Mudak, who were hotly pursued in close combat.

"No, this way!" Heidi shouted, turning her husband's head towards their farmhouse.

Four more gargoyles lay crumpled near Uud-Rement. The intense flurry of movement around the old warrior made it impossible to precisely count his remaining opponents, but Johann put the number at five.

"What do we do?" Heidi cried, choking on the fumes.

"Whatever we can!" Johann bellowed. Grabbing his wife by the shoulders, he pushed her up onto her feet and ran toward the barn. So far, it was intact and not the focus of any attacking gargoyle.

He led them on a weaving course, maximizing the smoke to obscure their movement. This tactic also obscured what was happening from them.

When they emerged from the cover of the nearest burning pile, Johann hastily scanned the field, calculating their risks and what course to take. So far, their enemies hadn't seemed to be interested in them.

While sprinting to the next mound, Heidi tripped and fell hard. Still, they went unnoticed. Johann wondered how long their good fortune would hold. He'd been in battle before and knew things could change at any moment, for good or ill.

They ran on, their lungs burning from the exertion as much as from the poisonous air.

As they cleared the final burning hay mound, one of the attacking gargoyles suddenly emerged from the smoke and flew over their heads.

"Oi!" Johann cried, ducking low. "Watch out, Heidi!"

Turning to face this threat, Johann gasped. When the attacker tumbled into the field, it broke in two, its lower half severed from the torso above.

"One less, thanks to Uud-Rement!" he bellowed, grabbing Heidi again.

Both struggled to run quickly across the loose furrows. The sounds of shouting gargoyles and exploding fireballs continued to fill the toxic air.

Bursting through the barn's tall double door, Johann ran to his wall of hand tools. Grabbing a wide pitchfork, he tossed it to Heidi, handle first. He owned numerous scythes for harvesting the grain crops. Their curved blades were nearly as long as a sword and easily mowed down grass and wheat like a scissor slices through paper. Seizing the biggest scythe, he ran back to the still-open door. He didn't want to be caught inside the stout, wooden structure with fireball-wielding foes on his property.

Stopping at the doorway, each leaned against the inside of the frame and furtively peered around.

Horror met their gaze.

To the right of the barn, Conomorg and Ita-Mudak remained in pitched battle with three opponents. Immediately, Johann saw that both were injured.

"I'm going to help them, Heidi!" he said into her ear. "I love you. Keep your head down," he added, before sprinting towards their friends.

As Johann neared them, it became all too clear that Ita-Mudak was terribly wounded. But it was obvious he'd given much worse than he'd got; he was actually standing on a mound of his foes.

Conomorg was locked in a battle with a swarthy-colored beast, from a class that Johann had not seen before. It was very thick, with wide shoulders and huge forearms. Conomorg kept his opponent's left arm gripped fiercely in his right hand, making it difficult to threaten his foe with much harm, since Conomorg was right-handed. Each would lunge at the other, with the defender twisting away as far as their locked arms would allow. Both showed multiple lacerations, but none appeared to be life threatening.

At the speed he was running, Johann knew he had only moments before he'd be in the thick of the fight. He scanned back to Ita-Mudak, assessing where his first blow needed to land. As Conomorg's fight shifted away from blocking the view of Ita-Mudak, Johann had his answer.

Ita-Mudak's left arm was unmoving, except for swinging lifelessly whenever he shifted his weight, which was often, as he defended against two attackers.

No time to waste! One-armed, against two foes...no time! Ah, he's got one of them! Johann charged forward.

Beginning his swing two paces before he reached the nearest of Ita-Mudak's combatants, Johann used his momentum and weight to maximize the speed and impact force of the long-bladed scythe.

Jumping as high as he could manage, so that the blade would hit the midsection of the beast closest to him, Johann roared defiantly. Ita-Mudak's attacker twisted his head over in dismay, just in time to see the blade slice through his waist. Because the beast was also elevated, standing on his dead comrades to be at the same height as Ita-Mudak, Johann's scythe was now head-high against Conomorg's assailant.

Twisting hard in the air, Johann continued the blade's deadly arc, lopping off the right hand of the remaining beast. In a final deft maneuver, Johann tucked his head into his chest and tossed the scythe away to his left, before tumbling into the field's dry soil. There was no good way to fall to the ground holding onto a blade half as long as he was.

As he rolled immediately back onto his knees, he seized the scythe and leaped up to reengage. There was no need. Conomorg's left-hand talons were still embedded in his foe's throat. With his right foot, Conomorg simultaneously shoved his toe-talons into the enemy's chest and shoved him backwards, pulling out all the talons at the same time.

Feeling a sudden surge of triumph, Johann was about to exult in their success. The war cry stuck in his throat when he heard the scream of his wife.

"Heidi!" he roared, shocked at what he saw. "What are you doing?"

Heidi Skulstad was no wallflower, introverted farmer's wife. It is what attracted Johann to her in the first place. Generous and kind to a fault, she was also assertive and forthright. She was confident and held her own with all the merchants they interacted with for their farm. As he'd always said of her, "She's as beautiful on the outside as she is on the inside." Naturally brave, she could sometimes be almost as rash as her husband. This was one of those times.

"I should have known better than to leave her to keep her head down! What was I thinking? Svarte!" he yelled, sprinting towards his house, unaware whether his gargoyle friends were coming to assist.

Heidi was jumping awkwardly as the squat gargoyle swung wildly at her with both hands. What separated them was the length of the pitchfork Johann had given her minutes earlier. The long tines glinted yellow from nearby flames behind the gargoyle's upper chest. She'd pierced him through and now held him at bay with the length of the fork's handle, waiting for him to fall. But the creature wasn't going down.

Again, Johann dashed towards the action while assessing the situation. Uud-Rement lay sprawled on the flowerbed next to the quaint farmhouse. *That doesn't look good.* The farmer didn't expect any reinforcement from Ita-Mudak, either. So, unless Conomorg proved combat functional—and joined him in the next few seconds—Johann was on his own to defend his wife.

But, unlike Johann's last opponent, whose back was to the farmer during the battle, this gargoyle could see him charging like a bull. An unworldly snarl erupted from the beast. Seeing the futility of reaching Heidi, with his right hand he swung his talons through the handle of the pitchfork, while simultaneously swinging at her with his left. She leapt back holding a much shorter handle with a ragged, sharp point.

The gargoyle spun to his right, reaching for the handle's stub. In a fluid motion that defied the pain it must have inflicted, he yanked out the broken fork and hurled it at Johann, tines first.

Johann instinctively swung the scythe's handle outward to block the wicked projectile, hoping he could stop it and that its handle wouldn't break in half. Heidi's broken fork slammed into the scythe's handle with such force that it splintered down the middle and knocked Johann off into the air. His feet flew out in front of him, and he landed hard on his back, nearly knocking the wind out of him.

Realizing the farmer was a greater threat than his wife, the gargoyle abandoned her and attacked Johann while he was still sprawled in the dirt.

As the creature leapt at him, Johann bellowed and rolled hard to his right, just as the creature's feet crashed down, talons first, where he'd just been lying. He knew the creature would be on him in a moment and there'd be no time to get back on his feet. *Whatever I'm going to do, it better be fast!* Seizing the scythe with his left hand, he held the handle's end in the dirt and pivoted the blade upward in an arc.

Unaware the curved, sharp blade—nearly a meter long—was already in motion with nearly the same force as the farmer could have mustered against a stand of wheat, the swarthy foe turned to kill Johann.

Whuck.

The sneer still on his face, the gargoyle's eyes looked down towards his chest. Slowly, the sneer faded and was replaced by dismay. Yet, the beast stood.

Johann gawked in disbelief. "Come now, foul spawn!" he cried. "Go down! For pity's sake, go down!"

Instead, the creature stared at Johann, and his eyes flashed a deeper red glow than before.

Now, Johann was the one dismayed.

His enemy, even wounded as he was, clasped the scythe where the blade curved up and into the handle and began pushing it away. A faint creaking came from his chest as the metal scraped against the beast's torso.

Johann threw his weight against the handle again, but to no avail. Even as the blade came further out of the beast's chest, Johann rolled onto his knees while still clutching the handle.

You know, he's sure to do the same to this implement what he did to Heidi's. Slice the handle in half and then throw the scythe's blade at me, while I attempt to retreat. This doesn't look good.

Impulsively, Johann wrapped his knees around the handle's tip and kept it in the dirt. At the same time, he grabbed the handle with both hands and threw his weight against it, plunging it back into the beast. It howled in pain and frustration.

Furious at Johann, the creature simply stepped back, still howling. The blade came free and hovered in midair, still propped up by Johann.

Clearly wounded, the creature's movements were slower. But it was plain what his intent was.

Johann reared back onto his feet, clutching the scythe, surprised he still had a useful weapon. Then, he realized that the gargoyle's movement wasn't that of hand-to-hand combat.

"Oh, blast!" Johann cried. "After all this, a fireball?"

Knowing he couldn't outrun such a weapon and that trying to dodge it at this close range was pointless, Johann charged at his foe and shouted, "Well, at least the farm will be here even if I'm not!"

But as Johann hurled himself at the beast, confident that his final blow would kill it even if he was killed in the blast, he saw the fireball's aim wasn't at him, after all. And it was aimed too high.

He's misfired!

There was no time to gloat. Johann felt the blade connect again with his foe just before he crashed into it. A crack more felt than heard announced to Johann that the impact with the squat gargoyle's head had just dislocated his own shoulder. Tumbling over the beast, Johann landed hard in the dirt onto his left hip.

In a fog of pain, Johann looked up at his enemy. Given its labored movement, he was sure it was finally mortally wounded. But it was still coming at him.

Weaponless and broken, Johann had nothing left. Staring at blue sky above the smoky haze, he yelled, "Well, at least you're done, you vile spawn! Ha! Even if you have me in the end."

Whuck.

"Not this day, husband!" Heidi cried. "There will be no end for you, not this day!"

Following the sound of her voice, Johann looked up at the gargoyle again.

"I don't recall you wearing that accoutrement before, beast! It becomes you…or, rather, unbecomes you!"

The remainder of Heidi's pitchfork handle skewered the gargoyle's neck, left to right.

Even as the gargoyle tipped forward and fell directly in front of Johann's prostrate body, it no longer blocked what Johann hadn't yet seen.

The farmhouse was on fire. His dead foe hadn't misfired, after all.

"It is time," Zarentil announced.

Danielle mindlessly picked at a pimple on her neck. Pacing back and forth helped dissipate only some of her tension. Pain jolted through her when she picked a little too hard.

"Ouch!"

"Eh, what's that?" Anders murmured a moment later, slowly turning to look at her. "Is something wrong?" he added, as he struggled to focus his attention.

"No, nothing," Danielle said, looking quickly at her finger and then wiping the blood off on her pants.

"When will we know something?" Freida asked, agitated.

Bettina said nothing. She furtively glanced back and forth.

"It is not for us to know before parting," Lohxnahr rasped.

"You mean we're not going to know before we launch our rescue mission?" Anders cried. "We won't know?"

"No, unless soon they return."

"But why, Lohxnahr?" Danielle said, her voice catching. "This is so important to all of us."

"Indeed, it is, child," Lohxnahr replied, smiling wide.

"Yet, there are times when even our greatest needs are left wanting," Zarentil rumbled. "There are times when others' needs must come before our own."

Quickly, tears welled up in Danielle's eyes and ran down her face. "But...I need to know...my parents..."

"And mine," Freida choked out.

"And mine," Bettina whispered.

Everyone knew she meant her mother and brother, so none bothered to correct a simple error in grammar. It didn't matter. What did matter was that all three girls had their most important family members at great risk, and none of them knew their status. Each was finding it terribly difficult to concentrate on anything, let alone something so important as engaging in a desperate rescue mission.

Zarentil stepped over and stopped in front of Bettina. Motioning with his hands, he signaled her to sit before him, which she did.

"Child, it is time for you to use your heart's eye. You can assist in guiding us to your mother, your brother. Place your hands in mine."

Bettina carefully placed her hands in his palms. Then he gently wrapped his long thumbs around her delicate hands.

Danielle was struck by the queer image. It was like Bettina's hands were wrapped in steak knives.

"Join you, I would," Lohxnahr hummed.

When Zarentil nodded, Lohxnahr placed his hands on Bettina's shoulders.

"Follow me," Zarentil said, looking intently into Bettina's eyes.

For Danielle, Freida and Anders, there wasn't much to see beyond a little swaying back and forth at first, which seemed to be led by Zarentil. But for Bettina, it was anything but gentle and quiet.

It was as if he'd manually shut her eyes with the command to follow. If she'd not spent this recent time with gargoyles learning their ways, she was sure to have gone mad.

At first, they were soaring, very high in a cloudy sky, higher even than birds fly. She felt the cold but it mattered little because her breath was taken away by the stunning vista of clouds piled up like mountains of colors. Subtle blues, deep greys and pale lavenders surrounded them, but far ahead explosions of yellows, oranges and reds beckoned. Above them, azure so brilliant it made her heart ache. Below, clouds overlaying more clouds. Bettina could feel a furious desire forming inside: now that she'd seen it, she never wanted to leave this place of beauty and peace.

But that was when Zarentil's flight—because she was flying, she remembered with a start—immediately angled down, plunging them into ever-increasing gloom. Bettina quickly felt choked off from the light and beauty and so claustrophobic it was hard to breathe. The peace that had enveloped her was soon replaced by clawing fear.

Further and further they plummeted. The darkness of the clouds now spirited away the joy and comfort she'd experienced just moments earlier.

No! No, Zarentil! Let's go back. Oh, please, please, take me back! Even in the dimness, she could make out shapes in the clouds, just as she did as a young girl lying in the clover fields with her father.

"Papa! Why did you have to go?" she cried, rolling over on the fragrant field. Waves of remorse and sadness swept over her. Reaching out to stroke his face—oh, the face that she missed so hard that the intense pain of its loss angered her—Bettina recoiled. Her hand no longer caressed the face of her beloved father but that of a monster, his eyes grown red with malice, set within a head of stone. She pulled her hand away but it didn't come. He held it fast to his face! Frightened, she pulled harder, yet it still wouldn't come. Bettina's heart was now pounding so loudly she wished to swat it away, like an annoying wasp. *If this pounding doesn't stop soon, my head will be crushed.* Twisting violently, she still could not break free from the creature.

Suddenly, she felt her stomach convulse. *But this isn't real!* her mind shouted. *I can still see clouds…and those aren't real, either, are they?*

"Are they not?" Zarentil replied, his voice deep and soothing.

Bettina thought it strange that his voice was also so gentle and quiet.

"But we're plunging through the mounted clouds of an angry sky, Zarentil. Yet, your voice is soft. I should hear only the roaring of the wind."

"Does that make it not real?"

And then, like coming back up to the surface after a deep dive into the lake near home, Bettina's mind went from a jumble of colors, bubbles and noise to bursting through to life-giving air.

Still clearly seeing that they were plummeting down through the mountainous clouds, Bettina saw also the face of her father behind the face of the creature. She sucked in her breath as she made out shreds of her friends surrounding them, too; Zarentil still held fast to her hands.

"So, is this real?" she whispered. "*All* of it?"

"Yes," Zarentil replied, "and no. The body that carries your mind yet remains in the place we left, surrounded by your friends. The vision of your father is much as it happened in your youth, as best you recall it from those many years ago. The apparition of horror is your dread and anger mixed with intense suffering at your father's loss, for these partings come with a lingering price. And, in a moment, we will arrive at the lair in which your mother and brother are held, for it is a real place, and these clouds are ascended up over its mountainous defense."

No sooner had he spoken the words than Bettina gasped. The thick, dark clouds quickly thinned, and they broke free from them. Before her body could release the scream that formed in her mind, they hurtled into the snowy upper region of the nearest slope. She knew that it should be pitch black within the solid rock, but a faint glow lit the quickly passing formulations of stone. More than ever, Bettina was struck by the coppery translucence of Zarentil.

The rasping sound in her ear made her twitch. She'd forgotten there were three in their party.

"Child, relent from nurturing your fear," Lohxnahr murmured. "Now is the time to release that which you know is within you."

Intuitively knowing what he meant and that, in moments, she would witness the threats facing her mother and brother, Bettina still asked, "What is within me, Lohxnahr?"

"This, well you know. Even with your question, shelter your fear, you do."

"This is weird," Danielle muttered. "It seems like something should be happening, doesn't it?"

Freida nodded. For many minutes, she'd been staring, along with Anders and Danielle, at Bettina holding hands with Zarentil while Lohxnahr's talons draped over her shoulders. All three were motionless.

"How long have they been gone? Well, you know what I mean," she asked. "It seems like close to an hour."

"That's about right, I think," Anders replied, still staring at their motionless friends. "And yes, it's weird, Danielle. No movement at all. Like they're dreaming with their eyes open. I guess this is what parting without leaving looks like…just their minds go."

While Anders struggled with his own anxieties and fears—for he'd grown to love each of Danielle's and Freida's parents as if they were his own—he recognized that he'd need all of his wits about him for this mission to succeed. *In fact, I'll need enough to share with the girls,* he realized, chewing on his lip.

The only indication that the reconnaissance was over was when all three relaxed. It was so anticlimactic that Tiny didn't even lift his head.

Lohxnahr and Zarentil released Bettina at the same time, and she immediately stood up. There was a fierceness in her eyes that hadn't been there before, almost like a different girl returned. It was striking to the other kids. Freida and Danielle exchanged glances before looking at Anders with raised eyebrows.

"What happened?" Anders asked after a moment.

"I released that which was always within me," Bettina replied, smiling wide. A confident smile, full of resolve. "That was the point of our trip, was it not, Lohxnahr?"

"Only in part, child," he replied, turning to bow. As he did so, his wing stretched out and brushed against Anders, almost knocking him over.

"Pardon, please, my boy!"

"Quite all right, Lohxnahr," Anders smiled. "I'm surprised it hasn't happened before, actually. Not just with you."

"And, in part, not," Lohxnahr said, returning to his original conversation, puzzling all but Bettina. "Must see, we did, the enemy's lair."

Taking a deep breath first, Anders swallowed hard. "So, Lohxnahr, now that you have seen it," he said with as much confidence as he could muster, "what do you say we come up with a plan?"

Lohxnahr beamed at Anders. "Yes, lad! A plan we shall make and a good one will it be!"

As Zarentil shuffled over from the rock he'd been perched on, Anders gathered his comrades into a circle and, over the next hour, drew a diagram in the dirt with his dagger, based on what he heard Zarentil, Lohxnahr and Bettina describe.

"I wonder how our friends are," Amy whispered, the air cool upon her face.

Peter turned away from staring at the cabin's door. Kimar had parted them into the clearing to the west of where Lohxnahr had been blown through the tree by the hybrid. It was deemed to be a relatively hidden spot while still close to the cabin. So far, there had been no sound except a great many birds still chirping in the midday warmth. They'd been in a little copse of trees near the door of the cabin for only a minute or two. Anja fidgeted between them, sniffing vigorously.

"Yeah, I know what you mean, Ames," Peter replied. Focusing on the task at hand, he added, "Do you really think the Hudsons are here, trapped or something, after all the uproar the last time we were? The door is still blown off its hinges, so it's not a very hospitable place to stay."

"It was the first place to check since it was the last place they might be," Ercen replied.

Peter opened his mouth and shut it a moment later. He found the logic of gargoyles confounding, at times.

"Couldn't they be anywhere?" Amy asked, agitation edging the question.

"It is possible," Ercen replied evenly. "This is the place to start."

"Okay, Ercen," Peter said. "We're just pretty wired because of the Skulstads. We're worried about Heidi and Johann, not to mention Danielle and her group's mission—whenever that happens—so we're a bit short on patience for, well, anything else. At least, I am."

Amy nodded.

Anja nuzzled her wet nose into her master's armpit. Since they were all kneeling to maximize the cover provided by the buttonbushes surrounding their little stand of trees, this was easy for Anja to do.

"As am I," Ercen replied.

Peter couldn't tell whether she meant that she shared their anxiety or that she was also impatient. *Probably both, I suppose.*

"Kimar needed to rule out that the Hudsons were here, whether held captive...or otherwise," she said quietly, "and, if not, to determine if the hybrid worked alone or with others because this may provide a clue for our next mission."

"And if they aren't here," Peter began and then shook his head and rubbed his unshaved chin, "I just hate to think about what's happened here and what it might mean for our friends."

Amy clutched his hand. "I know, Hon. I know."

"Because I...how will we live with ourselves if we've somehow brought..."

"And how did they even become part of this?" Amy asked shrilly.

"Kimar believes you were watched or, more accurately, were watched *for*," Ercen replied.

Peter breathed deeply, centering himself before asking, "What does that mean, *watched for?*"

"We believe that Kahrnahrgx was able to track you through time and space to the region in which you live."

"Our town, you mean?" Amy asked, incredulous.

"Yes."

"But wouldn't that mean—*how couldn't it*—that a gargoyle would be running amok amongst our town? Kind of hard to hide something like that," Peter said.

"Unless the spy was hidden in plain view."

"How's that, Ercen? You mean, like a government spook?"

Ercen ignored the unfamiliar reference. "Is there not an old stone church in your town?"

Amy and Peter stared at each other. In unison, they cried, "The Anglican cathedral! That's *our* church!"

"At least, it is when we go," Peter added, embarrassed.

"Does the cathedral house gargoyle statues?"

"Uh, it doesn't house them inside the cathedral, but it is decorated with them—a lot of them, in fact—all along its complicated roofline, corners and capitals," Peter replied.

"Are you saying that not all of those little gargoyle statues are...statues?" Amy wondered.

"Who would look to see? Who would count them enough to notice if an additional one or two appeared one day?" Ercen replied. "It is quite possible."

"Oh, that's simply creepy!" Amy exclaimed.

"How would they know to look for us?" Peter asked. "I mean, how would they know us from among everyone else walking around in town?"

"Do you remember when it was explained to you last year that it is possible for gargoyles to dream together?" Kimar asked, startling the Wheelens, who didn't hear him come up.

After a flustered moment, Peter answered for both of them, "Yes."

"The scouts of Kahrnahrgx would have known what you look like, based upon those dreams my brother permitted others to share. Once they had experienced you in that way, all they had to do was wait and watch," Kimar said matter-of-factly.

"But, Kimar," Peter cried, "they didn't know what town to look for us in, let alone which state! That would have required hundreds, no thousa—"

"Thousands," Kimar completed Peter's sentence.

"Oh, now," Amy cried, "that's even creepier! Much, much creepier." She vigorously rubbed her hands on her arms, which would have looked right if it was cold outside.

"So, you're saying it was just a matter of time before they found us? That it was inevitable?" she continued.

"Yes," Ercen replied, shuddering.

Peter could only stare while he processed this information. After a moment, he turned to Kimar.

"What did you find? Any clues as to the whereabouts of our friends, the Hudsons?"

"Unfortunately, yes," Kimar replied.

Amy's heart flopped like a fish just released from its hook onto a dock.

Peter grabbed her hand. "And?"

"Because they are not here, there are three probabilities: they are held captive in their home, they are dead or they are held captive elsewhere," Kimar answered firmly.

"And?" Amy whispered.

Kimar's face grew grim. "We will search their home, but I expect to find it empty like the cabin. Unless his minions are foolish or rogue, the Hudsons have been taken captive. As you know, Kahrnahrgx has more leverage with a living captive."

Reaching out his hands, he added, "There's nothing more to see here. Let us go now."

A moment later, a rustle of leaves marked their departure.

Heidi wept silently next to Uud-Rement. She stroked his wide, rough forehead as a mother caresses her fevered child.

The legendary and fearsome warrior, the great leader of generals, had fought his last fight. His slain foes littered the ground around him, ten in all. He had died protecting the Skulstads and their home. He knew what these dwellings meant to humans and that they valued them no less than a gargoyle does a choice eyrie or spacious cavern.

Even as Heidi had dispatched the last enemy standing, Ita-Mudak was hobbling over to see to Uud-Rement, but it was already too late. To the minions of Kahrnahrgx, General Uud-Rement had been their bane for many generations. Though wounded grievously on many occasions, Uud-Rement would not be vanquished. Thus, over time, his body became the patchwork of crisscrossing scars that was so alarming to behold.

With Ita-Mudak's blessing, Conomorg had flown to the roof of the farmhouse and, using his wings, slapped the fire down. Later, the Skulstads would find that, the fireball hadn't done much harm to their home besides a partially ruined attic and some smoke damage to Freida's bedroom. They'd been very fortunate.

Conomorg immediately flew down to Johann and quickly pressed into his shoulder and hip, healing his wounds.

"Jah, my hulking friend, that was the right order of importance. I could wait. The house could not!" Johann quipped. "But does not Ita-Mudak need attention even more?"

"It is not the proper order of things. We tend to humans first."

"Very well, then. Please see to him. You have made me right as rain," Johann replied. Lowering his voice, he added quietly, "I, too, am grieved by the loss of Uud-Rement. A mighty soldier he was...and I am honored to have fought alongside him, if even for a brief time."

Conomorg's eyes softened as he looked at Johann. Tipping his head low in acknowledgment, he said, "Indeed, the mightiest he was. Our loss is great. Very great."

Given the extent of Ita-Mudak's wounds, Conomorg spent more than an hour repairing his friend. Sometimes, while pressing his palm against a wound, his hand would glow a deep orange, and Johann and Heidi could hear a slight humming. Other times, his palm would glow red and, as he pressed it against one of Ita-Mudak's wounds, a wisp of smoke would follow a hissing sound.

Feeling helpless and a little awkward, Johann and Heidi walked around their farmstead to take stock of what they'd lost.

There were three remaining hay mounds. While this wasn't good, it could have been worse. Because their hay crop had yielded more than they needed, they'd be able to get by. But there was no hay to spare and nothing left to sell. The more difficult discovery was the losses of their dairy cows. It was all too clear that several of their best milk cows had been blasted by a fireball. It was a gruesome sight and would be not easily forgotten.

His voice thick, Johann muttered, "At least it was quick for them."

Heidi clutched his hand and leaned against his healed shoulder. Soon, he felt her tears bleeding through his heavy shirt.

"We should be grateful we still have a farm to come home to, Heidi," he said gruffly. "Last year, our friends did not. Ah, *spytte*, you know I mean they did not have a home to return to."

Heidi patted her husband's hand. "I know, my husband," she whispered. "I know what it is you mean. And I am very worried about them, also."

"As are we," Ita-Mudak stated from behind them.

Turning around, Heidi smiled wanly at the sight of their renewed friend. Conomorg stood next to him, his face grim.

"We believe it would be best to clear the slain from your land," Conomorg said. "Is there a place we may lay them?"

A few hours later, the enemy's strike force lay beneath a mound set just beyond the pasture fence, hidden in a tight stand of towering pine trees. For many years after, the herd avoided that corner of the pasture.

Johann had been impressed and grateful when Conomorg aimed his fists toward the small meadow and, suddenly, the ground peeled back, heaping up onto itself. It reminded him of watching Heidi in the garden, pulling a furrow with a hoe. In Conomorg's case, he was pushing the soil and didn't need a farm implement. Still, it was difficult to move so many fallen, and all were weary and covered in dirt and mud by the time it was done.

Acrid air from the still-smoldering hay mounds caught in Johann's throat, but that's not why his voice was thick. "It ought to be safe for us to part. Even should a wind kick up, these mounds are nearly out, and a rain is coming soon from the look of those clouds."

Swallowing hard, he struggled to get the words out, "Let us bring your friend home."

"*Our* friend," Heidi said tenderly, tears streaming freely down her smudged face, creating clean lines in the dirt on her cheeks.

Conomorg carefully lifted the body of his fallen comrade, General Uud-Rement, into the arms of Ita-Mudak. Without a word, he placed one hand on the shoulder of Ita-Mudak and the other into Heidi's hand. Johann understood. Clutching Heidi's other hand, he completed the circle when he touched Ita-Mudak's other shoulder. A funnel cloud rose two meters into the air as they parted away.

The battle for the Skulstad farm was ended. High, indeed, was the price of victory.

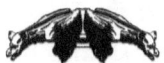

The Hudsons' modest brick house, nestled in the middle of an old subdivision, included a long-established back yard with several mature maples, a large oak, a lovely perimeter ring of flowers and raised garden boxes. It provided shelter from neighbors' prying eyes.

Immediately upon arriving in the deep, midday shadow of the oak, Kimar and Ercen concentrated on the home, sensing who might be within it. Peter and Amy watched the strange, slow movement of the gargoyles' arms, straight out with talons facing the sky, as they moved from the right side of the house to the left. It reminded Peter of elderly practitioners of Tai Chi he'd seen during a long layover in Japan.

Amy, hardly breathing, cupped her face in her hands, so her fingers stood like a picket fence in front of her mouth.

Ercen and Kimar dropped their hands.

Kimar said quietly, "We sense no one in the dwelling. Since, as you say, the floor is all wood, then you should check to make sure. Otherwise, we would leave impressions on their floor, as we did on yours. Keep in mind, though, that the hybrid's level of deceit may have reached the ability to remain hidden within, even as we search so close. I think not, but some have surmised it may be so."

Peter nodded and was about to say something when they heard voices. Neighbors' voices. Children squealing.

Kimar tipped his head towards the sliding door, indicating to Amy and Peter to get inside the house.

A moment later, Kimar and Ercen were squatting at the edge of the concrete patio, each looking as an overly large stone statue should.

Peter hastened to the sliding back door, pleased to discover that Caedmon Hudson left it unlocked. Quickly, he slid it open and Anja stepped inside before he could, with Amy on his heels. They left the door standing open.

Normally, Aleira Hudson kept her kitchen spotless. It was a point of pride for her, Amy knew. Except now the kitchen was a disaster, with entire cabinets torn from the walls, their contents strewn across the vinyl floor. Two forks and one steak knife had fallen, points down, with enough force to puncture the subfloor. Plates, bowls, cups, saucers, pots and pans littered the once immaculate kitchen.

"Oh, no," Amy whispered. "Oh, no…no, no, no."

Anja let go a high-pitched whimper in reply.

"Hang on, Hon. We don't know much yet," Peter whispered. "We need to search the whole house to see…to make sure."

Stepping gingerly around the detritus of the kitchen, they made their way into the large front room adjoining the kitchen via a small dining room. Anja's nose was twitching as she took in all the smells.

"Oh, no!" Amy cried out in a high-pitched whine. Some of Aleira's inheritance of fine china lay scattered across the mahogany dining table; the rest were heaped, broken, on the carpet.

"More of the same here," Peter said, motioning to the front room. Pictures hung askew on the walls. Plants were disgorged from their pots. Furniture was toppled. A sofa was slashed end to end by huge blades.

His voice a little louder, Peter said, "Whatever happened here happened a while ago."

"How do you know that?" Amy replied, her voice quivering.

"The plants have browned already."

Amy's gaze took in the entire room. All she could do was shake her head in slow dismay. "Still, shouldn't we look through the rest of the house?"

"Yes. Of course, Ames," Peter replied gently. "Anja's already started doing that."

It didn't take long to go through the bungalow; the other rooms were untouched. About the same age as Peter and Amy, Caedmon and Aleira were childless. All the Wheelens knew was that there was some kind of medical condition involved in making it impossible for the couple to conceive. Other than that detail, the Hudsons hadn't shared any more and the Wheelens didn't pry; some things you just don't ask. Peter and Amy knew their friends grieved at being unable to have a child of their own. Yet, they'd become the preferred caretakers for Danielle and many other neighbors' kids, because they made such excellent babysitters. Peter and Amy had entrusted Danielle to the Hudsons' care many times and they had all become very close friends in the process.

Stepping onto the patio again, Peter and Amy dropped to their knees beside Ercen and Kimar. Torrents of squeals rolled over the fence.

"They're not here," Peter said. "You were right."

Kimar remained unmoved.

Peter glanced at Amy, puzzled.

"Ercen?" Amy asked softly.

Ercen didn't flinch.

"What's going on with them?" Peter snapped. "Hey, Anja, come back here!"

Anja was jaunting over to the fence nearest the sounds of playing.

"Hey, mister!"

Peter jumped at the unexpected voice and glanced around the yard, uncertain where it had come from.

Amy's tapping him on the shoulder diverted his attention. The impish grin on her face puzzled him even more.

Her eyes twinkling, he looked in the direction she'd indicated with a tip of her head. The sounds of squealing continued with bursts of a young boy shouting, "Hey, that big piece's mine!"

About halfway down the yard, in between a pair of manicured pink hydrangeas, a small waving hand poked through the fence where a large knot had been. Anja stopped directly under the hand. When the hand brushed up against her, it suddenly stopped waving and began feeling around the hairy shape. In the process of exploring Anja's head, the child's hand nearly poked her in the eye, then played with her ears and lifted her jowls. Once the creature was deciphered, the boy patted Anja on the head. Then the hand vanished into the hole. A moment later, the hand was replaced by an eye. A moment after that, the eye was replaced by a mouth.

"Hi, mister! Is this your dog? What are you doing at the Hudsons'?" The mouth vanished; the eye returned, twisting back and forth for a good vantage point.

Peter was stumped about what to do. Their friends weren't here, so it was a certainty they, too, were captured. Soon, Danielle and her group would attempt a rescue of Paign and his mother. But now, it looked like there would be two more humans in need of immediate liberation. They needed to leave! They needed to alert and warn the others before their mission was launched. In the confusion caused by the discovery of attacks on the Hudsons' home and the Skulstads' farm, Peter couldn't remember any promises to wait for the diversionary forces to return. Would the rescue team leave without them? It was imperative to get back as soon as possible. But, apparently, Kimar and Ercen were unwilling to be seen by the child.

"Yes, that's Anja. And we're looking for our friends," Amy answered the boy. She couldn't see enough to know for sure, but guessed the boy was about eight or nine years old. "Do you know where they are, young man?"

"No ma'am! Haven't seen 'em for a couple of days. And my name is Charles! I like your dog."

"Did you see them leave, then?" Amy continued, grinning. "Yes, ma'am!"

A young girl's voice erupted from the other yard, "I'm going to get you for that, Ryan Whiner! That wasn't very nice!"

The eye was replaced by an ear, as the boy turned to see what was happening on his side of the fence. Tousled blond hair sprouted through the empty knothole.

The mouth returned. "You should see this, mister! I guess Ryan just smashed cake into Alice's hair, and she's hopping mad about it. That makes sense since it's her birthday party!"

Peter couldn't help but grin at the queer sight of lips in the fence, jabbering away. *Talking fence. Hmphf.*

Then the eye was back, squinting through the hole.

"And how did they leave, Charles?" Amy asked, returning to their pressing need for answers. "By car?"

"No, ma'am!"

A screech sundered the air, and a plume of water droplets flew up above the fence top. "Hey, Alice! That's *cold!* Knock it off!" Apparently, Ryan Whiner was receiving some payback from Alice, and he didn't much like it.

"Ryan is such a jerk!" cried the boy behind the fence, his voice muffled due to the fence slats, with only his eye visible again.

"Son," Peter said firmly. "Can you tell us how the Hudsons left? And when? It's very important, Charles! We're trying to help them."

The eye was replaced by the mouth. "Sure, mister!" the boy smiled, revealing a missing front tooth. "It was about this time, day before yesterday, I'd say. I was on the swing, blowing off some steam, see? It's been kind of a pain getting everything ready for Alice's party—she's my sister, you know, and since she's turning ten—well, now she is ten, I guess. Anyway, I got bored and went to swing for awhile, you know? And I'm getting really good at going high. I mean, really high! Higher than she goes, anyway, and she's two years older than me...at least until my birthday, which is next month, and then she'll only be one year older than me again. Like it's a big deal!

"Anyway, so I'm swinging really high and I see, just for a moment, mind you, 'cause the fence keeps getting in the way 'cause I'm swinging fast—you have to, to swing high, right? So, the Hudsons are in the backyard 'cause it's a really nice morning, and they're not doing much but sitting at that table next to you, drinking coffee, I suppose. There's not much to see, really, as I'm swinging back and forth, but I holler, 'Hey!' and they holler 'Hey!' back, and then there's this creepy thing all of a sudden standing there next to them, taller than they are, all shimmery black, and Mrs. Hudson screams, and then I can't see them because of the fence and the oak tree, and then there's two more creepy things, sort of like the first one but shorter and greyer, kind of like they're smudged from dirt and mud, I guess."

The eye replaced the mouth. Apparently the boy wanted to make sure his listeners were still there. More screams from Ryan Whiner cascaded over the fence, preceded by another plume of water glistening high into the air, sending up a rainbow that vanished with the falling droplets.

"Keep going, kid!" Peter encouraged.

The smiling mouth was back. This time, Peter and Amy could make out a little glint of white where the adult tooth was coming in to fill the toothless gap.

"OK, mister!" Charles cried. "So, I was swinging so fast there was no way I could jump off without flying into Alice's room or breaking my neck, right? Well, next thing I could see was the Hudsons being led back into their house by those things. And I haven't seen them since. Of course, no one believed me when I told them what I saw. My dad isn't around as much as he used to be, and my stepmom just didn't buy it. Told me I should stop reading my comic books! Can you imagine that? And I'm sure you know what Alice thinks of it, right?"

Again, the eye came into view.

Amy and Peter nodded. A peel of laughter washed into the yard. Apparently Ryan Whiner was a sight to behold.

Before the eye vanished again, Peter blurted out, "So, son, these creepy things—what did they look like?"

The eye squinted and then the mouth came into view. "Are you kidding, mister? Hey, I gotta go. Looks like Ryan needs some help, even if he is a jerk. He's my best friend, after all."

"Just a minute, young man!" Amy said, commandingly. "Why do you say *kidding*?"

"Look, lady. They looked pretty much like the two you popped in with just a while ago, at least before they went all lumpy-like. Are they supposed to be statues or something? Hey, I gotta go, like I said. Looks like the fight is coming my way. Yikes!"

Just after the face vanished from the knothole, a rifled spray of water burst through it. Another boy's voice joined the chorus of wailing kids.

Kimar and Ercen immediately stood up as Anja trotted back to the patio.

"Looks like your stealth wasn't necessary," Peter quipped.

"Or successful," Kimar added, smirking.

"But now we know the Hudsons were abducted, like Paign and Gudrun," Ercen said.

A chorus of girls' piercing cries burst over the fence as the group parted away. Ryan and Charles had retaken control of the hose.

CHAPTER TWENTY-FIVE

REDEMPTION DRAWS NIGH

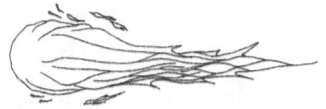

Paign knew, just knew, that this was his mother's last day. Her weakness had deepened, even though there was no outward cause for it. She wasn't old. At least, not old like the elderly farmers and their wives back home. She wasn't hurt. Not that Paign could see. It was this that troubled him most. *Perhaps she's got something wrong inside of her...something I can't see.*

Yet, he suspected—and, deep inside, knew the truth of his suspicion—that his mother had just given up. She didn't seem uncomfortable or in pain. In fact, when she was awake, she seemed almost at peace. Her nerves were shot, of course, whenever their jailors were in sight and especially so when they brought the meager excuse for what they called "food and drink" once a day. At those times, she'd curl up in a ball with her back to the gargoyles and her face to the wall, quivering until she fell asleep. He couldn't blame her for avoiding the food, which was vile, and the drink, which was filthy subterranean water with a strong and bitter mineral taste.

In his darkest moments, Paign wondered if she wanted to free him of herself. That she was actually willing herself to die, so he might escape. While his odds at such an endeavor were poor, at best, what chance did he have with his tottering mother in tow? He knew that she knew he would have dared to try it, to risk an escape, but now she was far too weak even to shuffle across their cell. Now, all he could do was wait. She'd know that.

But wait for what? Rescue? He could remember little else but waiting. Waiting and regret.

"Maybe I should just give up, too?" he whispered.

His mother stirred, her head still in his lap. He lightly pushed the dirt-matted hair away from her pale, smudged face.

"Roald, let us leave this base, my darling," she murmured, barely articulate, her dry lips garbling the word "place."

A deep sadness welled up in Paign, as if the very cave in which he was held captive cracked open wide, releasing a hidden lake of frigid, black water above, pouring through the rent in the stone, quickly filling the chamber.

He wondered about his friends, the Skulstads, especially Freida and Tiny, whom he shared so many adventures with. He wondered about Anders, his cousin and best friend. How he regretted the harsh words he'd hurled at Anders, and how wrong he'd been to do so. He wondered about the Wheelens. *Where are they now? And what are they doing? Are they safe?*

And then, though he wished it otherwise, his thoughts turned to Danielle. He wondered if she could forgive him, once she knew he'd brought this on because of his jealousy of Anders and the silly, but powerful, hope he'd harbored about seeing her again. Now that Paign had seen Danielle—and the horror in her face at what he'd become—he deeply regretted his actions. He was willing to do anything to have everything be as it was before his argument with Anders. He fervently wished he didn't so well understand the phrase his father used to say so often, "Be careful what you wish for!"

Suddenly, he was stung with a pang of guilt. "Bettina! I've nearly forgotten my own sister!"

"Hmm?" his mother murmured, without waking.

"I can't believe I've not considered her before now," he whispered. "How will she know what's become of mother and me?"

Even as the cold depths of despair swept over him, Paign's vision filled with a different place. Though he could still plainly see his cell and the slight movements of his jailors in the stone hallway beyond, he could also see a diagram in the dirt, about the size of a small wagon wheel, almost close enough to touch. A dagger's tip moved confidently through the dirt, a dagger with intricate runes etched into the blued steel, carving paths and positions.

"That's Anders's blade!" Paign choked out, straining to remain quiet.

As Paign watched, the blade furrowed the soil, back and forth, as it laid out a diagram...of...

"What is that? It looks like—wait a minute—that's our cell!" Paign's right hand reached into the air as he tried to touch the diagram. "But this area outside this cell, we've never seen before. How would he know what's out there?"

Still, the blade point swept across the dirt, sometimes stopping, only to be replaced with Anders's hand rubbing away the line to start fresh.

"It's like he's sketching out this floor plan based on someone else's description. But whose?"

Like a phantasm, a slender, delicate hand appeared over the lines Anders had just rubbed away. It moved back and forth, marking out where the lines needed to go.

Without thinking, Paign's hand—still outstretched before him—reached for the slender, pointing hand. When his fingertip touched the longest finger of the other's, his body jolted ramrod straight.

Bettina! How? Where?

Immediately, Paign realized the perspective he'd been viewing of the diagram and the knife was that of the person with the slender hand. Bettina's hand. That hand was flailing wildly now.

Paign was seeing through his sister's eyes the face of Anders, who looked startled.

"What is he saying? Something about *connection or maybe its detection.*"

Anders's mouth moved so slowly it was hard to tease out what word he was saying. But his face told the story of great surprise.

Still struggling to sort out whether his cousin's reaction was a good one or not, Paign reared back when Lohxnahr's face blocked out everything else from view.

Paign felt the little gargoyle's hands on his shoulders— *Wait! They'd be on Bettina's shoulders, wouldn't they?*—pressing down. Or were they pushing in? Squeezing?

Blinking back tears, Paign was stretched between two places, his own and his sister's. He could feel her tears roll down his cheeks. Or maybe it was the other way around. Did it matter?

What is happening to me?

You are connected to your sister, my boy! Lohxnahr buzzed in his head. *Well done! Unexpected this was and timely it is. Most timely.*

But I haven't done anything, Lohxnahr! What's happening?

Behold, we come for you.

The peculiar sensation in his shoulders intensified. While not painful, the pressure he felt wasn't comfortable either. He wasn't even sure if it was a physical sensation. One moment, it was like waking up to the first day of spring; the next, it was the dread of an expected exam. Paign wondered if Bettina could feel it, too. At the same time, he felt both freezing cold and ready to burst into flames. But more than anything else, he felt wild, frenzied hope expanding through his body, ever so slowly but with the irresistible power of a monstrous glacier.

So frightened that his breath came in gulps, Paign wanted to explode for the joy blooming within him.

A subtle shift in the pressure provided the clue that it had now entered into his mother. The tears flowing down his cheeks were now certainly his. This he knew, just knew.

They're coming for us. They're coming for us!

"Time for haste is now arrived," Zarentil rumbled. "This unexpected turn magnifies our opportunity and squander it, we cannot."

"But we can't do that, Zarentil!" Danielle cried. "We don't have our loved ones back yet—I'm sorry, Bettina…you know what I mean, right?—and they may have something important to report to us. Desperately important!"

Freida nodded vigorously, with Tiny's head propping up her hand.

Anders nodded but felt very conflicted. No words came. While he had loved ones everywhere, he knew that his cousin and aunt were at grave risk and intervention was needed immediately. He could only hope that the others were all safe, but the urgency for rescue was immediate.

"Trust, we must," Lohxnahr hummed. "In Providence, we trust. Easier this is, with this unexpected revelation of oneness between the sister and her brother. Insight it provides. Timely, yes, but gossamer-like. Transitory. Little time to tarry. Go, we must. Trust, we must."

With a foreboding she couldn't explain or shake, Danielle consented to the guidance of Lohxnahr. It was easier to do so because of Anders diagramming, as best he could, where they'd be going and what they might face. She was also encouraged by the change in Bettina. While she'd already seemed bolder and more confident after her inward journey with Zarentil and Lohxnahr, now that she'd somehow connected with Paign, her attitude was intense and focused.

Anders scurried around quickly, gathering up his weapons retrieved a day earlier with the help of Lohxnahr.

As he did so, Tiny sensed the energy shift and suddenly splayed his front paws out low so that his chin nearly touched the ground while his tail stood proud. Beginning at Freida, he growled and then ran around to each of the other kids to announce his readiness for action.

The moment had come. Lohxnahr, grinning so wide it tilted his horns, reached one hand out to Danielle and the other to Freida. Anders worked Tiny in between him and Freida. Bettina clutched Danielle's free hand. Zarentil waited until all were ready and in position before stepping into the gap. Both Anders and Bettina leaned down awkwardly to reach his hands. Zarentil reached up in turn to take their hands, then nodded slightly to Lohxnahr.

They were gone. The desperate mission to rescue Paign and his mother, from the very stronghold of Kahrnahrgx, had finally commenced.

There would be no diversionary assault, after all.

Danielle was growing impatient, and she knew Anders was, too, because his knee was bobbing up and down against hers. It was an inhospitable place to linger, high atop the craggy mountain peak that vaulted into the heavens above the chamber holding Paign and Gudrun. There was no good place to sit and countless ways to fall. The wind, while not howling, certainly didn't help in keeping one's balance. She sat awkwardly, feeling the variable speed of Anders's nervous leg.

Freida stood leaning into the mountainside, slightly below and to the left of Danielle. Positioned on the only relatively flat section of rock, Tiny quivered between his mistress and the harsh ridge. Once in a while, he'd whimper his desire to leave the place no dog should be.

"This is terrible!" Anders muttered. "I get my nerves hardened for a fight in the very halls of Kahrnahrgx and then, poof, we wind up here, parked on the high side of this hateful mountain! I thought we were a rescue party, not an ill-equipped climbing team attempting a new summit." His knee stopped as soon as he laced his fingers over the top of it. "Paign would like it here, though, apart from all this drama, you know. It is quite majestic, once you get past the blast of wind and sheer drops!"

Hundreds of meters below them, a massive cloud bank encircled the huge peak. Lesser peaks in the range stood to their right and left. Sunlight cast deep shadows into the cloud heaps, leaving a web of variegated greys and purples.

"It's like a child went crazy with loads of mashed potatoes," Danielle nodded in agreement.

"What potatoes?" Anders replied.

Freida gave no indication she'd even heard Danielle. Her focus was on keeping Tiny as calm as possible.

"Peace to you!" Lohxnahr said over the gusting wind. They hadn't heard him settle above their heads on a jutting finger of darkened granite. He'd flown over from the nearest spur of rock, where Bettina and Zarentil had sheltered.

Anders and Danielle craned their necks up and around to look at him. Freida laid her right hand on Tiny's head and kept it there before glancing up at their guide.

"Lohxnahr, we'd feel more peaceful if we weren't here, stuck on this perilous rock, waiting for…waiting for…what *are* we waiting for, again?" Danielle retorted.

"Opportunity!" Lohxnahr replied merrily.

"And what opportunity is that again?" Anders said surlily.

"Strengthening."

"But this place is anything but strengthening to us, Lohxnahr," Danielle interjected.

"Zarentil has chosen to tarry for a moment, as the connection between sister and brother empowers the mother. The elder female regains purpose and hope, even now as we wait upon the mountain's slope," Lohxnahr hummed. "This is an unexpected mercy and great help in a time when they are far from the other. We do well to receive it, as a weakly woman is more difficult to rescue. Yes?"

"Hm," Anders said, nodding. "In that case, we might as well be strengthened, as well." Fishing around in his small canvas satchel, Anders handed Danielle an apple and tossed another one to Freida.

Bettina sat on a spur of rock, about eight meters to their left. The spur had a horn of rock protruding up like a saddle. Zarentil was perched atop it and faced Bettina. Neither of them had moved for several minutes.

"So, is that what Zarentil is doing with Bettina? They look sort of like they're in a trance together," Danielle said. "Or praying." Then she took a huge bite from the apple.

"Trance, no," Lohxnahr replied. "The deepest of concentration, yes. Focusing one's attention intently on the single purpose of helping another is a blessed thing. Trances too often mean the emptying of one's attention, allowing another's to inject a new purpose of their making."

"That's creepy sounding, Lohxnahr," Danielle said, her nose wrinkled.

"Quite so!" he replied.

"How much longer will we be?" Anders asked, just before taking three bites of apple, making it hard to shut his mouth.

Glancing over at Zarentil, Lohxnahr leapt up, using his wings to balance himself against the wind. "Now, it appears! Quickly now."

With no chance of finishing what he'd started, Anders spit out the remaining apple chunks, only to have them fly back at him because of a strong gust.

"Ah, for pity's sake!" he cried. "Blast!" Bits of partially chewed apple clung to his patterned wool sweater.

Grinning, Danielle reached for his nearest hand. "Hopefully, you don't smell up the chamber with enough apple scent to alert the bad guys!"

Anders smirked but had no chance for a snappy retort. Zarentil had just flown over with Bettina.

"As your plans have placed us within the chamber, Anders," Zarentil intoned, "so let us take them. The sister's work is done, as far as time and urgency permit. Now we trust to hope, that with a good will and courageous hearts, we may find a path that leads to the rescue of those dear to us."

Reaching out to each other, the party quickly formed an awkward ring, using each other for balance as they prepared to part.

"Careful now!" Lohxnahr buzzed. "It is my belief that Zarentil's presence will be felt by our enemies as nothing more alarming than the hybrid. Given the small size of our group, it is my hope that fortune smiles on us and we remain unnoticed until we have affected the release of our companions.

"From our earlier scouting, two guards at the door of their cell we expect there to be. Troubling it is, more we did not see. Great our risk is that the hybrid happens nearby during our sortie. Even the dimmest of guards will know the presence of two hybrids, identical in sense, cannot be."

Danielle hadn't thought of that. From a stolen glance at Anders, she knew he hadn't either. Bettina still looked to be in a trance—or concentration, as Lohxnahr called it—and showed no sense of alarm or concern.

"Well, the sooner we get away from here, the better it will be for Tiny," Freida said flatly. The huge dog wobbled on the uneven surface.

"Very well!" Lohxnahr smiled as he reached for those nearest to him.

"Let us trust then to providence," Danielle said, paraphrasing Lohxnahr with as much confidence as she could muster. "May we find success in our rescue. Let's get our friends back!"

"But that's nuts!" Peter cried. "They needed to wait for us to get back, Prohximus. They *should not* have gone!"

"You must take us to them," Amy declared, "at once!"

"That I cannot do," Prohximus replied evenly. "The success of the rescue party is based on stealth and speed. We know not their progress or precise whereabouts. To go now would subject the entire operation to almost certain doom… the doom of those you wish to join, as well as those you wish to save."

Quarastohr nodded solemnly, but said nothing.

Kimar and Ercen stood motionless next to Peter and Amy.

"You don't understand, Prohximus!" Peter continued. "We have news. Those held captive also include our friends, the Hudsons. They were taken from their house, presumably within the past week or so by a number of obsidians, apparently just to get back at us!"

"Such was our fear," Quarastohr said, shaking his wide head. "Yet we do not know that these Hudsons are kept in the same stronghold as the boy and his mother."

"We have no reason to believe otherwise," Kimar interjected. "You already know full well my doubts concerning my brother's behavior in all of this. While I do not know the meaning of what I deem to be rash actions—precisely the abduction of these Hudsons—I remain unconvinced that

Kahrnahrgx would find any tactical value in it. Something strange is at work here. Something we do not yet see."

"Be that as it may, Kimar," Prohximus replied testily, "what would you have us do? Empty the surrounding land of the Ten Pinnacles and send all of our fighters to one place? All for the rescue of two—or, as you say now, four—humans? Would this not, too, be rash?"

"While I sympathize with your concerns and questions, Commander Kimar," Quarastohr said smoothly, "I trust you can see the point Prohximus makes. Neither does it make military sense to launch a huge force against one stronghold to rescue two or four humans, nor is it wise to deploy our scouts without more information than we currently have. The world is large."

"Well, waiting is not an option!" Peter spat.

Anja barked her disapproval. She hadn't much liked the process of going to a town she was familiar with, visiting her friends' house with her alpha persons, then hurrying up and doing nothing but come back. *And it did sound like those children were having fun on the other side of the fence. Pity we could not join them. We haven't had much fun in a long time.* No one noticed her sad face.

"Peter is right. No, it is not an option to just stay, doing nothing!" Amy bickered, agitation fueling her words. "How do we get to where Danielle and the others are? They still need the diversionary strike, don't they? How is it that we are just standing here talking about this? Talk, talk, talk! My little girl—*our* girl!—and her friends are in harm's way, at great risk. Ercen, please help us get to them! Now! Please!" Amy's arms flailed back and forth as she tried to make her point unmistakable and utterly compelling.

Ercen looked stricken and muttered, "We do not know their whereabouts, Amy."

"You *what?*" Amy and Peter cried, in unison.

"Zarentil knew of Paign's and Gudrun's location through his connection to Bettina. Lohxnahr may also have known it. We do not. In the great haste of preparations, as well as our sortie with you—seeking the Hudsons—we did not learn of their place of captivi—"

Kimar interrupted Ercen abruptly, "Although we may not know their whereabouts, it doesn't forego our learning it. We may, even now, discover it by communal dream. But should they be under deepest cover, Zarentil and Lohxnahr may be indecipherable to us, and we'll have only a vague sense of which hemisphere they've gone to. With some small fortune, we'll narrow it down to the continent and, perhaps, even the mountain range."

"That's it?" Peter cried. "That's the best you can do?" A vein in his left temple throbbed.

"Peter, you must understand that Lohxnahr and Zarentil do not want to be found out by the enemy," Ercen added. "Stealth is of utmost importance and critical to their success… as well as the safety of Danielle and the others."

"What happens if their attempts at stealth fail?" Amy whispered.

It was such an odd feeling. Danielle felt two feelings, actually, she realized. Like when she was little and would hide from her mother under the thin bed sheet. Now, of course, she knew her mother would have immediately seen the lumpiness beneath the cover and recognized her precocious daughter as the lump source. But then, Danielle could see her mother, oddly colored through the hues of the fabric, while remaining completely hidden. Or so she believed. While the memory of those moments of play and surprise often brought warmth and comfort to Danielle, here they seemed so terribly out of place.

She could see everyone in her rescue team very clearly. Anders was crouched low near the opening to the cell. He had already stealthily pulled his sword free. Freida stood slightly behind him with her dagger drawn. Bettina was walking un-evenly towards her loved ones, her left hand clamped over her mouth as if to keep it from crying out to them; her right hand was clutching Lohxnahr's left. The gargoyle that had become so dear to Danielle struggled to maintain his balance, as well as Bettina's. Zarentil squatted in the middle of the chamber with his head bowed low. Danielle was grateful that Tiny sat right next to her. She patted him gently and realized he was strung very tight and absolutely alert.

But when Danielle looked at Paign and Gudrun, it was if she was playing hide and seek again with her mother, looking through a drab and colorless sheet. Not only were they both slightly out of focus, their movements were glacially slow. And it was clear that, unlike Danielle's mother during their little hiding game, Paign and Gudrun were not yet aware of anyone else inside their prison.

So far, so good, she smiled to herself.

And that's when everything went horribly wrong.

Amy held Heidi close, her right arm stretched across her friend's shoulders. Heidi's body shook, but no sound could escape because her face was cupped into her hands.

A pleasant coolness brought up from the valley's lake on a slight breeze was a welcome comfort. The setting sun, already vanished behind the western rim of the Pinnacles, cast deep, hot shadows onto the eastern wall.

Grim, Peter stood next to Johann, who was spitting out his account of the catastrophic mission to the farm. Anger and grief spilled out of him like rain through a broken gutter. Because he had reverted to his native Norwegian, Peter and Amy didn't understand many of the words, but his intensity, well, that was unmistakable.

In the space between them lay the body of Uud-Rement. Conomorg stood next to the head of the legendary warrior; Ita-Mudak, with his own many wounds still visible, stood at the fallen general's feet.

Those listening to the report were many. Prohximus stood next to Conomorg, his arms folded across his chest. His gaze slowly shifted between Johann and a vague spot on the dais. Quarastohr, standing near Ita-Mudak, never looked away from his fallen comrade. Scores of other gargoyles encircled them. Many more looked down from the eyries and high places nearest the dais.

"My anger soon will turn to resentment if we remain here!" Johann bellowed. "If you somehow believe that the squad of enemies that came to destroy our farm—and would have succeeded if not for your fallen friend—wasn't part of a larger plan, then you are not the creatures of wisdom I took you to be."

Squatting down next to Uud-Rement's body, Johann continued his plea. "Do you not see that even as great a fighter as the mighty Uud-Rement was overmatched by the enemy's devious plan? What chance, then, do our—"

The entire valley grew silent as the farmer struggled to compose himself. Though his face was tilted towards the body of the fallen general, all could still see the evidence of emotions washing over Johann. He shoved a hand violently through his hair. His mouth opened as if to continue speaking, but no words came. His head slowly shook back and forth.

Heidi hastened over and stood directly behind him. Before placing a hand on her husband's thick shoulders, she swept angry tears from her face.

Johann gently stroked Uud-Rement's face, wiping away dirt and grime.

A murmuring rippled across the assembly. Such a thing as this had never been witnessed before in the gargoyle stronghold: a grown man—mighty in his own right—honoring one of their own. That he honored one of the greatest warriors in their long history, in a manner of such deep reverence and fondness, deeply moved every gargoyle in attendance.

Then, in the quintessential bond of friendship, Johann leaned over until his forehead touched the forehead of the great warrior.

Overcome by the simple tenderness and grace of Johann's action, Peter's vision clouded from hot tears and his throat hurt. He guessed that Amy must have felt it, too, from the gentle sobs he heard next to him.

A small gasp brought Peter's attention to Ercen, who was bowing towards Johann in a manner not unlike a school girl's curtsy. She was staring at something overhead.

Ita-Mudak and Conomorg had drawn closer to the body, leaning forward with arms raised over their commander. Kimar stepped up to the waist of Uud-Rement and did the same. The three gargoyles' talons met and entwined high over the center of the general's body, forming a protective canopy.

Only a moment did Johann hold this position of complete openness. When he stood again, his wet face told the story of grief, sadness and resolve. His eyes glinted fire.

In an instant, Peter and Amy knew they'd never forget this moment, for Johann's eyes didn't reveal only the fire within him—the anger at the loss of his crop, the shock of the attack, a desperate battle and the terrible fear that his farm would be lost along with those dear to him...even the death of the mighty Uud-Rement. While all of these were clear upon the farmer's face, the glinting fire in his eyes came from another source.

Silently, the entire host of gargoyles within the Valley of the Ten Pinnacles—those near, as well as those spread across the valley's floor and up into the heights of the tallest peaks—were pulsating all the shades of fire. Some glowed red. Others, yellow and orange. Combined in close quarters, it was as if a monstrous flow of lava had simply stopped moving after spilling down the mountainous rim of the valley and pooling upon its floor. The flaming hues burst through the hairline fissures and joints in the gargoyles bodies, just like fire erupts from molten rock.

Johann, with Heidi behind him, didn't move.

Peter and Amy, along with Anja, twisted around like dismayed children until they'd taken in the entire valley. Even in the darkest recesses of the valley where the forest was most dense, a pall of dim firelight glimmered on the treetops. The hundreds of shallow caverns, escarpments and deep caves that pockmarked the cliffs shown as if each one had a small wood fire within it.

Quarastohr raised his right hand high into the cooling air. His talons glinted as if they were on fire.

"Attend me, my brothers and sisters!" he said, looking first towards those on the heights, then at those surrounding him.

Prohximus stepped over to join him.

"As you have all witnessed here, the human known to us as Farmer Johann has brought the greatest of honor and reverence to our fallen comrade, Uud-Rement…" Quarastohr continued firmly until coming to the name of his friend, when his voice fell faint.

A moment later, Prohximus intervened. "The final parting of our legendary general, Uud-Rement the Powerful, is a great and terrible loss. You have heard testimony of how this came to pass, as well as the cause he willingly sacrificed himself to protect." He stopped for a moment, glancing at his friend to see if he wished to continue.

Quarastohr gave him a quick nod and a faint smile before resuming. "My countrymen, long have we served humankind. For generations upon generations have we lived—and died—as their protectors. Throughout the ages have we rarely known the bonds of fellowship with those we serve. Since our commission is one of secret protection, rarely have we become familiar to humans. And yet, be it known to you that these bonds of friendship are all the more dear to us, due to their great rarity. Indeed, they are most cherished."

All the while he spoke, Quarastohr stared at the body of his friend. Quivering for a moment, he continued, "Not unlike those bonds of fellowship we have with…our closest comrades.

"In all of those rare and treasured companionships—all of them dear to our kind, save one—we have not collectively witnessed such a demonstration of camaraderie as this."

As Quarastohr and Prohximus turned to face Johann, a collective murmur of agreement swept down from the heights like an incoming wave breaking upon a rocky shore.

Both generals bowed toward Johann. The sound of a second wave of ascent broke across the valley's floor.

"We are moved by your act of deep friendship to our dear friend, Uud-Rement," Prohximus said.

"It is a reminder of the union we were called to at the Beginning," Quarastohr added. "It recalls for us the strong story in your scriptures about the valiant warrior named Jonathan and his sworn friendship with the general known as David, even unto his death."

Johann nodded, his eyes shimmering with the colors of fire.

"That is the name from which *Johann* is derived," Heidi whispered.

Lifting his arms high, Quarastohr turned around slowly to indicate that all in the valley pay heed. His color changed suddenly from a pulsing red to a stunning, intense white that cast long shadows across the dais.

"We are moved, Farmer Johann, by the honor and fondness you have bestowed upon our great general," Quarastohr intoned solemnly. His voice carried the length, breadth and heighth of the valley, though he didn't shout. The intensity of his grief carried the words.

"You have renewed the bonds of fellowship, one with the other, humans and gargoyles, which has not been seen for many spans of human lives."

"We will do all that is in our power to locate the rescue party," Prohximus added.

"We will now conduct the collective dream!" he bellowed, so there was no mistaking his intention, even to the remotest eyrie.

Bettina stood directly in front of Paign, her hand still clamped over her mouth. Lohxnahr glanced back at Danielle, grinning enough that it made his horns wiggle slightly. It looked so strange to Danielle, given the desperate seriousness of their mission. And, yet, it brought her some small comfort and hope, exactly when she needed it most.

For when Bettina's right hand reached out, quaking from the great fear she struggled to conquer on behalf of her beloved mother and brother, it was clear to Danielle that Paign still did not see anything—or anyone—else. Somehow, what appeared to Danielle as the ephemeralness of Bettina and her rescue team was total hiddenness to Paign and Gudrun.

Paign's eyes widened as his sister's hand clutched at his shoulder. Not seeing any reason or cause for the sensation of touch, he recoiled, startling his mother.

Alarmed, Bettina let go of Lohxnahr's support and grabbed her brother by both shoulders, shaking him.

"Nei, nei, Paign! It is Bettina, your sister!" she cried. "We have come for you."

While it was clear to Danielle that they couldn't be seen by the captives, they could be heard.

Paign recoiled backwards from the disembodied voice of his sister, hitting his head hard against the stone wall behind him.

Gudrun, who had been resting with her head in the lap of her son, reared up at the sound of the spectral voice, smashing her head into the unseen arm of her daughter. Both women cried out in pain.

Danielle had no idea what to do, observing the scene as she might watch her tropical fish at home. But she was certain that the cries of alarm weren't helping their prospects for success. Surely someone would hear them.

Movement in the center of the prison cell grabbed her attention. Zarentil was standing there now with his face toward the roof of the cavern.

As Paign and his mother angled away from Bettina's fervent whisperings, she held on tightly with her good hand.

Zarentil swung both arms down in the direction of the family. His talons pointed at Bettina.

Danielle could see something change even to her view of Bettina. She was sharper now, though not completely. But it was enough.

"Bettina!" Paign cried. "You're here?"

"Oi! My child," Gudrun choked out, before grabbing her daughter around her waist.

What Danielle had feared came true.

Two obsidians appeared in the doorway of the cell, holding long metal pikestaffs. One stepped two paces into the chamber, looking throughout it for the sound of the unfamiliar voice. His head tipped back and forth as he peered intently at Paign and Gudrun.

Danielle couldn't believe it. Not only was Bettina somehow still hidden from the guards, the one standing in the cell was within reach of Anders and Freida, unaware of the imminent threat.

Again, Danielle saw the definition of Bettina's image strengthen as she tearfully embraced—and was embraced by—her mother and brother.

But now, so could the obsidian. Atmospheric shreds of a third person flashed before him in the midst of the boy and woman he'd guarded since their arrival. Quickly assessing where the interloper's midsection must be, he immediately hoisted his pike to his shoulder, gripped it tightly and cocked his arm. It was the last thing he ever did.

"No, you don't!" Anders surged up in front of the guard and plunged his sword into the gargoyle's chest.

The second guard, plainly confused by what it, too, was seeing, saw his comrade tip back from the impact of the sword strike. Though he didn't see the sword, he understood his partner's motion. As the second guard stepped into the room to defend the other guard, Anders removed his sword and became momentarily visible.

Even as the first guard crumpled to the cell's floor, the second lunged at the place he'd seen Anders, swinging his outstretched arms towards where Anders's head was.

Freida, who had remained squatting on the floor during the first fight, hurled herself into Anders's midsection, knocking him out of the way of the arcing talons. She felt a rush of wind as the talons swept over her head. Before the guard could try again, she stabbed him with her dagger.

Reflexively, the obsidian swept its arms away from its chest. Without knowing what he struck, Freida was backhanded across the room, sliding into Tiny.

Infuriated by this assault on his mistress, Tiny bounded towards the creature, howling revenge.

Only the now unconcealed sounds of the rescuers provided clues to the remaining guard. Not understanding what he confronted, he turned to face the howling ghost, squatting defensively low just as Tiny leapt. Had the obsidian been able to see the dog, Tiny would have been doomed. As it was, the guard leaned forward and reared up just as Tiny reached the height of his leap, ramming his stone-like shoulder into the dog's ribs. With a sickening crunch, several ribs were shattered and Tiny fell in a heap on the far side of the chamber. Only his whimpering told Freida and the others that he'd survived the blow.

Enraged, the obsidian roared out, "Show yourselves, cowards! You are thieves and knaves to do battle as apparitions!"

"I would if I could, you fell beast!" Anders bellowed in return. "I don't know why you can't see us. Perhaps you'll see this!" he yelled, brandishing his sword in the air as he ran to engage his foe.

Before Anders could say anything else, the obsidian was on him, swinging his talons at the area the voice seemed to come from.

Anders barely deflected five consecutive blows. The harsh clanking of talons against his heat-seasoned sword rang out like a church bell.

Narrow black, leathery wings suddenly snapped out from the obsidian's back and began flapping furiously. Immediately, Anders found it difficult to keep his balance, let alone make forward progress towards his foe. A plume of dust enveloped the chamber, causing all of the humans to cough.

"Ah!" cried the guard. "Now, I perceive your number—those already here I can see, the boy and woman, as well as those I cannot."

As sand and grit filled Anders's airway, a racking cough seized him.

"I have you!" the guard cried wickedly, sweeping his wings in the direction of Anders's hacking.

Freida had lifted herself onto her hands and knees, intent on making her way over to Tiny, who was breathing heavily at the other end of the cell.

Horrified, Danielle realized that the cloud of particles flying up from the floor before the obsidian's wings had changed her perception of Anders. No longer did he appear obscured in any way. The flying dust and grit overwhelmed the distortion.

"Ha! I can see you now, human! A boy, from the likes of it. Nothing more than a single, human boy?" Increasing the thrumming of his wings, the obsidian sent a cloud of grit at Anders as he pulled his right arm back to thrust a flying fist.

"Nei! Not a single, human boy—two!" Paign yelled. He could now see Anders just as clearly as the guard, but already knew of his presence, certain of the voice of his cousin and best friend. During the pitched battle, he'd nudged Bettina down onto the stone bench as best he could, only by touch. He'd gathered her hands around their mother's hands and stood up, weaponless. The guard had barely noticed that his captive showed signs of life. Until now.

Paign barely dodged the flying fist originally meant for Anders, rolling away to his left towards where Tiny lay.

In that momentary shift of attention towards Paign, Anders reengaged the guard with a vengeance, raining down a storm of blows. The obsidian's defensive skills were very good. He met every strike from Anders with a block, then a counter-strike. With the advantage of two sets of wicked talons against one sword and no shield, Anders was soon besieged.

The entire battle so far had lasted no more than a minute, Danielle guessed. She could hear voices outside the cell's doorway. The rescue party didn't have long. Loud yells and louder footsteps were coming.

A high-pitched wail—Freida's wail—broke over the noise of oncoming reinforcements.

Danielle's attention snapped towards Freida, who was pointing at Anders. He'd been cornered by the obsidian, not far from where Tiny lay still. The obsidian was oblivious to everything except the insolent boy. Paign was of little concern since he was weaponless. The only other person whose location he was certain of was the old woman. He'd surmised where the other humans were from the noise of their feet upon the ground, and he assumed a gargoyle must have parted them into the cell and then completely lost his nerve.

With supreme confidence and conceit, the guard raised his hands high over his head for the killing stroke, while keeping Anders occupied with one of his feet. Though he stood on only one foot, the gargoyle was incredibly agile and quick, even making stabbing thrusts with his other foot while defending against Anders's sword work.

There was too much distance for Freida to cover to give the guard a new target. She flipped the handle of her dagger so that the blade lay in her palm. Deftly, she flung the two-sided blade. It announced its arrival in the guard's neck with a *thwap*.

Twisting in agony, the guard turned to stare in the direction the blade came from and wildly hurled a flying fist. Only because his opponent was hidden did he miss Freida. But the erupting stone behind her blew dust and detritus into a cloud surrounding her.

"You're next, woman-child!" Reaching over his head, the guard pulled the dagger of his neck and flung it back at Freida. It impacted the cell's wall so hard that it caromed off and nearly hit Paign before clattering to the floor.

"Let's finish this!"

Cornered as he was, Anders had no chance. The speed and agility of the guard matched his own, but without freedom of movement, he was too limited in his offensive strikes. All he could do was block, and that wouldn't be enough for long.

Paign quickly assessed that his cousin was going to die while trying to save him—all because of Paign's own stupidity and stubbornness. The others were all at risk, too. He knew Bettina and Freida were there along with his mother. Perhaps Danielle was, too. While he didn't know which gargoyles had brought them there, he was furious they remained hidden. All the rage he'd been feeling—from the time of his idiotic argument with Anders to his torment by Rance-Dahl, up to the realization that he'd put all of his loved ones in danger—all erupted at once.

The guard again raised his hands into the air for the killing strike. Powerless to do anything else, Freida and Danielle sprang towards him, just as Gudrun seized Paign by his legs. "Nei, Paign! Nei!"

Impulsively, intuitively, with no time for any other action, Paign's hands pulled back to his chest even as he clenched them tightly into fists. As the guard's hands began arcing down to dispatch Anders, Paign's fists pushed violently away from his chest. "Nei!" he bellowed.

In the chaos of battle, no one had noticed Tiny stirring to his feet. Instinctively, he leapt in the direction of the fighters, but angled his body towards Anders, rather than his opponent. Having seen plenty of flying fists used by other gargoyles, Tiny knew that Anders might be crushed by the impact of the weapon on the guard. There'd be time later, he hoped, to learn how it was that a human could throw such a powerful device.

Even as Tiny crashed into Anders, knocking the boy into the open doorway, Paign's flying fist slammed into the back of the guard, violently spreading his wings outward while hurling him headlong into the airborne mastiff. The breadth of Paign's blow was wider than the gargoyle and blew around it and into the wall with such force that the ceiling fell down onto the guard, crushing it to the floor.

Freida screamed at the sight of Tiny's paws sprawled out from under the guard's body and mounds of broken stone, still roiling in a plume of choking dust. A moment later, she and Danielle were blown off their feet from the force of Paign's throw as it rebounded back into the cell.

When Danielle raised her head and sat up, everyone was clearly visible. Dust and grime lingered in the air. Freida was already busy lifting stones off of the gargoyle with Anders's help, so they could get to Tiny. Miraculously, Tiny's muffled whimpers could be heard coming from beneath the guard.

Lohxnahr, only a meter away to her left, was helping Zarentil back up to his feet. They, too, had been knocked down by Paign's blast.

When Danielle looked towards Paign, at first he was mostly hidden by Bettina's embrace. But even with the brief glimpses, she could see that there was a look of dismay—even alarm—in his eyes. She was alarmed, too. *How did he do that?*

How would he know how to throw a flying fist? I'd be worried, too, if I were him.

"Quickly, now!" Zarentil hissed. "There's no time to squander. The ruse was broken by the boy's spell. Quickly, Lohxnahr, gather everyone together! The enemy draws near."

Pitched so high, at first Danielle didn't recognize it for the scream it was. As she turned back towards Paign, she was stunned that Gudrun could make such a sound. Primal, the very essence of terror, her scream hurt Danielle's ears.

Paign's eyes grew wider, even as Bettina's scream joined her mother's.

"It's too late!" he cried. "They're already here!"

Danielle spun on her knees to face the doorway. It remained empty, as before. Only the first guard's body was near it. Twisting back to Paign, she saw he was pointing over her shoulder. Indeed, that was where Bettina and Gudrun stared, gaping. So, Danielle arced her body around, angling her head up towards the prison cell's wall, about halfway between the entrance and the stone bench that Paign and his mother sat on. She was just in time to see a large section of it become elastic and ripple. Ten irregular lines formed in it, from the floor of the cell almost to its ceiling. The areas between the lines shifted, protruding out near the ceiling and the floor, quickly taking on form and substance. First, horns appeared at the top of the shape nearest the doorway. A foot with long talons stepped out from the base of the dissolving wall. It took only seconds before nine obsidian gargoyles stood inside the prison cell, facing down three girls, two boys, a broken dog, a mature woman and two ancient gargoyles, who were finally visible to Paign.

"What have I done?" Paign whispered. "It's come to this… because of me."

"No! No, Paign! This is not your fault!" Danielle cried. "None of this is! This is a lie, Paign…a lie they want you to believe! Not this, Paign. Don't believe it. It'll make you like them. Don't—"

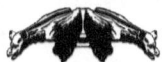

Quarastohr and Prohximus began pulsing an intense white light. Amy hastened over to Heidi, while Peter grabbed Johann's hands. The four of them stood in a tight circle, with Anja tucked into the center. The generals lifted their arms up and out, as did Ita-Mudak and Conomorg, as if embracing their comrades throughout the valley, all the way up into the heights.

Soon, the pulsing light radiated everywhere, accompanied by a deep, thrumming beat that punctuated each burst.

"Now, Kimar!" Quarastohr cried. "We are unified!"

Kimar, who had been standing just beyond the generals at the very edge of the dais, knelt onto one knee. Ercen positioned herself behind Kimar and laid her hands onto his head, so that his horns were wrapped by them. He turned his palms upward and lifted his arms high. A ball of brilliant white formed within his palms, pulsing to the same rhythm as the rest of the gargoyles. But even as it did so, its color began shifting. First to a pale grey, then to a pewter hue. Only a few seconds passed before it was barely visible at all, as if it was becoming the absence of light. As the shape shifted into blackness, it grew in size until it was much larger than Kimar himself, obstructing the view of everything beyond it. The pulsing light cast by each gargoyle lanced the black sphere and vanished within. Only the contrast of where the growing orb blocked others from view revealed the final size of it.

Johann exclaimed, "That's big enough to fit my largest wagon!"

At the moment it stopped growing, a subtle purple began pulsing from its core, quickly intensifying to violet. The cadence of the orb's light was opposite the collective beating of white. A moment later, a deep blue burst from the orb.

"Ames!" Peter cried. "Is this what I think it is? It's like a rainbow's seed!"

There was no answer. Amy stared in wonder at the huge sphere resting in Kimar's hands. But she was nodding.

The fluid indigo lightened for a moment before twisting into a dazzling green. It was twisting now, as if the changing colors danced and played within the sphere, chasing each other until the earlier color gracefully bowed out. So it was that green relinquished its role in favor of yellow's predominance.

"It's as if they…as if…they live!" Amy choked out. "These colors are alive, Peter!"

"*Nydelig!*" Heidi whispered loud enough the others could hear her over the thrumming.

"Jah, it is beautiful…wondrously beautiful!" Johann cried.

Orange began swirling within the orb, intricately lacing around the yellow, back and forth for a moment, until yellow took its leave.

Even as red burst out from the center of the sphere, casting the entire valley into shocks of pink as it blended with the still-pulsing white from those in attendance, its cadence ebbed into the rhythm of the white. The thrumming increased in tempo. The hundreds of points of white light within the valley, each belonging to the gargoyle from which it came, now surrendered to the sphere's red. First, the white points nearest the orb quickly shifted to match the red of the orb. The color shift continued outward, evenly, until red was racing up the slab-like walls hemming in the valley. Soon, the entire valley darkened as the gargoyles matched its hue. Rather than creating an unsettling sensation, which Peter had expected from everything being bathed in a blood-red, it quickened his expectations.

"Ames, I think they're shifting into a light register we can't see!" he said, as the valley continued to darken.

Just as the humans expected all to go black until only the stars above would be visible, the sphere over Kimar bloomed all of the colors of the rainbow, with blues chasing greens and oranges, reds yielding to yellows, each dancing with the other until they began to slow and gather themselves.

"No! I don't believe it!" Peter cried as Amy gasped.

"What is this thing?" Johann said, breathless.

"It's earth!" Peter replied.

"But more beautiful than ever we've seen it," Amy added.

"You have *seen* this before?" Heidi asked, wonder and fear framing her question.

"Uh, of course," Amy replied, absently, as she stared at the earth, in all its resplendent glory, perched over Kimar's hands. "I...we...oh, wait! I'm sorry, Heidi and Johann. I just assumed...yes, this is how earth looks from space—"

"Better!" Peter interrupted. "This looks better than any image from space. It's breathtaking, isn't it? I mean it's just—"

Prohximus lowered his hands, his palms facing the humans. They all recognized the signal for silence.

Quarastohr turned to look at Ercen. "Has he located them? Many of us sense tremendous urgency is called for. Has Kimar found them?"

Suddenly, a pinpoint of bright light flared on the surface of the sphere facing the humans.

"Yes!" Ercen cried, pointing at the globe. "Yes! He's located them!"

Amy gasped, pointing at the spot. "Peter, look! It can't be there. That puts them in Chile."

"What is the meaning of this?" Johann said.

"It appears that our loved ones are being held near—or in—Aconcagua. It's one of the tallest peaks on our planet. It's nearly impossible to get to."

"Not with us!" Kimar cried, standing up as he lifted the sphere high over his head. It now hovered. "You are correct, Quarastohr," Kimar added. "We must go with all haste. Whoever goes with us, join us now."

Conomorg and Ita-Mudak immediately strode over, flanking Kimar and Ercen. Anja jumped into the arms of Ita-Mudak, spoiling for a fight to rejoin her mistress, Danielle.

Peter glanced around the dais and realized more than twenty warriors had joined them, which greatly encouraged him.

"I, too, would join you," Prohximus intoned, tipping his head towards Kimar, "if you would permit it, Commander."

"Of a certainty, General," Kimar replied, a hint of a grin wrinkling his face. "Hear me!" Kimar roared. "As we part, I will split our party into two groups. One will go to where the Hudsons are held. There I send Ita-Mudak and Conomorg, along with the dog since it wishes to be in the company of them; so, too, will Prohximus and most of the other warriors.

The parents we will take to their daughters and companions, who are already harassed in battle."

Reaching up his right hand, he placed his index talon on the brilliant white point of Aconcagua.

"In the next instant, you will be at war!" he cried.

With a great rush of wind, the war party shrank into a gossamer band of light and, like an arrow, shot into the white point.

A moment later, the sphere of earth vanished.

CHAPTER TWENTY-SIX
GREAT SUNDERINGS

Greatly disoriented by gusts of wind, flying grit, acrid smoke and little light, Peter had difficulty getting his bearings. Glancing to his left, he realized he was on his hands and knees. Blood was dripping on his left hand. His blood.

What's happened? he wondered in the stillness. There seemed to be a lot of movement around him. Mostly it was grey movement. Shifting back and forth. He could make out feet sometimes, but the motion was very quick. Frenetic. A wing tip would sweep just over his head, blowing his hair all over. *Ah! That's where the grit is coming from. These wings are swirling it up off the floor.*

Peering beneath the shifting greys, he could see beige beyond them. *Walls? Wings and walls? Where am I and what's going on here?*

Suddenly, a pair of feet appeared next to him. Regular feet with no talons. Feet wearing Keds. *Keds? That's right! Danielle wears Keds.*

More blood dripped onto his filthy hand. Enough of it had pooled on the back of his palm that it finally ran off onto the dirty stone floor. *What happened?*

His shoulders squeezed together. Someone was tickling him. *No, that's not right. Lifting...*

Ah, Danielle! Her face came into view, but no words came to complete his greeting. Peter squinted at his daughter. She was talking to him. At least from the motion of her lips, he assumed that she intended to talk to him. *She really needs to speak up. We taught her better than this.*

"Dad!" Danielle yelled at him. *What else could she be saying? Bad? Mad?*

Peter was growing annoyed with Danielle and felt a surge of anger rising up within. But the incessant hissing in his ears was even more aggravating. That and the spots dancing before his eyes. *Where am I? Why is she taunting me? I'll have to talk to Ames about this because this is unaccepta—Ames? You're here, too?* Before Amy could answer, he felt consciousness slipping away.

Vaguely aware that another set of hands slid under his arms, Peter's head tipped back and he was staring at the ceiling. *No, that's not right. This isn't a ceiling. It's a...it's a...ah, what are these called again? Cave roof? Yes, that's it. Cave roof. Except this roof is very high. But I—we—were in a cave just now and...where'd Danielle go?*

A grey wing passed over his head, blocking his view of shimmering stalactites high overhead. This infuriated Peter. He tried thrusting his right hand through the gap in the wings just as a plume of fire burst over the gap. The veins in the grey canopy stood out harshly, as dark lines across now orange-colored wings.

Whoa! I really don't feel well. His left eye stung ferociously from the blood sliding into it. Dark spots chased around his right eye, blocking most of his remaining vision, until he slipped back into darkness.

Again, he felt someone lifting and dragging him. Looking down, he saw that the hands were as big as pie plates, with muscled forearms. *Why do Amy and Danielle keep pestering me like this?* The fingers were thick and calloused. *Wait. Danielle was just yelling at me. How did her hands get behind me?* Slowly, his mind repeated the observation: fingers…thick and calloused. *Johann!* "What are you—"

But then Danielle was staring at him again. *Where did Johann go?* He stared at her blankly from one eye. The other, clenched shut, was already swollen. His hair was matted from blood and grit.

"He must have a concussion!" she yelled over his shoulder. *Who is she yelling to? I wonder who has a concussion and why does she sound so strange? And will someone please get those idiots with the jackhammers to stop their incessant hamme—*his head drooped—*ham…hammering!* Silence stole over Peter, even as he vainly fought the impulse to sleep.

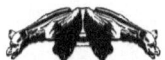

About fifteen minutes earlier, the second rescue team had parted into the chamber, nearly in the center, and immediately faced the nine secret guards, just as they unleashed a volley of flying fists at the Macys. What they couldn't see was Lohxnahr clapping his hands together just behind them. If Danielle had had time enough to yell a warning, they would have ducked. She'd seen the little gargoyle use this weapon to devastating effect within the special chamber beneath the temple of Kahrnahrgx the year before.

Though Kimar and Ercen had erected their wings in time to form a canopy, it was still in motion when the blast of Lohxnahr's clap hit them from behind. At the same moment, the collective flying fists from nine enraged guards, hit them from the front. While the majority of the impact flowed over and around the protecting wings, the initial blast slammed one of Kimar's wing tips into Peter's forehead and he went down like a felled lodge pole.

From then on, it was chaos.

Danielle had helped Bettina get Mrs. Macy into a recessed corner in the cell, where two huge gargoyle friends of Kimar sheltered the women, while two more fought against four of the hidden guards who had broken off from the main group.

Hearing a high-pitched cry, Danielle struggled to look past the battle just a few feet from her. She spotted Freida, holding Tiny's head in her lap, screaming at a guard towering over her. Though flashing greys, clattering talons, flailing arms and glinting swords blocked much of her view of Freida, she saw the swift arc of a wooden staff slam its large burled knob into the head of the guard. He toppled sideways onto the floor and didn't move again. "Mrs. Skulstad is here, then! And she came armed," she cried.

The noise within the cell was deafening, mostly from gargoyle shouts and the clashing of their talons. But Danielle also heard people shouting, of course. Her mother's voice wailing over her father's condition. Anders yelling for Paign. Gudrun's constant high-pitched wail almost in her ear. Johann shouting at Heidi and Freida to stay low. Her head throbbed from the noise and clamor. She wished Anja had come, and she wondered desperately what had become of her dog. Her breath was ragged and she was nearly hyperventilating. The dust and dirt in the air was choking. She so wanted to cower where she was in the vain hope that all would grow quiet and she'd wake up in her bed in Illinois.

But that was impossible, because more than anything, Danielle worried about her father. She dropped down on her hands and lifted her knees like a sprinter settling into the blocks just before a race. She could see her father trying to sit up on the floor, but there was no way he could manage it with all the movement of legs and wings swirling around him. It looked like her mother was trying to lift him, but she kept getting jostled out of the way.

Behind the mass of feet marking her father's location, Danielle could see evidence of other gargoyles. Some were the grey warriors who had come with Kimar's group. Some were the black obsidian of the hidden guards. Several of the obsidians were lying on the floor, motionless. She wondered if the blast of Lohxnahr's clap had felled any foes. The confines of the prison cell made fighting in close quarters especially horrifying. Danielle realized that she'd seen no fireballs hurled by either side because it would be suicidal within the prison cell. She couldn't see what was beyond the cell's doorway, but feared they must all get out that door soon or they never would.

As the granite protectors standing over her finally felled the guards attacking the Macys, Danielle saw an opening and dashed across the clearing to the canopy protecting her father. Quickly pushing her way through a gap in the convergence of wings, she was immediately knocked over and landed on top of a gargoyle's foot. She couldn't tell if it belonged to Ercen or Kimar.

Good thing their talons are only sharp on the bottom and tips, or I'd be missing fingers!

Before she could get herself upright, Danielle glimpsed Lohxnahr again, only about seven meters away. Zarentil was next to him. Both held their hands palm up as if warding off

blows. She couldn't see more than the feet of their attackers
before they were concealed again.

It was too loud to hear her mother, but Danielle understood plainly enough. Her mother's goal was to get them out
of the cavern and into the open. Danielle wasn't the only one
fearful of being trapped. Amy slid her left arm under Peter's
right and signaled for Danielle to do the reverse on the other
side. They were able to lift Peter for the first time. Though the
fighting was intense, Kimar and Ercen stole a quick glance
and nodded their approval and understanding. Slowly—so
slowly—the collective mass of humans and gargoyle protectors inched towards the opening.

Danielle hadn't forgotten about her friends, but in the
chaos there had been no time to wonder. It was Freida's scream
that changed that.

Just as Danielle tried to look in between the winged
canopy, her father's foot snagged on something. Or maybe
Kimar or Ercen stopped. Danielle couldn't tell. All she was
certain of was that Freida's scream came from outside of the
prison cell; there was an echo. For just a moment, she caught
sight of her friend pointing to the left, beyond the cell's wall.
Danielle had no idea what Freida was pointing at but knew it
was bad. Freida was flanked by Anders and Paign, who were
looking frantically to their right. They were dragging her in
that direction, but she seemed to be fighting them.

Something thudded hard, behind her mother, and suddenly the canopy of wings lifted. Danielle awkwardly lowered
her father to his knees, spent from the effort of moving him.
Peter was semiconscious and muttering gibberish. Turning
around to survey the room, Danielle gasped. Behind them lay
three obsidians. Towards the center of the room, Lohxnahr

and Zarentil were brushing themselves off; two more obsidians were heaped on the floor. At the far wall, two of the guards who had come with Kimar were gently helping Bettina and Gudrun step over two more obsidians. But two of their comrades had fallen while protecting the women.

She'd already seen the obsidian fall from the blow rendered by Mrs. Skulstad's staff. That brought her count to nine obsidians. But when Danielle finally turned around to face the doorway, she cried out. There was the reason they'd made so little progress. It was clear that the nine hidden obsidian sentries, plus the remaining prison guard, had exacted a high price for the liberation of the prisoners by the rescue teams. Two more obsidians were sprawled into the opening, but six granite gargoyles lay dead around them. Johann was trying to clean his sword on the stone doorway. Heidi leaned against the wall next to him, her face ashen and spent.

"They're coming, Kimar!" Paign yelled back into the cell. "You must get them out now! This way is our only chance!"

For reasons she couldn't guess, Danielle plainly saw that Freida struggled in Paign's grip. But looking at Kimar and Ercen for direction brought no comfort. Both were a patchwork of wounds and panted heavily from the exertions of defending Peter from a squad of elite fighters.

Instinct drove her now. Danielle pulled her father back to his feet. Kimar took a deep breath, shoved himself away from the wall he'd been leaning against and physically pushed the mass of dead gargoyles out of the way. Amy quickly slid her arm under her husband's, and they staggered through the doorway. Glancing over her right shoulder, Danielle saw the granite warriors emerge with Bettina and Gudrun.

In a moment, Paign's warnings became obvious. The prison cell was hewn into the wall of an enormous, deep cavern. To their right, a carved pathway ran nearly straight and level, before curving into an inky blackness. To their left, the pathway widened for several hundred meters until it joined a broad passage. Vast sections of the path were elevated, like a stone bridge spanning unseen depths below. The entire pathway to their left was lit from unseen lights high above them. But directly in front of them, the light vanished into an abyss. Danielle had a vague impression that the other side of the vast cavern was at least a hundred meters away. Their only option was to retreat down the narrowing path to their right or plunge over the side, for a large gargoyle host was rushing down the route to their left.

Freida's cry suddenly pierced the gloom. "Nei! We cannot leave without him! I will not go…I will not…go!" Her scream echoed in beyond the ledge they were perched on. Anders and Paign, looking stricken, released her.

Quickly, Johann strode over to embrace his daughter.

Danielle felt her heart stop when she saw her closest friend pound Mr. Skulstad on his shoulders, wailing hysterically, as he held her tightly around the waist.

"Nei! Nei! Neiiii!" Freida shrieked as she stomped hard on her father's instep. Johann fell back, releasing his daughter with a terrible howl of pain.

Dismayed, Danielle reached out to Freida, but her friend took no notice and raced by her into the prison cell.

"Go! Quickly, sweetheart. Go!" Amy cried, gripping Peter tightly.

Danielle released her father, turned and ran back into the cell, skidding to a stop just after entering. "Oh, no! No, no, no…it can't be," she whispered, falling to her knees.

Just a few paces in front of her, Lohxnahr was hunched over the body of Freida's beloved companion. Tiny, broken inside from a crushing blow by the obsidian, was motionless. Freida wept over him. A faint, red haze encompassed Lohxnahr, Freida and the broken dog.

Danielle crawled over to them. "Lohxnahr?"

"Yes, my child?" he replied. The gentle smile on his face reminded Danielle of the elderly neighbor man back home when she'd greeted him a few weeks after his wife had died. It was a sad smile of loss.

"Can nothing be done?" Danielle choked out, placing her arm tightly around Freida.

"This brave and faithful friend will not be leaving with us," Lohxnahr replied, wrapping Tiny's listless face in his hands. Then, the gargoyle mystic leaned over and placed his forehead against Tiny's, whispering something as he did so.

Danielle couldn't be sure, due to the racking sobs next to her, but she thought he'd said, "Be at peace now." She couldn't hear the rest of his blessing.

"We must go now, girls!" Johann bellowed into the chamber. "In great haste!" he added, rushing in and lifting Freida off of the floor. He tucked her under his arm like a sack of potatoes and dashed for the opening. He stopped at the doorway and turned, setting Freida back on her feet. "Goodbye, dear Tiny. We will miss you, boy." Spinning on his heels, he shouted, "Come now, Danielle! Bring Lohxnahr with you!"

"Yes, it is time!" Lohxnahr said, jumping up to his feet. Taking Danielle's hand, he ran back to the pathway. She

glanced to her right and saw her group vanish around the outcrop where the path narrowed and turned. Her heart, already
heavy, instinctively knew that their enemy was nearly upon
them. A great shout had gone up as soon as Lohxnahr appeared in the open. Yet, turning to face the oncoming hoard
still shocked her, for the host was beyond numbering. While
most of their foes ran with great speed upon the sloping path,
some were in flight. Out of the corner of her eye, she caught
a flicker of light reflecting in the deep gloom far to her right.
She guessed there were four or five obsidians already in pursuit
of her parents and the others.

"Lohxnahr, what do we do?" Danielle cried. "What hope
do we have?"

"Child, there is always hope, even in the darkest hours,"
Lohxnahr replied, fluttering off the pathway. "And these are,
indeed, dark hours," he added, grinning. "Let us hope the
more deeply in Hope!"

Danielle jumped at a scratching noise coming from the entrance of the cell. Her heart leapt, expecting to see Tiny. Turning
to welcome the dog, she recoiled in horror as the hybrid stepped
onto the pathway, only three meters from them.

It took a tremendous amount of trust to be parted anywhere at the hands of another. More so when the one doing
the parting didn't accompany the group. Only the deepest
trust would explain the madness of being parted directly into
an enemy stronghold, especially when those enemies are expecting the raid.

Conomorg, Ita-Mudak and Prohximus landed facing a throne, lit by huge braziers suspended from the high roof of the throne room, piled high with glowing stones. The throne was about twenty meters away and slightly to their right. Conomorg stood just in front of Prohximus, while Ita-Mudak stood to the right of Conomorg. Prohximus stood just to the right of a massive pillar of glistening, polished marble. The throne room was ringed by over a dozen such columns and was dazzling bright. Too bright.

The high-pitched whine of a dozen fireballs resonated in the giant hall.

"Screen!" Prohximus bellowed.

Ita-Mudak immediately jumped around Conomorg and dropped to one knee, next to Prohximus, raising his hands up to shoulder height, facing outwards. Quickly, Ita-Mudak pulled his shoulders back and pushed them outward again, just as the first volley of fireballs reached the rescue party.

Shards of flame lanced through the invisible screen, but most of the fireballs' power glanced off of the shield, sending them to either side of the group or into the ceiling above. Exploding against the pillar and surrounding area, the fireballs sent fume and grit everywhere, obscuring the rescuers' view of the throne. Several long stalactites overhead sheered away and fell like knives into Ita-Mudak's screen, piercing the top of it. The protective dome slowed the speed of the shards enough that no one was skewered by them.

"Did you see them?" Conomorg shouted.

"Were they near the throne?" Prohximus replied.

"Along with Kahrnahrgx!"

"Comrades!" Prohximus bellowed. "We are here to retrieve the humans. We are greatly outnumbered, even in this chamber, so now is not the time to engage in battle unless absolutely necessary. Trust in Providence!"

Ita-Mudak again pushed his hands out, but this time the screen sprang forward, expanding as it went. A second volley of fireballs exploded into it. More shards got through, but with nearly all of their speed and power removed. Bits of fiery embers showered across the expanse between the edge of Ita-Mudak's shield and the company it protected.

Prohximus leapt high into the air, latching onto the column with his feet near its top.

Eight of the accompanying granite gargoyles, led by Conomorg, sprinted towards the throne, throwing flying fists into the dim expanse between the columns nearest the throne. They couldn't clearly see the obsidians lurking there, but they knew it was where the fireballs were coming from. The concussive blast shattered sections of the columns down onto their enraged opponents.

Even as Conomorg neared the throne's large dais, he saw that the hostages were alive. Briefly encouraged, he then saw Kahrnahrgx smirk. Raising his right hand, he made a fist, flaring out his long, curved talons for the killing strike. The humans were already kneeling before the ruthless gargoyle.

"No, Kahrnahrgx! No!" Crying out, Conomorg hurled a flying fist at Kahrnahrgx, knowing too well that it would not be speedy enough to matter. Just as he did so, the floor upon which Conomorg ran exploded upwards, sending sharp chunks of stone blasting into his comrades and knocking him into the air.

With bitter irony, Conomorg realized that the very trick he and Ita-Mudak had employed against the hybrid, lying hidden in the stone floor entryway of the Wheelen's home, had just been unleashed upon his squad with brutal consequence. Even as he crashed hard into the ruptured floor, Conomorg was set upon by three slate gargoyles. At least three of his mates had been killed in the violence of the sprung trap. The remainder was accosted by more slates that had lain in wait, disguised as a huge section of floor.

Furious that he'd been surprised by the trap, Conomorg unleashed a lethal counterattack on the slates, while still working his way towards the humans. Stealing a glance at the Hudsons, he saw his enemy's hand sweep down at them. Then his view was blocked by a slate dodging his blow.

"No!" he bellowed again, knowing it was already too late.

In the tumult of battle, none of the rescuing gargoyles, including Ita-Mudak, remembered they'd brought Anja. Right away, she spotted the Hudsons, whom she thought of with great fondness. Twisting out from under the gargoyles surrounding her, she immediately bounded into the darkness behind the marble column. Knowing she'd be hard to see and completely unexpected by their foes, she sprinted along the edge of the throne room and past the left edge of the dais, until she was hidden in the gloom behind the throne. Spires of stone, some carved into grotesque shapes and others made of natural stalagmites, cast frenzied shadows from erupting fireballs. Here, she slowed and moved with stealth, keeping her head low to the ground, slipping quickly from shadow into shadow, growing ever closer to where the Hudsons were kneeled on the harsh surface of the dais.

Anja's ears perked up at the cry of the big gargoyle friend of her mistress. She peered over the edge of the dais and saw Conomorg under attack from the slate gargoyles hidden as part of the throne room's floor.

Her head tipped to one side as she noted the furtive glances he kept making in her direction. She followed his gaze and—*No!*

Anja saw the glittering talons hovering above the Hudsons' heads. She was less than seven meters from them, and she knew there was no creature in this chamber as fast as she was in a dead sprint. With a massive thrust of her powerful thighs, Anja launched onto the dais, covering a third of the distance. Then she ran full out directly at the hulking gargoyle threatening her mistress's friends. Even in the din of battle with skirmishes throughout the great hall, Anja's claws were audible, clicking upon the dais.

Just as the gargoyle's fist swung down at the Hudsons, Anja sprang at his arm, snarling.

Kahrnahrgx caught the barest glimpse of motion coming at him fast. Instead of completing his executioner's swing, he swept his arm over their heads, minimizing his arm as a target. He knew nothing of dogs and therefore had no frame of reference by which to judge Anja. Little did he know she weighed more than most male Akitas and was enormous for a female. When she clamped onto his unprotected arm, he howled in fury and pain. Her momentum carried her past the gargoyle, but she wasn't letting go. Kahrnahrgx's shoulder was nearly wrenched from its socket before he unwillingly pivoted on his feet and flew backwards off of the dais.

Anja released her grip on the beast's arm and landed deftly on her feet, sliding quietly on her pads to a stop. Immediately, she snarled at him and prepared to pounce. He crashed hard onto the floor and nearly slid into the melee with Conomorg.

Ita-Mudak had freed himself of all his assailants just before Anja's attack on Kahrnahrgx. The bodies of slates ringed the area around him. Having spent the most time with the canine companions of the humans they protected, he knew that Anja's luck with Kahrnahrgx had been based on stealth. Her advantage was gone, but she didn't know it. The bloodlust of battle filled her nostrils. Too far away to engage Kahrnahrgx directly, Ita-Mudak cast his invisible shield at the dog, enveloping Anja just as Kahrnahrgx flipped over, pushed up by a tremendous snap of his leathery wings. Dog and gargoyle stared the other down, a fearful growl coming from both. But Kahrnahrgx knew it was pointless to fight the dog. In fact, it played into the hands of his enemies, distracting him from his objective: the captives.

Turning back to the Hudsons, Kahrnahrgx was surprised that Prohximus blocked the way. He'd dropped down from the pillar's height at the same time that Anja sprang from hiding, but she was the quicker.

"You will not pass, Kahrnahrgx!"

Snorting his disgust, Kahrnahrgx replied, "And who will stop me, ancient one? The general in you is old and decrepit, a shadow of the warrior of the elder days. Would you have me bow, Prohximus, for old time's sake?"

Now it was Prohximus who snorted. "Ha! I believe we are long past that path, General Kahrnahrgx."

"What, then?"

"Surrender!"

"I prefer not to."

"Your preference notwithstanding, you must surrender!"

"Prohximus," Kahrnahrgx sighed. "Need I remind you that you came with a small raiding party to cause havoc and annoyance? In this you have succeeded. However, you have failed in your grand plan of rescuing those humans I've held captive. Even these two who cower behind you yet remain in my chamber, yes? Your fighters have done splendidly within my throne room, I grant you. But you must know, Prohximus, that I command a legion of loyal soldiers within this mountain alone. What hope do you have of escape? Do you not recognize that, while we made it only somewhat difficult for you to enter here, we wanted you to come? Now that you are here, along with my brother and his ragtag band of followers, you shall find leaving my fortress *exceptionally* challenging. Parting out of here you will find to be impossible."

"Hm," Prohximus replied. "Nice speech, Kahrnahrgx. I found it very moving." Reaching behind him, he waved for Caedmon and Aleira Hudson to grab his wings. Bruised and very pale, still both stood firm and did as he indicated.

"You will note, Kahrnahrgx, that of the sorties we brought to your throne room, we were the victors," Prohximus continued, surveying the fallen within the great hall, "although the price was high. Many of these, my comrades, you knew once. And I, yours. This is wanton senselessness."

"Only because you and your followers—Quarastohr, Lohxnahr, the dim-witted Zarentil and, of course, my brother and his mate—because you all refuse to see the truth," Kahrnahrgx replied, yawning while drawing attention to the battle's results with a grandiose sweep of his arm. "Indeed, the losses are regrettable…but necessary. Let us not quibble about such things. I grow weary of this conversation. Long has it been since you were my master. Now, I am the stronger. Relinquish the captives and promise your warriors will desist and I will release you. Even the dog."

As the parrying continued, the companions of Prohximus quietly gathered near where they'd parted in. Ita-Mudak eventually coaxed Anja to trot over to him.

"I think not. We have what we came for. You have cleaning to do, my student. And you seem to think that you learned all of the lessons I could teach. In this, you are woefully mistaken."

"Perhaps it is you who are mistaken. I hear your comrades gathering in the darkness beyond, like cowards in retreat. I say again...you cannot part out of the fortress, old fool!"

"Indeed, they are," Prohximus grinned. "And who said anything about parting out of this mountain?" With a nod from their senior commander, Conomorg, Ita-Mudak holding Anja, and the remaining rescue team vanished from the throne room.

Danielle reared back from the approaching hybrid and, in the process, let go of Lohxnahr's hand. So great was her fear that she couldn't make any sound erupt from her throat. Instead, she flailed her arms at the creature as if to swat away a wasp. Paying no heed to anything around her—even the quickly advancing squads of Kahrnahrgx —she tripped over a protruding stone in the pathway, losing her balance. Suddenly, she was waving her arms in a vain attempt at keeping herself from toppling into the abyss.

Finally, a scream came. "Lohxnaaaaaahr!" exploded from her, as gravity trumped her effort at staying upright, and she tipped over the edge. She couldn't twist fast enough to grab any part of the ledge. It would have made no difference since there was nothing growing either on the sheer rock face or upon the path.

Danielle cried out as she tried to stop her body from its chaotic tumbling. She flailed in the whistling air with her arms and struggled for breath against the force of the wind in her face. Fear and regret billowed up in her heart. What would become of her parents? Of Anja? Of all the people they'd come to rescue—and the ones who made up the rescue team she'd come with? Of her dear gargoyle friends? She couldn't help but stare down into the abyss, wondering how far she had to fall. The inky darkness provided no answer. Yet, Danielle's thoughts and feelings coalesced into a single focus: hope. Not for herself. But for the others—without understanding why— she sensed everything would be all right. Not in the way she'd expected, of course. Already, there had been great loss and, somehow, Danielle knew there would be more loss: failures, setbacks, injury, even death. And yet a burning confidence grew inside her, like a fast-growing flame. With nothing left to do, she surrendered to the inevitable, let go of her fear and closed her eyes for a moment.

Bursting through her closed lids, a deep gold flushed.

Is this death? she wondered. *No...I still hear the wind rushing past my ears.*

Opening her eyes brought Danielle face to face with the hybrid, flying straight down the sheer wall. Aghast, she felt an urge to panic, to scream, to resist. But there was something strange about the hybrid.

What is it? Something...something.

The hybrid's wings flared out wide at the precise moment it grabbed Danielle's hands.

Copper...copper eyes?

In an instant, Danielle was on the back of the hybrid, riding it as she had Kimar the year before. As the pleasant memory filled her heart, she marveled that the feeling she had now—riding on the back of her mortal enemy—was not one of dread and horror, but…

COPPER EYES!

Squeezing her thighs securely around the gargoyle, Danielle sat up straight and threw her arms wide, giggling.

"Dear me!" she laughed. "How did I not see it before?"

"You weren't looking!" a familiar voice buzzed next to her.

"Lohxnahr!" Danielle cried. "You knew all about this, didn't you?"

"Indeed!" he grinned. "But Zarentil was the original schemer."

Danielle rocked back and forth as the gargoyle beneath her affirmed Lohxnahr's assertion.

"So, not only can Zarentil throw off the sentries in this fortress—or he *did*, anyway, so they didn't recognize him for what he is—he can actually take the shape of the hybrid! You're not done yet!"

"Truth!" Lohxnahr chirped.

All the while, the three had been plummeting towards the bottom of the chasm, almost vertically. Now that they were closer to the ground, she could finally make things out. Danielle guessed they had already dropped about 150 meters and still had another 120 meters before they'd reach the highest stalagmite spires.

"Then, where are we off to now?"

Despite the rush of wind, Danielle heard Zarentil's deep voice reply, "Into the heart of this kingdom!"

With that, both gargoyles trimmed their wing position and arced their flight slightly upwards, towards the far end of the long cavern. They seemed to be making for a point roughly sixty meters below the junction where the path to the Macys' prison cell joined the highway. Danielle guessed that the patch of darkness against a dimly lit rock face marked a cave.

Only seconds from it, she heard Lohxnahr hum, "You would do well to duck your head, child."

She snuggled down, so that she was nearly prone across the back of Zarentil. With no change in their speed, they disappeared into the hole a moment later.

A pale radiance instantly emanated from Lohxnahr, lighting their way down the passage, for the cave was more like a tunnel, going relatively level and straight back into the center of the mountain.

Zarentil weaved easily back and forth with subtle movements of his wings. Their speed was breakneck and made Danielle giddy. At the same time, the excitement brought her uncontrollable giggles.

"This would make such a fun ride back home!"

"Eh?" Lohxnahr replied.

"You know, an amusement park ride. We could call it 'The Zarentil'! It would be so great," she chuckled.

Danielle noticed a different light coming from far down the tunnel; it flickered yellow, like a fire does.

"In a moment, I'll need to leave you for a time," Lohxnahr smiled in return.

Immediately, the gravity of the situation rushed back into Danielle's mind, choking off the giggles. "OK, Lohxnahr. What do we need to do?"

"Complete the deception, of course!" he quipped, spreading his wings out. Quickly, Zarentil's speed carried Danielle away from her guide.

Before he was out of sight, she heard Lohxnahr add, "And spring the trap!" The pale light surrounding Lohxnahr quickly dissipated, and he shrank into the tunnel's gloom.

"I'll go back," Anders offered. He knew it would be too hard for Freida or either of her parents to go, with the loss of Tiny just minutes earlier.

"Nothing doing, Kimar!" Peter snapped, opening his eyes unnaturally. "She's my daughter and I'm going."

"No, you will not," Kimar replied, "either one of you. By now, the prison chamber has been overrun, or will be by the time you get there and"—he held his hand up to cut off Peter's retort—"while your heart is great, my friend, your weapons are insufficient to this task. And you have only now been barely healed from a blow I never meant to give you."

"But—" Amy began.

"He would have no chance, Amy," Kimar continued, "and neither would you. Two things I take comfort in. First, though Danielle is missing, so are Lohxnahr and Zarentil. It is inconceivable that they are not to be found together. So, though she is not with us, she is therefore with them. What you cannot understand is that, though small in size, even childlike in manner and shape, these two are perhaps the most dangerous gargoyles within this mountain fortress. Thus, your daughter is under the protection of *most powerful* defenders."

"OK," Peter quickly relented, dropping down into a squatting position on the ledge and slowly rubbing his head. "What's the second thing?"

"That the pathway between us and those pursuing us is narrow. This requires most of his minions to fly."

"And that helps us how?" Amy snapped.

"It is much harder to aim when in flight, Amy and Peter," Ercen interjected.

"Especially when you're being fired upon by gargoyles on a ledge?" Anders surmised.

"Yes, Anders," Kimar replied. "Our situation is very serious, it is true, and I do not make light of it. In spite of that, it is imperative to understand that the defenders of Kahrnahrgx do not have any advantages over us at this time. And we have succeeded in rescuing the Macys. This angers them, yes, but it also demoralizes them. They believed their trap to be inescapable. Yet here we are. We have the advantage."

"Let's get moving, then!" Paign barked. The surviving granite gargoyles who had defended Gudrun and Bettina in the cave flanked Paign and his mother and sister. "And the advantage seems pretty slim to me."

"Jah, my thinking, also!" Johann blurted out.

"Indeed," Kimar chuckled. "I'll investigate where Danielle and the guides have gotten to. Ercen will lead you farther into the rear of this chasm. I'll return as soo—"

"Kimar?" Freida said, stepping forward.

"Yes, Freida?"

"Will there be other gargoyles ahead, hidden in the walls… or the pathway, I mean?"

Kimar took a deep breath. "No, it is unlikely. Kahrnahrgx may be ruthless, but he is not stupid. Rather, he is a brilliant tactician, which we saw today in the prison cell. But it takes away critical resources when he dedicates his elite soldiers to hiding. Even with the nine he utilized in the prison, it was not enough. So, no, I don't expect any hidden enemies."

"Well, I guess we'll be the ones to find out," Amy muttered. Seeing the look on Freida's face, she quickly softened and hugged the girl with as much of a smile as she could muster. "I'm sorry, sweetie. I'm just grumpy and upset about what's happened already."

With a nod to Ercen, Kimar turned and ran down the narrow ledge. No one moved until he rounded a corner about thirty meters back. But just as he reached the corner, he disappeared even before he went around it.

"Whoa!" Peter exclaimed. "Maybe I'm not as healed up as I thought. Either that or my eyes are playing tricks on me. Didn't Kimar just—"

"Fade," Ercen replied, finishing his question.

"I'm sorry?"

"Kimar faded. It is a less complete version of what the gargoyles hidden into the walls did. When a gargoyle is utterly still, the illusion is quite complete, as you noticed with Ita-Mudak and Conomorg hidden in your own floor. Because Kimar needs as much stealth as possible, he's faded. This makes it nearly impossible to see him without the enemy looking directly at him when he is stationary. The illusion is not as powerful as when hidden, but it is close."

"And if he's moving?" Anders said.

"Less hidden," Ercen replied. "His colors shift to imitate his surroundings. But the greater his speed, the more difficult that becomes."

"So, it would be kind of like seeing something familiar but through the shimmering waves rising off of the hot ground of midsummer? Like heat devils?" Amy asked.

"Or a fast-changing chameleon," Peter quipped.

"Yes, those are good images. An observant guard might notice an odd movement of colors."

"How far is it that we need to go, Ercen?" Peter asked, slowly getting up from the floor.

"With luck, we should be there in less than a quarter of your hours," Ercen replied. "Prohximus is to meet us there with his squad once they have rescued the Hudsons."

"Please, rest here," Conomorg said to the Hudsons.

"Sure," Caedmon replied, helping Aleira sit on the interior of the vast ledge where the cavern wall formed a deep hollow. "Thanks."

While otherwise whole, the Hudsons had been subjected to overwhelming fear since their abduction. It had taken the greatest toll on Aleira, who was gentle and shy. Anja sensed this and snuggled up to her, nuzzling the woman's face. Aleira quickly buried her face into Anja's scruff and wept.

Ita-Mudak stepped over to Prohximus, who was leaning over the edge of the yawning precipice using his outstretched wings as a counterbalance. "Any sign of them, General?"

"Not as yet," came the reply, as Prohximus stared down the length of the pathway their friends were traveling. But the leader also scanned into the depths below for signs of movement.

"How long do we wait, sir?"

"As long as it takes or until the enemy arrives, whichever comes first."

"And if the enemy arrives first?"

"Then we stay as long it takes, until our comrades arrive."

"Understood, sir," Ita-Mudak replied, nodding once. "I'll make arrangements."

Ita-Mudak waved over Conomorg and the remaining eleven gargoyles in the elite rescue unit. "Lads, even if the others join us before our enemies discover us, it is improbable that we won't be attacked before we all leave this kingdom of darkness. Find positions of concealment and tactical advantage. I leave those locations to your choosing, but make all haste. The hour draws near."

In a flash, five of the soldiers dispersed to dim pockets and recesses in the cavern's walls, high over the ledge where Ercen's group would soon join them. Four more split off to either side of where the Hudsons huddled. The remaining three jumped over the edge and scaled down the face until they found dark hollows. Prohximus remained where he was with a commanding view of the huge chasm. Conomorg and Ita-Mudak lifted off of the ledge and flew to a colossal stalactite not far from the high plateau. They crawled around its huge base along the ceiling of the cave until they found concealed areas to hang from.

No sooner had they positioned themselves than Prohximus hissed, "They're here!"

Conomorg looked quickly towards Prohximus and then in the direction the general was pointing. Where the pathway leading to the plateau came into view, Anders was leading Kimar's rescue team. Freida and Bettina helped Paign's mother with as much haste as the fragile woman could manage. Heidi and Amy were clearly assisting Peter, who appeared unsteady on his feet. Ercen walked behind them several paces, constantly scanning the chasm below and above them. Johann and Paign brought up the rear, their swords at the ready.

"Where is the dog, Tiny?" Ita-Mudak whispered.

"I know not," Conomorg replied softly. "Something has happened already. An attack? Ambush? We won't know until we—"

"Conomorg!" Ita-Mudak cut him off. "Below Ercen!"

Barely visible against the gloomy depths of the cavern's steep walls, Conomorg perceived vague movement. He guessed they were obsidians or slates because they effortlessly blended into the dense shadows below the pathway.

"How many, Ita-Mudak? I'm having trouble seeing them. They fade well!"

"Indeed! There are five by my count. They'll be on Ercen in moments if we do not engage them. The others can't see them due to their angle of vision on that section of cliff."

Their hidden position was meant to be used to the greatest effect during a full-on assault on the huge ledge guarded by Prohximus. By engaging the faded gargoyles, their position would eventually be revealed.

"Agreed!" Conomorg hissed. "Use the fists for now. Perhaps we can get them all without disclosing our location. Once we use fireballs, our advantage is gone."

Ita-Mudak had already hurled two fists by the time Conomorg was done speaking. Given their distance from the sheer face, it was several seconds before impact, so they had to calculate each gargoyle's climbing speed and lead the shot.

Ercen and the others were as yet unaware they were near their friends, let alone about to be attacked. The sundering of rock four meters below her changed all that. Ita-Mudak's shots slammed into the nearest gargoyle, dislodging him completely and sending him tumbling chaotically into the abyss. The climber below him was barely able to cling to the rock by jamming one set of talons into a crack in the face. His fade vanished. Even as the first gargoyle was blown off the cliff face, Ercen aimed a fireball into the second foe, finishing what Ita-Mudak had begun. The bright explosion glistened off of the remaining faded beasts. Stripped of the advantage, four enemies launched off the wall, diving into the abyss below.

"You misjudged by one, my friend," Conomorg cried to his friend. "Turns out there were six attackers."

Prohximus bellowed, "Ercen! Get them over here. That was only the advance team. Many more are coming up the narrow divide at the base of the chasm! We're under attack!"

So focused had Conomorg and Ita-Mudak been on the crawlers, they had failed to see a large cluster flying up out of the gloom below. Already, the general and the sentries had launched fists and fireballs into the region below the rock shelf.

The noise was staggering between the concussive power of flying fists impacting enemy or stone, the explosions of fire-balls preceded by their high-pitched howl and the screams of gargoyles—some in pain and many more in anger.

Anders grabbed Gudrun and sheltered her between him and the rough wall vanishing into the darkness over their heads. Wrapping his arm around her waist, he made as much speed as she could manage. Freida and Bettina were right behind them. Still, he kept scanning the path before him and the chasm off to his left. He was grateful the way before them was nearly flat and that someone—unseen—had hurled down the bat-like gargoyles that nearly climbed up onto their path. "Quickly now, Mrs. Macy! I've got you."

There hadn't been enough time to completely restore Peter from the accidental blow he'd suffered in the prison. He was doing the best he could, but he wondered if his best would be good enough. He, too, was grateful there were defenders nearby, but he couldn't see any of them in the gloom, and the massive noise was affecting his balance. With one hand, he held tight to Amy and, with the other, he waved wildly against the sounds.

Heidi kept her head low and her hands tight around Amy's waist so that, between them, they could force Peter up the slight incline. She understood the physics of keeping a body in motion.

Ercen, recognizing how dire their situation was, scanned beneath their path. She could see Prohximus and was aware there were other defenders, suspecting that Conomorg and Ita-Mudak had engaged the gargoyles that had nearly reached her. She plainly could see movement below. Stretching her wings high and backwards, she curled her wing tips into tiny cracks in the wall, allowing her to lean far over the edge while providing enough space for Johann and Paign to pass.

A moment later, first Paign and then Johann ducked under her wings and trotted through. Johann bellowed back, "Ercen, we'll have company very soon. There are some fast runners in hot pursuit." As Johann and Paign ran towards the others, plumes of dust shook off them, leaving a trail.

"Where are the others, Ita-Mudak?" Conomorg cried. "Ercen isn't waiting. There's no sign of Kimar, Danielle or the mystics! This doesn't bode well."

Ita-Mudak wasn't listening. The depths of the abyss, directly below their perch, grew suddenly bright. From the top of the massive stalagmite that was the sister to their stalactite, three attackers had alighted, aimed and launched six fireballs at the company of humans. Spread across thirty meters of path, Ercen had no chance of protecting all of the humans.

Nor did anyone else. The speed of the incoming, flaming orbs was faster than any gargoyle could fly.

Ercen reacted immediately, releasing one wing from the wall, twisting around so she faced into the path, jamming the free pinion into a crack, releasing and jamming again, alternating back and forth so that she faced inward, then outward. She advanced on Johann and Paign with such speed that she overtook them in seconds, her wings already spread to protect those she could.

At the same, Anders reached the vast ledge and hurled Gudrun towards a cavity that sheltered humans he'd never seen before. Bettina and Freida ran after her, crouching low.

Peter reared back as Prohximus bellowed, "No! Hold your ground!" Along with Amy and Heidi, Peter dropped to his knees on the narrow pathway, completely exposed. Prohximus's wings snapped up and outwards, even as his arms reached high over his head. His arms swung down in the direction of the incoming fireballs, as his wings snapped forwards so hard that Prohximus tottered back from the edge. Peter had never seen a flying fist before, only the results of one. But this one just fired by Prohximus was enormous, disrupting smoke and fume already filling the cavern's expanse. Multiples larger than even the biggest fireballs, the flying fist pushed so much air in front of it that a vacuum formed in its wake.

"Ames, he's thrown a curve!" Peter yelled.

The flying fist howled past, dropping ten meters underneath them but still nearly pulled them off the narrow path. Then, it swung away and towards the very stalagmite where the attackers wailed in anger and fear. As their fireballs flew through the roiling air left by Prohximus's weapon, the trajectory of the flaming orbs veered right, sending them exploding well below their targets. A scorching plume roared up and over Peter, Heidi and Amy, but they were unharmed.

The most forward fireball, however, bounced over the fist's trail, deflecting it higher. Ercen had time to pivot over Johann and Paign, but not fully spread her wings into a canopy before the fireball cratered into the stone six meters over them. A shower of ruptured rock and grit fell onto the men. Ercen's right wing no longer held and she swung out violently. Johann lunged at her, seized her hand and hauled her back in. Her free wing snapped over their heads even as a large section of fractured wall let go and collapsed, deflecting it just in time.

A second later, the massive flying fist launched by Prohximus detonated across the upper third of the stalagmite seventy meters below where Ita-Mudak and Conomorg were perched. The top of it vaporized in a blinding burst of light, taking the three attackers with it. Much of the remaining upper section disintegrated into hundreds of mineral shards flying out in all directions. Because many of the attacking host were still near it, countless obsidians and slates were struck down or severely wounded. Those unhurt quickly retreated back into the depths of the abyss.

Anders rushed back down the path to assist Peter. Soon, Peter was leaning heavily against the wall next to Caedmon. Amy dropped to her knees and embraced Aleira. Johann and Heidi embraced for a quiet minute with Freida squished between them.

At first, Anja was delirious with excitement at the sight of her persons. But when she realized her mistress, Danielle, was not with them, she quivered uncontrollably, whimpering.

Ercen strode up to Prohximus, just as Conomorg and Ita-Mudak landed on the outcrop next to him. The other soldiers remained at their stations.

"Ercen, are you damaged? That was a near miss," the general asked.

"Nothing serious," she replied.

"Hm. Perhaps in a moment, it won't be serious," Conomorg chuckled, pressing his right hand against the wing she'd deflected the falling boulders with.

"What of the others, Ercen?" Prohximus continued, urgency driving his words. "Where is Kimar? Lohxnahr? The Chosen One?"

"I know not. We believed them to be behind us around a turn in the path. When it became clear they tarried, Kimar hastened back towards the prison cell to learn the reason."

"And he has not returned?"

"No, Prohximus."

"We must leave him to his own devices, Ercen. We have the humans we came for against all odds. It is a certainty that they will be lost should we linger here much longer. Though highly skilled, our force is small, and ill equipped to withstand another wave of enemy forces. We threw down the vanguard, but more are coming up the pathway, and I sense a huge force assembling in the abyss below. We cannot stay. I wish it were not so."

Dismay and comprehension mixed on Ercen's face. She nodded curtly.

"Kahrnahrgx boasted that we would not be able to part out of this mountain. I have yet to test his assertion. But at all costs, it must be done. Our time grows perilously short."

"No, Greatness. Our time is up," Ita-Mudak shouted, as he launched a fireball at the far end of the pathway. Several obsidians were swept away, but many more charged up the narrow passageway. More leapt off, flying away from the fireballs while shooting their own.

All eleven gargoyles of the elite squad unleashed a volley of weapons. Conomorg and Ita-Mudak remained at the edge of the plateau, using their vantage point to see what was coming from the abyss.

"A great swarm is coming from below, Prohximus!" Conomorg howled, pulling Ita-Mudak away from the edge and diving to the ground. A wall of fireballs rocketed upwards like a flaming curtain, throwing brilliant heat into the back of the recess.

Prohximus ran to the humans with Ercen just behind him. Hastily, they gathered all of the humans into a mass, cloaking them inadequately with only two sets of wings.

A giant rush of wind passed over their heads as the five elite guards nestled above loosed a torrent of fire just beyond the edge of the plateau. Not a second later, they were blown off the rock face by a wicked barrage of returning fire.

"Now, Ercen. To the Ten Pinnacles! We must part now!"

And nothing happened.

CHAPTER TWENTY-SEVEN
TECTONIC SHIFT

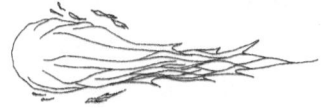

Lement-Nor exulted in how his elaborate plans were coming together. He'd woven a complex tapestry of deceit, dissembling and misdirection. It was his masterwork. How well he knew the chronic suspiciousness of his "master," Kahrnahrgx. It would be the rogue leader's downfall. More pleasing still, Lement-Nor waited to pull away the veil he'd spun before the Preceptor and reveal his actual objective. The hybrid chuckled as he visualized that moment. It would be a special time, meant for savoring deep and long, when he threw down the two who each considered himself Lement-Nor's master, one completely unaware of the other's involvement in his downfall and both unaware of Lement-Nor's true intention. He suffered no internal conflict about the role of gargoyles in the lives of humanity. The source of the conflict between the followers of Kahrnahrgx and those of his troublesome brother, Kimar, meant nothing to the hybrid. Along with the ever-present distractions, scheming about tactics and the absurd waste of resources, Lement-Nor found the opposing arguments tedious. He had been designed to best his opponents, and he intended to do so. Since he'd come to realize this truth—that at its most elemental, all creatures were his opponents—his purpose had been clear.

Being summoned back to the throne room was an annoyance. *What else is there? Prohximus got away with the human couple. What of it? He'll fail at the critical moment, unaware that they cannot hope to part out of this kingdom because of one in their midst.*

Striding confidently into the long chamber from its little-used rear entrance, Lement-Nor was stunned to see the human girl sitting cross-legged before the throne, facing into the great hall. Though her head hung down, with hair concealing her face, he immediately recognized her as the "Chosen One." Puzzled greatly by this unexpected good fortune, Lement-Nor jumped into the air and flew the length of the hall, landing on the first step of the dais, directly in front of Danielle. A small swirl of dust blew up around her.

She looked up and stared at the hybrid. "What is it you want from me?"

"Everything," Lement-Nor smirked, "and nothing."

"Why did you bring me here?" the girl sneered.

The insolence of her tone infuriated the hybrid, but the question itself threw him. A scowl wrinkled his face as he tipped his head. "Why do you ask?"

"Surely your lord, Kahrnahrgx, wanted me here to bring his revenge on me for my part in the destruction of his temple."

"This is…perhaps…how did you get here?"

"You brought me. As an offering."

"I, uh…"

"As a sacrifice," the girl continued.

"How did you get here?" Lement-Nor demanded.

"You brought me…or your twin did."

"My twin was killed by you and your protectors. He lived long enough to explain this to me before I dispatched him for his failure, his weakness. The Lord Kahrnahrgx has been less enthusiastic about your return to his kingdom since then, seeking other means by which to destroy you and your kind."

"You mean Paign?"

"How did you know that he—"

"I've suspected since he used a flying fist to destroy one of your comrades in his prison cell. But you just confirmed it for me."

"Don't toy with me, child! You think me a fool, do you? He's incapable of doing any such thing. We've marked him, yes, but empowered him? And as one of us, this would be madness."

"Then you are mad!" Danielle snapped back. "It is impossible to mistake what he did."

"I ask a final time, spawn of Eve," Lement-Nor snarled. "How is it you came to be here?"

Danielle sat up straight, stood slowly, stepped back and hopped up onto the throne. Smirking at Lement-Nor, she replied, "And I will say a final time…you brought me. Or, more accurately, your doppelgänger!"

"My what, you insolent human?"

"Me!"

Lement-Nor wheeled around to face the voice behind him…his voice.

Shock and dismay swept over the hybrid, for there before him—alive—was his twin. But he'd seen him die. He'd slain him personally. It couldn't be. But what other explanation could there be?

"You! You summoned me here?" Lement-Nor fumed.

"You are an abomination," his twin uttered, contempt filling each word.

Lement-Nor stared uncomprehending at his apparition until the eyes turned to polished copper. Rearing back, he roared, "No! It is not possible. I dispatched you myself, Zarentil. You *were* dead and you *will* be again soon enough!" Immediately, the hybrid lunged at Zarentil.

Danielle watched, aghast, since the violent exchange was like a warrior fighting an opposing mirror. Blow for blow, defense for defense, Lement-Nor grew furious. It was as if he were combating himself because, in truth, he was. Just as he had absorbed the essence of Zarentil, so had Zarentil been imbued with the same from Lement-Nor. Thus, no sudden movement intended to surprise Zarentil worked, since it wasn't a surprise. It couldn't be.

Lement-Nor jumped back from the conflict. Only his next words provided Danielle the clue as to which Lement-Nor was speaking: her enemy or her friend. During the combat, she had lost track of which gargoyle was Zarentil.

Seething with malice, the true Lement-Nor railed, "This is all very clever, Zarentil! You are impossible to best, so it would seem, at least by me. It dawns on me that the transfer of knowledge and understanding was not just from you to me. I see that now. A miscalculation on my part, I grant."

Bowing in mock deference, Lement-Nor said, "It matters not! You will find the task of fighting a host of this fortress's guards beyond your meager ability to mirror or distract. In but a moment, you will die, old fool! You and your pathetic friends."

Immediately, Zarentil shrank back to himself, small, childlike and translucent. "Again, I confess that you are an abomination. Further, you are, for all of your conceit and arrogance, oblivious to the obvious. For all of your intelligence and scheming, you failed to see the simplest fact. You cannot hope to kill what has already died."

Finally, the truth of what had really taken place with Zarentil registered on the face of the hybrid. But before the hybrid could react, Zarentil struck him down. Danielle witnessed no blow. Zarentil simply closed his eyes, whispered something unintelligible and the hybrid collapsed, dismay now frozen in his eyes. "There are powers you've closed your mind to, creature of darkness. Even you could have chosen the way of redemption, but instead your embraced raw power, evil and death. A pity this is."

Zarentil reached down and touched the body with his palm, and it vanished from the room. Shuffling over to Danielle, his words came quickly, "You have done superbly, young one. But we are not, as you say, 'out of the woods' yet. With the real hybrid gone, Lohxnahr can again join us, since I will not raise the alarm of his presence, as the real hybrid would have once it sensed his presence."

"Okay, Zarentil."

Already, a faint light was growing larger and brighter, flying in from the other rear entrance to the hall. A moment later, Lohxnahr alighted on the dais next to Danielle, who immediately threw her arms around him in a fierce embrace.

"You have been brilliant, dear one," he buzzed into her ear, careful with his talons as he patted her on the back. "The next stage is more complicated, I must say."

"They come, my old friend," Zarentil murmured in his own deep voice, not the higher voice of Lement-Nor. The copper hue of his eyes transformed into glaring red. "Let our ruse continue to unfold. Yet we trust to hope." The expectant phrase sounded wrong to Danielle as, once again, Lement-

Nor's voice came from Zarentil, and his body transformed back to the size and shape of the hybrid.

Lohxnahr gently released Danielle from his embrace and moved her behind Zarentil. Then, he shuffled into the deep shadows behind the throne, just as a phalanx of imperial guards ran through the enormous archway between the throne room and the bridge connecting it to the central hub of Kahrnahrgx's mountain kingdom. Each soldier ran to his appointed station, carrying a huge, mineral torch, as if they were specially formed, identical stalactites. On the end of each was a bright, pulsing stone. Simultaneously, all the torches were raised high to the twelve embrasures attached to each massive column within the chamber. Once lit, each soldier stood at attention facing into the main hall. None of them paid any attention to those already there.

A large number of soldiers strode into the throne room. Danielle guessed their number to be more than fifty. Many glanced at the hybrid but none held eye contact long, save one.

Danielle found this "second phase," as Lohxnahr called it, much more difficult. With so many of the enemy in one place, it was already harder to believe what she knew to be true: Zarentil was just *posing* as the hybrid. But when the one, massive gargoyle stared at the hybrid she knew to be Zarentil, her skin crawled. He walked on a stump of a leg and appeared to be the most senior commander in a hall full of soldiers. His stare was fierce. *He knows! Somehow he knows!*

Yet another soldier entered the hall only as far as the center of the archway and stopped. Standing to attention, he declared, "The Lord Kahrnahrgx!" With the exception of the guards standing under the lamps, all in the room bowed, even the massive one, as best as he could.

Danielle's heart grew cold when Kahrnahrgx strode into the great hall, stopped and surveyed those in attendance. Immediately, she moved slightly so that she stood directly behind Zarentil. Her fingers dug into his shoulders and she started hyperventilating. *Kimar! It's Kimar!*

No, child! Lohxnahr whispered into her mind. *He is the twin of Kimar. They are twin brothers, with Kimar being the elder of the two. It is true they look the same, but as you know full well, they are of very different spirits. In the end, that is all that matters.*

Danielle had no time to consider the situation more deeply, because as Kahrnahrgx surveyed his assembled warriors, a frown immediately furrowed his face. Turning away, he spoke into the ear of a tall gargoyle next to him. While Kahrnahrgx was still speaking, a robed figure standing behind him tapped Kahrnahrgx on the shoulder and pointed at the dais.

Danielle held her breath as Kahrnahrgx spoke.

"Ah! Lement-Nor, you are here, though uninvited at this time. This meeting is for weapons and tactical experts."

He even sounds like Kimar!

"And am I not both, my master? Both a weapon of your making and an expert tactician? As you have given me leave in other matters, so I exercised discretion in—"

As soon as Zarentil began speaking, Danielle put her fear and dismay in check, knowing that their success was already, at best, perilously doubtful. She slowed her breathing and released her fingers from Zarentil's back, grateful that, posing as Lement-Nor, he was so tall that no one could have seen her. Even the other soldiers would only perceive she was cowering behind the hybrid. She lowered her head as she had at first and took a submissive posture.

Good, child! Lohxnahr hummed into her mind.

Why didn't you tell me, Lohxnahr?

Kahrnahrgx held his hand up abruptly. Zarentil immediately stopped speaking.

"General Uu-Descah!" Kahrnahrgx cried.

"Your highness," the fearful soldier replied, shifting his weight.

"The battle in the upper hall goes well. We will have them all cornered soon enough. According to plan, they are inhibited from parting out of this mountain kingdom because of one in their company."

"Yes, sir." Mostly hidden behind Zarentil, Danielle peered through her fallen hair, watching Uu-Descah closely. Again, she was convinced the huge fighter knew more than he disclosed in words.

"Yet," Kahrnahrgx said quietly, "the battle should have been faster—indeed, over by now—save for the abject failure within the prison cell. How is it, General, that a small band of humans was able to defeat nine of your elite warriors in such close quarters?" From the tone of the feared leader, it was clear where he meant to lay blame for the disastrous mission.

The robed figure nodded approvingly and appeared to whisper something into the ear of Kahrnahrgx.

"Unknown, your highness. There have been fleeting sensations of other gargoyles within the kingdom, other than General Prohximus, of course, who have already visited this chamber."

Though Danielle saw no perceptible movement in the hall, she felt the tension go up exponentially. The massive general had just reminded his lord that the first battle was lost in his own throne room, under his watch, when General Uu-Descah was elsewhere.

Ignoring the slight, Kahrnahrgx continued, "Where was the promised squad of soldiers posted in the corridor outside the cell? They were, for reasons that escape me, *gone* when it mattered. How do you explain this?"

"Redeployed, your highness," General Uu-Descah replied, with the confidence that comes only from countless battles. There was in his voice an air of not just unconcern, but boredom.

"You countered my order?" Kahrnahrgx growled out each word.

"No, sir."

"Then who did?"

"Your hybrid."

As his head turned towards Zarentil-Lement-Nor, Kahrnahrgx's eyes twitched.

"And why would you do this, Lement-Nor?"

Zarentil bowed slightly. "To bring you a gift…something that will help our warriors in the upper hall secure a quick and permanent victory, my lord."

"And…that is?"

Zarentil stepped to one side, revealing Danielle to Kahrnahrgx.

Everything moved slowly, like cool molasses. Paign was already highly agitated from the moment the first rescue team arrived with Danielle until this moment, when from all appearances, the rescue failed and they'd all been plunged into hell. More than anything, he was distraught over his use of a flying fist. Confounded and shocked, he struggled to understand how he'd done such a thing. Doubt gnawed at his heart as one question hammered at him with each heartbeat: *What has become of me?*

But it was hard to think about that now when the world was on fire. Everywhere he looked, flaming orbs intersected the sky—such as he could call the air within the vast cavern they were trapped in "air." A wave of bitterness and regret surged through him as the utter destruction of his friends, his cousin, even his mother and sister, grew so unavoidable. Greatly outnumbered by an incensed enemy force, it was clear that being unable to part out of the mountain kingdom had dealt a crushing blow to those committed to protecting him and those he loved. Already, several of the gargoyle force deployed high above them before the battle commenced now lay dead not far from where all of them were pinned down. Conomorg and Ita-Mudak stood side by side with Prohximus along the very edge of their ledge, fully exposed to the tectonic forces aimed at them. All three had dealt devastation of enormous magnitude, to the extent that, so far, not one foe had set foot upon the plateau. Yet the price they paid for it was severe. It couldn't last much longer before one, or perhaps all three, together fell. Ercen was unable to assist in any offensive maneuvers, given the large number of humans she defended. Of course, against such an array of weapons, the humans could do nothing, save for shouting, until an enemy actually was within reach of a sword or staff.

Looking at his mother and sister wailing silently next to the Skulstads and Anders, nearly frozen in time, ignited a resolve deep within Paign. Seeing the horror-stricken faces of

Danielle's parents was like throwing kerosene on it. *On account of me!*

Rage burst up inside of Paign like bile, so strong that he suddenly felt nauseous. Rage at himself. Rage at the others for pursuing him. Rage at the situation over which he had no control.

He swatted at his ear and noted it was the only motion in real time; everything else remained impossibly slow. The noise hissing into his head was painful. He swatted again. *Ouch! What is this?*

Paign, you have a choice.

Lohxnahr? Where are you?

With you, child.

What do you mean, choice?

You have a choice now. Choosing to wallow in your suffering at the expense of the others is strong in you. Yet you know there is another choice available to you.

To act on behalf of the others?

Have they not acted on your behalf?

What can I do? Here? In all of this?

More than you believe. Therefore, you must believe more.

I might be killed.

And of what other outcome can you see if you do nothing?

As Paign heard Lohxnahr's voice utter the word *nothing*, the edge of the plateau grew bright and small globs of flame burst slowly in all directions. The three commanders guarding the ledge slowly flew up and backwards from the blast.

Our time is up, Lohxnahr. With me?

Of a certainty, child.

Paign jumped to his feet and wove his way through the falling bits of flame, fractured stone and debris. As he came to each of the fallen commanders, he laid his hand on their foreheads and bowed a moment.

Glancing over his shoulder, he shouted, "I'm sorry, all of you! I never meant for this to happen." Turning back, his eyes welled with tears.

As he neared the line marking the end of the ledge and the beginning of the void, Paign noticed noises, none of them pleasant, quickly increasing. Other sensations were returning as he approached the edge. Heat. Pain. Stench. Fear was already with him.

Peering over the edge, Paign was staggered by the number of gargoyles advancing on their position. Many were scaling up the tallest stalagmites, then jumping to a long stalactite. Many more were in flight. Filled with wonder at the bravery of Prohximus, Conomorg and Ita-Mudak at defending their ledge in the face of such an overwhelming force, Paign's knees buckled under.

Here, Lohxnahr?

Of a certainty, brave one.

What can I do, Lohxnahr? I'm just a simple farm boy.

Nei! Paign found the use of his language at such a time as this to be very comforting. *Nei!* Lohxnahr repeated. *You were never a simple farm boy, as no boy on a farm is simple, as no boy or girl is simple, wherever they grow.*

What can I do?

You have done it already.

Vaguely aware of motion through the tears flowing down his face, Paign felt a wall of heat increasing stunningly fast. His ears confirmed for him that untold fireballs were streaking up at him.

Thank you, Lohxnahr. You have always been a faithful friend.

Before any reply came, the edge of the plateau was engulfed in a conflagration of hundreds of fireballs, rupturing it violently upwards, turning Paign ghostly white. Huge fissures formed across the front third of the ledge, and all at once it cracked, slid over the cliff face and plummeted into the abyss below.

"You!" Kahrnahrgx exclaimed, his eyes shifting from a dull orange to a glowing red as he glared at Danielle. "*The Chosen One*," he smirked.

Turning back to Lement-Nor, Kahrnahrgx's eyes narrowed. "How is it that *she* will bring victory to my forces in the upper hall?"

"Ah! My Lord Kahrnahrgx," Zarentil-Lement-Nor began, tipping forwards in a nearly imperceptible bow, "you pose a question to something which was not said."

"Ever you would play the clever one, Lement-Nor," snapped his master. "You appear to operate under the illusion that because I created you, I would never destroy you. In this, you are quite mistaken!"

Several of the soldiers arrayed throughout the hall murmured their agreement with their lord.

"Now, answer my question, Lement-Nor!" Kahrnahrgx yelled, pouring contempt into the name of his creation. "How will she bring a swift and definitive ending for my warriors fighting above?"

"Forgive me for my lack of sufficient clarity," Zarentil-Lement-Nor bowed lower, his voice bouncing up from the dais. Danielle shifted her feet slightly, so that she ended up with Zarentil between her and Kahrnahrgx. "In the matter of a 'quick and permanent victory' you are quite correct, Lord Kahrnahrgx. This I declared, for it is true. As you well know, the boy known as Paign has suffered much in his short life—not the least from the fool, Rance-Dahl, as well as from your dutiful servant. Indeed, the boy was to be your brilliant device, serving both as bait to bring your enemies into this fortress, then to bring the doom you have so long planned for them, is this not so?"

Kahrnahrgx nodded slowly, while whispering into the ear of his slender attendant.

"For this intricate plan to function, it was necessary for your servant to dispatch the ancient mystic known as Zarentil, effecting a ruse so deep that all of your enemies would be deceived, thus allowing your servant opportunity and access to weave his tapestry of duplicity. In this manner, your servant could bring torment to the human boy with specific intent, unimpeded."

"What of it, hybrid? Do I need you to recount for me my own plans?"

"Verily, Lord Kahrnahrgx, it is due to your utter failure of these plans that I engage in this tedious recounting."

A great murmuring arose in the hall.

Danielle stepped back at the flaring of Kahrnahrgx's eyes. She expected fire to come from them, they glowed so fiercely.

"Have a care, my hybrid," Kahrnahrgx hissed. "Bring your tale to a hasty close before I do the same with you."

"As you wish," came Zarentil-Lement-Nor's unconcerned reply. "It is thus. What you failed to discern is that, even as your servant dispatched Zarentil the Mystic and, in so doing, absorbed all of his characteristics and knowledge, something unforeseen resulted. In like fashion, of all of Rance-Dahl's ministrations imparted to the boy, one of particular importance failed your notice."

Several soldiers shouted epithets at Zarentil-Lement-Nor, including the hulking Uu-Descah.

Kahrnahrgx's wings snapped out. "You will bait me no longer, Lement-Nor," he whispered. "Your insolence brings your doom, swift and certain."

Zarentil bowed low, pressing his palms down on the dais for a moment before standing at his full height.

"Of course, Lord Kahrnahrgx. It is your prerogative to assert these claims, as well as to execute me. It is just that I have yet to answer your first question, which I feel I must do before you dispatch me into the eternal abyss."

The hooded figure whispered something to Kahrnahrgx before stepping away towards to the entrance.

"I did *not* say that the human child known as Danielle, called the 'Chosen One' by your enemies, would bring a swift and definitive ending for *your* warriors but for *ours*."

What had been an escalating undercurrent of grumbling within the hall throughout Lement-Nor's speech exploded into howls when Lohxnahr stepped out of the shadows behind the throne, with Kimar at his side.

The Preceptor turned swiftly on his heels and stole away across the massive bridge leading to the great hall.

"What do you mean, I have done it already?" Paign wondered out loud, remembering shreds of a conversation he'd been having. But he was baffled as to why he was standing at the edge of the precipice and, come to think of it, what had happened to the edge of the precipice? Here was the edge with his toes jutting over the lip, but it was now much closer to where everyone huddled.

Do you not know? Lohxnahr replied, soundlessly. Paign could hear the smile in the gargoyle's tender question.

Paign rubbed his hair a long time before answering. "Maybe…"

Like everyone, Paign, you always have a choice. You have experienced terrible things in your short life. Heartbreaks. Deep confusion. Great loss. Abiding questions. Much of these came to you from afar. And some you brought from within.

Paign nodded as he stared into the nearly tangible stillness of the abyss. All the smoke and fumes had disappeared, except for the seething cloud of dust roiling far below where the missing plateau had crashed moments earlier.

It appears that in your captivity, during your abuse by the tyrant tormenting you, something happened, something unexpected…that in some way, part of his powers were transferred to you. This became evident in the prison cell holding you and your mother.

"When I killed the gargoyle with the flying fist?"

Indeed. And yet it appears that more was transferred, more than just the power of his skills.

"Rance-Dahl made me very angry, Lohxnahr, so angry… enough so…"

Did he? Or was the anger already there? You see, brave one, he couldn't put into you what was already there. There was much for you to be angry over. Much.

"Then it wasn't wrong of me to be angry, Lohxnahr?"

Indeed not. Did not Danielle warn you of this in your prison cell? Many creatures experience anger. Humans. Gargoyles. Others. But do you discern what else Rance-Dahl transferred to you?

Again, Paign rubbed his hair absentmindedly. He was surprised by how much dust flew out. Finally, he replied, "The belief that my anger justified my desire to make others suffer as I had."

Hm, yes. The terrible belief that it was "your fault." Is this not what you believed within your prison? And yet, before, you also believed everyone else was at fault, thus giving you the justification for making others suffer. One's suffering and pain are not relieved by meting out more suffering and pain. This is the lie of which Danielle warned you. Anger, even at oneself, is not a worthy end in itself, but a signal to something greater. Well done. Many never make the connection you just did.

"Am I dead then, Lohxnahr?"

No and yes! Yes and no! Lohxnahr hummed merrily. *In some ways you are more dead than those not dead yet. There is a part of you that died in the inferno you absorbed on behalf of your friends and loved ones. But that is not a part of you to be missed and even less to be grieved. And there is a part of you—the growing core of you—that is more alive, more true, more you now than it was just moments ago.*

Paign grinned. He found he liked the feeling that came with it. He realized he also liked the feeling that prompted the grin in the first place.

"So, is there a point you're not talking to me in my head? I would much prefer we could do this face to face," he chuckled.

A curious snorting sound took Paign's grin to a wide smile. After a moment, the snorting stopped and Paign received his reply: *Soon. There is another matter to bring to a close.*

"Brother," Kimar shouted over the din, throwing his arms wide in ironic welcome, framed by his outstretched wings.

Clearly shocked, Kahrnahrgx would still not have disorder within his kingdom and held his hand aloft. The hall grew still immediately, except for the echoes of the outburst when Kimar and Lohxnahr came out of the shadows.

"What is the meaning of this, Lement-Nor?" Kahrnahrgx hissed.

"Yet another truth you failed to see, Kahrnahrgx. That your unfaithful servant always sought to double cross you, intent on seizing this throne for his own."

Kahrnahrgx's face contorted from rage to confusion and back, until it mixed both together. "Before I send you all into the depths of the eternal abyss, why is it you tell me this now, Lement-Nor?"

"Ah! Quite simply...I am *not* Lement-Nor," Zarentil-Lement-Nor announced. First his eyes transformed to a brilliant copper even as his wings thinned and his body shrank, shifting from glistening black to the subtleties of pearl. "Your hybrid failed to recognize that he imparted more to me than I to him. I returned from death, while he will not. It was she whom you mock, the Chosen One, who spoke truth into the falseness your minions infused into the brave one known as Paign, dissolving its power upon him. Rather than direct the power of his suffering into the birth of yet more suffering, he chose another path. Not the path of your choosing. Thus it was that out of an abiding sense of grace and love for his friends and family did Paign just absorb the full onslaught of your warriors in the high hall. And, in so doing, he defeated all of them while purging himself of the great lie you sought to enslave him with. You heard what you wished to hear, Kahrnahrgx. In bringing this liberating truth to Paign,

Danielle provided the gift that helped our warriors in the upper hall secure a quick and permanent victory, just as I said. The only difference is that they defeated *yours*, Lord Kahrnahrgx."

When Zarentil spoke the name of their nemesis, he abruptly spun around, cloaking Danielle with his small arms. Lohxnahr, hidden behind Kimar, was already blurred in a blinding spin.

"No!" Kahrnahrgx roared, even as Kimar dropped to one knee, with his wings draped over him, and Lohxnahr instantly stopped moving. A silver wave burst away from the little gargoyle, hurling every warrior off his feet and into the far recesses of the hall. Only Kahrnahrgx remained in place, having lanced the floor with his talons just before the blast impacted his generals, commanders and finest soldiers.

Danielle still couldn't believe that Kimar and Kahrnahrgx were identical to look at. Only their words were different, and that difference meant everything. Kimar's sought reconciliation, while Kahrnahrgx wanted nothing to do with it.

"Brother, why continue?" Kimar said, dismayed. "We have liberated the humans. Much has been lost. Why persist? You heard that the boy, Paign, willingly offered himself for others, including our kind! He was willing to sacrifice himself to protect not only humans, Kahrnahrgx, but gargoyles. Your countrymen, brother! Old friends from time immemorial. Will you not see this? This has not been done since the Beginning."

"It matters not!" Kahrnahrgx snapped. "It does nothing to change the calculus of humans and our kind: humans are vulgar, self-possessed and without any passion. They live only for the day they are in, caring nothing for the needs of those around them. And if they care nothing for their own—allowing suffering to continue without abatement—then why should we? We have done so for generations and what has it provided us? Disregard, at best. More often, suspicion. They are not worthy of us!"

Danielle couldn't help herself. Without thinking, she blurted out, "I suppose you're right, Kahrnahrgx. I'm sure not in a position to talk for everyone—all humans, I mean—but it's true what you say, even for me. Sometimes I do pay more attention to what's important to me than what's really important. You know, little things. But that doesn't mean it's all the time. And even if it was, it doesn't mean it's that way for everyone else, and it doesn't mean that I can't get better."

Kahrnahrgx said nothing, but stared curiously at Danielle. Finally, his eyes turned and fixed on Lohxnahr. "That was well delivered, Mystic. You have taught her well."

Lohxnahr beamed. "That it was! But that came not from my teaching. It came from her own."

"Come with us, brother!" Kimar cried. "Let us end this conflict. It is all for naught."

"I think not, Kimar. While your spokesperson—this Chosen One of yours—makes a great speech, she does not wield power enough to change the human race."

"Nor do you, brother."

"Perhaps, perhaps. There is always tomorrow and a new day. Your time is nearly gone. My companions begin to recover from Lohxnahr's spinning blow. It is, as always, little one, impressive. Until next time, brother."

And he was gone.

The desperate rescue missions of the Macys and the Hudsons, in the depths of massive Aconcagua, were fulfilled.

CHAPTER TWENTY-EIGHT
LOSSES AND GAINS

"So, explain it to me again, will you, Paign?" Johann said, smiling as he shoved a small, round loaf into his mouth.

Paign grinned. He'd been doing that a lot lately. It felt good. Since they had returned to the Valley of Ten Pinnacles, he couldn't remember a time when he wasn't grinning. Holding up his finger in a gesture that he needed a minute, Paign took a long draught of pure lake water and marveled that a clay cup could be fashioned so thin that he could see light through it. He was thirsty from talking so much. "All right, then. It was like this…" And so he began again recounting what had happened on the cliff's ledge.

In the past three days, Paign had lost count of how many times he'd told the story. But there had been so much else to do. Numerous wounds to heal on so many. Peter had needed special attention to restore his memory and vision. Because his initial healing had been interrupted and incomplete, more damage had taken place during the hours of their retreat up the pathway and the lengthy and fierce battle on the plateau.

Then there were the gargoyles. Prohximus had been terribly wounded, along with Conomorg, in the concussive blast that threw them down onto the ledge. Ita-Mudak, who had already been wounded at the Skulstads' farm, was nearly killed by it. Each of the warriors had learned from Lohxnahr it was Paign's touch that had stayed the damage from worsening until care could be applied by gargoyles trained in the healing arts. It was another unexpected but welcome skill imparted to Paign from his horrible encounters with Rance-Dahl and Lement-Nor. He hoped it would linger.

The toughest time had come on the first day when the bodies of Tiny and Uud-Rement, along with the elite soldiers who had perished, were laid to rest. Paign had wept along with Freida and her parents, knowing that Tiny had sacrificed his life saving his. Anders and Danielle had stood alongside him. It had been a lovely memorial for the mastiff, with words of great fondness and respect shared by many. The most moving were those from Ita-Mudak, who had grown to love the dog deeply and, of course, from Freida, whose expression of loss was felt by all. But perhaps the most poignant moment came when Anja had lain down at the head of Tiny's grave at sunset and stayed there until sunrise. Freida and Danielle had joined her, a comfort to each other, all three wrapped in blankets.

The next day, Uud-Rement received the full pomp and honors appropriate of a legendary general. Many gargoyles from all ranks spoke of his valor and character. A long list of accolades was read. But it was the simple word of praise and gratitude from Johann that was most meaningful. None of the kids, of course, knew what had happened at the Skulstads' farm. Freida clutched at her heart, realizing how close she'd come to losing both of her parents, and wished she'd gotten to know Uud-Rement. Prohximus was healed just enough to share, along with Quarastohr, some reflections about their lifelong friend, especially the humorous banter they'd shared together the moments before they'd left for battle. Their deep fondness for each other was palpable to the humans.

The humans were moved by the unassuming tenderness and affection shown to the fighters who had sacrificed themselves on their behalf. While all of the humans were touched by their memorial, it was felt most deeply by Gudrun, who went to each of the fighter's surviving family to thank and honor them for their sacrifice, as one who knew well what that sacrifice meant. Her fervency brought abiding comfort, especially to the grieving mothers, widows and children.

The Hudsons couldn't seem to express enough gratitude to satisfy themselves. Caedmon enjoyed exploring much of the valley with Peter, who grew stronger every day from the strong air and clear water. Aleira, for her part, spent the most time with Amy and Heidi. But in the evenings, she'd stroll hand in hand with Danielle and Freida, talking quietly about matters of the heart. Anja would trot alongside them until a careless rabbit hopped out of its hole in the large meadow between the lake and the dais. Then they would laugh at the antics of Anja chasing the rabbit around as if she meant to threaten it, until finally the much-annoyed rabbit would turn and chase Anja.

Gudrun and Bettina Macy were inseparable during their stay under the sheltering peaks. Both could often be found giggling and smiling, having left their great fears behind them in the deep shadows under Aconcagua. Paign was often with them with a look of deep contentment on his face.

On the evening of the second-to-last day, Lohxnahr came to join the families during their supper. While there was much laughter, he also answered the many questions lingering for everyone. No, they didn't know where Kahrnahrgx had vanished to, but they knew he'd never use the vast kingdom below the peaks of Aconcagua again. Yes, he believed what was imparted to Paign would remain, both the protective and healing skills, and it was up to Paign to use each more wisely than those who had unwittingly imparted the powers. No, they were not sure if there was another hybrid, but he hoped not, saying, "Two were worse than one and three would be too many!" He explained Zarentil would soon return to see them off; he and Quarastohr were busy repatriating several of the warriors who had heard Zarentil's speech in the throne room about the noble exploits of the human known as Paign, as well as the words of the Chosen One. Their view of the human world had been forever changed.

Kimar and Ercen were often seen strolling alone together. It was plain that, for Kimar, the refusal of his brother to return and face justice for his crimes was a terrible blow. Danielle feared that Kimar took far too much responsibility for the outcomes of decisions his brother made alone. But at times, there was something else about the way he and Ercen walked, something that didn't feel somber.

On their last day together, everyone again grouped together for a final breakfast. There was much joy in the companionship to be sure and new stories, as yet untold, being shared. But there was an underlying sadness, too. Danielle didn't have much of an appetite and strolled down to the lake's edge by herself. Peter glanced over at Amy and was surprised she was already looking at him with a mischievous grin. Before he could do anything, she tipped her head to one side, indicating he should look in that direction. His left eyebrow immediately went up; Paign was walking down to where Danielle was sitting at the lake's lip, her feet splashing in the water. Peter turned back towards Amy with both eyebrows raised and shrugged. She was grinning ear to ear and tipped her head again. Peter's eyes bugged out when he saw Anders walking slowly down to the lake.

Johann burst out laughing and slapped Peter on the back. "Ha, my friend! You should need to—how do you say?— 'pickup the space'! Have you not noticed Paign and Anders talking all afternoon yesterday? They have come to an understanding from what our Freida tells us."

Heidi, whose arm was wrapped around their daughter, gave her a little kiss on the head. Freida turned crimson, jumped up and ran into the field with Anja in pursuit. They had found great comfort in each other, feeling Tiny's absence intensely.

"Ah…oh!" was the best Peter could come up with. Heidi winked at him, while Amy shook her head at her husband and muttered, "Men!"

In the hour before their departures, Zarentil arrived and joined Quarastohr, Prohximus and other leaders on the dais. None of the humans seemed in haste to leave. Paign and Freida chatted quietly, their feet hanging over the dais and bouncing off the granite slab. The adults, including Bettina and Gudrun, stood clustered together, sharing heartfelt hugs and well wishes.

Peter glanced over his shoulder, still wondering where Danielle was, when he noticed her walking out of a nearby copse of willows. One hand held Anja's scruff. The other was delicately touching Anders's, their fingers barely entwined. Though his eyebrows furrowed, a bemused smile grew across his face.

Though it took nearly another hour, finally everyone had shared hugs, kind words and firm handshakes. It was time to go.

"There is plenty of work to be done on our farm before the season changes. Repairs to be made on our home are the most pressing, but Anders, Paign and Bettina won't take no for an answer. The more the merrier, I say—or, at least, the more *the quicker!*" Johann chuckled, slapping Peter on the back and giving Amy a fierce hug.

"You, young lady," he continued, his face growing serious as he addressed Danielle, "you I expect to see again *in our world.* Be kind to an old farmer and bring your parents along and Anja, too!"

Danielle blushed and glanced automatically at Anders, which was the very last thing she meant to do. Anders became suddenly interested in the dais, studying the mineral patterns surrounding his feet while his neck reddened.

Kimar held his right hand aloft. "Partings such as these are difficult because of the strong bonds of affection we have for one another, even as we wish to return to the familiarity of our lives as they were. And yet, because of the challenges that brought us together, our lives will never be the same. That is as it should be. Before you return to your homes and eras, Zarentil would speak to you. Ercen and I would have you know that you will remain in our hearts no matter the distance between us."

The most diminutive of all the gargoyles, Zarentil jumped onto the top of a pedestal normally used for braziers and surveyed the group with his bright copper eyes. The Hudsons, who had never heard him speak in his own voice, gasped when a deep rumbling sound came from him.

"Peace be with you!" he intoned. "On behalf of all in this community housed among the Ten Pinnacles, I bring you thanks and blessing. Again, the Chosen One joined us in battling the evil of separation and the fanatical patriotism of Kahrnahrgx and his disciples. Yet the foundation upon which their zealotry is built has been cracked by the selfless actions you have demonstrated. Several of his warriors and commanders have renounced his view and, in time, will return into our rookery. For their return, we rejoice, even as we trust to Hope that, in time, more will come home. We do not see our role as caretakers of humans to be a burden but an honor of the highest order, graced upon us by the Giver. Thus, we are grieved by the perversion that alienates us from our brethren.

"As a parent with their child, we would wish for you only safety and joy. Our wish isn't enough. Therefore, we act. Though you see us not, ever will we be vigilant…ever watchful. You will not be alone, even as we pursue Kahrnahrgx and his deceived followers, trusting to Providence for direction and supply. Our goal, as it has ever been, is reconciliation, not sundering.

"Many new questions surfaced within the throne room. These we seek to resolve, as Lohxnahr has already made known to you. We suspect but must confirm, despite the woe that is uncovered."

And with that, he hopped off of the column and tottered over to Danielle.

"As you have been much in the company of our kind and have interceded on our behalf, we would grant you certain gifts it is within our power to convey," Zarentil said before tipping his head to Lohxnahr.

Springing nimbly off the dais, Lohxnahr fluttered over to Danielle.

"Dear one," he began, "as a kindred spirit—you, your parents and their friends—we wish for you to have the freedom to abide with us, should you ever desire it," he said, beaming.

Danielle struggled to get words to form and mumbled, "Do you mean what I hope you mean?"

"Of course!" Lohxnahr quipped. With his wings beating faster than a hummingbird's, he leaned in slowly until his forehead touched hers.

Amy clutched at Peter, while he dabbed his eye and whispered, "As much as we hated that key you discovered in Nepal, Ames, think what we would have missed without it!"

A tiny point of light flared for a moment where Danielle and Lohxnahr touched. Then Lohxnahr fluttered up a little, kissed Danielle's head and settled back to the dais. "Visit any time you wish!"

Danielle was speechless from boundless joy and smiled at Anders with shining eyes. Paign slapped him on the back and burst out laughing.

EPILOGUE

Had they known the name for the temple plateau on which they stood, it wouldn't have mattered to Kahrnahrgx or the hooded figure. The pyramid at Tula, Mexico, was important for its violent history, not what its witless inhabitants called it.

"All is not lost, Highness," the figure said lazily. "It is nothing more than a setback…an opportunity for enhancing your strategic planning." His tone was conversational and easy, as if he were enjoying a pleasant afternoon, even though they stood in the stark light of a chill moon.

"The betrayal of Lement-Nor seems to have caused you no alarm or introspection, Preceptor. Almost as if you expected it."

"Ah, my lord, you go too far. Should it surprise when such a creature, born out of vile intent and incubated in deceit, should be somewhat less than, shall we say, honest?"

"Perhaps not."

"And you have one more at your disposal. Would not an appropriate response be to monitor him more closely?"

Kahrnahrgx, still shaken by the remarkable assertions he'd been subjected to by Zarentil, the imposter, as well as the most unfortunate deployment of the spinning fist by Lohxnahr, found it unnerving that the boy, Paign, had acted with such selflessness. Then there was the girl.

Competing emotions surged within him. He needed time to think, to assess what went wrong and develop plans impenetrable by his opponents. Though he benefited from the wisdom of his teacher, the Preceptor's instruction sometimes felt sadistic, intending to harm more than help. *Perhaps that is not accidental. But what would be his desired objective from doing so? Does he not know that I could dispatch him in less time than he could scream?*

"A recommendation, my lord, if you would permit me."

"Of course, master."

"Redirect your efforts away from the humans. There is little to be gained—and too many resources required—in relentless pursuit of the girl…and now, the boy. Rather, strike at the source of your opposition. Wield a blow the likes of which has never been seen before. Regather your warriors. Attack the Ten Pinnacles and the other rookeries. Bring your wrath unto them when they are all ill prepared to launch an adequate defense."

"During the birthing season?"

"When better, my apprentice?"

It felt so weird to be home again. Danielle had helped her parents sweep their entryway, rehang pictures and try to make their home feel more like a home than a battle zone. That would take more than a day. Having a ring of dining room chairs and a long ribbon around the gaping hole in the entry floor left when Conomorg and Ita-Mudak suddenly emerged from it served as a glaring reminder.

As they sat down to their first meal together as just a family in too many days to count, Danielle giggled.

"What's up, kid?" Peter asked. "Know something we don't?"

"Well, actually, yes!"

"What is it, honey?" Amy grinned. "You remind me of the Cheshire cat in Wonderland."

Danielle giggled again. "You know when Lohxnahr touched his forehead to mine and, well, uh, granted me the ability to part whenever we want to?"

"Which is awesome, by the way!" Peter cried. "Just terrific!"

"That's the truth," Amy agreed.

"Well," Danielle murmured, "he also whispered something to me. Something so wonderful it almost killed me to not screech or freak out or something."

"Wow! What was it he said?"

"Oh, Dad, it's *so* cool! Ercen is pregnant! Kimar and Ercen are going to have their first little gargling!"

BEFORE YOU GO...

If you enjoyed *All His Wrath*, please consider adding a review on Amazon. You'd make this author very happy. I'd be grateful if you could spare five minutes to do that. It need only be a line or two and it makes a massive difference.

Best wishes,
Brandon

PLEASE LEAVE A REVIEW

APPENDIX ONE

GLOSSARY

Alcove	A recessed space; vaulted room
Archaeologist	A scientist who studies ancient peoples, species or civilizations
Detritus	Debris; disintegrated material; small particles broken or worn away from a mass
Escarpment	A long, cliff-like ridge
Eyrie	A lofty nest, house, or fortress, located high on a hill or mountain.
Glimmer	A device used by Rance-Dahl, in part a prison, in part similar to a straight-jacket
Nodule	A small, rounded lump or mass *[Book One]*
Portico	A structure to fortify a gateway, usually attached to a building as a porch *[Book One]*
Repatriate	To return, or be sent, back to one's own country or people
Roiling	Combining the words "rolling" and "boiling"; disturb; stir up
Rookery	A nesting area for winged creatures, typically very high up and sheltered among cliffs

Scree   A steep mass of detritus on the side of a mountain *[Book One]*

Stalactite   A mineral deposit, shaped roughly like an icicle,
hanging from the roof of a cave

Stalagmite   A mineral deposit, shaped roughly like an icicle,
that rises from the ground; made from drippings
from stalactites

Umbrage   Annoyance; displeasure *[Book One]*

Verbatim   To repeat something (a phrase, quote, even a
whole conversation) word for word

APPENDIX TWO

CHARACTERS

CREATURES

Anja

The Wheelens' Akita, a large and strong dog. She is a protector to Danielle, obtained after the Wheelens experiences fighting against Kahrnahrgx and his followers. Friendly after getting acquainted with others, but defensive until then.

Gyrfalcon

Largest of all falcons, it breeds on Arctic coasts and the islands of North America, Europe, and Asia. Some gyrfalcons travel much further when it has a mind to. There are populations in north America, Greenland and Northern Europe. It was a prized hunter to the Vikings.

Tiny

The Skulstads' enormous dog, a mastiff. Very protective of his family, especially of Freida, his mistress. Fond of Anders Knutson and Paign Macy, Freida's best friends. *[Book One]*

Vannveps

Literally means: water wasps. Very dangerous, especially when flying in large numbers. *[Book One]*

Vanntorden   Literally means: water thunder. Very dangerous, but slower than their cousins, the Van-
nveps. It is unlikely they would sting their
opponents, because they cannot fly. Their
roars generate the destructive force of a hundred years of glacial movement, condensed
down to moments. *[Book One]*

GARGOYLES

Ahkzita   Pronounced: "Ock-zee-tah." Obsidian class.
Promoted to Hunter-Seeker Unit Com-
mander, after his leader is destroyed.

Bahlkrum   Pronounced: "Ball-crum." Minion of Kahrnahrgx, middle rank. Obsidian class.
[Book One]

Conomorg   Pronounced: "Con-oh-morg." Superior
fighter. Granite class.

Ercen   Pronounced: "Ur-sen." Mate to Kimar.
Protector, especially of human children.
Granite class.

Evalcohr   Pronounced: "Evil-core." Commander.
Ruthless. Obsidian class. *[Book One]*

Gahrspat   Pronounced: "Gar-spat." Minion of Kahrnahrgx, senior rank. Obsidian class. *[Book One]*

Gustlab   Pronounced: "Goost-lab." Superior fighter.
Basalt class. *[Book One]*

Ita-Mudak   Pronounced: "It-ah-moo-dack." Superior
fighter. Granite class.

Kahrnahrgx	Pronounced: "Car-narx." Brother to Kimar. Leader of the gargoyle rebellion. Created the powerful and dreaded Key of Kahrnahrgx by murdering the Widow Vellhelmina. Killed Osberg the Great. Granite class.
Kimar	Pronounced: "Key-mar." Mate to Ercen, brother to Kahrnahrgx. Leader of the gargoyle defenders and protector of humans. Granite class.
Lement-Nor	Pronounced: As it reads. Obsidian hybrid. Incredibly dangerous and devious. Perfectly imitates creatures (gargoyle, human, other) that is kills, absorbing their behaviors and speech.
Lohmong	Pronounced: "Low-mong." Superior fighter. Granite class. *[Book One]*
Lohxnahr	Pronounced: "Locks-nar." Friend of Kimar and Ercen. Guide for Danielle. Slate class.
Mahtrance	Pronounced: "Mah-trance." Superior fighter. Basalt class. *[Book One]*
Nahgflint	Pronounced: "Nog-flint." Comes to the Wheelens' home to capture Danielle. One of Kahrnahrgx's special hunting units. Slate class. *[Book One]*
Osberg	Pronounced: "Oss-burg." Great leader of the gargoyle clans. Killed by Kahrnahrgx while capturing the Key. Gabbro class.
Quarastohr	Pronounced: "Koo-war-uh-store." Senior commander of forces opposed to Kahrnahrgx. Leader of the War Council. Soapstone class.

Prohximus   Pronounced: "Procks-e-muss." Senior commander. War Council member. Very tall. Supremely intelligent. Limestone class.

Rance-Dahl   Pronounced: "Rance-Doll." Keeper of the Glimmer. Basalt class. Sadistic.

Recknab   Pronounced: "Wreck-nab." Superior fighter. Granite class. *[Book One]*

Rutahn   Pronounced: "Rue-tan." Superior fighter. Soapstone class. *[Book One]*

Sedig-Tahr   Pronounced: "Said-ig-Tar." Obsidian hybrid. Assassin, wicked, shape shifter.

Sepanyahd   Pronounced: "Sep-an-yod." Hunter-Seeker Unit Commander. Friend of Kahrnarhgx.

Stenring   Pronounced: "Stenn-ring." Superior fighter. Granite class. *[Book One]*

Strohrnahq   Pronounced: "Stro-ar-nock." Fierce, very mean. Gahrspat's brother. Obsidian class. *[Book One]*

Tiunarz   Pronounced: "Tea-oo-nar-z." Senior squad leader. Obsidian class. *[Book One]*

Uu-Descah   Pronounced: "Oo-Desk-ah." Uu sounds like "ooze" without the "ze." Mighty warrior. General and senior commander opposed to Karnahrgx. Close comrade to Quarastohr and Prohximus. Basalt class, largely scoria stone.

Urchzahv   Pronounced: "Urch-zahv." Superior fighter. Granite class. *[Book One]*

Uud-Rement	Pronounced: "Ood-rement." Battle-seasoned general of opposition. Gabbro class.
Zarentil	Pronounced: "Zair-entill." Mystic High Priest and prophet. Ancient. Copper class.

HUMANS

Aleira Hudson	Friend of the Wheelens. Preferred babysitter of Danielle as an infant.
Amy Wheelen	Mother of Danielle. Archaeologist. Professor. Curious, caring.
Anders Knutson	Cousin to Paign Macy. Smart and brave. Friend of Freida Skulstad.
Anna Vellhelmina	The widow of Parson Vellhelmina. Murdered by Kahrnahrgx. *[Book One]*
Bettina Macy	Paign Macy's sister (older). Independent, sometimes headstrong.
Caedmon Hudson	Husband of Aleira. Friend to the Wheelens, especially Peter.
Danielle Wheelen	The "Chosen One." Only child of Amy and Peter Wheelen. Hunted by Kahrnahrgx and his minions.
Freida Skulstad	Inquisitive, hard-headed friend of Anders Knutson and Paign Macy. Becomes best friend to Danielle Wheelen.
Gudrun Macy	Paign Macy's mother. Strong, lonely.

Heidi Skulstad	Mother to Freida. Fierce but sensitive.
Johann Skulstad	Burly father to Freida. Primarily a sheep and goat farmer.
Paign Macy	Cousin to Anders Knutson. Friend to Freida Skulstad. Name pronounced like "pain." Courageous to the point of being rash.
Pers Olson	Wealthy Honellaken merchant. Believed by some to have killed the Widow Vellhelmina. Leader of a secretive society of merchants and important townspeople. *[Book One]*
Parson Pearsson	Pastor to the people of Honellaken. Confidant to Freida, Anders and Paign. *[Book One]*
Peter Wheelen	Husband of Amy. Father of Danielle. Professor. Witty. Athletic. Brave under pressure.
Preceptor	Shadowy figure. Most senior advisor to Kahrnahrgx.
Roald Macy	Paign Macy's father. Soldier.

APPENDIX THREE

PLACES

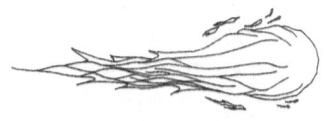

Aconcagua, Argentina	It is the highest mountain peak outside of Asia, making it the tallest point in both the Western. Hemisphere and the Southern Hemisphere.
Cave of Osberg	A chamber of special significance to those opposed to Kahrnahrgx. It was Osberg who retrieved the temple key from Kahrnahrgx until it was discovered by Amy Wheelen.
Cavern of Zarentil	Special, extremely remote lair for the gargoyle's great High Priest.
Ghorlikharka, Nepal	The area where Amy and Peter Wheelen discovered the remains of Osberg the Great, along with the Key of Kahrnahrgx.
Honellaken Valley	A mountainous Nordic valley, where Freida, Anders, Paign and their families live.
Mount Thor	Located on Baffin Island, Nunavut, Canada, this mountain features Earth's greatest vertical drop of 1,250 m (4,101 ft). Thor's cliff overhangs at roughly 15 degrees from vertical, creating a negative pitch.
Ruar's Ridge	A ragged ridge, vaulting high above the Honellaken Valley. Named after the historic Norwegian adventurer Hans Ruar.

Strahl Lake	A picturesque lake in Southern Indiana, located in Brown County State Park. The Hudson's cabin is near the lake.
Taksar Bhojpur, Nepal	Taksar is a village in the Bhojpur district of the Kosi zone in eastern Nepal. It is about 96.5 km (60 m) south of Mount Everest, the tallest mountain on Earth.
The Temple of Kahrnahrgx	An ancient place that had originally been the primary worship center for all gargoyles. Site of battle between the followers of Kahrnahrgx and those loyal to Osberg the Great. Now a ruin.
The Rookery of Ten Pinnacles	The majestic, rugged primary nesting grounds for the granite, basalt and slate gargoyle classes.
Tula, Mexico	Tula is an archeological site, which was at its height the capital of the Toltec Empire. The main feature is the Pyramid of Quetzalcoatl (the feathered serpent god), topped by four, 4 meter high basalt columns carved in the shape of Toltec warriors. Though Tula fell around 1150, it influenced the Aztec Empire, with its strong emphasis on myth.

ABOUT THE AUTHOR

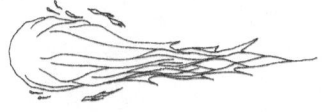

Brandon King is an award-winning novelist, as well as a non-fiction writer. He spent too many years believing he *should not* write because he had a busy career and a family to support. When he finally started letting words flow out of his head, down his arms and through his fingers onto a computer keyboard, he regretted how much time he let flow past. At least now he is wiser (a little) and more focused (a lot). *If you have an itch to write, then do it. Now. Put this book down and come back after you've written your book. Or at least a chapter.*

Mr. King lives in southwestern Idaho, where the mountains are near enough to feel. In just a few minutes he can be sitting on a column of basalt nearly 100 feet high. His wife is an accomplished singer-songwriter, with a love for Americana and blues. Their daughter became a published fantasy novelist at 17; she is now studying to become an engineer…while she continues writing her book series. They share their home with lots of beloved pets adopted from their local shelter.

Learn more at BrandonKingAuthor.com

WANT TO PREVIEW

THE QUEST FOR THE TEMPLE KEY?

Download your preview here:

www.ingramcontent.com/pod-product-compliance
Lightning Source LLC
Chambersburg PA
CBHW030546260626
47157CB00006B/2205